What the reviewers are saying...

ഇ

Transformations

"A great read and an excellent anthology for lovers of erotic shapeshifter romance." ~ *Paranormal Romance Reviews*

Foxfire

"FOXFIRE is a delicate weave of old magic in a modern day, rustic setting...a pleasant read, and a great addition to any TBR pile." ~ *Romance Reviews Today*

"To say Ms. Carter did her homework for FOXFIRE would be an understatement; she went above and beyond the call with her work." ~ *Novelspot*

Taking Shape

"Ms. St. Clare does an excellent job of building the sexual tension...Tally and Nick's attraction grows from 'I really like" to 'I've gotta have" through surprising twists and turns." ~ *Romance Reviews Today*

"The sex has never been hotter and the rubber ducky scene wins hands down." ~ *Fallen Angel Reviews*

MARGARET L. CARTER
LIDDY MIDNIGHT
TIELLE ST. CLARE

TRANSFORMATIONS

ELLORA'S CAVE
ROMANTICA PUBLISHING

An Ellora's Cave Romantica Publication

www.ellorascave.com

Transformations

ISBN #1419954458
ALL RIGHTS RESERVED.
Foxfire Copyright© 2005 Margaret Carter
Survivor Copyright© 2005 Liddy Midnight
Taking Shape Copyright© 2005 Tielle St. Clare
Edited by Pamela Campbell and Briana St. James
Cover art by Syneca.

Electronic book Publication October 2005
Trade paperback Publication July 2006

Warning:

The following material contains graphic sexual content meant for mature readers. This story has been rated E–rotic by a minimum of three independent reviewers.

Ellora's Cave Publishing offers three levels of Romantica™ reading entertainment: S (S-ensuous), E (E-rotic), and X (X-treme).

S-*ensuous* love scenes are explicit and leave nothing to the imagination.

E-*rotic* love scenes are explicit, leave nothing to the imagination, and are high in volume per the overall word count. In addition, some E-rated titles might contain fantasy material that some readers find objectionable, such as bondage, submission, same sex encounters, forced seductions, and so forth. E-rated titles are the most graphic titles we carry; it is common, for instance, for an author to use words such as "fucking", "cock", "pussy", and such within their work of literature.

X-*treme* titles differ from E-rated titles only in plot premise and storyline execution. Unlike E-rated titles, stories designated with the letter X tend to contain controversial subject matter not for the faint of heart.

Contents

Also by Margaret L. Carter

ଞ

Dragon's Tribute

Ellora's Cavemen: Legendary Tails II *(Anthology)*

New Flame

Night Flight

Things That Go Bump In the Night II *(Anthology)*

Virgin Blood

About the Author

ଞ

Marked for life by reading DRACULA at the age of twelve, Margaret L. Carter specializes in the literature of fantasy and the supernatural, particularly vampires. She received degrees in English from the College of William and Mary, the University of Hawaii, and the University of California. She is a 2000 Eppie Award winner in horror, and with her husband, retired Navy Captain Leslie Roy Carter, she coauthored a fantasy novel, WILD SORCERESS.

Margaret welcomes comments from readers. You can find her website and email address on her author bio page at www.ellorascave.com.

Foxfire

By Margaret L. Carter

એ

Author's Note

❧

All the powers attributed to Kenji come from authentic Japanese mythology. Two Internet sources I used for kitsune legends are *Kitsune Lore*, www.comnet.ca/~foxtrot/kitsune/kitsune1.html, and *The Kitsune Page*, www.coyotes.org/kitsune/ kitsune.html.

Chapter One

વ્ર

Anger and frustration hammered at Tabitha like a fist pounding on a door. She felt like clamping her hands over her ears to shut out the racket, but plugging her ears couldn't block noise that existed only in her brain. Besides, her sister would get the wrong idea. It wasn't Chloe's voice that made Tabitha's head hurt, but the feelings behind the words.

"I know damn well you don't want me here, Tabby."

Tabitha winced at that nickname. The kittenish overtones clashed with the negative emotions and made her skull jangle even worse. "I never said that." She kept her tone low in hopes of soothing Chloe. Sometimes her curse of perceiving other people's emotions enabled her to give them a gentle nudge in a different direction.

"You don't have to. If I'd phoned first instead of just showing up at the door, would you have invited me to come?" Her anger bounced off the walls like a steel sphere in an old-fashioned pinball machine. Her chin quivered like a sulky toddler's, oddly contrasting with her porcupine-spiked, blood-red hairdo, the black jeans and halter top, and the silver ankh necklace. Tabitha, with her brown hair, light sprinkle of freckles and discount-store wardrobe, felt drab by contrast, but she liked herself that way, comfortably inconspicuous.

"I might have tried to talk you into making up with Mom and Dad. That doesn't mean I don't want you around."

"You don't want anybody around. Why else are you hiding on a mountaintop in the middle of nowhere?" A wave of Chloe's hand, fingernails polished with silver glitter, encompassed the living room with its wood paneling, braided rug, bare ceiling beams and the pine trees visible through the window.

"Not quite in the middle of nowhere. There's a town less than half an hour away." Tabitha rubbed her forehead. She couldn't deny she lived in the Blue Ridge Mountains, though on more of a hillside than a mountaintop, to keep her distance from other people. That didn't mean she never wanted to see her family again. She just wanted to confine that contact to small doses. It didn't help that her parents suspected she was a little nuts. Chloe, who seemed to have a faint trace of the emotion-sensing talent Tabitha had inherited in such unwanted abundance from their grandmother, might have understood, except that most of the time she preferred to deny any such ability existed. "Look, Chloe, I understand the folks can be a giant pain about guys and stuff. And I don't mind having you hide out here for a while. But aiding and abetting you with outright disobeying them is a whole 'nother thing."

"Bottom line, you won't help me."

"I thought letting you crash here was helping. Bottom line, I won't let you meet your boyfriend in my house. Mom and Dad would never let me hear the end of it." Their parents would phone from Norfolk and badger her for hours about supporting her little sister's rebellion. Listening to them yell hurt less when distance kept her from sensing their anger directly, but she still wanted to avoid the ordeal. Chloe's anger felt almost as harsh. Desperate for fresh air, Tabitha opened the door and stepped onto the porch to inhale the pine-scented mountain breeze.

Her sister trailed after her. "I should've known you wouldn't understand. It's not like you've ever dated much." Planting her hands on her hips, Chloe fired the lethal shot. "You being a freak and all."

The scorn in her voice stung like a swarm of wasps. Tabitha sensed the accusation as half sincere, half chosen because her sister felt how much pain it would cause. Unfortunately, Chloe's mild hint of empathic talent didn't seem to serve any other purpose. It certainly hadn't won Tabitha an ally against their parents, who found her ability embarrassing when they didn't deny it altogether.

"This isn't about me. It's about you disappearing. Mom's worried. She called a few hours ago, before you got here, asking if I'd seen you."

"So now I guess you're going to phone and tell them I'm here?"

"Not yet. Don't know what I'll say when they get desperate and call me again. You're not eighteen yet. They'll drag you back home sooner or later." Tabitha sighed. "I wish you'd go on your own though. A guy who'd expect you to vanish and let the folks think you might've been slaughtered by a serial killer or something can't be worth much."

"Like you know anything about guys. You turned down every boy who wanted to go with you." Chloe's words felt the way petting a porcupine probably would.

"That's not exactly true." Tabitha had accepted a few dates in high school and college. Every time, close contact with the feelings of a casual acquaintance had made her feel like creeping into a burrow and hiding like a rabbit. Especially when those feelings became intense—male sexual desire mingled with worries about how she would respond and whether his performance would live up to his own image of his studliness. "Why don't we calm down and talk about this later, maybe after dinner?" She visualized herself stroking those porcupine quills very carefully, in the right direction to make them lie flat.

Chloe drew back like a cat with ruffled fur. "I don't want to calm down and quit trying to make me."

"What do you mean, make you?" She knew her voice sounded defensive because she'd gotten caught trying to steer her sister's emotions onto a smoother track. Their grandmother had possessed the power to calm people. Tabitha wished she'd inherited more than a trace of that.

"You're sneaking into my mind, the way you used to when we were kids." The only person who really believed in Tabitha's wild talent, Chloe had never gotten straight the difference between emotion-reading and mind-reading.

At this moment, Tabitha felt more glad than usual that she couldn't decipher her sister's exact thoughts. The part she could perceive was bad enough. "Think what you want. I'm tired of fighting. I'm going for a walk."

"Yeah, go on, run away like you always do."

Tabitha stomped down the porch steps, already ashamed of acting like a brat herself. She couldn't stand the hostile emanations any longer though. The atmosphere inside the house felt like a toxic fog that made her stomach churn. The moment she got a few yards away, and Chloe stormed inside and slammed the door, the air felt clearer. Negative emotions still buzzed around her, but the closed door dulled the impact.

She savored the crisp aroma of the pine trees and the lush fragrance of honeysuckles that festooned a nearby fallen tree trunk. Eager to escape the remnants of her sister's anger, she jogged down the gravel driveway to a one-lane road that connected her land with the highway a couple of miles down. She didn't exactly live in the middle of nowhere, the way her family always put it. The ten acres she'd inherited from her grandmother bordered another residential lot, inhabited by a man who seemed as much of a recluse as Tabitha herself. She was thankful that she hardly ever saw him. She preferred loneliness to the stress of armoring herself against random emotions from strangers.

By the time she reached the end of the driveway, she couldn't feel Chloe at all. Birds and animals lurked, easily ignored, in trees and underbrush. Those creatures had refreshingly one-dimensional feelings—hunger, thirst, fear, aggression, lust. With none of it aimed at her, she could treat it as background noise like the breeze rustling the leaves overhead. Human emotions, too complex and too strong, battered her mental walls to splinters. She'd often gotten into trouble by caving in to avoid that assault. Agreeing to let Chloe stay at her place instead of phoning their parents the minute her sister had appeared at the door that day was just the latest instance. She didn't gain much by providing a hideout because she still had to deal with verbal and emotional whiplashing. She drew the line at letting her sister use her house to hook up with the boyfriend their parents had banned.

When had her relationship with Chloe become such a wreck? When she'd acquired a little sister at age seven, she'd felt protective toward the new baby. Unlike their parents, she could identify the cause of each cry and tell Mom what the baby needed. Though Mom and Dad had never stopped acting leery of Tabitha's ability, they'd accepted her help with translating the baby's demands. For a while, she enjoyed the role of useful child instead of difficult child. "Difficult" was how Mom described Tabitha as an infant and toddler, constantly screaming for reasons her parents couldn't figure out. Now, from an adult perspective, she knew she'd sensed the pain, anxieties and anger of people around her and reacted with panic.

Shaking off the memories of her parents' disapproval, she left the road and veered into the woods, following a narrow trail where she often ran. Her skin grew damp from the late afternoon heat, with her shorts and T-shirt sticking to her. She slowed her pace, pushing up her collar-length hair to let the breeze cool the back of her neck. A feeling, not her own, drifted toward her with the breeze. A glow of admiration she could bask in like sunshine, if only it would stay at that level. That kind of reaction always morphed into something more demanding though.

A split second after she sensed a watcher, she caught sight of a moving figure among the trees ahead. Kenji McGraw, her nearest neighbor, strode in her direction, gliding through the brush so smoothly she couldn't hear his footsteps. She halted about ten feet from him. When his glance met hers, he stopped too. He brushed a stray lock of black hair, growing to just above the nape of his neck with raggedly trimmed bangs in front, off his forehead. She sensed his discomfort in the hot, humid air. Feeling his eyes on her, she realized the T-shirt clinging to her moist flesh outlined the curves of her breasts and the peaks of her nipples. She wore no bra, as usual when she planned to spend the day at home. A blush spread over her face. She waved a greeting to him, and he raised his hand in reply. Though his face showed no more than a faint smile, she felt heat rising from within him to match the warmth of the summer day. His cheeks reddened too.

He wore less clothing than she did. Besides sneakers, he had on only a pair of satin jogging shorts that clung as tightly as hers. They'd talked only a few times since she'd moved in. After that, she'd occasionally glimpsed him from a distance during her daily run but never this close before. He always detoured in the opposite direction when they stumbled upon each other. Every time, they exchanged casual greetings and headed their separate ways, as if he preferred to avoid people too. That behavior pattern suited her fine.

Now he changed course to retreat into the denser growth. She leaned against a tree and watched him. Only a few inches taller than her own medium height, he had a compact build without a visible ounce of fat. She'd never seen him shirtless before, and she enjoyed the glimpse of muscles flexing under the skin. The shorts outlined a tight rear end, a view that provided a welcome distraction from the fight with her sister. Even if Tabitha's sensitivity to others' emotions kept her from dating, she figured she could still indulge in an occasional fantasy. Good thing he couldn't read her reactions the way she did his.

So why did he radiate embarrassment? Simply because she'd noticed him watching her? She felt something else from him, a wave of arousal that made her skin tingle. The cloth of her shirt abraded her nipples into harder peaks. She hugged herself to press her forearms against them. Kenji's excitement drifted toward her like a spicy-scented mist. Awareness of inciting that desire made her breath catch in her throat like a trapped butterfly. Warm liquid welled between her legs.

By now he'd disappeared from sight behind a misshapen giant of a fallen oak tree festooned with ivy and honeysuckle. He hadn't withdrawn out of sensing range though. She still felt his arousal. If anything, it grew stronger by the minute instead of fading. She knew she ought to turn around and run until she couldn't feel him anymore. Eavesdropping on emotions he wanted to hide amounted to voyeurism. Besides, why torment herself with the aroma of a banquet she could never taste?

Her body didn't listen. Her throat went dry, with her heart racing and her breath accelerating to keep up. In spite of the breeze, the temperature seemed to rise until she felt as if she stood in front of a roaring campfire. The blaze came from him, no more than twenty feet away. If she charged up to him and touched his naked chest, it would scorch her.

But of course she wouldn't do that. He would think she'd gone crazy. She fell to her knees on the leaf-strewn ground and cupped her breasts with her palms. The ache spread from her nipples across her chest as if a pair of hands larger than her own were splayed over her bare flesh. Her breasts felt heavy, too swollen for the clinging T-shirt. Invisible ants scurried over her skin. She wanted to rip off the shirt and rub herself everywhere at once.

The air thrummed with passion like the beat of music amplified to a deafening level. Not her own passion, but it engulfed her and made her heart pound in cadence with it. She could almost see the waves distorting the world around her, blurring her view of the trees, like a mirage on heated asphalt. Her whole body felt like a single expanding and contracting heartbeat.

She squeezed her breasts, trying to bind her awareness to her own flesh. *They're his feelings, not mine!* But the pulsation only grew more intense by the second. The emptiness between her legs hungered to be filled. A rush of hot wetness made her press her thighs together, trying to quell the gaping need. At the same moment, she felt a hardness that yearned to thrust into that cavity and bury itself in that moist embrace. A rising pressure on the verge of explosion.

I'm feeling his erection! She struggled to block the relentless waves of arousal. Too late. His need swept away her mental shield like a dam of twigs in a flooding river. She couldn't pretend the excitement didn't belong to her as well. She wanted to strip off her pants and plunge her fingers deep into her sheath, as a substitute for the male organ she never expected to welcome there. Instead, she just cupped her mound through her shorts, pressing hard in rhythm with the accelerating contractions.

A crimson haze veiled the trees around her and the path under her knees. She closed her eyes, but the redness glowed behind her lids. The flesh between her legs started to throb. She felt the pressure reach its peak with a starburst of blinding sparks on the insides of her eyes. Her hips involuntarily jerked with each spurt of hot liquid. Her vagina and clitoris contracted in a dozen short, sharp pulses. In the background, scarcely penetrating her awareness, the keening of some animal ripped through the silence. She bit off a cry, curled into herself and soared with the whirlwind of sensation until it faded.

A languid sigh of relief loosened the tightness in her chest. His relief. Hers too though. Had she screamed aloud in her climax? A flush of embarrassment swept over her. She couldn't deny her ownership of that last feeling. In the back of her mind, she sensed Kenji's presence becoming fainter, drawing away, finally fading completely.

She sat up, hugging her knees to her chest, tears leaking from her eyes. If only she could share that experience, face to face, with a man who cared for her. But she knew she would never get any closer than what had just occurred, a spontaneous merging with a near-stranger. Such a thing had never happened to her before. She'd shied away from men who lusted for her before their arousal could trigger hers beyond control. She would have to make sure it didn't happen again. Worst of all, she couldn't face Kenji again, couldn't even cherish a daydream of friendship.

Chapter Two

ஐ

When he practically ran into his neighbor jogging through the woods, Kenji indulged a few seconds of fantasy. He could stop and say hello instead of fleeing in the opposite direction. They could carry on a normal conversation, the way he'd sometimes chatted with her grandmother. The old lady had radiated a calming aura. Having her for a neighbor hadn't threatened his peace at all. He'd carved a coffee table out of an oak tree stump for her, and she'd praised his craftsmanship. He wondered whether her granddaughter still used that table. Why didn't he drop by sometime and ask?

Because of the inescapable difference between an elderly widow and a sexy, single woman almost his own age. Because every time he laid eyes on Tabitha, he wanted to lay hands and other appendages on her, and that couldn't happen. He couldn't forget the disasters that had resulted every time he'd tried to get close to a woman. So he allowed himself only a peek at Tabitha's nipples outlined by the damp T-shirt and her legs exposed by the brief, snug shorts before he retreated into the undergrowth.

One peek turned out to be too much, combined with the salty scent of her clean sweat. He couldn't resist inhaling deeply even while he walked away. No perfume, just the tang of her female flesh. The breeze wafted the fragrance toward him, tormenting his senses. He knew his face turned red to match the pinkness of hers. Had she noticed the bulge of the hard-on in his shorts? He definitely had one by the time he got out of sight behind the bulk of the fallen tree.

His keen ears, as well as his nose, told him that she'd stopped instead of moving on down the trail. Why? He sniffed the humid air and smelled female secretions. She felt an attraction too. Their brief meeting had made her wet. His erection grew, tenting his pants. It felt so long and hard he could close his eyes and imagine it jutting out like a steel rod.

Crouching on the ground, he pressed a hand to his aching shaft. No way would he make it home now. Already he could feel the shifting joints and muscles and the prickles under the skin that sexual cravings always triggered. All strong emotions had that effect, but none worse than this kind. She couldn't see him. He'd be safe enough seeking his release right here. In the back of his mind, he knew he'd do it even at risk of her catching him in the act. Her intoxicating scent wouldn't let him crawl out of range. He hungered to savor that aroma while he relieved the pressure it caused. He peeled off his shorts, not wanting to get tangled in them while his excitement ran its course, and shuffled out of his shoes and socks with one hand already massaging his penis. He shouldn't have let so many nights go by without sexual release. His mother had warned him, in an awkward speech when he'd turned twelve, how he would have to feed that craving regularly. She hadn't explained how to take care of the need when he couldn't risk seducing women. He'd figured out the makeshift solution on his own soon enough. By now, he should know better than to let the tension build up this way. If he hadn't, he'd be able to control himself long enough to get to shelter.

Too late now though. His sharp ears picked up the acceleration in Tabitha's breathing. He could tell she tried to suppress it, probably worried about his being close enough to hear. No normal man could have, at this distance, but he had no trouble catching every nuance, every hitch in her throat and rustle of leaves when she rolled on the ground. The tang of her scent confirmed the cause of her restless movements. He was already squirming himself.

He imagined plunging deeply into her, reveling in the union he'd never shared with any woman. He visualized what he could never know in reality, soft arms around his neck, lips parted under his, smooth legs clamped around his hips. For a second he flushed with self-contempt at the memory of the only way he had experienced mating, but need quickly drowned shame. He rubbed his cock harder and faster, his breathing labored as the pressure intensified beyond bearing. He imagined her slick sheath clenched around him.

A spasm of ecstasy on the edge of pain contorted his body. His joints cracked as his limbs shrank, bent and realigned. A crawling sensation coursed over his bare skin. His nose elongated while his ears grew pointed, fangs sprouted in his jaws, and a new appendage erupted from the base of his spine. The world fractured around him then reshaped itself in his altered vision. The light breeze carrying the woman's musk to him tickled his whiskers. Panting, he tasted the air. All scents instantly became more pungent, so vivid he could almost see them shimmering in the humid atmosphere, making up for the sudden change in his vision that attenuated colors to pastels and grays. His nostrils flared to inhale the smells of moist loam, pine needles, small animals scurrying through the underbrush, and above all the humid flesh of the female a short distance away. He could almost feel her pussy squeezing his eager cock.

He no longer had hands to pump his erect organ. Instead, he dug the claws of all four feet into the soil and sprawled on his belly to thrust through the final convulsions. A high-pitched howl burst from his throat at the same instant that he shot his juices into the leaf-mold.

He lay on his side, panting, until his heartbeat slowed to normal. He picked himself up and slunk homeward, leaving his clothes on the ground to collect later. If he could have shed tears in his nonhuman form, they would have leaked from his eyes now. In this shape, he only dimly recalled the cause of his despair, but the inarticulate state of his thoughts made them no less painful.

* * * * *

The near-miss encounter only confirmed Tabitha's usual practice of staying out of Kenji's way. Not that she disliked what little she knew of him. He earned his living by custom woodworking, and last fall she'd commissioned him to make a set of monkeypod salad bowls as a Christmas gift for her parents. In casual conversation, she'd found out his father had been an officer in the Navy who'd married a Japanese woman. Both were dead, and Kenji had lived alone on the mountainside for several years longer than Tabitha had owned her place. During her two visits to his house, first to discuss the job and later to pick up the finished product, she'd felt that warm glow from him. It had disturbed her less than similar reactions from her few dating partners. Kenji had seemed embarrassed about noticing her figure, eager to withdraw from contact rather than determined to foist his attention on her like most men. She remembered how he'd practically pushed her out the door with her purchase the second time she'd dropped by his place. He seemed as reluctant to associate with people as she was.

On the way home, she couldn't help comparing what she'd just experienced to her few dates in high school and college. Suppose she did work up the nerve to pursue a relationship with her neighbor instead of avoiding him? If that kind of passion overwhelmed them when they met face to face, would she react any less disastrously than she had with other men? She remembered writhing in silent embarrassment in the passenger seat of a boy's car after leaving a movie one Friday night. The movie itself had shielded her from the full force of his desire, which skulked around the edges of her mind like a coyote stalking a flock of sheep. In the car, with no distractions, she had to keep pushing away his lust like a hairy, clumsy dog jumping on her. And he hadn't even touched her since they'd left their seats in the theater. She remembered how she'd tensed up when he'd parked the car under a tree on a dark side street outside a vacant house. His lust had felt greedy, a hunger she couldn't possibly sate. It crept under her skin and made her body tingle in response, but she knew that need belonged to him, not her. She hadn't even found him that attractive. As a casual friend and president of the chess club rather than a class leader or star athlete, he'd impressed her as somebody she could date without feeling threatened. The feelings that lurked behind his bland

couple of years of office work following college, she'd networked into freelance copyediting and technical writing jobs she could do online, from home. Inheriting this secluded house had formed the final step in her plan to construct a life where she never had to encounter people unless she wanted to.

So, yeah, Chloe had a point in accusing her of running away from things. Who could blame her, Tabitha thought, considering what happened when she did associate with family members, such as now? Although the two of them didn't raise their voices or make any hostile remarks, the atmosphere continued to twang with tension through dinner, dishwashing and an hour in front of the TV watching sitcoms on satellite channels. Tabitha, relieved when Chloe withdrew to her bedroom at nine, retreated to her own room to distract herself with a new mystery novel. She made sure to stow her purse, with car keys zipped inside it, in her closet. If she had to take temporary responsibility for her sister, reasonable precautions against impulsive acts such as "borrowing" her car made sense. That way, her parents couldn't accuse her of letting Chloe run wild during the visit that, with luck, would be brief.

* * * * *

She woke to darkness and silence, except for crickets chirping outside the open window. The fragments of a dream shredded and drifted away, a luscious dream of rolling in Kenji's arms on the cool, pine-needle-carpeted forest floor. Her nipples and clit tingled. She pressed a hand against the wetness between her legs and waited for her heartbeat to stop pounding in her head. Within seconds, her breathing slowed to normal. For a minute she strained her ears, wondering what had shattered her sleep. Nothing. When she woke to full consciousness, she realized she sensed a vacuum where a hazy cloud of muted emotions should emanate from Chloe's dreaming mind. Tabitha glanced at the luminous digits of the clock on the nightstand. Five minutes past midnight.

She got out of bed, her skin prickling with the coolness that nightfall brought to the mountains, even in mid-June. Without stopping to throw on anything warm over her flimsy nightgown, she tiptoed into the hall. Maybe her perceptions had failed her for once, and Chloe hadn't really left the house. She turned the doorknob of the other bedroom inch by inch until she could ease the door open. One glance showed her that the sheets were flung back and the bed was empty. A quick check of the bathroom confirmed her sister's absence.

Don't tell me she went for a walk in the woods in the middle of the night! I can't imagine her stumbling around under the trees in the dark.

Unless she'd gone only as far as the driveway, for a little fresh air. Tabitha had trouble visualizing even that much of a midnight foray, considering Chloe's pose of big-city boredom with nature in the almost-raw. Another thought sent her to the kitchen, where she found one of her two flashlights missing. So Chloe had expected to need light, a bit of preparation that indicated she'd planned her expedition. Tabitha flicked on the floodlight over the back deck, slipped her feet into the flip-flops she kept by the kitchen door and hurried outside. No sign of her sister behind the house. A circuit of the yard brought no results. Chloe had definitely sneaked away.

If she'd simply wanted to leave, she'd have waited until daylight and said so, probably asking for a ride to town. So she must have a reason for secrecy. Remembering Chloe's nervous behavior at the computer, Tabitha went into the living room and booted it up. She knew her sister's screen name, of course. She typed "ScarletWings" into the box. As for the password, when Tabitha had lived at home, Chloe had used the same three passwords for all Internet activities and not bothered to hide them from the rest of the family. With luck, she'd remained predictable that way.

She had. The second letter combination Tabitha tried, RavenX, accessed the account. Without the least twinge of guilt, she opened the in-box and clicked on the most recent message, dated that afternoon. Somebody labeled ShadowElf wanted to know where Chloe was and when they could meet. Tabitha switched over to the "sent mail" folder and quickly found the reply: "I'll be on Route 29 where my sister's road joins it about 12:30 tonight. Wait for me if I don't get there right on time 'cause I'll probably have to walk." The e-mail then described the landmarks that identified the crossroads of Route 29 with the narrow lane meandering up to the house.

Fuming, Tabitha logged off. It didn't take much of a leap to figure out "ShadowElf" was the forbidden boyfriend. So much for trusting Chloe not to get herself and Tabitha into deep trouble with the folks. On the other hand, if Chloe intended to run away permanently, she wouldn't have to face the trouble. She'd have left it all for other people to clean up.

Especially me, Tabitha grumbled to herself. It occurred to her that she still had time to head off this rendezvous. Without access to the car keys, Chloe had to reach the highway on foot. Catching up with her before she met the boy shouldn't pose a problem. Tabitha scrambled into jeans, a T-shirt, tennis shoes and a lightweight denim jacket and tied her hair out of the way in a lopsided ponytail. Grabbing her purse and the flashlight, she dashed to the car, backed out of the driveway and headed down the hillside. She gritted her teeth, fighting anger that for once she recognized as entirely her own, and debated whether to phone their parents to collect Chloe before or after shoving the brat into a bedroom and barricading the door.

Chapter Three

ဆ

The winding, one-lane road had no street lamps. Tabitha had to drive slowly, scanning the shoulders by the headlight beams alone. Unless Chloe glimpsed the lights around a curve and hid in the bushes, though, she'd be impossible to miss. With the windows down and her mind wide open, Tabitha would sense the girl even if she didn't see her right away.

But she felt only the fuzzy consciousness of night birds and small animals she couldn't identify. No hint of movement, aside from shadows thrown by her headlights, broke the stillness of the road. She drove to the Route 29 intersection at a crawl, much slower than she usually covered the distance. Surely Chloe couldn't have beaten her to the spot. No, not even at a run.

At the bottom of the lane, Tabitha parked the car under the trees and got out, locking the doors. With her purse slung over her shoulder and the unlit flashlight in one hand, she crept toward the highway, though her sixth sense told her nobody waited there. The night remained silent except for the chirping of crickets. A lamppost across the road cast a circle of light whose outer edge she avoided. She lurked behind a huge, double-trunked oak tree looming next to the wooden sign that was supposed to mark the turn-off toward her house. Years of weather had worn the words "Honeysuckle Way" to illegibility. With only two properties on that road, hers and Kenji McGraw's, the loss didn't matter. Anybody who'd visit here would get directions from one or the other of them.

She leaned against the tree, watching fireflies and checking the time every few minutes. Chloe must have tried a shortcut through the woods. Dumb thing to do, but her behavior hadn't demonstrated much wisdom so far. Still, if she kept going downhill, she had to end up at the highway eventually. Tabitha nibbled on a fingernail and tried not to worry. If her sister got hurt wandering around the mountains at night, their parents would skin both of them alive. With a nervous laugh, Tabitha reminded herself how tame this "wilderness" was, even with the Shenandoah National Park a few miles away. Bears weren't common enough to constitute a realistic threat. Lesser predators avoided people. *What do I think could happen to her, she'll get gored by a deer?*

Or maybe she might stumble over a skittish skunk, a fate that would serve her right, except that Tabitha would have to live with the fallout too. She sighed and rubbed her eyes, longing for her bed and the interrupted dream. Before her thoughts could drift too far in that fruitless direction, a car engine broke the silence. She peeked around the tree.

Some kind of sports car roared to a stop, a two-seater with a motor too loud for its size. The driver turned off the ignition, stepped out and lounged against the hood. A boy in his late teens with silver-tipped black hair, he wore dark pants and a T-shirt, cut off to expose his abs, with a logo of an unidentifiable fanged monster on it. She read nervousness and impatience in the glances he darted from side to side. He took a pack of cigarettes from his pocket and struck a match.

No sense dragging out an unpleasant scene. Tabitha strolled around the tree and said, "ShadowElf, I presume?" She couldn't help gloating a little when he jumped and dropped the match on the pavement. A spike of alarm shot from his mind.

When he saw only a woman, he calmed down. "Sorry, I'm waiting for somebody else." He fumbled the matchbook open again.

"Don't bother to light up. You won't be here long enough." She folded her arms and glared at him.

He frowned back at her. He didn't need to speak for Tabitha to sense his resentment at her giving him orders.

"I know you're supposed to meet Chloe. She's not coming." She saw no need to mention that she had no idea where Chloe was at this moment. Let the guy think he'd been stood up.

"You've got to be her sister. The weirdo who reads minds. What did you do to her?"

Tabitha ignored the tiny stab of hurt caused by those words. By now she should be used to that kind of reaction. "Not a thing. But she isn't going anywhere with you. You might as well split."

"You've got no right to tell us what to do. I'm not leaving without her." His simmering resentment heated toward anger.

"Then you'll have a long wait." The cloud of negative emotion emanating from him started to seep into her head and fill it with a dull ache.

"Where is she? Did you lock her up or something? How do I know she's okay?" He took one stride toward Tabitha.

She fought the impulse to back away. "No, I didn't lock her up. What makes you think she didn't just change her mind?"

"She wouldn't. We love each other." In the light from the street lamp, a blush showed on his face. Anxiety tinged his anger, along with embarrassment at making that claim out loud. "Come on, give us a break. Why are you siding with your folks? You're not that old yet."

A flush of annoyance swamped her momentary sympathy for him. "Old enough to want to stop her from acting like an idiot. Love, huh? What did you plan to do, run off and get married?"

"Yeah, why not?" Defiance mingled with guilt seasoned the words.

"That's crap. For one thing, you know she's not old enough."

Though he gave no outward sign, she felt him flinch at the direct hit. "She'll be eighteen in a few months. Then we can—"

"You're lying. You never thought of it until a minute ago."

Now he was the one who backed up. "Hell, Chloe was right. You're reading my mind."

"Then you don't deny it?" She crowded him against the car, brandishing the flashlight like a weapon. "You've been stringing her along, just playing her, right?"

"No way!" His hand clamped onto the driver's side door handle.

"Then what do you feel so guilty about?"

"Get out of my head!" His fear and anger hit her like a fist to the jaw. He flung open the car door, jumped inside, slammed the door, switched on the ignition, made a wide U-turn and accelerated up the highway.

Tabitha staggered into the shelter of the trees and leaned against the huge oak. She trembled with relief at the fading of the boy's turbulent emotions. Slowly, her breathing settled to normal. She'd disposed of the immediate problem. Now she just had to find her sister. Why hadn't Chloe shown up yet? With a flashlight and the slope of the ground to guide her, how lost could she get? Tabitha dredged a heavy sigh from deep in her chest. *Idiot, what possessed her to leave the road in the first place? Probably expecting me to follow her, just like I did. Now I'll bet she's roaming around in circles somewhere up there.*

Tabitha knew she'd get nowhere striking out aimlessly through the underbrush herself. Maybe if she hiked up the road toward the house, periodically venturing a few yards into the woods and calling her sister's name, she'd get lucky. Even if Chloe refused to answer verbally, she couldn't hide her emotional reaction. Muttering curses under her breath, Tabitha turned on the flashlight and started walking.

Fifteen minutes of trudging uphill, with detours into the trees to yell herself hoarse, produced nothing except a dry throat and sore leg muscles. At least now she didn't have to worry about getting chilled by the night air. She was beginning to sweat in her lightweight jacket. She would have been falling asleep on her feet too if she weren't too exasperated to feel drowsy. When she finally caught up with Chloe, her pain-in-the-butt sister would pay for this.

At the bottom of her neighbor's driveway, Tabitha switched off the flashlight and paused to rest by the mailbox. Maybe she wasted time and energy searching by herself. Suppose she asked Kenji for help? He'd lived here longer than she had and probably knew the trails through the woods a lot better. In any case, two searchers could cover ground more efficiently than one. What the heck, the worst he could do was say no and yell at her for waking him up. Which she couldn't imagine from such a sweet-looking guy. Sure, he'd practically thrown her off his front porch when she'd picked up the salad bowl set, but he'd done it quietly.

When she reached the top of the driveway and stood in front of the house, she considered how dumb she would look if Chloe had come to her senses and simply gone home to bed. *I've gone this far*, Tabitha thought, *no point in turning back now*.

An A-frame with wood siding stained a rich reddish-brown, his home looked less rustic than hers. He kept the shrubbery around his porch trimmed, something she didn't bother with. She paused on the bottom step and turned off the flashlight, swallowing a lump of nervousness. Was he asleep or awake? A mental probe through the walls yielded no sense of a presence at all, though a car sat in the driveway. Had he gone for a walk at this strange hour? Well, at least three other people were out and about, including herself. She smiled ruefully at the thought of the anticlimax if she worked up the nerve to knock at Kenji's door and he wasn't even home.

Then another mind brushed hers, but not from inside the house. She felt some live creature moving under the trees not far away. It didn't feel human. She froze, not wanting to scare away whatever it was. The feral consciousness she touched radiated pleasant weariness and the satisfaction of a full stomach. It glided toward the deck at the rear of the cabin. Holding her breath, she watched a shape emerge from the undergrowth and pace into the clearing behind the house. It didn't seem to notice her. Maybe the breeze blew the wrong way to carry her scent. She glimpsed the glow of the animal's eyes for a second. With her vision adjusting to the moonlight, she could distinguish its outline. It had the plumed tail and pointed muzzle of a fox, but it looked bigger than any fox she'd ever seen, the size of a small collie. Before she could get a better look, it disappeared around back.

Too worried about her sister to wonder about the animal for long, she knocked on the door. As she'd feared, she got no answer. Yet a few seconds later a sense of Kenji's nearness blossomed out of nowhere. He was inside the house after all. Why hadn't she felt him before? He hadn't simply awakened from sleep. She knew what that shift in awareness felt like. If he'd just come back from a midnight stroll, she would have sensed him from farther away, and she would certainly have seen or at least heard him walking up to the house. She could only guess that the clash with the boy had rattled her enough to dull her empathic perception temporarily.

Now she read Kenji's emotions as strongly as ever. When she repeated the knock, a haze of drowsy satiation morphed into mild annoyance. So he didn't want to be bothered. Too bad. She felt him moving through the house in her direction, though she didn't hear footsteps until he got almost to the door. When it opened, his irritation changed to surprise at the sight of her.

His black hair, tousled as if he'd just gotten out of bed after all, gleamed in the overhead light. His bare feet accounted for her not having heard him walking on the polished hardwood floors. Most of the rest of him was bare too. Just as he had earlier that evening, he wore only a clingy pair of navy blue shorts. Dragging her eyes away from the shape those pants outlined, she moved to the safer territory of his face. Or maybe not so safe, because she'd never studied his brown eyes so closely before, and she discovered fascinating flecks of gold in the irises. A faintly Asian slant to his features gave him an exotic charm she hadn't taken time to appreciate during their previous meetings. Those enchanting eyes looked at her without much sign of friendliness, yet he projected a conflicting push-pull of impulses. He wanted her gone instantly, but an aura of arousal surrounded him like steam from boiling water. She started to simmer too, feeling the excitement her eyes had already noted in their travels over his body.

When his face reddened, she felt hers doing the same. Was he thinking of their chance encounter in the woods? He couldn't read her mind or emotions, as far as she knew, so why did she blush deeper at that assumption? It didn't help that she stared at him with her lips parted, trying to catch her breath instead of stating the request she'd come to make. His mouth opened and his breath became rapid and shallow too, as if her nervousness were contagious.

Finally, he broke the silence with, "What do you want?"

She tensed at the way this unpromising welcome rasped on her nerves. "Sorry to bother you, but my sister's missing, and I'm worried. I'm hoping you can help."

"How?" He sounded only a shade less annoyed. Meanwhile, he scanned her in a way that made her acutely conscious of her braless condition. Fortunately, the jacket covered her pebbled-up nipples. Or unfortunately, depending on whether she wanted to feel more of that leashed excitement from him.

She shook her head, forcing herself to think of Chloe, lost in the dark somewhere on the hillside between here and the road. Regardless of how tame these woods were, people still got hurt in them every year. Worrying about her sister provided a barricade against the tendrils of arousal emanating from Kenji and swirling around her. "Can I come in and explain?"

"Okay." His grudging tone echoed the reluctance in his thoughts. Stepping aside, he made room for her to enter. The fragrance of wood shavings that drifted from his workroom tickled her nose. The front door opened into a living room no bigger than her own, furnished with a long, low couch, a low table of shiny black wood, surrounded by plump cushions scattered on the floor, an entertainment center on the opposite wall featuring every sound and video component a stereotypically tech-obsessed guy could dream of and a bonsai tree on a stand in a corner. The slanted walls drew the eye to the exposed ceiling beams. "What's up?" he asked, plopping down on one of the cushions. His trimly muscled legs crossed in a graceful half-lotus.

Her eyes couldn't help flicking to the front of his shorts. From the deepening of the flush on his cheeks, he thought of the accidental word-play the same instant she did. She squashed the thought, hoping her own blush would fade if she ignored it. Since sharing the floor with him would feel too intimate after that remark, she sat on the couch.

Oh, no, I hope he doesn't think I'm making an excuse to drop in and hit on him. She swallowed her nervousness and said, "Chloe ran away from home, sort of, because she had a fight with our folks over a boy. A little while ago she sneaked out to meet him. I read her e-mail…"

Kenji interrupted with a teasing smile that made the invisible hedge of thorns bristling around him vanish. "You read your sister's e-mail? Isn't that against the sibling code of honor?"

"Normally, yeah, but I was desperate. If Mom and Dad knew she got into trouble while I was supposedly responsible for her, they'd kill me. Even if I didn't invite her here in the first place. Anyway, I headed off the guy and got him to leave, but Chloe never showed. I think she took a shortcut through the woods and got lost."

He leaned back on his elbows, looking at her upside down. "What makes you think I can find her any better than you can?" A tinge of suspicion colored the question.

Suspicion of what? Tabitha felt as if he were hiding something that he feared she might discover, but she couldn't imagine what. She pushed the idea away, deciding her worry and confusion made her perceive layers of meaning that didn't exist. "I just thought two of us would have a better chance. Also, I figure you know the area better. You've lived here longer."

"True." He stared into space for a minute, a blend of unidentifiable emotions churning in his head. It felt like a ball of yarn with so many strands that the only threads she could untangle were a hunger to draw her close and a fear that something terrible would happen if he surrendered to the desire. "Okay."

She jumped at the abrupt reply. "Great, thanks. Let's get going."

"Not you, just me." He unfolded his legs and stood up in a single, fluid motion.

She sprang to her feet. "What?"

"I'm going alone. I know where to look, and you'd only slow me down, maybe scare her away if she's trying to avoid you. You wait here."

"No way! That's my sister we're talking about." His argument sounded too flimsy to be worth refuting, and besides, she heard the unmistakable taint of a half-lie in his voice.

Already halfway to the door, he turned toward her. "That's the deal. If you want my help, you let me do it my way."

Chapter Four

ഓ

"Where do you get off issuing orders? Of course I'm going."

"If you did, the whole thing would be a waste of time. We wouldn't find her." He meant that, she could tell. He had access to a search method he was sure would work. But that wasn't the whole truth.

"What's your real reason for not wanting me along?"

He blinked in surprise. She felt him flinch the way people always did when she probed their motives. As usual, any chance of simple friendship was already sliding downhill. "I don't know what you're talking about," he said with an overly casual shrug. "If you don't need help after all, let me go back to sleep." She sensed that he did want to help her, whether from sheer altruism or from a desire to know her better, she couldn't tell. His determination to search alone, though, grew more unmistakable by the second.

"Oh, all right, have it your way. I'm not getting anywhere on my own, that's for sure." Realizing how ungracious she sounded, she forced a smile and added, "Thanks. Sorry to make such a hassle out of it."

"No problem." He opened the door and said, "You stay here. From the way you sound running on the trails, she'd hear you coming a mile away." He grinned to soften the insult. "This shouldn't take long. Don't worry."

Before she could construct a snappy retort, he hurried into the back room, to reappear a minute later in tennis shoes and a T-shirt. Without another word, he disappeared out the front door. She realized he'd left without so much as a flashlight. Did he have eyes like a cat or what? Well, maybe he kept a flashlight on the porch or in his car.

By the time she opened the door and followed him outside, he was nowhere in sight.

* * * * *

As soon as he reached the shelter of the trees, Kenji stripped naked and prepared to search. He would have to backtrack toward Tabitha's house in hope of crossing the girl's trail. Since Tabitha's and Chloe's should be the only human female scents in the area, finding the spoor shouldn't pose a problem.

Tucking his clothes into the fork of a branch for safekeeping, he wondered what had possessed him to agree to this quest. He couldn't fool himself that he'd just wanted to do the neighborly thing. He liked Tabitha and didn't want to see her worried and scared. He lusted after her and wanted to make a good impression, regardless of the impossibility of a relationship. Neither of those impulses justified putting himself in the risky position of having to explain how he could find a teenage girl in the woods in the middle of the night. He groaned to himself at the memory of the lame excuse he'd given Tabitha for making her stay behind. With luck, she'd feel so relieved to have her sister safe that she wouldn't think to ask for details right away, and he wouldn't give her a chance to ask later. They wouldn't see each other again except for their usual chance meetings on the trails.

Why did that prospect depress him so much? Until tonight, he'd thought he'd become resigned to his solitary life.

Naked, he crouched on all fours and willed the change.

He transformed more smoothly than when strong emotion made him shift involuntarily. Now his bones and muscles melted into their new shape with a sensuous pleasure like hot water flowing over his bare limbs. The fur that enveloped him felt more natural than skin, as if he'd awakened from a dream of bipedal awkwardness and returned to his true self, with the claws of all four feet denting the soft loam. Darkness became shades of gray and silver in the moonlight. When human, he could see in the dark better than normal people, but nothing like this. His whiskers twitched at random puffs of wind, and his nostrils flared to absorb the odors of the forest. Rabbits, squirrels and raccoons crouched or crawled in the underbrush and tree branches. Ordinarily, he might hunt one of them for the sport even though he'd already fed on a rabbit earlier that night. Now, though, he had a job to do.

He shook his head, aware of how quickly his human purpose had escaped his mind. Getting distracted by animal sensations and appetites was always a hazard when he changed. Normally it wouldn't matter if he let instinct sweep thought into the background. But he couldn't succumb to that temptation at the moment.

He trotted uphill in the direction of Tabitha's house. His ears twitched at every sound. He heard no human noises, only an owl hooting overhead and small animals scurrying out of his path. Along the way, he disturbed a doe with a pair of fawns, who bounded through the trees to avoid him. He scented the footprints of a bear, left over from at least a day ago, nothing to worry about now. At the bottom of his neighbor's driveway, he circled, sniffing the ground, in search of human traces. His plumed tail lashed with pleasure at Tabitha's aroma, permeating the area. He forced his mind back to the reason he'd come here. Casting a little farther from the house, he picked up the scent of another female. With a low bark of satisfaction, he followed the track downhill.

In the daytime even human eyes could probably have tracked the girl. She'd left footprints in the damp soil and broken twigs on bushes. Shortly, she'd stumbled onto one of the narrow trails and followed that in the general direction of the road. For most of its length, this trail stayed on level or gently sloping ground. Farther on, though, it bordered a steep bank on one side. That was where he heard labored breathing from human lungs. A broken thorn-bush and scuffed dirt showed where the girl had tripped and failed to catch herself. The breeze carried the scent of blood.

He edged around the spot until he reached an easier point to climb down into the ravine. He conjured a ball of foxfire to augment his night vision in the shadowed hollow. The girl lay on her back with her left shin bleeding. A flashlight, still glowing, had rolled out of her reach. An occasional whimper punctuated her rasping breaths. She didn't catch sight of him until he'd approached close enough to touch. With a shriek, she snatched up a small rock and flung it at him. It bounced off his flank.

He growled at the sting and dodged the next stone. He couldn't do anything for her in this shape. Extinguishing the foxfire, he clambered up the bank and trotted along the trail to its juncture with one that led near his house. Able to make good time on the cleared surfaces, he reached the place where he'd left his clothes within a few minutes. After dressing, he hurried back to the spot where Chloe had fallen. Cutting through the brush and climbing down the bank to reach the girl gave him a few scratches on his arms and legs, but no discomfort he couldn't ignore.

He picked up the flashlight when he reached the bottom, more to let her get a look at him than because he needed it himself. "Chloe?"

"What? Who's there?" She unthinkingly rolled toward him and yelped in obvious pain.

"Take it easy and don't move. Tabitha sent me to look for you. I'm her neighbor, Kenji McGraw."

"How'd you find me?"

"Luck, I guess," he said, hoping to sound convincingly casual. "I figured you'd stick to the trails, so it was just a matter of checking them until I came across the spot where you fell."

"In the dark?" She tried to sit up and lay back with a hiss through clenched teeth. "I think my leg's broken."

He trained the flashlight beam on her left calf. The blood oozed from superficial scratches. No bone pierced the skin. "Good thing it's not a compound fracture. If that's the only serious injury, I think the best idea would be for me to carry you back to my place. Then we'll call for help." It crossed his mind that if he'd been thinking like a normal man, he would have brought a cell phone, and the paramedics could meet them at the house. On the other hand, how could a fox carry a phone?

He smiled at the thought of rigging a collar to support necessary items like that. Not that he expected another emergency of this kind to pop up anytime soon. Of course, if it did, he could plan ahead next time and stash a phone with his clothes.

"Wait here a second. I don't want to pick you up until we get that immobilized." A rapid survey of the surrounding trees revealed a straight limb of suitable length a few yards away. He trotted over to it, snapped off a two-foot section and cleared it of twigs and leaves. With his T-shirt as a bandage, he strapped the stick snugly to the broken leg. From a long-ago Red Cross course, he knew a bulky item of clothing would make a better splint, but he didn't want to leave Chloe again to get one.

"Let's go." He sank to one knee and put an arm under her back. "Can you hold onto my neck? I'll try not to hurt you too much."

* * * * *

Tabitha alternately sat on Kenji's front steps and paced up and down the driveway for what seemed like hours. As much as she itched to charge into the woods after him, she knew blundering around out there would do no good. She'd be lucky not to get lost or hurt herself. As fast and quietly as he seemed able to move, she didn't have a hope of catching up with him. And though she hated to admit his orders made sense, it was true that two people together couldn't search any better than one alone who knew where to look.

How did he know? He'd sounded more confident than he had any right to. From the way he'd acted so far, she didn't expect to get a straight answer out of him on that point.

She'd cycled back to the step-sitting phase of her vigil when she spotted a light floating up the driveway. She jumped up. Kenji strode into the circle of light from the porch lamp with a flashlight in one hand and Chloe in his arms. He'd taken off his shirt, now tied around her leg. A fog of pain hovered around them.

"Oh, thank God, you really found her." Tabitha dashed to his side.

"Yeah, I said I would, didn't I? Let's get her inside and call 911."

"What's wrong with her?" She flung the front door open and looked around for a phone.

"Kitchen," Kenji said, gesturing with the flashlight.

Tabitha sprinted through the door he'd indicated, saw the phone on the wall next to the refrigerator and made the call. Back in the living room, she found her sister lying on the couch. Sweat plastered Chloe's hair to her scalp, and tears stained her cheeks. She emitted shame and frustration underneath the drumbeat of the pain.

"What happened?" Tabitha said.

"I tripped and fell, like a total dork. Broke my leg, I think."

"I just hope I didn't make it worse carrying her here. It seemed like the right thing to do." His concern felt genuine. Tabitha let it wrap around her like a well-worn blanket.

She bit back the impulse to yell at Chloe for acting like an idiot. Starting a fight would add emotional distress to the physical pain she could barely fend off by itself. That dull throb got worse minute by minute. Thirst and exhaustion lurked somewhere in there too. "Kenji, do you think she could have some water?" She thought about asking him for aspirin, but suppose Chloe had a concussion? They'd better wait for the professionals to decide about drugs.

He went into the kitchen and came back with a glass of ice water and a handful of damp paper towels. Tabitha accepted them, blotted her sister's forehead and swabbed the blood and dirt off her leg while Kenji supported Chloe in a half-reclining position to drink. Under the improvised splint, her calf already showed bruises and swelling. "Did you get hurt anywhere else?" Tabitha asked.

Chloe shook her head. "Just bumps and scrapes." She grimaced. "You probably guessed where I went."

"To meet the boyfriend, right?" Tabitha didn't think it would be a good idea to mention reading her sister's e-mail.

"Now he'll think I bailed on him." A stab of emotional pain echoed the physical one.

While Tabitha debated whether to admit she'd intercepted the boy and chased him off, sirens wailed up the driveway. Kenji let in the paramedics, both men, one young and wiry, the other middle-aged and burly. She stood off to the side while they unfolded a gurney and prepared Chloe for transport. Every movement shot another dart of pain into the leg and into Tabitha's head.

Fear sharpened Chloe's anguish. "Mom and Dad will kill me. Tabby, do you have to tell them?"

"Did your brain get damaged too? You know I have to. For one thing, how else is your hospital bill supposed to get paid?"

Chloe shut her eyes, fresh tears leaking from them. Her distress pulled Tabitha down like quicksand. She caught herself clutching Kenji's hand as if it could haul her out of that pit. Bracing herself, she watched the paramedics hook up an IV and wheel her sister to the ambulance. The husky one told her their destination, the small community hospital in the nearest town, and reassured her that Chloe seemed to have a fractured tibia. Nothing life threatening.

When the cloud of pain vanished into the distance with the siren, Tabitha shuddered in relief. She realized she still gripped Kenji's hand and let go of it, dimly aware that she'd unconsciously dug her nails into it. He didn't step away from her, as she expected. Instead, he wrapped his arms around her. Trembling, she leaned on his slim, firm body. She found his shoulder just the proper height for resting her head.

"Shh, it's okay. They said she'll be fine." He radiated caring and comfort that nobody had offered her since her grandmother's death. When was the last time anyone had held her this way? Her parents, when she visited at Christmas, gave her awkward hugs, with contact only at shoulders and cheeks, as if they didn't want to risk touching their mind-probing daughter more than necessary.

Tabitha realized she was still shaking. She didn't want to let go of him. Her knees might collapse under her. "How did you find her that fast?"

"Just lucky." The full truth hid in a corner of his mind like a mouse in its burrow. She didn't challenge his evasion, since she couldn't explain how she knew he was withholding information. "You want to go to the hospital now, right?" he said. "Should I drive you to your place to pick up some of your sister's clothes and stuff?"

"Thanks." She raised her head and wiped her eyes. "Then could you run me to the crossroads to get my car?"

"Are you kidding? You can't drive when you're upset like this. I'm taking you to the hospital."

"You don't have to do that, not after I dragged you out in the middle of the night."

"I want to." The sincerity behind the words enveloped her like a thermal blanket on a chilly evening. He didn't make any move to release her and lead the way to his car though. His brown eyes softened with warmth she couldn't bring herself to turn away from. His embrace tightened and his hand massaged her back in slow circles. She sensed hunger in him, lurking under the impulse to help. With her breasts flattened against his chest, her hips fitted to his, she felt a swelling hardness between his legs. Their heights matched so well that the apex of her thighs cradled his erection.

Embarrassment, his and her own combined, surrounded them as hot as the vapor from a steam bath. She knew she ought to pull back. His mind projected the same feeling. But neither of them made a move because the other emotion, the need, overwhelmed good judgment. She couldn't help thinking of their earlier meeting. At the memory of sharing his climax, she melted inside, already as wet as if they stood there naked together.

An answering surge of desire welled from him. How did he know how she felt? Or did he? Maybe his lust sprang up spontaneously. She had trouble visualizing herself as an irresistible sex object, yet the attention felt good, not like the crude appetites of her past would-be boyfriends. While he continued rubbing the middle of her back, sending spirals of warmth through her body, his other hand stroked her hair until she wanted to purr. Cupping her head, he nuzzled the side of her neck. Tiny electric shocks zapped her spine. He nibbled along her jawline. A moan escaped her throat. She tilted her head, her lips parted.

With a hissing breath, he brushed his mouth over hers. She sensed him holding back, his desire straining at its leash. Why did he fight the hunger to kiss her? Her tongue teased his lips in one rapid flick that was all her own self-consciousness allowed. He gasped and covered her open mouth with his. Sliding his hand down her back, he clasped her bottom and wedged her against his hardness. His tongue darted in and out of her mouth in vigorous thrusts that she sensed he could barely keep his pelvis from imitating.

Though his teeth scraped the corner of her mouth, the minor pain hardly registered. He suckled alternately on her upper and lower lip as if trying to devour her. He obviously had no more experience with kissing than she had. But the awkwardness didn't matter. Panting, tasting, groping, she wanted nothing more than to rip off their clothes and beg him to fill every hollow space inside her.

A strange sound rumbled in his chest, something like a growl. A new emotion overshadowed his arousal. Fear verging on panic.

He tore his mouth free of hers, pried her hands off him and whirled around. With his back to her, he shuddered, his fists curling and uncurling. He exhaled fear with every rasping breath. She sensed that he believed sharing sexual pleasure with her would make something terrible happen.

She struggled to catch her own breath. At last he turned around and spoke, his voice harsh. "We can't do this. It's wrong."

Chapter Five

&

Her cheeks burned as if she'd just stepped out of a sauna. "You're right," she mumbled. "We have to get going." What had possessed her, making out while Chloe was being rushed to the emergency room with a broken leg? Maybe, Tabitha thought, her folks were right about her freakishness. And what was wrong with Kenji? Did he have some kind of phobia or guilt complex about sex so severe that even kissing triggered panic? Yet he seemed normal most of the time, quiet and kind.

Without another word, he retreated into one of the back rooms. Grateful for the respite, she waited for her face to cool and her heartbeat to slow down. Kenji reappeared wearing a shirt, tennis shoes and khaki shorts and dangling a set of car keys. The two of them didn't look at each other while they walked outside and got into his car, an economy-style compact not much different from her own. By the time they fastened their seat belts and he pulled out of the driveway, humiliation over the way she'd almost eaten him alive had wiped out her excitement. His feelings echoed hers, the lust and fear receding as embarrassment took over. She had no idea why a moment of near-intimacy had thrown him into a panic, but this was no time to puzzle over such things. At her house, she dashed inside to throw a few of Chloe's things into an overnight bag. The task reminded Tabitha to focus on her sister's predicament, and having a couple of walls and doors between Kenji and herself helped to cool her the rest of the way.

When they reached the town after a silent half-hour trip, he dropped her at the hospital's emergency entrance and drove off to find a space in the parking lot. Tabitha gritted her teeth and squared her shoulders, symbolic acts that wouldn't add a fraction of an inch to the layer of armor around her brain.

Against the psychic barrage she knew she would face inside, that armor would feel more like a sheet of tinfoil.

The moment she walked through the automatic doors, pain and fear slammed her from all sides. And the emergency room, not much bigger than her living room, wasn't even especially crowded. In one corner sat a mother holding a feverish little boy who whimpered with a headache. Across the room, a woman with stomach cramps waited her turn. Beyond the swinging doors leading to the treatment area, somebody had a crushing chest pain, endurable because the walls partly blocked it. His fear of a heart attack echoed the physical distress. Last, Tabitha sensed Chloe's consciousness, blurry as if she'd been medicated

At the window Tabitha introduced herself to the receptionist, who gave her a clipboard of paperwork to fill out. She sat on one of the molded plastic chairs and started writing, using the routine as a shield against the swarm of emotions and sensations. She glanced up when she felt a soothing presence reach out to surround her. Kenji sat next to her. Concern swirled around him like an aromatic mist.

"You look like you're the one who got hurt," he said.

She realized she'd knotted her forehead so tightly her brow ached. Forcing her muscles to smooth out, she said, "I'm okay." To her surprise, she did feel the emotional clamor around her less acutely with his warmth muffling it. She puzzled over the blank lines on the form in her lap. She knew her parents' health insurance company, of course, but not the policy number. That question reminded her she would have to call them soon.

She'd just handed the clipboard back to the receptionist when a slim, black nurse opened the swinging door and called her name. The inner room smelled like disinfectant with a trace of vomit in the background. On top of the pain from the man with the heart attack and the miasma of fear emitted by him and the woman sitting beside him, the odors made Tabitha queasy. Now that she'd left Kenji behind in the waiting room, she realized how much his caring had shielded her against the negative sensations. She drew shallow breaths through her mouth and followed the nurse to the corner where Chloe lay. A doctor with a high forehead and bushy mustache was examining her leg.

He introduced himself and shook Tabitha's hand. He projected confidence under a layer of mild fatigue. "Fortunately, your sister has only a simple fracture. She'll have to wear a cast for a couple of months. I understand you're not her legal guardian?"

"No way!" The horror of that notion made the emphatic denial leap out of Tabitha's mouth before she realized how rude it sounded. "She's just visiting. Our parents live in Norfolk."

"Did you tell them yet?" asked Chloe, her voice slurred by painkillers.

"No, I'll do that in a minute. They'll want to come pick you up, I guess." She clasped her sister's damp hand. A dull ache from the broken bone and anxiety over their parents' probable reaction seeped through the contact, fogged by the drugs.

Chloe's eyes drifted from Tabitha to the waiting room doors. "What about Shawn?"

"Who? Oh, the guy you were trying to meet?"

A small nod. "I've got to let him know what happened to me."

Tabitha debated for a few seconds whether to leave the subject hanging. No, she had to tell the truth eventually and might as well get it over with. "Don't worry about that. I met him and told him to stop bothering us. He left."

"You what?" A whiplash of anger crackled from Chloe. She tried to sit up and yelped in pain. The doctor made her lie flat again.

Tabitha winced at the double sting. "Listen, I may not be your guardian, but if I'm temporarily responsible, I'm not about to let you run off and elope or something."

"Elope? It's not like we were planning to get married." Her voice dropped to a drowsy mumble.

"I sure hope not. What did you think you were doing?"

"We just want to be together. He loves me." She believed that claim. No trace of doubt colored her thoughts. "Where do you get off butting in? And how did you know where to find him anyway?" The anger swelled into fury. "You read my e-mail, didn't you?"

"I was trying to do what's best for everybody."

Chloe snatched her hand away and closed her eyes. "Don't do me any favors." The words felt like a slap in the face.

The doctor said, "Let her get some rest. You can settle this later." Impatience and faint disapproval of their public bickering tinged the orders.

Tabitha turned away, half blinded by a gray cloud of negative emotions like a gathering thunderstorm, and staggered into the waiting room. When a hand gripped her arm to guide her to a chair, the cloud vanished.

Kenji's touch lingered as he said, "You don't look too good. Maybe I should take you home."

"In a minute. I have to call my folks." She rummaged in the bottom of her purse for her cell phone and started for the door.

He followed her outside. "Will your sister be all right?"

"Yeah, it's just one broken bone, the way you thought." The cool air, even with gas fumes from the parking lot, smelled better than the atmosphere in the ER. More important, the doors protected her from most of the turmoil inside. She flipped the phone open and punched her parents' number while Kenji walked off, probably to the car.

Tabitha's throat clogged when the phone started ringing. The prospect of this conversation felt like the time she'd stayed too late at a party in high school and tried to sneak in after curfew, or like scraping the car's fender and having to explain the damage to her father. She combed her fingers through her hair in an exasperated gesture, wishing she could scoop the irrational anxiety out of her brain. She wasn't a teenager anymore. They couldn't ground her or dock her allowance. And over the phone, she didn't have to worry about feeling their emotions.

Her father's voice barked, "Hello? Who's this?"

"It's me, Dad. Chloe's here." She hastily added, "She's going to be okay."

"What do you mean, going to be? She isn't now?"

Tabitha's pulse pounded in her temples. She had to gulp a breath to keep from stammering. "She fell down on one of the trails." That explanation sounded less dire than tumbling into a ravine. "She broke her leg, but it's not too bad."

On the other end, her father relayed the information to her mother. Tabitha heard her mother say, "Give me that!" and then, "Tabby, what on earth is going on? When did Chloe get there?"

"Late this afternoon."

"And you didn't bother to call us?"

"I'm calling you now, aren't I? I didn't want to upset her into running away from my place too." The excuse sounded as weak in her own ears as the one she'd given for a failed test in junior high school science.

"That wasn't for you to decide. I'd think by this age you'd have better judgment."

Before Tabitha could come up with a defense, her father reclaimed the phone. "What hospital is she in? Do you have the address and phone number?"

She recited them from the notes she'd jotted down while filling out the paperwork. A siren wailed a few blocks away, and she covered her free ear to muffle the noise.

"Fine, we'll be there in the morning." His voice warmed a fraction of a degree. "Don't mind your mother. She's just upset."

From the background came, "I am not —"

"Bye, Dad. I'll see you tomorrow." Tabitha glanced at her watch. Almost three a.m. "I mean this morning, I guess." She switched off before her mother could jump into the conversation again.

Only then did she notice Kenji's car idling at the curb. Dropping the phone in her purse, she started in his direction. He stepped out and strode around to open the passenger door. At the same moment, the siren's scream rose to a crescendo and cut off as an ambulance pulled into the bay next to the pedestrian entrance. Halfway into the front seat of the car, Tabitha watched the paramedics lift a gurney out of the vehicle and wheel the patient into the ER. She caught a glimpse of a young man with the sheet covering his torso soaked in blood. His agony stabbed her in the gut.

She doubled over, clutching her stomach. A groan erupted from her clenched jaws. Her head reeled with the man's terror and the tension that reverberated between the two EMTs attending him. Tendrils of black and crimson swarmed in her vision.

She felt hands settling her in the car and buckling the seat belt around her, heard doors slam, sensed an arm around her shoulders and breath ruffling her hair.

"Tabitha, what's wrong? Should I take you inside and get a doctor?" The words quivered with the strain of Kenji's fear for her.

"No, not that!" Shaking, she forced her voice under control. "I'm not sick. Just get me away from here, and I'll be okay."

She closed her eyes and breathed deeply while the car pulled out of the hospital lot and accelerated onto the road. His concern lapped around her like wavelets in a tide pool. After a few minutes, the effects of the most recent psychic barrage faded. She looked over at him, and he met her glance with a brief smile.

"Feeling better? Can you tell me what happened back there?"

Tell him? And have him write her off as either a nutcase or a mutant? "You wouldn't believe me."

A shadow flitted across the surface of his mind. "You'd be surprised what I'd believe." He cast her a look weighted with trepidation. She felt he wanted to explain further but couldn't bring himself to take the risk. "Come back to my place for a while. I don't want to leave you alone like this."

"Okay." She released the tightness in her chest in a long sigh. She knew she shouldn't expose herself to the naked emotions of any man, no matter how sweet and seductive, because the shattering of the fragile union would only hurt more than keeping her distance. But she couldn't resist a few hours of pretending she could handle intimacy like a normal woman.

When they reached the intersection with their road, Tabitha blinked at the unexpected sight of a two-seater sports car parked on the side of the highway. "That car looks familiar."

As soon as they turned into the lane, a figure stepped in front of Kenji's car, waving. With a muttered curse, he screeched to a stop. Tabitha recognized the silver-tipped black hair at once. "That's Chloe's boyfriend."

The boy—Shawn—circled to the passenger door and yanked it open. "Where the hell is she?"

Tabitha braced herself to keep from cringing. "What are you talking about?"

Kenji got out and walked around the front of the car. "I suggest you back off and leave her alone."

"Not until she tells me where Chloe went." Shawn clutched Tabitha's arm. Kenji grabbed him by the shoulder to pull him off.

"No, wait," she said. She sensed more anxiety than rage emanating from the boy. "Chloe's in the hospital, but she'll be okay. She fell down and broke her leg trying to get to that meeting with you."

"You're lying. You just don't want us together." Behind his belligerence lurked honest worry about Chloe's welfare.

"You know I'm not lying." Tabitha reached out mentally to collect the strands of his tangled emotions and weave them into a smoother pattern. For a second she had a grasp on the threads, but they slipped from her fingers. "What are you doing back here anyway?"

"You didn't think I'd let you chase me away permanently, did you? I figured, so what if she can read my mind."

"I can't—" She glanced at Kenji, whose outrage at the attack mingled with confusion. *Oh, hell, now I'll have to come up with an explanation whether I'm ready or not.*

"So after I got over whatever you did to me," Shawn continued, "I drove up there looking for your house. Only two houses, so it wasn't hard to find. Nobody was home. With your car still parked here, I decided this was the best place to wait. I figured you had to show up eventually."

"Well, here I am, and I told you what happened to Chloe. She's in the hospital in town, and our parents are coming to pick her up in a couple of hours."

"Just like that? Damn it, I'm not letting you take her away until I see her."

His rage scalded her. His fingers dug into her arm hard enough to bruise. She probed the surface of his thoughts again, trying to calm the storm enough to make him listen. He did care about Chloe. She didn't want to fight with him. She pried his grip loose from her arm and whispered, "It's all right. You can contact her later. There's no reason to get upset."

"You're inside my head again. Bitch freak!"

Kenji seized his shoulders and spun him around. "That's enough! Get the hell out of here!"

Shawn pulled back his right arm for a punch. Kenji dodged the blow and raised both hands, palms out. A gesture of surrender?

No. Something that had to be an illusion. A basketball-size sphere of flame appeared in the air in front of him.

Chapter Six

∞

The greenish fire dazzled her eyes. How did Kenji do it? Some kind of magician's trick? Where in the pockets of his shorts would he have room to carry the supplies? And how did the sphere float toward Shawn when the boy backed away? How could it follow his every move while he ducked and swerved in his retreat?

"Go!" Kenji yelled. "Now!" The last word sounded more like a howl than human speech. With his back to Tabitha, he chased Shawn toward the highway, with the fireball dancing in midair between them. She stood up, straining her eyes to follow their movements in the shadows under the trees. The fireball vanished while Shawn disappeared into the darkness, and seconds later his car engine accelerated in the distance. Kenji leaned over, facing away from her, his hands on his bent knees. His emotions whirled like a tornado.

She staggered toward him. His loud, harsh breathing echoed the turbulence in his head. She thought she heard an animal's growl, but that had to be her imagination. Any normal wild creature would flee from the noise of human voices and footsteps. Just before she got close enough to touch Kenji, he shouted, "Stay back!" She could hardly understand the words, thick and guttural.

Was he sick? The chaos of his fury, panic and despair buffeted her like hurricane winds. She collapsed to her knees, hugging herself to form a flimsy barrier. Squeezing her eyes shut, she prayed for the storm to die down before it ripped her apart.

Little by little, it faded. She heard his breathing slow to normal and felt him lock his emotions inside whatever cage they had escaped from. She opened her eyes and used a low-hanging branch to pull herself upright. With soundless, hesitant steps, Kenji came to her side. Momentarily, she thought she saw golden sparks gleaming in his eyes. No, only an illusion. They were gone now. When he touched her forearm, his fingers felt as hot as if he had a fever.

"Did that jerk hurt you?" His fingers slid up her arm to her shoulder, slipping under the short sleeve of her shirt. Though his skin scorched hers, the contact made her shiver.

"No," she whispered. Still trembling, she hugged him around the waist and rested her forehead on his shoulder. She felt him hesitate for a second before putting one arm around her. His body radiated heat while his mind emitted a tangle of fear, anger and desire.

He wanted her as much as she wanted him. Or did she? Why did lust ignite within her every time they touched? Was she feeling her own need, born of lifelong celibacy and years of loneliness? Or did her hunger only echo his?

This has to be real. I have my own feelings, I know I do. She'd felt attracted to him the other times they'd met. Only her emotional bruises from past attempts at intimacy had kept her from acting on the attraction. To prove that claim to herself, she raised her head, stood on tiptoe and pressed her lips to his.

She heard a hitch in his breath, felt his surge of gratitude for the gesture, blurred by the same strange apprehension that had tinged his feelings before. Her tongue probed between his lips. The tip of his tongue flickered to meet hers then retreated. With a shuddering sigh, he moved his mouth over hers as if sampling her flavor.

She wondered whether he was erect. The thought made warm liquid gush from her slit. Shifting her legs, she tried to press her hips against his.

For a second she felt his hardness, and his lips parted. Their tongues met again. A miniature bolt of lightning flashed through her. The next instant, he broke off the kiss.

"I'm sorry." He stepped back, his breath fast and shallow. "I shouldn't hassle you that way on top of what that guy did."

Tabitha shook her head. She had to wait for dizziness to fade before she could speak. "I'm okay. And he's not as bad as I thought he was. He's really worried about Chloe." The remark slipped out before she realized Kenji would wonder how she knew Shawn's state of mind.

He didn't seem to catch the discrepancy though. Anxiety about her overshadowed his thoughts. "Then what was wrong with you a minute ago? Are you sick?"

She almost giggled, hearing him ask the same thing she'd wondered about him. "Like I said, you wouldn't believe me."

"And like I said before, you'd be surprised how easily I'd believe a lot of strange things." He slid his arm around her waist again, lightly this time, to guide her back to the car. "Come to my place, the way we planned, so you can rest until you feel better and explain what's going on. Unless I've scared you away." The tremor in his voice confirmed his worry about her reaction.

"Scared? No." But she was more intrigued than before. "So you can believe six impossible things before breakfast, huh?" she said after getting into the car.

"I hope you can too because I want to show you one of them." Though his voice held steady, she sensed the trepidation behind it. Whatever he planned to show her, he feared scaring her with it. What secret could he have that was weirder than her own?

"That'll work out," she said, trying to keep her tone light, "because breakfast is still hours away."

"Sorry, I didn't think about that. You must be hungry. I'll fix you something."

"Food hasn't even occurred to me. After all, I don't usually eat at midnight, and I've been worrying about Chloe." Her insides still felt tied in knots from barricading herself against more physical and emotional pain than she normally confronted in a full year.

A few minutes later, they pulled into Kenji's driveway. Just inside his front door he paused to take off his shoes, so she did the same. Again the clean aroma of freshly cut wood wafted from the back of the house. She retreated to the bathroom at the end of a short hallway, a welcome refuge from the puzzling blend of eagerness and nervousness that swirled around him. She splashed water on her flushed cheeks and drank a glass to quench the thirst she hadn't noticed until then. The emptiness in her stomach might be hunger or simply the void left by wrung-out emotions. She couldn't tell for sure.

When she returned to the living room, she found Kenji sitting on the floor pouring tea from a porcelain pot on a tray on the coffee table. Beside two handleless cups in the same flowered pattern as the teapot sat a plate of rice crackers along with a rectangle of some brick-red substance. "Sit down and have a drink," he said, "and tell me your unbelievable secret whenever you feel ready." His shy grin lit up his face. "I promise I won't run screaming into the woods."

"It's not that horrible," she said, "just weird." She blew on the steaming liquid in her cup and took a sip. Green tea, with a delicate flavor that reminded her a little of the aroma of freshly mown grass. "I don't want you to think I'm either a lunatic or a mutant. The thing is, ever since I can remember, I've been reading people's feelings, emotional and physical."

She sensed his heartbeat skip in momentary alarm. "You can tell what I'm thinking?"

Her spirits sagged. *Here we go again. It's been nice meeting you, hope you enjoyed the tea, so long.* How did she dare imagine he'd react differently from anyone else? "Not thoughts. Just emotions and sensations."

"Oh." The ruffled surface of his mind smoothed over. "I'm not surprised."

"Huh?" With a shaky hand, she set the cup down with a slosh.

"I knew your grandmother for years. I suspected she had some kind of power like that."

The world froze like a stopped clock. She forced herself to breathe, and everything started up again. "How did you guess?"

"I felt it. Whenever we met, she projected an aura of peace. I always felt calm around her. It was like she knew when I happened to be upset about anything, and she soothed it away."

"Did you know her well?" Surely not, or Grandmama would have introduced them.

He shook his head. "Not really. I made a coffee table for her." He looked down into his cup. "I've wondered if you still have it."

"The one carved out of a tree stump? I love it."

He flushed with obvious pleasure. "After that, we met casually now and then, and every time she filled me with…" He seemed to grope for a word. "Serenity."

Tabitha nodded. "She did that for me too. With her was the only time I felt completely relaxed."

"Can you do that the way she did?"

"I wish. She did try to teach me to shape people's emotions. It doesn't usually work for me. Maybe I'm trying too hard, because they seem to pick up on it and get more disturbed instead of less. I can only influence animals."

"Yeah?" An odd tinge of hopefulness colored the word.

"Well, and sometimes little kids. I could make Chloe calm down until she got old enough to notice what I was doing. But the cat couldn't resist. Nobody else in the family could lure him into his cage when he had to go to the vet." She smiled at the memory. "I felt where he was hiding and coaxed him out by imagining I was touching him, stroking his fur flat instead of all bristly. I got along fine with pets. I just had trouble with people."

"Even your parents?" The question held wistful overtones. She remembered his folks were both dead.

"Half the time they thought I was making up stuff and yelled at me for lying. The other half, they believed in my abilities and tried to hide how nervous they felt about the whole thing."

"So you moved here after your grandmother died."

"Yeah, she left the place to me. I think she must've needed shelter almost as much as I do, except that she could shield against the stress better. She had that control I couldn't develop. The cabin used to be hers and Granddad's summer place. After he died, she had it fixed up and moved into it full time. She invited me to hide here whenever Mom and Dad would let me." Her throat clogged with sadness. Since Grandmama's death, she hadn't been able to discuss her "problem" with anybody. Not until this moment.

"You miss her a lot," Kenji said softly.

"Yeah." She swallowed. "She practically rescued me from going insane by leaving me the house. I love the isolation. It saves me from constantly getting battered by people's emotions." She nibbled a rice cracker. "Thing is, every time I get into a group of people, it seems worse than the time before. Like tonight at the hospital. It felt like getting caught in a hurricane. High wind, deafening thunder and pounding rain all at once."

"That's a special case, isn't it?" He cut a slice of the reddish substance on the plate. "Other than hospital emergency rooms, is it possible the problem's getting worse because you're out of practice?"

Her eyes widened. "I didn't think of that. Maybe." Her shoulders sagged. "But after tonight, I don't think I could get up the nerve to test the theory anytime soon." She accepted the slice he handed her on a napkin. "What's this?"

"Red bean paste."

It tasted like firm, mildly sweet tofu. "What inspired you to live out here in the middle of nowhere, as my folks call it?

Grandmama mentioned it to me when you started building the house. She said she wouldn't mind having a neighbor as long as he wasn't right next door. That was just a couple of years before she died."

"I needed a refuge too." Tabitha noticed he didn't volunteer the reason for that need. "After Mom died, Dad went downhill pretty fast. He wasn't very old, but he didn't want to live on without her. Maybe it sounds hokey, but they had a super romantic relationship."

"Doesn't sound hokey to me. It must be great." She couldn't suppress a sigh at the thought that she'd probably never have a love like that.

He smiled. "Right, though it's a little weird thinking of my parents that way. Anyhow, he had three heart attacks, and the last one killed him. He'd made good investments after he retired from the Navy, and he left a big life insurance policy too. So I decided to buy this land and become a hermit."

"You didn't have any other relatives to hassle you about that?"

"No. Dad was an only child and so am I. I've wished I had a brother." He grinned. "Although now I'm not so sure, after watching you and Chloe."

"Oh, it wasn't always this bad. As my baby sister, she was kind of fun to have around." She sighed at the memory of acting out adventures with dolls as fairy princesses riding pastel, plush unicorns, with a stuffed tiger standing in for a fierce dragon. Tabitha's empathic gift had served as an advantage then, enhancing the imaginary peril of the games. "We got along okay until she turned into a smart-mouthed teenager. She thought I was invading her mental space, so she threw fits every time I looked at her the wrong way."

"And I bet that made things worse because her negative emotions hurt you."

"That's right." His ability to discuss her power so calmly made her muscles slacken in release of a tension she hadn't realized existed.

"I heard her call you Tabby. That sounded kind of cute, like she doesn't exactly hate you. Should I call you that?"

She said with a wry smile, "Depends on how long you want to keep living. Do people call you Ken?"

He chuckled. "Not if I can help it." He unfolded his crossed legs and stood up. "Now I want to show you something. I promised you something impossible. It runs in my family, the way empathy does in yours."

"You have a deep, dark secret too?"

He nodded, quietly serious, with trepidation leaking through his calm facade. She followed him across the room.

Two doors led from the living room into the back half of the house. One, she knew from previous visits, opened into the hall that connected with the kitchen, bedroom and workshop. He headed for the other exit, which led to the corridor that ended in the bathroom. Two closed doors occupied the wall to the right of the bathroom.

"This is just the linen closet," he said, indicating the one on the left. "But this…"

Good grief, what does he keep in there, a bunch of dead wives like Bluebeard? She could almost hear his heart hammering with nervousness.

Kenji hesitated with his hand on the doorknob. "I've never shown this to anyone before. I'm trusting you to keep it to yourself."

"I promise."

"Good," he said with a sudden grin, "because this is definitely something nobody would believe."

"Like that ball of fire you chased Shawn with?"

"Stranger than that." He opened the door and turned a dial just inside. A diffuse light came on. He raised the level to a gentle glow, too dim to read by but enough to banish the darkness. Other than noticing the room had no windows, Tabitha didn't waste time looking for the source of the illumination. She was too stunned by what the light revealed.

She stood on the threshold of a square space that looked larger than all the other parts of the house combined. At least, it appeared square from what she could see of the walls, camouflaged by potted shrubs, flowers and dwarf trees. She saw peonies, purple irises and other blooms she didn't recognize. A blossomy fragrance permeated the cool air. Just inside the door, a pond sparkled with the silver of lazily swimming fish. A miniature waterfall cascaded over shiny pebbles into the pond. Lily pads floated on the surface. A stone lantern about two feet high stood next to it.

Her eyes tracked the paths — darker wood inlaid amid the golden hardwood — that wound among the shrubbery. Against one wall she noticed a hibachi with a black lacquer cabinet beside it. A high screen painted with drooping willow trees hid one corner. In the opposite corner the path led to a sunken whirlpool tub, bordered with marble. Cushions in assorted sizes covered the floor nearby.

She'd unconsciously taken a couple of steps into the room, she realized when she heard Kenji shut the door behind her. In the silence, softened only by the waterfall's ripple, she heard him hold his breath, his mind taut with anticipation.

Finally he whispered, "Well?"

She whispered back, half afraid the place would pop like a bubble if she spoke too loudly. "You're right, this is impossible."

"I told you," he said in a more normal tone, "six impossible things before breakfast." He waved a hand. A flame leaped up in the stone lantern. Another wave, and a fireball floated to the ceiling. He dialed the electric light back to its dimmest setting.

"No, I mean *really* impossible." Her lungs felt as constricted as if she'd hiked to the top of a mountain. "The house doesn't have nearly enough space to hold this room. This should be a closet."

"For anybody else, it would be a combination broom closet and half bath. Only I can open the door and find this space. I and anybody I've escorted here. Which means only you."

Her next breath turned into a gasp. She drew a deeper one and said, "Why would you trust me that much?"

"I want to know you better. That can't happen if I keep hiding everything about myself. You saw the fireball, so you're bound to have questions. This seemed like the next step. Anyway, you trusted me with your secret." With a hand on her shoulder, he guided her to the cushions and lowered her to a seat like a courtier settling a princess on a throne.

"Yeah, but this is a whole different order of strangeness. How?"

He shrugged. "Call it magic if you want. A talent I inherited from my mother."

"Okay, this makes two impossible things so far."

"No, three, counting your emotion-reading power."

"So what are the other three?"

A shadow flitted across his face. "Let's hold off on them for now, okay?"

"Your mother, huh? She could make whole rooms appear out of nowhere? What else could she do?"

"Lots more than I can. Seduce men."

"I guess you inherited that power too. To seduce women, I mean. I've seen a sample." Their eyes met, and she felt her face flushing at the same time as his reddened.

"I didn't plan that. It just happened." The words rang true. Tabitha had sensed how he'd tried to quench his arousal. "Mom warned me, said I'd have to be careful."

Careful how? Why? The evasive shifting of his eyes didn't encourage questions. "Men fell for her? Like your father?"

"Maybe it started with the magic. I know she loved my dad though. Enough to give up her home and live halfway around the world." Sadness shadowed the words. "That's probably why she died so young. Pneumonia, they said, but I think she pined away because she was cut off from her land. That's important to our people. Our family. That's why she created a place like this for herself. It helped for a while."

"So why aren't you pining away?"

"Virginia is my home. I was born here, so this is the land I'm tied to."

She scanned the room again, still dazed by her surroundings. "Is any of this real? What about the fish?" Tabitha stood up and walked to the pond. A foot or two long, the fish swam in lazy circles, displaying their black, scarlet, and silver bands.

"Of course it's real. You're seeing and touching it, aren't you?" He took a mundane-looking can of dried shrimp out of the cabinet. "They're koi. Want to feed them?"

She accepted the can and sprinkled a handful of shrimp flakes on the water. The koi rose to the surface and gulped the fragments. "Granted, they look solid enough."

"Oh, they're for-real real. I can't produce live animals. Mom could have, maybe, but I bought these at a pet shop."

"And you just conjured up everything else." She retreated to the cushions and sank into the soft heap, her breath escaping in a gust of amazement.

"Mom taught me, before she died. She needed a refuge of her own that no outsider could find, and she knew I would too. We practiced together until I got it right. Little things. She let me help redecorate her secret garden sometimes." His eyes seemed focused on a distant vision. "Hers wasn't just one room. It was like stepping into another world."

"Where did she get this magic from?"

Kenji sat down next to her on the cushion and dragged his gaze back from whatever memory had snared him. "Like I said, it runs in the family. Just think of it as inscrutable Oriental lore."

Though she sensed the lid he kept on the rest of the truth, she couldn't insist on prying open that locked box. Not yet. If she'd found a man who could accept her strangeness without freaking out, though, surely he would eventually show her his innermost secrets. "So the magic made the plants and the hot tub and all this stuff?" If she hadn't felt his emotions as keenly as ever, she might have suspected herself of dreaming. But her power never operated in dreams.

"Want to try it out? The tub, I mean."

Her cheeks warmed. "In what? You don't have a woman's bathing suit around, do you?"

"What's wrong with underwear? It covers as much as swimsuits." He stood up and took her hand to help her to her feet.

Her pulse quickened at the clasp of his fingers. "Why do you want to do that? I can tell you're nervous about it. Scared."

He winced. "This empathy stuff will take some getting used to. I'm inviting you because I want to prove I can. To prove we can share a simple hot tub like friends, and I can stay in control."

Control of what? she wanted to scream. But of course she didn't. He'd already revealed more to her than she'd dared hope, and she sensed that, unlike her, he hid more layers of secrets. Did he fear their mutual lust would turn him into a raving maniac? The idea of that almost made her giggle aloud. Nobody had ever accused her of being an irresistible sex goddess. If that was his secret dread, she wouldn't push him to confess it.

"Okay, I'm all for friendship," she said.

"I'm glad." His fingers skimmed her hair. "I've decided I don't like being a hermit as much as I expected to."

"Me neither."

With a sigh, she involuntarily swayed toward him. He fingered the nape of her neck. A shiver trickled down her spine, and she felt a shudder run through him too.

He removed his hand, stepped backward and said, "Just friendship. For now."

Her throat closed up. She could only nod her agreement. For the first time, she let herself hope they might share something more.

Chapter Seven

ဢ

After a couple of deep breaths, he spoke in a more normal tone. "You'll find a robe behind the screen there, if you want to wear it."

It turned out that the screen hid a sink and commode. One of the hooks on the wall above the towel rack held a jade green, kimono-style garment. After peeling off her shorts and shirt, she slipped on the robe over her bra and panties and tied the sash around her waist. The silky fabric shimmered over her skin like a cool breeze.

Wide-eyed, she stared at herself in the mirror. *Okay, I'm dreaming, right? Not that I'm in a hurry to wake up, but this can't be real, can it?* She might have believed that claim, except that she'd never had a dream this long and detailed, nor one in which she could read emotions. In dreams the clamor of feelings and sensations that normally plagued her fell silent.

She expelled pent-up breath in a long sigh and stepped around the screen. The overhead electric light had been switched off. In addition to the fireball hovering in the middle of the ceiling, swarms of greenish sparks like fireflies danced above her head. A lush jasmine scent permeated the room. Kenji already sat in the foaming whirlpool bath, submerged to mid-chest. His glossy black hair, damp and disheveled, made her long to rake her fingers through it. Steam hovered in the air over the water. A stack of beach towels had materialized next to the sunken tub. "Come on." He beckoned to her. She thought she glimpsed a glow in his eyes again. The surface of his mind rippled with suppressed eagerness like a lake ruffled by a breeze.

Swallowing the lump that still clogged her throat, she shrugged off the kimono and draped it over the nearest shrub.

She felt his gaze alight on her breasts then dart aside. Thankful that she'd worn a bra this time, she stuck one foot into the water. The heat, just short of scalding, made her halt with a hiss of shock.

"Go ahead, you'll get used to it in a minute."

Eager to hide under the bubbles, she gritted her teeth, put both feet on the ledge at the side of the tub and lowered herself onto the seat across from Kenji. The hot water that enveloped her up to her shoulders made her gasp. "Wow!"

He grinned. "Great, isn't it? Have a drink." He reached onto the marble deck for a porcelain cup, one of two sitting next to a matching blue and white decanter. He gently set the cup on the surface of the water and let go of it. Instead of tipping and spilling, it floated on the current produced by the whirlpool pump.

Tabitha watched it sail in a circle around the edge of the tub. When it came near her, she plucked it out of the eddy and found it half full of clear liquid. She took a sip. Warm sake. An involuntary "Mmm" escaped from her. The semi-sweet rice wine settled in her stomach and radiated comfort through her veins. Already she felt the water's heat as pleasant instead of near-painful. The froth made her nipples tingle, and the bubbling outflow from the pump behind her tantalized the space between her thighs. Her muscles seemed to melt in the steam. No chlorine stung her nose and eyes. Maybe the pool stayed clean by magic instead of chemicals.

Kenji filled his own cup and emptied it in one shot before setting it on the tub's rim. "This is one of my favorite places. It always calms me down. I hoped it would do the same for you."

She nodded and stretched her arms along the edge of the pool. "I wouldn't mind having one of these myself."

He spread his own arms until their fingertips almost brushed. "You can use mine anytime. Now that I've invited you in, why waste it?" His gold-flecked, chocolate-brown eyes silently begged for a favorable answer.

"I'd like that." She leaned her head back on the rim and watched the firefly lights circle the ceiling. "You're sure this place won't go poof and vanish while we're in it?"

"Not a chance. As long as I live, it'll stay solid."

"I still don't understand how it can exist. It wouldn't fit inside the walls of the house, so where is it?"

"If you can't accept that it's just magic, think of it as another dimension, a pocket of space at right angles to all the other dimensions."

"Including time?" A sudden memory from fairy tales and myths struck her. She sat up straight and shifted her gaze from the ceiling to his face. "Will I walk out of here and discover weeks have passed?"

He laughed softly. "Nothing like that. Mom's refuge worked in the opposite direction. You could spend as much time inside as you wanted and lose only a few minutes from the mundane world. I don't have that kind of power. Time in here runs the same as outside."

"Okay. I won't miss meeting my parents at the hospital. Not that I'm exactly looking forward to facing them." The understatement hid her true feelings, barely suppressed panic at the thought of their anger.

"Or all that hospital chaos?" His voice lapped over her as gently as the hot water. "Don't worry about that. I'll stay with you the whole time." He reached another couple of inches to lace his fingers through hers.

The jolt of electricity down her arm to her breasts distracted her from the sting of tears. Nobody else except her grandmother had ever reacted to her talent with sympathy. She drank the rest of her sake and wiped her eyes with the back of her hand. "That's the best offer I've had in a long time. The few people who know about me tend to run the other way."

He squeezed the hand he was still holding. "I'm the last person who has any right to do that, with my own deep, dark secrets. Except, well, I have to admit I ran for cover when we crossed paths yesterday."

She bowed her head, knowing the redness of her cheeks revealed her thoughts. He wouldn't have to share her psychic ability to guess what she was remembering. "I can't blame you there," she murmured. "I didn't mean to invade your privacy." She blushed hotter, with the lame apology digging her into a deeper pit of embarrassment.

"I should apologize to you. You shouldn't have had that forced on you. You felt when I got aroused, didn't you?"

She nodded. "I didn't feel forced," she whispered.

He tugged on her hand. She glided over to him, careful to keep most of her bra-line under the water. "I couldn't help it," he said. "You looked so cute in that clingy T-shirt. I hope that doesn't sound like a pickup line."

"Not to me, because I can tell you mean it." Hovering between his splayed legs and gazing down at the bubbles, she added, "I think you're pretty cute, yourself."

"Thanks, I don't hear that much," he said with a chuckle that quickly faded away. He cupped her chin to raise her head so that their eyes met. His cheeks were as flushed as hers felt. "Simplifies a lot, doesn't it? If you can tell I'm sincere, that should eliminate a ton of misunderstandings."

"Most people don't see it like that. They're afraid of having somebody know when they're lying, even little social lies."

"Up here in the woods, I don't have much chance for social anything, including lies. Which is how I liked it, until you came along." He fingered the side of her jaw. She felt her pulse jump. "You'll know I'm not lying when I say I want to kiss you."

"You want more than that." The air crackled with his growing arousal. Her nerves sparked in response.

"Can we start with kissing? I thought the water might relax me enough that we could go that far, and I could stay in control." His tongue flicked between his parted lips. The pulse fluttered in her neck at the thought of tasting him again.

Who needs control anyway? Was he afraid of spooking her, since he knew she could feel his excitement? She suppressed the impulse to tell him to unleash the passion she felt straining inside him. She wasn't yet sure she really wanted that.

She floated close enough to touch her lips to his cheek. With his hand clasping the nape of her neck, he rubbed the side of his face against hers. Fuzz on his cheeks rasped her skin. She heard him inhale deeply, as if he were savoring her scent. He licked her earlobe. "You taste delicious."

When he turned to plant his mouth on hers, she gasped. His tongue slipped between her parted lips. Clouds of sensual longing emanated from him in tendrils of invisible mist that wreathed around her like incense. She stroked his sleek black hair and brushed back the locks that tumbled over his forehead. He twined his fingers in the loose hairs under her ponytail, while he continued nibbling her lips, and his tongue teased hers. With every breath he exhaled, the mist of arousal that enveloped them grew denser and more fragrant. She tried to close the space between them. Her breasts ached to press against his chest.

To her surprise, he grasped her upper arms and held her off. "I think that went pretty well." His shallow, rapid breathing undercut the flippant comment.

"It went great. Why'd you stop?" She sensed his heart racing as fast as hers.

"I'm not sure it's safe to go farther."

"What do you mean, safe?" His firmly muscled body, slick with a sheen of water, irresistibly tempted her to explore it. She laid her open hand on his chest, where his heart pounded. When she slid her fingers over to graze a nipple, firm as a pebble, he grabbed her hand. "Remember, you can't hide your feelings from me," she said.

He flushed deep red. "Yeah, I know. Yesterday in the woods, you felt when I—came, didn't you?"

"Yes." Her face burned too. It didn't seem right to strip his feelings bare without offering the same honesty about her own. "When you had a climax, I did too."

He didn't look surprised. "Then there's no use denying I want you. But there are reasons why it might not work."

"What reasons?" A tingle in her nipples and clit echoed what she knew he felt at that moment. The tightness and heat grew stronger by the second, swamping any sensible caution she might have exercised. "I want the same thing." She straddled one of his legs and sat on his thigh before he could stop her. The pressure on her slit made her dizzy with pleasure. She sensed his erection without touching it, and her clit thickened and stiffened in answer. She brushed a fingertip over his left nipple. "Do that to me, please."

He mimicked the action. Both of her nipples sprang to attention. A bolt of lightning zapped from them to the apex of her thighs. She rocked on Kenji's leg. The friction of her wet panties sliding between her cleft and his hard muscles drove her halfway to climax in seconds.

With a growl, he pulled her into his arms and closed his mouth over hers. He tasted like the sake he'd drunk, and she sensed his tongue sampling the same flavor on her. She luxuriated in the way the hug squeezed her breasts against his chest and his hands skimmed in circles over the slick surface of her back. She felt feverish, with her skin too tight. She hungered to eat him alive, or did she feel his craving to devour her? She couldn't separate his longing from her own. Though the torrent swept over her, for once she didn't fear it. His arms supported her and wouldn't let her drown.

When he tore his mouth away from hers, they both struggled to catch their breath. Shuddering, he leaned his forehead on her shoulder. She smoothed his hair, as sleek and soft as an animal's pelt. His teeth closed gently on the skin above her collarbone. "We should stop," he murmured into her neck.

"No, we shouldn't. I want more and so do you." She would never have had the nerve to push the issue so boldly if she hadn't read his desire. His muscles quivered with the strain of resisting his need, and his erection verged on pain. Sharing that sensation made her clit swell so tautly she couldn't hold still. Rocking her hips back and forth, she felt the pressure building. "I want more touching." With one hand, she fumbled behind her back for the hook of her bra. When she got it unfastened, she leaned back long enough to strip it off and fling it away then rubbed her bare breasts on Kenji's chest.

Again he growled, a sound that made her insides vibrate in harmony with it. He buried his face in her throat, planting his teeth there just short of biting down, and suckled. The heat of his mouth made her whole body more sensitive, so that each tiny shift of position made her nipples, the bare skin of her chest and midriff, her inner thighs and her cleft tingle as if a million ants crawled over them. The bubbles felt like fingers caressing her everywhere at once.

"I can't stand much more," he said, his lips still touching her neck. The tickle of his breath made her nerves hum.

"Me neither." She scooted forward on his thigh until his upright shaft bumped her abdomen. "You're so hard. You need a climax." Her face burned with self-consciousness at speaking the words, but her own urgency overrode the embarrassment.

"Yes, damn it!"

"Me too." She rocked faster. "I'm going to come any minute."

With a groan, he held her tighter, compressing her breasts and his cock between their bodies. "Oh, damn, that feels so great. I don't want to stop."

"Then don't," she gasped. "I don't want to—go without you." His lust and hers together felt like a swarm of wasps buzzing in her head. She realized she'd closed her eyes, and sparks flashed behind her lids. The tension in her clit kept building. She clamped her thighs around his leg, wanting him to press deeper into her slit.

"Maybe," he forced out, "maybe it would be — okay — if you use your hand."

She inched backward just far enough to wedge one hand between them. He wore briefs, molded to the hard ridge by the water. She reached under the elastic. His cock sprang up to meet her groping fingers. She wrapped her hand around the shaft and squeezed. The spike in his arousal instantly leaped to her and made her clit twitch on the edge of release.

"Please!" He thrust into her clasp with a frantic up-and-down rhythm. "Like this. Quick!"

She obeyed. The water made his penis slippery. It glided in her palm, driving him to heights of delirium that drew her along with him. His eyes closed as he abandoned himself to the rising pleasure. She sensed him on the verge of erupting. Her clit, echoing the tension in his cock, felt so swollen it might burst. She rubbed it more vigorously on his leg while she stropped his shaft harder, faster, as eager for his release as he was.

When she felt the hot liquid bursting forth, she knew he needed her to squeeze the tip and press her thumb into the ridge at its rim. At that instant, he threw his head back and howled while his semen fountained into the pool. The convulsion seized her at the same moment. The passion that she'd always feared would sweep her under like a tsunami, batter her to unconsciousness and drown her instead rolled over her in powerful yet gentle waves of ecstasy that she wished would go on forever.

Trembling, they sagged into each other's arms. She laid her head on his shoulder, keeping her eyes closed until the world stopped spinning. "Oh, Tabitha..." he whispered. "That was —" She felt him swallow. "I can't thank you enough. I've never done this before. Didn't dare."

"I never have either. With anybody." She lifted her head. "What do you mean, dare? You don't have my problem. Do you?"

"No, mine's worse. But maybe we won't have to worry about it." He let go of her and climbed out of the tub, offering a hand to help her out.

Her wet skin developed goose bumps in the cool air. Wrapping one of the oversized towels around her, he massaged her back through the fluffy cloth. "Can't you tell me about this problem?"

A door in his mind swung shut. "Like I said, maybe it won't matter anymore. We've gotten this far." With another towel, he started drying himself.

"Good," she said, "then we can do it again." She smiled at the surprise that emanated from him. "After waiting all this time, you think I'd be satisfied with just once?"

"Believe me, I'd love to make love to you again. And again and again. I've got plenty of lost time to make up for too." He dropped his towel and rubbed hers vigorously over her shoulders and chest. Her skin tingled with the friction. With her legs almost too jelly-like to stand on, she grasped his upper arms for support and sighed with pleasure. His delight in touching her swirled around her the way the water had a few minutes before. "You need to lie down," he said, his voice husky with longing.

He scooped her up in his arms. She gasped, her head reeling. A second later, he set her on one of the giant cushions a few feet from the tub. She lay back, gazing up at him while he stripped off his soaked briefs. Already his penis looked half-erect. He reclined on his side next to her and pulled a fresh, dry towel over both of them. "I don't want you to get chilled."

Basking in the warmth of his aura, she said, "I don't think it'll feel cool for long. But wet underwear isn't helping." She giggled at his blush, after what they'd just done together, though she felt her face growing pinker too. She guided his hand to her waist. He hooked his fingers in the elastic and peeled her panties down. For a few seconds her legs got tangled in the damp nylon, making them both laugh.

Giddy, she twined her arms around his neck and drew his face close to hers. Again his beard fuzz sandpapered her cheek. The prickles of sensation that started there spread all over her body. She teased his lips with the tip of her tongue.

He rolled on top of her. She spread her legs to cradle his pelvis between them. His stiffening cock wedged into the exact place to put delicious pressure on her clit. She felt his chest growing hot against hers, as if he'd suddenly developed a fever. A glow of arousal welled up in him. The next moment, though, he pushed up on his elbows and shifted his hips away from hers, dismay tainting his pleasure.

"What's wrong?" She wiggled, trying to fit herself under him again.

"I want to give you pleasure," he said, "but I can't come inside you."

Chapter Eight

છ

"Good grief, why not?" His palpable distress made her feel like crying. "If it's protection you're worried about, we can do without it this one time. It's nowhere near my fertile period." As for disease, she sensed the truth of his claim to virginity, so infection was a non-issue. She tightened her embrace around him. "You said you wanted to make love to me. I feel that in you, but I feel this other thing too."

He nuzzled her hair. "I do want to make love to you, over and over. I will. But without entering. Then maybe I can keep control. Keep what I'm worried about from happening."

"Why are you trying to scare me?" She dug her nails into his shoulders.

He winced. "I'm not. Just being careful."

Sensing how her questions upset him, she dropped the subject. Instead of speech, she answered with a tentative kiss. It still seemed like a miracle that she could share this intimacy with any man, open to his every feeling and sensation, with him fully aware of her power. The surge of joy from him confirmed that he too could hardly believe what was happening.

His mouth opened as if hungry to devour her. Parting her lips to meet the thrust of his tongue, she realized that eating image came from him. She didn't mind. The thought of his grazing on her made her melt inside. She wanted his lips and tongue on her whole body at once.

When he lifted his head to gaze at her, she breathed, "More," and pulled him down to bury his face in her neck.

He caught a fold of skin in his teeth, not hard enough to hurt. "I want to taste you everywhere," he murmured. The hum of his voice in the hollow of her throat resonated through her chest and stomach.

"Do it!"

Again he emitted that ravenous growl that turned her insides to molten lava. He licked his way down to her breasts and circled each one with rapid flickers that felt like dancing flames. Her nipples perked up, begging for attention. She guided his mouth to one of them. While he lapped it until she thought it should visibly glow with the heat, the other one ached for the same stimulation. She grasped his right hand and placed it on her breast.

"There," she whispered. He twirled the nipple to an even harder peak, with his tongue still teasing the other one. "Like this." She brushed his fingers over the tip. He strummed it in the same rhythm with which his tongue pleasured its twin. "Yes!" She arched her back, eyes closed, and basked in the ripples of sensation. Her cleft melted into liquid heat. She squeezed her thighs together to ease the fresh swelling in her clit.

He moved downward, leaving her moist nipple exposed to cool air. His mouth explored the valley between her breasts and the soft skin of her abdomen. She flinched when his tongue dipped into her navel, but in a second the shock yielded to a new rush of warmth. Meanwhile, his fingers played with both nipples at once. Through the crimson fog of her excitement, she felt his delight at pleasing her. She also felt his arousal growing again. His erection brushed against her leg, but he wouldn't lie on top of her the way he longed to. Why not?

The question fled from her mind when he nipped his way down to the triangle of hair. He rubbed his face against her mound. His hot breath made her clit twitch, and his morning whiskers rasped the insides of her thighs.

"You smell great," he said. A blush spread over her whole body. The next moment, he fastened his mouth onto her and his tongue flicked her clit. She squirmed and his hands moved down to clasp her hips. He licked from her slit to the tip of her clit. "Like that?" he asked.

"Yes!"

He repeated the motion, lapping the full length of her cleft over and over. "Delicious," he murmured. "I could taste your pussy for hours."

"Then don't stop!" The second's pause when he spoke left her already throbbing with impatience. She felt ready to explode, and she sensed his cock almost as near to bursting.

With a soft laugh, he resumed licking her, faster now. The long, methodical strokes left her craving more. "My clit," she gasped. "Stay on my clit."

He obeyed, flicking the firm tip while her hips pumped up and down. He gripped her thighs to keep his mouth on target. Though dizzy with pleasure at the hot, wet caresses on her clit, she needed still more. Her slit yearned to be filled. "Touch inside me!"

One hand moved to her inner thigh, and two fingers probed her vagina. Her clit pulsed in time with his tongue's rhythm, and her sheath contracted around his fingers. She heard a scream and realized it was erupting from her throat. The convulsions rippled through her over and over, until she melted into a puddle of sated exhaustion.

Only then did she float out of her own mind and tune in to Kenji's sensations once more. He'd snuggled up next to her, his muscles taut with unreleased tension, the head of his erect penis barely touching her leg. His arm lying across her chest seared her with its heat. She felt him straining to resist shoving his cock against her for relief.

"You need to come too," she said. "Why are you fighting it? Come inside me."

"No. Do me with your hand again." He held himself rigid as if frightened of what might happen if he moved. "That worked in the tub. It should be okay here too."

Impatience won over any caution his obvious fear might have implanted in her. She rolled on her side and cuddled up to press her body against the length of his. "You're the only man

I've ever wanted this way, knowing it's my own desire, not just an echo. I'm not letting you escape." His hardness and the arousal radiating from him stirred her craving anew. She draped one leg over his hip, silently inviting him to sheath himself in her. "My pussy wants your cock." Normally, she'd never think of speaking that way, and hearing the words from her own mouth made her blush, but she hoped they would stimulate him to forget his fear, whatever caused it.

"Oh, hell, yes!" To her shock, he grabbed her by the shoulders and flipped her onto her stomach.

Her breath rushed out in a whoosh of surprise. "What—"

"Maybe it'll work this way." His fingers dug into her hips to raise her onto her knees. She knelt with her legs folded under her and her face turned to one side on the cushion. His cock slid between her thighs, nudging the folds of her pussy.

She didn't think she could get wetter, but she thought wrong. Another gush of liquid answered his thrusts. She spread her legs, longing for him to plunge deep inside, even if it might hurt. Once more his passion blended with hers so that she could hardly tell them apart. Picking up his urgency, she felt herself nearing the verge of another climax. The head of his penis thrust into her. Somewhere in the background she felt pain, but the need overrode it. She also felt panic rising in him along with the hunger. He snarled aloud. A musky smell tickled her nose, and his skin grew so hot she wondered again if he had a fever. More strangely, the hair on his legs and belly, rubbing her thighs and buttocks, felt coarser and thicker than it should.

His teeth clamped onto the nape of her neck with a stab of pain-laced pleasure. A growl rumbled from his chest through the nerves of her spine.

Her head reeled with his excitement and hers but also with the terror and rage that howled inside his skull.

Abruptly, he pulled out of her. She rolled to her back just in time to see him dashing to the door.

* * * * *

The moment he mounted Tabitha, the fur began to sprout, and his jaws stung as his teeth elongated into fangs. Instinct drove him to bite her neck, to hold her still for his thrusts. He burned with the change boiling in his blood. *Faster, faster, got to come before I—* Along with the race toward his peak, the transformation surged over him.

Just in time, he caught himself. *Can't let her see this. Have to get away.* His cock already pulsed with the onslaught of climax. With an agonizing effort, he broke away from the satiny tightness of her vagina and fled. He barely made it to the front door and shoved it open before he fell to all fours, and the magic wrenched him out of human shape altogether. He raced onto the front lawn, where he couldn't resist the urge any longer. He convulsed and spurted into the grass.

The last of his human thoughts vanished when he came. The only awareness remaining was that he had to escape, hide, disappear. Anguish he could no longer frame into words overwhelmed him.

But at the edge of the forest he felt the touch of a mind probing his. It snared and tugged him like an invisible leash. Trembling between terror and longing, he waited.

* * * * *

It took her a minute to recover enough to realize he'd actually run out and another few seconds to catch her breath and force her wobbly legs to stand up. *He's not getting away with this! He'll confess what's going on if I have to strangle him!* She snatched up the kimono and shrugged into it as she hurried to the exit. When she emerged from the secret room into the hall, she heard the front door bang shut. He'd run outside. She charged after him. Halfway there, she felt the cyclone of his orgasm sweep over her. It forced her to the floor, where she crouched with her hands wedged between her thighs while she pulsed in release too. His emotions, already in jagged bits, shattered completely.

She no longer sensed Kenji at all, only a whirling chaos of animal urges and panic.

On the porch, she paused, struggling for breath, and strained her eyes in the predawn light. Under the trees at the edge of the driveway, a creature the size of a small collie lurked. When her vision adjusted, she recognized the shape as a fox, though larger than any normal beast of that kind. It shivered, paralyzed with yearning and fear.

She remembered glimpsing that same fox, for surely two of that size couldn't live in these woods, outside Kenji's house the night before. She also remembered how she'd felt his consciousness spring out of nowhere a minute later. Her head spun and the world turned gray. She grabbed a post to keep from collapsing. *Impossible! What I'm thinking can't be!* Yet Kenji had vanished from her perception faster than any human being could run out of her range. Instead, the fox crouched there, watching her as warily as she watched it.

"Kenji?" Her voice quavered. She swallowed and made herself speak more forcefully. "Kenji, if I'm not dreaming or nuts, I know that's you. I'm not going anywhere until you come up here and show yourself." She plopped down on the porch steps.

The fox whined.

"Right, you can understand, can't you? Get over here."

He slunk a few feet closer. *He does understand English. Oh, God, it's really him.* Seized by another wave of dizziness, she had to bow her head to keep from fainting.

Inside his motionless body, a tornado of clashing needs raged. She found it didn't lash her with agony like a human mind in the same condition. Although Kenji's personality lived in this shape, the animal form muted the intensity of the emotions.

She stretched out a hand. "It's okay. I know you won't hurt me." He took a few paces nearer, then pricked his ears forward and trotted up to her. Black hairs mingled with the russet of his fur, his paws were black, he had a snow-white chest, and a white plume tipped his tail. His eyes, though, showed the same liquid brown flecked with gold as Kenji's own. "So this is your terrible secret."

He crept close enough to lay his head on her knees. Panting, he let his tongue loll from his open jaws. Twin rows of fangs showed. He could rip her arm open before she could move, if he wanted to. But he wouldn't. She stroked the sleek pelt on his back. He let out a long sigh. The agitation in his mind settled under her touch. She found herself soothing him the same way she used to calm her cat. When she scratched behind his ears, his tongue flicked out to lick her other hand. He nuzzled her crotch through the robe. When she flinched at the tantalizing tickle through the silky fabric, he emitted a spark of alarm and pulled back. She stroked his head again and willed him to relax. He rolled on his side, with a low yip of a bark. She couldn't resist ruffling the soft, white fur of his belly. His back legs twitched in rhythm with her brisk rubbing. His penis poked out of its furry sheath, but only contented sensuality, not sexual demand, radiated from him.

"Can you change back?"

A shudder racked him. Heat rolled off him as if from an open fire. Under her palm, his flank softened like clay. The hair melted and vanished. A crimson haze fogged the air. When it evaporated, Kenji's naked body curled on the steps beside her, with his head in her lap.

She smoothed his hair. Still trembling, he hid his face against her stomach.

"You see," he whispered. "That's why I didn't want to take the chance."

"Making love changes you into a fox?" she said, trying to sort out her confusion.

"Any strong emotion, sex, anger, whatever. They all make it hard for me to keep control of the change, sometimes impossible."

She nudged him. "Let's go inside, and you can tell me about it."

He stood up, and they walked inside hand in hand. "You're not scared?"

With a shaky laugh, she said, "I'll let you know after I decide whether I'm dreaming or not. But seriously, why would I be afraid of you? I know you won't hurt me."

"The same reason people act afraid of your power, or more so," he said. "Because it's too strange to accept."

"So that's why you didn't have so much trouble with it."

Instead of heading for the secret room, he led her to his bedroom. With the curtains closed and the sun just rising, she could see little in the dimness, except for a general impression of serene simplicity. "I'm worn out, and you have to be exhausted too. If you're staying, we should get some sleep before we go back to the hospital."

"After we talk."

He folded back the covers of the king-size bed. "You're sure you want to talk, not run away?"

"This is the fourth impossible thing. I can't leave without knowing the whole truth."

He stretched on the bed and held out a hand to her. Struggling to slow down her fast, shallow breathing, she slipped off the kimono and lay next to him, side by side facing each other. He wrapped one arm around her, his palm tracing circles on the center of her back. "Okay, what do you want to know?"

Chapter Nine

ɛɔ

"How did you turn into a were-fox?" Her head buzzed with disbelief at hearing herself ask that question. Yet she knew she was awake. She felt the cool sheets and his warm, slightly sweat-dampened skin, smelled his faintly musky scent and sensed the tentative caress of his emotions while he luxuriated in their embrace.

He winced. "Not a were-fox. Kitsune."

"What's that?"

"Actually, I'm half kitsune. My mother was one, a magical fox that can take human form. I don't have her full powers because of my human father."

"How did they get together?"

"When Dad was stationed in Japan, he didn't stick close to the naval base and the big cities the way most of the officers did. He learned some of the language and roamed around the countryside on leave. He met my mother in a small village where his car broke down once."

"And it was love at first sight? That's so romantic."

He shifted position as if groping for the right words. "Well, according to Mom, it started more like lust at first sight." A flush reddened his face and chest. "Fox spirits are highly sexual creatures. A kitsune has supernatural powers of erotic attraction, and she, or he, uses that power to satisfy an almost insatiable appetite. They sicken and pine away without regular relief."

"And you've never had that because you couldn't risk anybody seeing you change."

"I tried once." Pain shadowed his words. "I went with a girl in college. We became close enough that she started wondering why we didn't get intimate. Finally, I couldn't stand being apart from her. I decided to try."

"It didn't work." His sadness made that obvious.

"I had less control then. I started to change even before I was ready to climax. I didn't get away fast enough. She saw — everything."

Tabitha squeezed his shoulder, trying to transmit comfort. She felt his tension slacken under her touch. *It works on him. He's different from other people that way.*

"She freaked out, of course. Screamed. Lucky the apartment had decent insulation so the neighbors didn't hear her and break in to investigate. She threw a lamp at me. At the time I was too panicked to feel it, but later, in human shape, I found cuts from the broken glass."

"Did you ever get to explain?"

"I never saw her again. She hung up on me the one time I called, and no wonder. Later I heard that she'd gone into therapy. She probably thought she'd had a hallucination."

"I'm not surprised you didn't want to risk that again." She brushed a kiss on his shoulder. "But your dad didn't react that way?"

"He'd heard the legends, of course, not that anybody who hadn't seen a supernatural creature face to face believed in them. So he was sort of prepared when Mom revealed herself. That was after they'd been lovers for a few weeks."

"She didn't have your problem?"

"Being full-blooded, she had control. She was more worried about another part of the legend, which claims men who take kitsune lovers usually waste away from the constant sexual drain."

"That didn't happen to your father, did it?"

"No, she wouldn't risk hurting him, and she didn't have to because they fell in love. At least, that was her theory. She said it turned out real lovemaking was much more satisfying than plain sex." Another blush heated his face. "She loved him enough to give up her home, which means a lot to a kitsune. Like I mentioned earlier, she died when I was just a teenager, probably because she'd been cut off from her home ground for so long."

"Didn't your father think of taking her back to Japan?"

"By the time he realized what was wrong and made the offer, she said it was too late. Anyway, she would never have left us, and she didn't want to drag me away from my home. Being self-centered like most kids, I had no idea what she was giving up. I took her for granted like any teenager with his mother."

Tabitha smoothed Kenji's hair back from his forehead, willing his sorrow and guilt to fade. "Judging from what I've seen of mothers, she enjoyed doing what she thought was best for you."

"She lived long enough to coach me through my first change and warn me what to expect. She taught me to conjure foxfire and create a secret space like the one here in the house. She explained about the tie to my native ground. She also warned me that I'd need lots of sex. What she didn't know was that my half-blood nature meant I wouldn't have her control over the transformation. As a teenager, I had a hell of a time with the change overwhelming me whenever I felt violent emotions. Not just sex, others too, like anger. When that Shawn guy tried to attack you, I almost lost it."

"So that's what was going on." She couldn't accept that she and Kenji could never share total penetration. The need to untangle the problem overrode her self-consciousness in discussing it. "If you got regular sexual release, maybe you could develop better control.

"Yeah, if I could ever get that intimate with a woman in the first place. You saw what happened."

"Now that I know what to expect, I won't be afraid." The hope rising in him compelled her to add, "Not much, anyway. I know you won't hurt me."

Gratitude welled up from him to flow around her like a warm breeze. His head sagged onto her shoulder, though, with the momentary spark of hope dying away. "What kind of relationship could we have if we can't consummate it? I couldn't ask you to live that way."

"Maybe how I want to live should be my choice." She skimmed a fingernail down the center of his chest to emphasize the point. "Wait, if you need sex to stay healthy, how did you get along all these years if you're still a virgin?"

"Quantity makes up for quality. I take care of it myself. Almost every day. I found out if I don't want to change while I'm coming, I can get relief in the shower. The water seems to give me a little more control."

"So that's why you decided we should make love in the hot tub."

"Yeah, but I don't think that would keep me from changing if I penetrated you. It's almost too exciting just to think about it. Or would be if we hadn't run out of energy."

"Speak for yourself." She gave him a playful slap on the arm. Actually, though, she felt more weariness than arousal too. Her eyelids were beginning to droop.

"Uh, to be completely honest, I'm not exactly a virgin. I've never been with a woman, but there are lots of wild foxes around here. In the early part of the year, the vixens go into season." He lay still, his muscles rigid, his thoughts taut with apprehension.

"You mean you—" She couldn't deny her first reaction was shock. "You fathered fox cubs?"

"I hope not, and if they exist, I hope they're ordinary foxes. I'll probably never know." She felt him collecting his courage to speak on. "I won't blame you if you never want to touch me again. All I can say is that when I'm transformed, my human thoughts get submerged unless I make a special effort, like when I hunted for Chloe. I think and feel like a fox, and I can't resist the scent of another fox in heat." Though he didn't move, she sensed that inside he squirmed with shame. "I would have gone crazy if I hadn't mated with them."

She swallowed. "I understand. I can't blame you. Even feeling your emotions, I can't fully imagine what it's like to become an animal."

He relaxed a little. "Even as a man, I have some animal traits. I see better in the dark. My hearing and sense of smell are keener. You have no idea how excited I got from your scent when you were aroused."

A hot blush suffused her. "That's what you meant when you said I smelled delicious?"

"Sure. When we met on the trail yesterday, I could tell how you reacted. That's what drove me over the edge so fast."

She hid her face against his chest. "I may never be able to look you in the eye again," she mumbled.

"Then don't look, as long as you don't stop touching. Now go to sleep." He turned on his back with one arm still wrapped around her. His contentment sheltered her in a warm nest. She laid her head on his shoulder, draped an arm over his chest and let herself drift into oblivion.

* * * * *

Sunlight sifting through the curtains woke her. Disoriented for a minute, she looked around the room, trying to figure out where she was. She lay alone in a wide bed. A door in the corner opposite the exit to the hall opened, and Kenji emerged. She realized that door connected to the hall bathroom. "Want to take a shower before we go to the hospital?" he said. "I've put your clothes in the washer-dryer already."

She sat up, shaking her head and combing her fingers through her hair to chase the cobwebs from her brain. Kenji's bare limbs and damp, tousled hair looked sleek and strokable.

Had she really seen him turn into a fox and then back again? His tentative glance at her confirmed that something strange had happened, and he worried about her morning-after reaction. But she couldn't talk about the strangeness until she finished waking up. Instead, she said, "You do laundry?"

He laughed. "I've lived alone for years. What do you think I do, replace my clothes every week?"

Swinging her legs over the side of the bed, she let her gaze roam up and down his body. His penis stirred. "Sure you don't want to get back in the shower with me? You said it helps you with control. Maybe we should experiment."

His luscious brown eyes lingered on her breasts before rising to her face. "Not if you ever want to leave the house. Your folks are probably at the hospital already."

A glance at the clock spurred her to jump to her feet. Past ten! She snatched up the kimono, rushed into the bathroom and switched on the shower.

When she emerged a few minutes later, wearing only the robe, she found Kenji in the bedroom fully dressed. He'd left her dry clothes on the bed. While she scrambled into them, he poured her a cup of tea and handed it to her along with a roll wrapped in a napkin. After gulping down most of the tea, she sampled a bite of the sweet bread. "I guess we'd better go." At the thought of facing her parents, she wished she could retreat into Kenji's secret den and hide there forever.

In the car she finished the roll, though it settled into her stomach in a lump. Kenji glanced at her from the driver's seat. "I can't read emotions the way you can, but I can smell your nervousness. Don't worry, I'll stick with you."

At the hospital, he held her hand while walking across the parking lot. She braced herself as they entered the main lobby. Fortunately, the atmosphere didn't bristle with pain and fear like the emergency room. The worst she felt was low-level anxiety hovering in the air like cigarette smoke. They headed for the front desk, where she identified herself and asked for

Chloe's room number. The receptionist gave her the information and directed her to the elevators around the corner.

On the way, Tabitha and Kenji passed another counter, where a stout, middle-aged man in a rumpled sport shirt barged up to the woman behind the computer and shouted something about a bill. The flare-up of his anger buffeted Tabitha like a shock wave from a grenade. She involuntarily lifted one hand in front of her as if she could raise an invisible shield to ward off the attack. Kenji glanced at her and slid his arm around her waist. "It'll be all right," he whispered. "Don't pay any attention. Focus on me. Concentrate on what I'm feeling."

She forcibly shifted her attention from the outraged man to Kenji. Caring and affection emanated from him. She basked in it like sunlight through the leafy branches of the woods in springtime. It surrounded her like a shimmering bubble. The man's anger receded into the distance, so muted it no longer made her head pound.

She met Kenji's eyes with a delighted smile. "It works. It doesn't hurt anymore."

His lips grazed her hair. "Great. Just keep focusing on me, and you'll be fine."

They had the elevator to themselves. She leaned back against him, with his arms around her immediately below the curve of her breasts. As long as he could surround her with this snug shelter, she didn't care whether he changed into a man-eating wolf every night.

All too soon, they disembarked at Chloe's ward. Odors of disinfectant and sickness hit Tabitha when they stepped out of the elevator. She noticed Kenji grimacing and remembered what he'd said about the keenness of his nose, even in human form. She curled her arm through his and whispered, "I know it's uncomfortable for you too. We'll prop up each other." She stretched out intangible tendrils to caress his mind and smooth its ruffled surface the way she had petted his fur a few hours earlier.

"You're doing something to my head, aren't you?" he said in a low tone. "Thanks."

Turning left, they started down the corridor. In the distance, Tabitha heard her mother's voice. She redirected her attention, like tuning a radio to a new channel, to Kenji's silent comfort.

A wave of anger burst upon them from behind. She turned to face Chloe's boyfriend Shawn.

Chapter Ten

ജ

Tabitha clutched Kenji's arm for support. "What are you doing here?"

"That woman in the lobby wouldn't tell me the room number, so I hung around outside until you showed up. I watched you get into the elevator and saw what floor you stopped at. I told you I wouldn't let you keep me from seeing Chloe." The boy's frustration and anxiety made the air in the hallway feel as dense and dark as a thundercloud.

"My parents are here. You sure you want to run into them?"

"I don't care." He charged ahead of them down the hall.

Tabitha quickened her steps, still clinging to Kenji, who kept pace with her. "You'll do fine," he murmured. They reached Chloe's semiprivate room a few seconds behind Shawn. They had to wedge in next to him on the room's threshold.

Chloe reclined, propped on pillows, in the nearer bed. The one next to the window was unoccupied and made up. Between the beds stood their mother, who clutched Chloe's hand as if to stop her from leaping up and flinging herself at the boy. Their father, arms folded, stood closer to the door, as if guarding it. The two of them glared at Shawn, who glowered back.

"What do you think you're doing here?" Her dad's voice sounded like a club hitting human flesh.

Her mother interrupted him with, "Get out. She can't see you," while in the background Chloe groaned, "Mom, Dad, please!"

Tabitha felt Chloe's humiliation, overriding emotional distress and the drug-muted throb of physical pain. The anger between their father and Shawn clashed like thrown boulders colliding. Their mother's tone sliced the air like a knife. Tabitha took an involuntary step backward. On one side she felt scorching flames, on the other an icy gale. *I can't take this.*

Kenji's hand squeezed hers. The gesture reminded her to focus on him. Again she deliberately shifted her attention like a weathervane turning in the wind. His affection enveloped her. She felt a rosy cloud cluster around her and cushion the floor under her feet. She floated on it, above the turmoil. With one hand still clasping his, she reached for her father.

"Dad, Mom, I'm glad you're here." That statement was true enough, if only from relief at transferring responsibility for her sister.

Her dad dragged his eyes away from Shawn and glanced at Kenji. "Who's that?"

Tabitha tightened her grip on Kenji's hand. "Mom, Dad, meet my neighbor, Kenji McGraw. He gave me a ride."

Her father granted Kenji a curt nod then focused on her again. His frown faded. "If you'd called us yesterday, this wouldn't have happened in the first place." But he accepted Tabitha's light kiss. His anger, now simmering instead of boiling, leaked through the insulation of Kenji's nearness.

"I hoped Chloe would do that herself. Hi, sis, how are you feeling?"

"Like you don't know." Chloe flicked a scornful glance at Tabitha then looked at Shawn. "I was going to meet you like I promised."

"Yeah, I know. Uh, I'm sorry you got hurt."

Chloe said with a small shrug, "It's cool. No big deal."

"No big deal? You broke your leg with that stupid behavior." Tabitha's mom circled around the bed and gave her a cool peck on the cheek. "And *you* let her wander around the woods at night."

Tabitha found that as long as she kept touching Kenji and focusing on him, she could maintain negative emotions at a distance like a lightning storm viewed through a plate glass window. "I didn't let her. She made her own decision, and I couldn't keep her locked up like a prisoner."

"You're older. You're supposed to exercise better judgment."

She could almost hear the familiar nagging: *If your sister jumped off a cliff, would you jump too?* "Come on, Mom, that argument worked when we were kids climbing trees in our Sunday dresses. She's practically grown up now."

"Too bad you didn't think about that yesterday," Chloe broke in. "Shawn, when I get back home, I'll go out with you anytime."

"No, you won't," her parents chorused.

"Where do you get off—" Shawn started.

The room felt like a hedge of thorn bushes. Tabitha edged closer to the protective blanket of Kenji's presence and held up her free hand. "Hold it. Time out."

Surprise at her speaking up stunned them into silence. She used the instant of quiet to probe the tangle of emotions emanating from all four. With Kenji's caring to steady her, she explored facets she hadn't been able to perceive before. She peeled back layers of feelings like strips of bark, to expose the green core underneath. Shawn worried about Chloe's injury, felt guilty that he'd persuaded her to go out in the middle of the night and fidgeted under the looming anger of her parents. Chloe's stomach was knotted with desire to be near him and the sour awareness of her parents' disapproval, along with a veneer of defiance to hide how much their rejection hurt. Their dad feared she might leave home and not come back next time. Their mother worried about how far Chloe and her boyfriend had already gone toward intimacy. At the deepest level, both of them harbored sorrow over the rift with their daughters.

Tabitha caught that thread and clung to it, letting the others slip to the edge of her consciousness. "Mom and Dad, you're right. I should have let you know where Chloe was right away."

When Chloe drew a breath to make an indignant protest, she said, "And I should have leveled with you the minute you showed up, not let you think I might support you running away. Shawn, I know you really care about her, and the folks should cut you guys some slack."

She felt Kenji's approval like a sunbeam through clouds.

After a moment of silent gaping, her mom said, "It's not your place to dictate how we raise your sister."

"No, I'm just saying what I feel you need to do if you don't want to drive her away." Both parents winced at that remark. "And you know my feelings are reliable, even if the idea scares you sometimes." Her dad stared at her as if she'd grown horns or wings. Neither of them had ever spoken about her power in such explicit terms before. "It's not my job to be a buffer between you and Chloe, much less make her do what you want." She glanced at her sister. "Just like it's not my job to cover up for you. So all of you just chill out and start getting along."

She spread her arms, with the fingers of one hand still twined in Kenji's, and drew on the affection he spun around her like a cocoon. She gathered invisible threads of that cocoon and broadcast them around the room to create a web of calm. To her astonishment, it worked; the web coiled around all four of the combatants and made the imaginary thorn hedges dissolve into nothing. No predicting how long the effect would last, but for the moment they'd become calm enough to listen to each other.

"Way to go," Kenji whispered.

"I know you all need to talk, so I'll head home," she said. "Mom, Dad, Chloe, I don't have any close deadlines coming up. How about if I drive down to visit you guys in a week or two?"

Her mother and father nodded. Chloe just stared. After giving each of them a quick kiss, Tabitha retreated into the hall with Kenji, who cast a general "nice meeting you" over his shoulder as they left. Pulling him along, she hurried to the elevator, half afraid the spell would wear off before they got out of range.

In the elevator she let out a long breath and sagged into his arms. "Wow. I've never been able to do that before. Thanks."

"For what? You did it all, not me."

"I couldn't have done it alone. Maybe I won't have to stay a hermit for the rest of my life after all."

He kissed the top of her head. "Can I hope I won't either? I want to be with you, but I admit I'm still afraid it won't work." His aura quivered with hope and apprehension.

"Why? The fox thing?" She still couldn't quite believe she'd seen what she had, but if not, their whole night together had to be a dream, and she needed it to be real. "I won't let you go because of that. If your parents could manage the situation, so can we."

The elevator slowed to a stop and the doors opened. They had to face the world long enough to reach the refuge of the car. Clasping hands, they strode through the lobby to the parking lot.

They didn't talk on the way to his house. Tabitha glowed with incredulous joy that he'd seen the negative as well as positive effects of her power and didn't shrink from her. She sensed the same stream of quiet happiness flowing through him, but disturbed by the undercurrent of fear that his animal nature would wreck their union.

At his place, she headed straight for the secret room. He'd claimed she had access to it now. Did she? With her hand on the doorknob, she held her breath, half convinced that she would find only a closet, that she had dreamed the garden chamber. If so, the fox transformation would have been a delusion too. She shut her eyes and flung the door open.

When she dared to look, globes of foxfire drifted near the ceiling, the fragrance of jasmine perfumed the air and the serenity of the garden surrounded her. "It's real," she whispered.

He embraced her from behind, his palms cupping the bottom curves of her breasts, his torso pressed against her back. "Yes, and so am I. With all the drawbacks you've already seen. Oh, God, Tabitha, I want to make love to you completely. But I'm not sure that can happen."

She rubbed her bottom against him and felt him harden. Excitement, his and hers mingled, hummed inside her skull like a hive of bees. Liquid welled between her legs. "So do I. You know that. And I won't take 'can't' for an answer. I didn't think I could face my folks, remember? But you helped me achieve that. The fifth impossible thing."

She twisted around to face him. The darkness that shadowed his eyes made her long to reassure him. With their heights so similar, she didn't have to stretch far to kiss him. With a sigh, he opened his mouth and darted his tongue between her lips. His hunger caught fire, and hers flared to meet it. His erection pressed into the V of her thighs. She shifted her legs farther apart to take full advantage of the tantalizing contact. They fitted together so well it seemed unnatural to think of parting. He licked the corner of her mouth and rasped his whiskers across her cheek. Her face heated, and the tingle spread downward, stiffening her nipples and clit.

"You make a persuasive argument," he said hoarsely.

"It's totally logical." Her breasts felt heavy, and she could almost see the blood pooling in her lower abdomen. "So quit arguing."

"I'm not. I'm ready whenever you are."

"Yeah, I noticed." She swiveled her hips to rub against the hard ridge in his pants. "I'll be right back."

He already panted as if he'd run a mile, and her breath came almost equally rapid and shallow. She struggled to fill her lungs while she ducked into the bathroom and undressed. The kimono had spontaneously hung itself back on the hook, unless a new one had appeared out of the ether. She decided not to wear it. She wanted them completely exposed to each other.

When she peeked around the screen, she saw to her relief that Kenji felt the same impulse. He stood naked in the middle of the chamber. She didn't see his clothes anywhere. Maybe he'd stripped in his bedroom and come back. A new aroma scented the air, sandalwood incense. She glanced at the lacquer table and noticed a cone of it in a dish.

In the eerie light of the foxfire, Kenji's bare limbs and torso gleamed. Passion poured off him in waves. She stepped into the fiery sphere that surrounded him. It bathed her so that she could almost see coruscations of light dancing on her skin, the same glow that radiated from the luminous globes. His arms enfolded her along with the sizzling energy. By now his cock had become fully erect. His tight embrace trapped it between their bodies and squeezed her breasts against his chest. To her heightened perception, his heart seemed to pound in time with the pulsation of his desire, and her heartbeat fell into sync with it.

"I'm so wet I can't stand it," she murmured into the hollow of his throat. Salt flavored his damp skin.

"I know," he said, his voice rough. "You smell ready."

"You can tell that way?" Her whole body flushed, heightening her sensitivity to the hairs that bristled on his legs and chest.

"Sure. I knew you were excited yesterday in the woods. Why do you think I couldn't wait to come?"

"Yes, I'm ready. I'm melting inside. And you're almost there too."

"Yeah, but not melting." He rocked his hips to emphasize the point.

She slipped her hand between them to fondle the rigid tip of his penis. "No, definitely not."

He groaned. "You smell so great I could eat you alive." Grasping her bottom in both hands, he hoisted her up.

She wrapped her legs around his waist, gasping when his cock pressed harder into the hair on her mound. "Well, do it!"

He carried her to the nearest pile of oversize pillows and lowered her onto her back. He broke out of her grip and swooped downward to plant his mouth over her clit. "Here?" he muttered.

"Yes, you know it, right there!" She couldn't help wiggling. He had to grab her hips and hold her still. He'd learned quickly from the first time. After a couple of long, slow laps that made her moan and clutch the cushion under her in both hands, he returned to her clit and flicked it rapidly back and forth, up and down, faster and faster as her hips arched to meet his tongue. The need built inside her until she saw lightning flashes behind her closed eyelids. "You too...come on."

He ignored her, though she felt his aura vibrating with hunger. Instead, he licked even faster. Her legs tightened, her nails gouged the fabric she lay on and her muscles quivered with rising tension. She blacked out, all sensation rushing to the swollen head of her clit and the well of molten liquid behind it. At last the explosion burst from her, the contractions rippling through her until she melted into complete relaxation.

When Kenji moved up to recline next to her, nuzzling her neck and fondling each breast in turn, she asked, "Why didn't you enter? You're on the brink too."

"I wanted to make sure you had satisfaction before we tried that. If I can't control the change, I don't want to leave you hanging." His eyes gleamed, and this time she knew the glow was really there.

His need made her eager to start over. "Don't think about that. Just take what you want."

"You know what I want," he growled. He crossed one leg over hers, rubbing the tops of her thighs. The bristling hairs drove her half crazy in seconds. The tickle spread to her clit, and her nipples peaked in sympathy with the swelling down below. She sensed anxiety crawling under his lust, but passion made him disregard his fears. When she spread her legs, he rolled on top. She cradled his cock at the apex of her thighs. He delayed the final joining by lapping her nipples, one after the other. She goaded him by flexing her hips up and down.

"Come on," she said. "I know you want to be inside my pussy."

With a snarl, he grasped her thighs, pulled them apart and thrust the head of his cock between the folds of her slit. The hot, slick tip made the sensitive nerves quiver in anticipation of his thrusts. The crimson haze of his passion surrounded both of them. Again she felt the pressure in his cock, and her clit echoed it with unbearable tightness in the cluster of tiny nerves and blood vessels. "Deeper," she gasped.

His teeth clamped onto the side of her neck. He plunged in to the hilt. A shudder coursed through both of them. In the back of her mind, she once again felt the stabbing pain of penetration. Most of her awareness, though, was filled to overflowing with his urgent lust. He slid halfway out, braced on his forearms, trembling with the effort.

"More!" she cried. She felt his cock start to throb, a sensation transmitted directly to her clit and vagina. Where his body pressed on hers, it felt hot enough to brand her.

The teeth at her neck changed, became needle sharp. He raised his head, emitting a howl that resonated with the cry of despair in his mind. The hair on his chest thickened, turned white and spread over the bare flesh. Russet hair sprouted on his arms. His face lengthened and narrowed, nose morphing into a muzzle. The musky smell that had lingered faintly on his skin grew stronger.

Though dizzy with desire, Tabitha couldn't squelch a mental leap of alarm. Kenji, only half human now, lunged backward. He crouched at her feet, panting.

Chapter Eleven

ဆာ

Gathering her wits, she damped down the momentary impulse to flee. At this point she couldn't tell for sure how much of that was her own and how much his. She raised herself on her elbows and extended psychic tendrils toward him. They twined through his aura and muted his panic a little.

Still, he edged away from her, toward the door.

She scrambled to her knees on the cushion. "Don't you dare think about running away."

He hesitated, tongue lolling between open jaws. His fangs looked completely vulpine now.

"It's all right," she said. "I won't rush out screaming if you change the rest of the way."

His taut grip on his animal self slackened. In a rush of heat, his body folded upon itself and flowed into fox shape. When she held out both arms, he trotted to the cushion and laid his head on her lap. The need for release still simmered in both of them. While one of her hands fondled his ears, his tongue lapped the other hand. Then he licked her stomach just above the triangle of hair. A shiver convulsed her. Whining, he drew back to rest on the cushion. His tail switched from side to side. Although a cloud of shame hovered around him, his hunger hadn't died. He involuntarily thrust into the cloth under his belly.

"Turn human." She ran her palm down the bristling fur of his back.

He growled. She caressed him with hands and mind, envisioning her fingers smoothing out the tangle of his need and fear. Again the scarlet cloud enfolded him. The fur shrank and vanished, his face flattened into human features, and his limbs and torso expanded to normal size. Under her touch, the scorching heat of his flesh faded to normal body warmth.

He hid his face on her lap, his breath hot against the hairs of her mound. Between that persistent tickle, the molten liquid inside her from his penetration and her awareness of his erection straining for relief, her head spun with the need to have him inside her. "See, the world didn't end. Take me, quick."

"I can't." His voice quavered on the verge of a sob. "I can't stand to have that happen again."

"Maybe it won't. It almost worked. We can't give up." She slithered down to lie beside him. Her fingers skimmed his firm nipples and crept down the front of his body to his cock. He groaned when she encircled his shaft. "Touch me."

He slipped his fingers between her moist folds and traced a path through her cleft up to her clit and back again, over and over in long, slow strokes. Equally slowly, her hand glided up and down his shaft, pausing to squeeze the tip at the end of each stroke. She felt the pressure building in him. "What else?" she whispered.

"Touch my balls." His guttural tone approached a growl, but his shape didn't change.

Her other hand cupped his scrotum and bounced it in her fingers. She could almost feel the semen ready to erupt from it.

"Can't wait," he gasped. "Have to come!"

"Well, come on!" Before he could resist, she rolled him onto his back and climbed astride.

Panic laced the flavor of his passion. He gripped her shoulders to hold her off.

"Listen, you! I want you this way, but if we can't, it'll be all right. If you have to change into a fox every time you climax, we'll work around it. It won't stop me loving you." The words escaping from her mouth startled her. For a second she felt about to drop off her own cliff of panic. Digging her nails into his chest, she forged on. "But I don't believe it has to happen that way." She lowered herself onto his shaft.

It pierced her to the core. When his hips pumped wildly, she fell into the rhythm with him. She felt his animal nature surge out of the depth of his being, along with the sliding of his cock in and out of her eager pussy. Fur again sprouted on his legs and chest. With a growl, he tried to push her off. She tightened her thighs and vagina around him. "Stop!"

He froze, his muscles quivering with tension. She ran her fingers over the russet hairs on his chest until they vanished into his heated skin. She tweaked his nipples, and he closed his eyes and moaned. His claws dug into the cloth under him, but otherwise he stayed human.

Only then did she start rocking again. After a few thrusts, the beast once more heaved to the surface. Fur coursed over his body, and he bared his fangs in a ravenous growl. Again she stilled him and imprisoned his body under hers while her hands and mind caressed the fox until it yielded to the man. His cock throbbed inside her.

"I need to come," he groaned.

Her channel was pulsing too. "Now!" she gasped.

With one part of her mind, she stroked the fox spirit into submission, while the rest of her luxuriated in the need that soared to fulfillment. She rode his thrusts to the peak. When he started to spurt, her clit throbbed with every pulsation and her canal rippled around him. He threw back his head and howled. When he felt as if he might fracture and melt in her arms, she embraced him so tightly both of them could hardly breathe. Together they glided through the final ecstasy to a peaceful release.

"You did something to me," he panted. "Controlled me."

"Tamed your animal self, the way I used to tame ordinary animals. Do you mind?"

"No, it's fantastic." His voice and thoughts dissolved into a warm fog.

She lay for a long time with her eyes shut, tasting the salt on his skin where her lips nuzzled his neck, feeling the heat of his body under her gradually cooling, basking in his contentment. His hands stroked languidly up and down her spine.

Finally he said, "The sixth impossible thing."

"Controlling your change?" she murmured.

"Not just that." His chest rumbled under hers. "You said something about love." His breath ruffled her hair.

She lifted her head. "Sorry, didn't mean to scare you with the L-word." She sensed, though, that his reaction held no taint of fear.

"Has your radar gone on the blink?" he said, echoing her thought. "You can tell I'm not afraid. Just having trouble believing it. I expected to live the rest of my life without the L-word." His gold-flecked eyes captured hers.

"Me too." Tears blurred her vision. "I guess I need more practice accepting the impossible."

"Let's practice together." He drew her down for a lingering kiss while sparks of foxfire danced above them.

Survivor

By Liddy Midnight

ဆာ

Also by Liddy Midnight

ଶ

Elementals 1
(*print anthology containing* Fire and Ice *and* Small Magick)
Ellora's Cavemen: Dreams of the Oasis I *(Anthology)*
Fire and Ice *(digital release)*
In Moonlight *(Anthology)*
Small Magick *(digital release)*

By Liddy Midnight writing as Annalise

Equinox II *(Anthology)*
Venus Rising

About the Author

ଶ

Liddy Midnight lives, loves, works and writes in the woods of eastern Pennsylvania, surrounded by lush greenery and wildlife. Although raccoons, possums, skunks and the occasional fox eat the cat food on her back porch, she's no more than half an hour from some of the finest shopping in the country. Situated in this best of all possible worlds, how could she write anything other than romance?

Liddy welcomes comments from readers. You can find her website and email address on her author bio page at www.ellorascave.com.

Chapter One

ࢲ

Doug alighted in the clearing, his bare feet sinking into the pine needles. The sensation of having been something else or somewhere else troubled him until midnight shadows folded around him like a cloak. Here, deep within the trees, was where he belonged.

She was there to meet him with open arms, her unbound hair gleaming in the moonlight. His pulse quickened at the warmth in her eyes, warmth that was both a welcome and a promise. Her full breasts rose and fell with each quick breath she took. The beauty of her full curves and her comfort with their nudity made his breath hitch.

Doug stared a moment, gulping in the sight of her. She stretched, hands braced on her lower back, legs spread, revealing the entire feast that awaited him. The nest of curls between her legs echoed the silver of her hair, bright against the mahogany of her dark skin. Between those pale curls, darker lips pouted. Moonlight glinted off drops of moisture there.

How long had he been gone this time? How long since he'd buried his cock in that hot, tight cunt of hers, fucked her until they both exploded? He wasn't sure. He only knew that it had been too long.

Welcome, my Chosen. I have missed you. She always spoke in his mind. He'd given up trying to figure out how.

And I missed you, too. God, you're just as beautiful as I remember.

Her response was amused. *Only one god? My people have many, although the First One is more important than the others.*

Just one. At least in my family. His uncle would have beaten him for even thinking about going outside the parish. *My world has many different belief systems.*

So has mine. As many as there are peoples. She stopped stretching and smiled at him. Her teeth flashed white against her deep red lips. Holding his gaze, she began to dance. Her feet rose and fell in a pattern that was as familiar to him as it was arousing. Arms lifted above her head, she swayed from side to side.

The flicker of the flames played over her swaying hips and the luscious globes of her breasts. He struggled to keep his mind on their conversation. *And you tolerate each other?*

We must. Once we did not, but the Great War taught us to respect others. How else are we to live together?

Yeah, our world is getting to that point. Although it took us more than one war. He followed her movements with his eyes, aware of his hands moving as if to touch her. He could feel the satin softness of her breasts against his fingers, though she stayed several feet away.

You learn slowly. He sensed no scorn in her voice.

He hadn't thought of it in that way, but she was right. *Yeah, I guess we do.*

The space between them grew heavy with arousal, both his and hers. He drew in a breath, savoring her scent. His mouth watered and his balls tightened with anticipation.

By the look in her eyes, she knew what he wanted. How could she not? He knew she was just as eager, knew by the cream frothing her thighs and the tight, hard peaks of her nipples. He could swear her breasts were larger than before, riding higher and fuller. His fingers twitched. He wanted to stroke her thighs. He wanted to pinch her nipples and watch the ripples of pleasure run over her skin. He wanted to taste her, drink her in, take her swollen clit into his mouth and suckle until she cried out for mercy. He would show her none, not until his hard cock was sheathed to the hilt with her hot, creaming cunt clenching around him.

Welcoming warmth grew into heat as she stared boldly at him, letting her appreciation show as she looked him over. *You are a great warrior.*

That's what I do, but I'm not sure I deserve being called great. He drew in a deeper breath, scenting the increase in her readiness. His cock jumped in response. Christ, was it possible for his balls to tighten any more?

She stopped her shuffling dance before a pile of furs and turned, slowly. Her lush curves called to him. With a small smile, she held out her hand. *Come and join with me, my Chosen warrior.*

This wasn't the first time she'd called him her Chosen and he still didn't know what she meant, but he had more pressing things on his mind. Like not turning down an offer like that. He covered her palm with his and wrapped his fingers around hers. She twisted in his grip until their fingers laced together. This close, he could taste her on the air.

When he moved, his erect cock bobbed toward her like a compass needle finding north. He followed its lead and tugged her against him. He couldn't suppress a groan as he claimed her mouth with his.

She opened for him immediately, sweeping her tongue along his, delving eagerly into his mouth while giving him plenty of access to her wet heat.

Sweet Christ, she parted her thighs to take the tip of his cock between them, moving her hips back and forth in time with their dancing tongues. The tangled curls between her legs rasped across the swollen head of his erection, the friction tempting him to drive deep inside her.

Could he grow any harder? The next slide of her hips confirmed he could. Need rocketed through him and his cock ached almost to the point of pain. His automatic response was to thrust his hips, to bury himself balls-deep, seeking relief from the pressure building inside him. Impatience goaded him to claim her in every way imaginable. She was his and no one else's. A primal impulse surfaced, driving him almost to violence.

Recognition pulled him back from the brink of insanity. He tore his mouth free and stepped away. *No! Not like this.*

She frowned at him, her lips forming a little "o" of disapproval.

The effort of holding back made his knees tremble and he sank to the heap of furs. When he opened his arms in invitation, she fell upon him like a hungry cat, licking her way down his chest and belly. Each stroke of her tongue was a flicker of flame on his skin, burning away the strange violent urge he'd had and feeding his excitement. He'd never dreamed his body could have so many erogenous zones.

She moved slowly over him, circling his nipples with little laps of her tongue, sweeping her lips across his ribs, piling on the sensations, until his body burned red-hot with need. One place she licked on the side of his belly, just below his ribs, made his scalp tingle.

He groaned and clutched the furs. Lower and lower on his belly she went, pausing to explore his navel. She swept her tongue along the length of his cock. Her hot, wet mouth closed over him and she tongued the slit before circling around and under the head.

He damned near flew into orbit.

She gathered his scrotum in a tight grip. When he was on the verge of coming, just as his balls tightened, as he was ready and willing to shoot his cum sky-high, she pulled on his sac and twisted her hand slightly. The pressure of her fingers pulled him back from the edge. Each harsh breath broke from his chest in a heaving gasp.

He jerked at the intensity as she slowly, far too slowly, lowered her head to take him in. Inch by excruciating inch. Deeper and deeper. She took her time, holding him back, not letting him find the release he craved. Her teeth scraped high on his shaft, up where he'd never felt a woman's mouth before.

His cock nudged the back of her throat and he groaned, fighting the sudden urge to thrust. Christ, this was something he'd never experienced, had never even imagined anyone would do to him. Not that he was about to complain. He'd gladly be her Chosen, for this alone. Hell, he'd become whatever she wanted him to be, if only she stayed right where she was.

Once she'd engulfed him completely, taken the whole length of his cock into the wet heat of her mouth, she began to stroke her teeth up and down his shaft. Each time she withdrew, night air washed across his cock. The contrast of alternating temperatures, her hot mouth and the cool air, was almost more than he could stand.

Each time he hovered on the edge of the abyss, straining for that elusive orgasm, she used her grip on his balls to pull him back. After an eternity of increasing need and escalating sensation, she finally released his scrotum.

The rhythm of her mouth never faltered.

Freed from her restraining grip, his balls tightened and throbbed. He threw his arm across his face and howled into his elbow. The fire engulfing him flared hotter, streaking from the soles of his feet to gather in his balls. The roof of the cave dissolved into a gray mist as ecstasy swept over him. His cum erupted into the furnace of her mouth.

Jesus, Mary and Joseph!

Another dream.

Doug sat up and blinked in the light, heaving and gasping. His stomach hurt from the intensity of his orgasm. The wail of a siren cut through the chaos in the barracks.

Another drill.

Since the World Peace Treaty nine years before, there was little for a standing Air Force to do but drill to keep their skills sharp. As if there would be another war, now that all countries had finally agreed on a single currency and were on track moving toward the Common Tongue.

So they drilled, fighting mock battles and learning increasingly difficult aerobatic routines. Those maneuvers wowed the crowds in public performances, at state fairs and air shows. He was a member of the elite Screaming Dragons, as popular for the colorful artwork decorating their aircraft as for the difficult routines they mastered.

This *was* a drill. That officious weasel Sergeant Holmes stood in the doorway, spectacled eyes glued to the stopwatch in his hand. Poor vision kept him grounded and he never missed an opportunity to irritate the pilots he envied.

"Move it, Phoenix!" Holmes poked at Doug's foot and yelled his call sign with a grin. "Time to fly!"

Holmes was just trying to piss him off. Doug scowled. Lacking a clever childhood nickname, he'd been dubbed Phoenix by his first unit. It struck a little too close to home, but the word was instantly recognizable on the radio.

Struggling to escape the sheets, Doug ran his hand through his hair. His palm came away soaked with sweat. Beneath the twisted cotton folds, his impressive erection still dripped the last of his cum. He didn't have a monster cock, but he knew he was above average. Let little-man Holmes get an eyeful of that.

"Come on, rise and shine!" Holmes moved on to another victim. "Wakey wakey!" He sniggered as Jet Wake shot him a murderous look.

With a curse, Doug tore the bedding apart and leapt to his feet. Mind-blowing wet dream or not, he was damned if he was going to be the last pilot on the tarmac.

* * * * *

Doug followed his squad, ducking under the low doorway into the bar. After the quiet of the deserted street outside, stepping into the raucous smoke-filled bar was a shock.

A huge flat-screen television hung in one corner. Baseball was good. Very good. He started to nod his approval but changed it to a disgusted shake of his head. Half the crowd clustered around the other end of the bar wore ties, for Chrissake. The rest were skinny nerds by the looks of them, complete with pale skin and narrow shoulders. He swore he actually saw a few pocket protectors.

The joint was packed. Doug took in the plastic New England Colonial décor. In Nevada, *rural* Nevada no less. Even the playoffs wouldn't make up for such tacky furnishings, and it was only the beginning of the season. "Who picked this place?"

Renegade evidently couldn't hear him over the televised sports commentary. Doug tugged on Wingnut's jacket and repeated his question.

His buddy leaned over and yelled, "Some babe Buffalo thinks is hot works here."

So their leader was sniffing around another prospect. With his shaggy bad-boy looks, Buffalo had his pick of women, but he only wanted the ones who didn't want him. Once again, he'd dragged his squad along for moral support. Not the first time, and surely not the last time.

Doug would give slim odds for Buffalo's success. At least the food smelled good. His lead man might not get laid, but they'd all get a decent meal out of the evening. Sometimes you had to settle for small blessings.

Jet Wake slid in behind a couple as they were leaving and claimed a large table, empty except for some leftover glasses and a jumble of change. "Look! Is this fate, or what?" He indicated the largest coin in the pile. It was turned heads-down, revealing an ornate Chinese dragon.

World currency was issued by every country and each put its own design on the back. The guys collected anything to do with dragons. Grinning, Doug pulled one of the same denomination from his pocket and swapped them. The one he tossed to the table came to rest with the harp of Ireland showing.

Fingering the coin, Doug settled on the bench along the wall where he could see the big screen. Having played ball all through college, he was the squad member most likely to appreciate a good game.

The shortstop made a leap to scoop a bounced ball out of the air over his head and fired it off to first base. The ump made the call and the manager walked over to dispute it. The score flashed on the screen and Doug snorted in disgust.

The Seattle Sandpipers hadn't played the Tokyo Tigers yet this season, and wouldn't for another week. This was a rerun of last year's game if he wasn't mistaken. A worse thought occurred to him. It might be older than that.

What the hell kind of morons watched reruns of ball games? It wasn't like the final score would be a surprise, and all the best plays had been rerun over and over during the original multicast.

The rest of the squad had scattered and came back with enough chairs pulled from here and there. The table was one of the largest in the place, but the six of them filled it.

The game was interrupted with a breaking news story. The screen filled with a tight shot of a blazing row house.

Doug shut his eyes, reliving the horror of fire hemming him in. His throat closed as though smoke choked him, and he swallowed hard to clear the way for his next breath. Damn, all these years later, the ordeal that killed his family still had the power to make him sweat in terror.

Renegade punched him lightly on the arm, bringing him back to the crowded bar. When he looked over, his buddy's dark eyes reflected the flames. It gave him the creeps.

"You okay?"

Doug managed a brief nod. He tried to shut out the reporter's words but the volume was way too loud and everyone else had stopped talking to watch the live feed. He found his eyes were drawn to the picture despite his fear of another flashback.

A fireman ran out of an alley to an ambulance, carrying a small form wrapped in a blanket. A young boy had escaped, the reporter said. The rest of his family apparently had not. Shit. That poor kid.

Someone at the next table muttered, "Poor little guy. I can imagine how he feels."

No, you can't. Doug glanced around the table and saw the thought reflected in his buddies' faces. Not for the first time, he realized that they shared a strong bond. They'd become the family each had lost in childhood. Every member of the Screaming Dragons was the sole survivor of some tragedy.

A shiver ran through him. What would he do if he lost these guys? It could happen so easily. They risked their lives every time they roared off the runway. Hell, they risked their lives on the local roads more often than that. So much of the world's resources had been gobbled up during the war that nobody had fully recovered yet, almost a decade later. Nevada was just getting around to dealing with battered roads and dangerously old vehicles. He shook himself. Thinking like that was a sure way to get depressed. Life was too short to spend in a black funk.

The game resumed on the screen, chatter carried on around them and the mood at their table lightened.

A pretty cocktail server came along and Buffalo jumped to his feet. His chair clattered to the floor behind him. Doug shook his head. Smooth. Real smooth.

Buffalo gestured to all of them and yelled something into the waitress' ear. She nodded, jerked her thumb towards the bar, scooped up the tip and dirty glasses and left.

Dolphin leaned across the table and hollered, "So, Buffalo boy, what's going on? This isn't our usual type of hangout."

"I know. I want to see if I can hook up with Shirley."

"Shirley?" Jet Wake sniggered. "Surely you don't mean Shirley?"

"Surely he does mean Shirley," Dolphin shot back. "But, Buffalo boy, surely that wasn't Shirley?"

Their banter earned them a long-suffering look. "You're right. That wasn't Shirley." Buffalo cocked his head at a stunning blonde working the bar. "*That's* Shirley."

Dolphin mimed a drool. Renegade clutched his heart and panted. Doug tilted his head and tried to look like a star-struck idiot. Wingnut and Jet Wake settled for exaggerated leers. They were doing a pretty good job of ticking off more than their buddy Buffalo, if the disgusted looks from the neighboring tables were anything to go by. Doug could tell from Buffalo's narrowed eyes and ruddy face that he was about to explode.

The sound on the television cut out just as there was a lull in the general conversation. Buffalo bellowed into the sudden silence, "Fucking assholes."

Chapter Two

ഔ

Two minutes later, they were back on the sidewalk.

Buffalo aimed a vicious kick at a pebble. It went soaring across the road and struck the side of a darkened warehouse. Hands thrust deep in his pockets, he watched the stone bounce back into the street. "Man, I'll be lucky if she ever speaks to me again."

Doug struggled to keep his mouth shut. His old man, God rest his soul, was right. Sometimes it was smart not to be so smart. They'd paid for drinks they hadn't had a chance to enjoy, there was no food in sight and Buffalo was pissed off. If he was honest about it, Buffalo had good reason. They were being assholes, but that didn't mean he had to announce it to the world.

Renegade pointed out, "You did damn near get arrested." Their left wing man didn't say much. Doug would have bet good money that he was upset with Buffalo's behavior.

Wingnut chimed in, "You didn't have to threaten her boss."

"How was I supposed to know he's her husband? She oughta wear a ring."

That had seemed a little too convenient, but Doug kept his mouth shut. If Buffalo thought he'd been lied to and hustled out of the place, he'd turn around and go back in, metaphorical guns blazing. Postponing dinner was an inconvenience. Getting hauled in for disorderly conduct was a more serious prospect.

"It's not like she was happy to see you," Jet Wake interjected. "You oughta do your homework a little better. How'd you know she works there?"

"Somebody mentioned it. Said the place was nice, and the food was great."

Doug frowned. "I don't want to say it—"

"Cut the bullshit, Phoenix. You can't wait to say it." Buffalo hunched his shoulders. "I'm the asshole. I just flew full-throttle into a rock wall. And here I am, still worried about her ever speaking to me again. She's married, for Chrissake, she never said a word to me, and I've still got a case for her."

Doug braced himself. Buffalo's temper was legendary. "No, I'm hungry."

To his surprise, all he got was a scowl. "You're just jealous." Buffalo turned and they began walking once more. "You've got no girl, unless it's that chick in your dreams. Still fucking your sheets, Phoenix?"

"Hey, she's better-looking than Shirley." Doug spoke mildly. He'd learned to deflect their jibes with a good-natured retort. Anything else led to endless idiocy.

They were all fucking assholes.

"Surely not," One corner of Renegade's lips twitched up as he muttered and Doug suppressed a chuckle.

Instead of rising to the bait, Buffalo said, "I always thought there was something off about her. She's damned hot, but a little odd." He planted a light punch on Doug's arm and laughed. "Man, you should've seen your face. You were afraid I'd take a swing at you."

"Superman would be afraid you'd take a swing at him," Wingnut complained. "You're nineteen feet tall, with hands the size of taxicabs and shoulders like a linebacker. You shaved right before we left the base but now you've got a five o'clock shadow that's edging into beard territory. I'm glad we have you along to scare away the bad guys."

"No wonder Shirley didn't want to stand up for you." Dolphin sniggered. "But now you won't get a chance to stand up for her."

Buffalo pointedly ignored this witty observation. "Not to change the subject, but how is your dream fuck, Phoenix? Still flying without a jet?"

"Yup. Every night, sometimes twice." It was a lie, but damned if he'd tell them the truth. He only flew to find his mahogany-skinned beauty now and then, although the dreams were becoming more frequent.

They all laughed, but something flickered in Renegade's eyes. Not for the first time, Doug wondered if he was the only one with strange dreams.

They rounded a corner and ran into a police barrier. Flashing lights rotated on the fire engines and rescue vehicles clustered a block away. The row house still burned, releasing a wide plume of black smoke. As Doug watched, the smoke took the shape of a huge dragon in flight. The wind changed. A spiny head formed between the great wings, the mouth open in a silent scream. The creature appeared to look right at him, through gaping holes the color of flame. A hissing cry rang in his ears. Before he could call the others' attention to it, the image blurred and became a column of smoke once more.

A chill ran through him. Was it protection the dragon offered, or a warning?

Buffalo rubbed his hands together. "Now, where are we going to get some food?"

* * * * *

She watched him come, bathed in moonlight, to the misty vale below the highest mountain pass. He swooped down the slope to land on a rock at her side, changing form in time for his bare feet to touch the stone.

His form was physical perfection, sculpted of muscle and sinew. He was truly a proud and mighty warrior, fit to guide her people to victory — and her to joy divine.

One look into his eyes, the color of the midday sky, and she knew him for who he was.

One touch of his hand and she was lost. Lost to the perfection of his body and the temptation of his lips.

She led him to her camp. The best furs awaited them, the finest food her enclave had to offer. Nothing was too good for her warrior.

Her mate.

Her Chosen.

He refused the meat. The goblet he accepted and drained in a gulp.

The look in his eyes told her what he wanted.

She stripped for him slowly, taking her time unknotting the ties and slipping her arms free. Tradition required her to give him the chance to view all that she offered, and the chance to refuse. Each time was like the first.

Each time, it was just as important that he agree. As her Chosen, he was the hope of her enclave and her key to a bright future. She must please him, no matter what it took. He had proven a gentle and caring lover. Giving in would be no chore.

He reached to help her, easing the garment free of her breasts and hips, dropping the cloth to the ground at her feet. An unexpected rush of shyness heated her skin. Resisting an urge to cover herself, she straightened.

She stood naked before him. As she had so many times before.

His touch sent a shiver through her. So many times they'd been together like this, and still he affected her in amazing ways. New ways, yet as familiar as the fields she worked.

With strong fingers, he lightly traced the contour of her shoulder, raising goose bumps on her flesh and pebbling her nipples. He stroked down, across the soft skin below her collarbone, and her breasts grew heavy in anticipation. Her slit swelled and grew damp. The slightly rough pads of his fingers brushed across the tips of her nipples. She shuddered at the sensations racing through her, lightning and desire and hunger, all rolled into a delightful wave of need.

He did not neglect any part of her. With touch and tongue, he explored her skin. He nipped the inside of her elbow and her anticipation winched higher. Light touches feathered across her rib cage. Brushing back her hair, he blew softly into her ear.

She shivered in his arms.

Supporting her torso with one arm, he bent her over backwards. Her breasts jutted up, presented for his—and her—pleasure. He kneaded the soft flesh and licked the taut peaks.

Sweet gods, this was exquisite! No one had warned her of the ecstasy she would find in her Chosen's arms.

Legend had it that those to whom the Chosen appeared in dreams were cursed, that this was a terrible thing to experience. These dreams were so wonderful she had trouble believing the dark warrior was truly the same Chosen spoken of in the legends. That her enclave now desperately needed a warrior to lead them was what finally convinced her.

Why did her people fear the warrior dreams?

Head down, eyes closed, she discovered her other senses heightened to compensate for not being able to see him. His harsh breathing filled the chamber, mingling with her whimpers and cries. Each breath filled her head with the rich fragrance of his male arousal. She would know him anywhere by his unique scent.

Thank you, she risked telling him. *I am so glad you are here with me.*

He smiled. *Wherever here is.* His fingers pinched and stretched one nipple, his lips tugged at the other. Lightning and fire raced through her, from where he played with her, straight to her womb.

This is a camp my people use, near the mountain pass above our enclave. Where you will join me soon, when the First One decrees.

I thought I was joining you now. He followed the jest with a quick grin.

It is foretold you will appear in the hour of our greatest need.

And I will satisfy all your needs. He sobered. *When you need me, I will come. Is it that important to you?*

Yes. She searched his eyes and found the truth.

Then I promise. Following the path of her desire, his free hand slid lower to the curls between her legs. He parted her lips to dip a finger into her wetness. With a firm massage, he spread the slickness over her before easing one finger inside.

She jerked at the delicious intrusion, parting her thighs.

More! More! Sweet gods, don't make me wait!

Rubbing and working her tight muscles, he stretched her, now with two fingers. She cried out as he thrust a third digit inside, bringing more of that delightful tingling fire to life. Her breath hitched.

Pulling herself upright, she stared into his bright blue eyes. "Please." The word came out in a soft sigh.

It was the first time she'd spoken aloud and he responded in kind. "Please what?"

"Please love me."

His hand moved in response, withdrawing almost fully before thrusting deep. He spread his fingers, opening her wide.

Moisture flooded his hand. Cupping his palm, he gathered the juice of her desire and brought it to his lips. His eyes remained locked on hers as his tongue flicked out to lap up her essence.

She almost climaxed just watching him.

Leaning forward to nip the skin behind her ear and press his hard cock into her hip, he whispered in her mind, *My mahogany-skinned dream, feel how I want you.*

I want you, too. I want you to fill me with your cock. I want you to fly with me to the highest peaks and back again.

Oh, yes, we will fly.

He lifted her and she straddled his hips. The muscles of his chest moved and flexed in the firelight.

He was her warrior, her strength and her salvation. Her destiny.

Slowly, so slowly, he lowered her onto his cock. Oh, dear gods, that hard, thick, ready cock.

Why did her people fear the warrior dreams?

He was her tender lover, her delight and her joy.

She came to rest against him, fully impaled on his hard length. Holding her in place, he strode about the cave. Each step ground her clit against him and she tightened around his shaft. His cock jerked in response. Seated so deeply, each tiny movement sent shudders of delight through her.

By the First One's wings, this was her most incredibly erotic dream yet. Surely that meant he would arrive soon.

He bent to gather up some furs, keeping her firmly seated on him. The dip and sensation of almost falling came close to making her swoon. Rising to spread the pelts across a ledge, he sat her on the cushioned edge and began to stroke his cock in and out of her. Each motion rocked her hips and increased her pleasure.

As her whimpers and moans grew, he laid her back on the mound of furs. The angle of his cock changed and he slowed his thrusts. He drove into her with measured, powerful strokes that caressed her just *there*, on the perfect spot to ensure her climax.

Her head thrashed back and forth when he cupped her breasts, scraping his thumbs across her sensitive nipples. Her cries increased as the sensations built, spiraling through her, carrying her into a realm of sensation and delight and sparkling joy.

The stroke of his cock and the rasp of his thumbs fired her blood. Heat suffused her, tracing a burning path from her breasts to her womb, rushing down to her feet and up her spine.

He reached back for her legs and repositioned her, pulling her feet up to his shoulders. Her hips tilted and her thighs spread apart.

Sweet gods, he thrust into her once more, twice, thrice, reaching ever deeper, and with the fourth stroke she flew apart, shimmering into the star-spangled sky and crying out her joy.

He roared his completion above her, spurting his seed deep within her convulsing womb.

They collapsed together in a heap, sated and panting.

She smiled. He had said he would help them. Hadn't he?

* * * * *

Darya slapped her hand on the table. "Rumors about the mages abound, that they are divided and disagreements within the Council are fast approaching war. The situation grows more serious with each passing day. We need a warrior to lead us. Where is your Chosen?"

Harna regarded Darya's steely glare with equanimity before turning away. Impatience would do her no good. Nor would haste. Around the chamber, those charged with guiding their enclave shifted in their seats.

Darya had been the settlement's elected leader for five years. When she began having dreams that were known only from legends, Harna had vaulted from obscurity as a widowed field worker into a place of importance. She now stood just below Darya in the hierarchy. When her Chosen arrived, Harna would eclipse Darya's current status, sharing with him the responsibility and honor of leading the enclave.

She turned away from the window and the glorious sunset it framed. The assembly awaited her reply. She took a moment to look over the room, hoping to find some way to answer a question she had often asked herself.

Their assembly chamber was no different than any other she'd seen. It was larger than some and smaller than others. Stone arches supported the ceiling above ranks of benches placed in a semicircle. Representatives of the enclave, one for each ten adults, filled fewer than half the seats. In her father's youth, the room had overflowed at every meeting. Or so he claimed. No one could explain their shrinking numbers, a problem that plagued every enclave. Was this the threat that summoned her Chosen? Or did her people need him to prevent them from being drawn into the mages' conflict?

No inspiration came during her perusal of the chamber. She took refuge in assurances. "He will arrive, Darya, and soon."

Darya's father, one of the eldest in the assemblage, thumped his walking stick on the stone floor and snorted. "You are a novice! How can you know this?"

Aye, she was a novice, but in this matter, they were all novices. She strove to master her temper and keep her voice calm. "I know by the dreams. They come more often."

Several of the others seated around the room cleared their throats or made sympathetic noises. None of them had walked her path, indeed none had experienced the warrior dreams in many generations, but all knew the legends.

"Are they still as intense?" Compassion replaced irritation in Darya's voice.

Harna thought of the ecstasy she found in her Chosen's touch and was heartily glad her flush didn't show under her dark skin. "Aye. They grow more vivid."

Legend did not disclose the nature of the dreams and she had never shared details of her night encounters with her Chosen. The thought of what reaction the assembly might have, should they learn how he had come to her, was mortifying. And humbling. They would surely strip her of her position. She did not want to return to the fields.

In the weeks since the warrior dreams began, she had grown accustomed to sleeping until dawn. Her back no longer ached. With the change in her status had come a nicer cottage, one she didn't have to share with her siblings. She had access to the best food the enclave had. Nothing about her new life resembled her former drudgery. Were it within her power, she would summon her Chosen immediately and secure her future.

As it was, she could only wait for him to appear. Legend said he would arrive in their hour of greatest need.

Darya turned the talk away to mundane matters, and Harna breathed a covert sigh of relief. Trade had to be reestablished for this season's bounty of hides, grain and cheeses. By tradition, each year the negotiations began anew. No trader, be he buyer or seller, was assured of continuing agreements. Every spring, representatives from each enclave must meet with those of the fisherfolk and the magefolk to discuss renewal of their ties.

A man, who resembled his neighbor like they were two peas nestled in a pod, rose and waited to be acknowledged. "I suggest that Harna be our representative this year." General agreement murmured through the room as the speaker returned to his seat.

Young Nodda's pronouncement caught Harna by surprise. He had not voiced any support of her leadership, had never said anything to indicate whether he was in favor of her or not. Was turning over this task to her meant to bolster her authority? Or was it relegating her to a lower status? Young Nodda whispered to Old Nodda beside him. Both turned their heads toward Harna and half-smiled at her. The softness in their expressions led her to believe they held her in favor.

Darya pointed at her father, giving him her attention. The old man waved his hand to indicate he preferred to remain seated. Harna waited for the thump of his stick, but he folded his hands over the knobby end and leaned forward to speak.

"It is long past time for the younger members of the assembly, and those in the enclave, to learn to deal with outsiders. Our stores remain half-full from last year's abundant harvest. Their dealings will not impoverish us should they fail to negotiate wisely for this season's reapings. I support that suggestion and further wish to send a group of untried youths. Doing is the best way of learning."

A murmur of agreement passed through the room, with a few snorts. Harna judged the snorts were very much in the minority. Darya must have as well, for she ignored them.

"There are so many among us who have not had this experience. Who shall go with Harna?" Darya kept her grip on power by letting general agreement determine most issues. Harna had learned much by observing her, both in her official role and in her dealings outside the assembly. "What shall be the means of deciding?"

Her father, long the elected leader during his prime, was no fool either. "If she is to lead them, let her choose. What say you all?"

To no one's surprise, the assembly agreed.

Harna breathed a sigh of relief. For now, she was secure. Should her Chosen fail to come, she wasn't quite certain what would happen to her.

Most likely, she would be reduced to her former humble position. Returning to the grueling work in the fields would be bad enough. She would also have to endure pitying looks from everyone in the enclave, from child to elder, those who now treated her with deference and respect. May the First One forbid that.

The trip to the coast would be important to her future. She'd work to charm the fisherfolk and the mages' representatives. She needed to build a good reputation as a trader. To do that, she'd need to make good bargains. No, merely good trades would not suffice. Only excellence would do.

She resolved to do anything she had to do to keep the luxuries she now had.

Chapter Three

✤

While the assembly members chatted in the aisles following the meeting, Harna lingered by the dais. She dared to sit in Darya's chair, to see how it felt and what the room looked like from this vantage point. This would soon be her place.

Shouts came from outside and commotion filled the assembly chamber as what looked like the entire enclave rushed inside. She hastily rose and stepped aside as the crowd parted to reveal two bards.

"We have news that cannot wait," the man gasped. His breath came fast, as though he had been running. The amulet he wore around his neck, the token of his position, hung over dusty and wrinkled garments.

Darya resumed her place and banged her hammer on the table. Everyone found a seat. The male bard moved to the center of the dais while his female companion remained in the front row. The woman did not return Harna's smile and, if anything, her expression grew graver. What could be so serious? Harna eyed her with consideration. There were few bards these days to carry word from enclave to enclave. What dangers did she face, traveling from one far-flung community to another? What brought someone to accept such a task?

The bard took a moment to compose himself before he bowed to the assemblage. "I bring you greetings from your sister enclaves. I come from our guild's main hall, and it pains me to bring you such news." He paused to clear his throat. "Harriers everywhere are more numerous this season, and a few months ago, they began to swarm in the eastern provinces."

A number of those present surged to their feet, protesting in a babble of voices.

"No! That cannot be!"

"Never in our history have they done so."

"Swarm?" Harriers looked like miniature dragons but there the resemblance ended. They were solitary and mostly scavengers, but sometimes one would go after a beast in a field. Chill horror spread through Harna at the thought of countless tiny needle-like teeth and razor talons wielded together in a coordinated attack. A single harrier presented a painful nuisance. A flock of them would be lethal. To anything or anyone.

The reason for dreams of her Chosen became perfectly clear. The enclave's need for a strong leader had nothing to do with declining numbers or the mages' troubles. Thank the First One that they would soon have a warrior to lead them.

The thump of Dorpa's walking stick quieted the room.

An ashen-faced Darya broke the silence. "How can that be? They are scavengers or solitary hunters."

"No longer." His words fell into the chamber like heavy stones. "I will explain. This is a long story, so let me speak. I promise you, I will get to the crux of the story in time.

"One of the eastern wizards has made a bid to head the Congress of Mages. This occurred after he was denied admission to the Council. The elder members of the Council have united against him. It is believed his ambition has overpowered his honor, for he thumbs his nose at the restrictions that are the foundation of the Council's rule."

A murmur of surprise ran around the room. The natural order of things was sacrosanct. The mages were devoted to maintaining it at the expense of personal concerns. Dragonfolk and the fisherfolk were pledged to support their efforts. Legend told of how, long ago, an upset in the balance ended with many people, mage, dragonkind and fisherfolk alike, being killed.

By the First One's wings, surely a disaster of this magnitude would be the only reason her warrior dreams had begun. There would be no avoiding the turmoil to come. Harna shuddered at the thought.

The bard continued. "One of the primary rules placed on the mages is a ban on upsetting the natural order. His rejection of this ban involves the line between domesticated and wild creatures. That line is of tremendous importance to the Council of Mages. You may not know, so far removed from there as you are, that they live by herding." He bowed to remove any hint of insult from his words.

"As do we, which you may not know, being a stranger." Darya nodded at him with more than a bit of condescension. She could be counted on to give as good as she got. Harna suppressed a smile.

"Initially, he trained a harrier as one would train a falcon or a goshawk. The Congress suspects him of teaching the harriers to cooperate while hunting in order to amuse himself and his followers. The harriers' behavior has spread farther and faster than he expected. We believe he no longer controls them."

A collective gasp echoed in the room. Harna swallowed hard. To meddle with nature was outlawed. Such infractions rightly carried severe penalties. Why had they not killed this upstart immediately?

As if she had posed the question aloud, the bard continued, "He has disappeared, most believe he has fled before the wrath of the united Congress. No one has seen him for weeks. Should he join forces with the Lords of the West and power their tek with his magic, we will be fighting for our lives on two fronts."

"To do that, he would have to cross the sea. I doubt he can overcome the mages' inability to survive the salt air." Darya regarded him grimly. "It sounds as though we will be fighting for our lives against the harrier swarms, whether he and the Lords come together or no."

"At our best guess, you have two weeks, no more, to prepare a defense or to flee." The bard's expression grew stony. "Already we have lost touch with three enclaves, those nearest the rogue mage's holding. We fear harriers have destroyed them." Cries of protest ran through the assembly at his words.

A nauseating mixture of anger and fear filled Harna. She was tempted to put her head between her knees, but such behavior was unworthy of one in her position. Darya asked through pale, tight lips, "Why have you not verified this?"

"One bard was in the region and has not been heard from. We only assume the harriers have killed her. Our leaders consider the risk too great to send another. There are too few of us now. To lose more would be detrimental to the remaining enclaves."

Darya asked, "Just which mage is it who dares challenge the Congress?"

"Perdin."

"Why, that insolent little firkin!" Darya's sire thumped his stick again, this time so hard Harna feared for the flagstone floor. "His beard is barely grown! What made him think he's qualified to lead those who teach him?"

"Hubris," Harna answered for the bard. "It will be his downfall. My Chosen is a mighty warrior." She joined Darya behind the table on the dais and looked around the room. The enclave members nodded their heads. The two bards stared at her. She'd wager no one had told them of her warrior dreams. At the next enclave, they would have welcome news and interesting gossip to relate along with the warning they carried.

"Mighty enough to challenge a renegade mage, as well as overcome swarms of harriers?" Darya's tone was dry.

Harna ignored her. "The news that harriers already swarm and hunt dragons close to our territory surely means he will arrive soon. I know he will find a way to conquer the harriers and save us."

The assemblage muttered and whispered but none contradicted her.

On occasion, being a living legend had its advantages.

* * * * *

Doug kept his eyes riveted on Buffalo's nozzles just ahead and above him as he maintained pressure on the stick. To keep his position within the narrow tolerances of the tight diamond formation, he had to be ready to mimic and match any moves his flight leader made in his point position.

Up, up and over they flew, into the loop that would bring them down for a low-altitude pass, still in formation.

He kept his flight path in sync with the other three, slightly lower to avoid his flight leader's jet exhaust. In his peripheral vision, at the zenith of the loop he was aware of the fighters at the corners of the diamond. Early sunlight glinted off the red and gold scales of the ornate dragons on each fuselage. The other two planes in the pyramid would be coming in now to make their low-altitude pass below, crossing within feet of each other.

Now came the diamond's descent.

His comm unit crackled in his ear with the expected grunt of a pilot taking more than four gees at the bottom of the loop. His brain registered the fact that it wasn't quite normal even as he tracked the bobble of the leader's tail, up and then down.

Shit. That dip was a bad thing. Buffalo's exhaust would wash over him and melt his windshield. Training kicked in. He pulled the stick up and shoved it to the left, pulling out of position. He kept his eyes glued to his flight leader's jet and wondered what had destroyed Buffalo's legendary concentration.

Doug's right engine flamed out, starved by a gulp of jet exhaust. Better that than losing his canopy. He moved to try a restart.

Hell opened up in front of him. Flame erupted, painting his vision in red and gold.

Before he could draw a panicked breath, Buffalo's jet, followed in formation by the other two planes, smashed into the ground and disintegrated.

The ground rushed up at him. He pulled the stick and leveled off with inches to spare.

The debris field from the crashes splashed up.

Blazing fuel and sharp metal.

Right in front of him. Shit. He was totally fucked. Panic froze his limbs and raised a chill sweat on his skin before instinct took over and he pulled harder on the stick, sending his nose higher and higher. His reaction to the tail bobble had saved his life—for now. He'd gone vertical.

Not soon enough. The instrument panel lit up. Multiple impacts, both large and small, peppered the fuselage all around him. Every gauge he had warned of impending disaster.

Ignoring the screamers, he focused on the altimeter and the airspeed indicator. When he was vertical, his speed bled away. The throb of the left engine stopped. No change in pitch first, just dead. FOD—Foreign Object Destruct. The aircraft had nothing more to give. He was losing fuel long before his airspeed slowed. No hope of a restart on the dead right engine now.

He got to sixty-five hundred feet. When his airspeed fell to zero, he punched out. Had to, or he'd ride the dead weight of the jet back down, into the firestorm below. A quick deep breath steadied his nerves and let his training kick in.

Reaching over his head, he yanked down the curtain, protecting his face from the four-hundred-mile-an-hour wind when he hit the outside air. The canopy blew and his seat ran up the rails and out of the jet. The explosion that freed him pushed the seat and the jet apart. The rocket under his seat would carry him further away, out beyond the debris field directly below him.

He braced himself for the jolt of the rocket.

One-Mississippi.

Two-Mississippi.

Three-Mississippi.

The rocket should have kicked in.

Four-Mississippi.

Five-Mississippi.

Six-Mississippi.

Where was that fucking rocket?

He was losing altitude quickly. If his chute didn't open before he reached two thousand feet, he was toast.

He whacked the harness release and shoved away from the six-hundred-pound seat.

The chute billowed out above him perfectly. His descent slowed.

Below him, three of the finest officers he'd ever worked with were spread out among the tangled wreckage of three of the best fighters ever built. No, not just officers. His brothers. Grief engulfed him, wavering his vision of the crash scene below, before he resolutely pushed it aside. If he didn't concentrate now, he'd wind up landing smack-dab in the fire with them. That wasn't going to happen if he could help it. Wingnut and Jet Wake, who'd cleared the area after their low-altitude pass, would need him.

In these situations, the massive amount of heat generated by the fire created a firestorm that sucked in anything nearby and airborne. He calculated his best odds at getting out of the conflagration and began to maneuver his chute. The burning debris field was well defined. Should be enough altitude to make it.

With a roar, the jet rocket finally deployed.

He shook his head in disgust. Lowest bidder. Had to be.

The seat arrowed down and away. Its exhaust melted a huge hole in his chute.

Doug cursed, grabbed his shoulders and pulled the capewells, freeing himself from the useless tangle of rope and nylon.

He was a dead man.

Again, instinct took over. He spread his arms and legs in an attempt to slow his descent. The action made no difference. He continued to drop like a fucking rock. Closing his eyes, he mumbled prayers for his fallen comrades, sparing a single request for his own safety.

* * * * *

He opened his eyes.

The morning sun no longer cast small shadows across the barren landscape of the extensive base. No scorching crash site sent smoke into the sky around him.

A forest stretched out below him, a vast carpet of treetops glowing brilliant green in the bright sunlight. What the hell?

He closed his eyes tightly, opened them and looked again. The view hadn't changed.

Toto, I don't think we're in Kansas anymore. Or Nevada.

This wasn't Tonopah.

Where the hell was he?

He spread his arms again to slow his descent and great wings unfolded on either side of him.

What the hell was he?

He blinked. Shit, this was one of his dreams.

Sure enough, now that he took a close look at it, the landscape was that of his dream world. Where he flew like a winged creature, without the encasing metal and electronics of his jet. Where he'd never actually seen what he flew as, until now.

Where the silver-haired, mahogany-skinned woman had sucked him off. Where he'd screwed himself senseless, buried inside her sweet, hot cunt.

His groin tightened at the thought.

He'd died in the fiery sky over the practice range—or he thought he had. Along with the other three pilots in the diamond. Damn. He remembered that look he'd seen in Renegade's eyes and hoped like hell they'd been having the same dreams. Maybe he'd find them here.

But this was just a dream. He'd never seen any of the guys in his dreams. Come to think of it, he'd never been anywhere in these dreams before unless he was with his dream-fuck. Why was this one different?

Most likely, he'd been critically injured and lay right now in a hospital bed on the base, in Intensive Care. This was a coma, there were drugs coursing through his veins, he was dreaming and all too soon he'd be back in his body, enduring the agony of broken bones and battered flesh.

Been there, done that. He was in no hurry to do it again.

If this was a dream, he'd go with it. Damn, this was an incredible dream world he'd created. Not bad for an altar boy from Chicago. His mind must be filling in the details, providing an escape from the pain and the drugs. He didn't feel drugged. He felt fine, although light as a feather. That was unusual.

He wasn't wearing a flight suit. He wasn't wearing armor.

Tilting his head to look down at his body, he saw a surface made up of small tightly overlapping—*scales*? Maybe he was wearing armor after all. It was just armor he hadn't seen before. He counted four feet, two on each side of his belly. No, they were four short thick legs, each ending in a set of powerful-looking claws. Tentatively, he tried to flex them. The sharp talons opened and closed at his command. Oh, yeah, they were his, no doubt about it.

He turned his head. A wide leathery wing extended from just behind what he thought was his shoulder. Jointed in the center, rigid at the leading edge, it moved as he flexed his muscles. The black matte surface absorbed the sunlight, giving off no reflection.

Way cool. He was a stealth dragon.

Impossible. He was a *dragon*.

Why not? This was a dream, after all. In dreams, all things are possible.

So, where was the hot babe? Oh, yeah. The woman of his dreams. How cliché. He snorted a chuckle and a trickle of smoke blew out his snout. *His snout?*

Intrigued, he laughed aloud. A gout of flame poured from his open mouth.

Oh, baby. He was a fire-breathing stealth dragon.

How fucking cool was that?

* * * * *

The sea pounded against the rocks, sending up spray that glittered in the sunlight. Cliffs dropped directly into the ocean, providing no beach that he could see, only a scattering of boulders in the shallows. Might be high tide now, he decided, and from the looks of it the receding water would allow a narrow beach. Well out beyond the surf, the boulders became massive and more numerous, forming a lethal barrier. Here and there bleached spikes, the masts of foundered ships, stuck above the expanse of rocks and foaming waves.

Doug wheeled and rose, seeking a higher vantage point. This was farther than he'd ranged in his dreams. So far, no sign of his silver-haired dream woman.

So far, no signs of life at all.

Flying without any instruments was weird. All of his flight training had drilled into him that his senses couldn't be trusted, yet now he had nothing else to rely on. He gauged altitude and wind direction with his eyes and his hide, adjusting the cant of his body and the strokes of his wings to get him where he wanted to go. A thermal washed over one wing in a warm breeze and he plunged into it, riding it aloft.

The wind sweeping in from the ocean carried a taste of salt. Higher and higher he soared, gaining a better view of the countryside as he gained altitude. A vast forest topped the cliffs, spreading far inland. Way off in the distance, he caught a silver glint that resolved into a city as he rose.

There were human inhabitants here then, and nearby. He might find her there, although he didn't remember any dreams that took place in what looked like a city. Not that he'd paid much attention to their surroundings, but he thought they always met in the wilds, a forest or heavily treed area. He'd always appeared in human form, too, not as a dragon. What if he remained a dragon here? That wouldn't be so cool, especially if he found his dream-woman.

The thought that he might not find her was unsettling and left him feeling empty inside. It was like returning to the barracks and finding the guys had never been there, like missing a dear friend. Whoa! How had he become attached to a figment of his imagination? He might be hard up when it came to women but he wasn't that far gone.

Now that line of reasoning was certainly depressing. And here he was, a fire-breathing dragon with a whole new world to explore. Time to leave the heavy thoughts behind and get on with the discovery thing.

In the other direction, away from the gleaming city, the forest gave way to grasslands. From this distance he couldn't be sure but it looked like lanes and low walls of stone separated a patchwork of fields stretching away from the sea to the base of the mountains. Those shadowed smudges clustered around a crossroads might be cottages and barns.

Movement along the cliff below him caught his eye. Another dragon swooped and banked near the water.

Not only life, but another dragon.

He had to investigate. He tipped his head down and pulled his wings in, descending for a closer look.

A sense of urgency filled him as he rushed down, a kind of battle lust. He felt compelled to attack something, anything. He'd never felt anything like this in training. Or in his dreams.

Shrieks filled the air. Small birds—or some kind of flying thing, he couldn't be sure what they were—swarmed around the dragon, darting close and retreating. They stayed well back, attacking the trailing edge of the wings and avoiding the thrashing tail.

He counted eighteen of the winged things. The dragon's flight pattern was an attempt either to avoid its attackers or to get behind them. Whichever it was trying, it wasn't succeeding very well.

All right! This he could handle. No missiles, no targeting computers, but he certainly had a powerful weapon at his command.

He dove in from the rear, hosing the creatures with a roar of fire and anger. They crisped in a heartbeat and their smoldering remains fell into the sea.

Way cool! Toasting the critters with an angry breath went a long way to appeasing his battle lust and was much more satisfying than strafing an enemy with bullets.

His blood pounded in his ears. Wheeling and turning, he made a second pass over the beleaguered dragon. He flamed six more of the little bastards before the others broke off the attack, disappearing along the cliffs the way they'd come.

The dragon had descended close to the water as he attacked the attackers. Now, it rose and approached him, flying just below the cliffs. A familiar voice sounded in his head.

I thank you, stranger, for your timely intervention. If you will, follow me and accept the hospitality of our enclave.

The woman of his dreams. Could she also become a dragon at will?

Hell, it was his dream. Why not?

Could he answer her by speaking into her mind? He tried. *Thank you.*

Follow me. She turned and led him back along the coastline. They skimmed along above the water. The cliffs broke in one place, allowing the sunlight to reach her. He sucked in a breath.

Numerous gaping wounds peppered her back and tail, harsh red against the deeper red-brown of her scales. Her wings were shredded at the back. Blood spattered off each down stroke, falling to disappear in the surf.

Rage gathered in his belly. Those, those things—whatever they were—had dared to attack his woman! He roared his anger in a great stream of flame.

Did they injure you? Her calm attitude shamed him.

No. I'm furious because they hurt you.

Had they not surprised me, I would be unhurt and home by now. I had no desire to lead them to our camp. Fatigue colored her tone.

You've gotta rest. You need medical attention.

There are no healers here and I cannot take the time to find one. I must return and warn my people that the harriers have reached us.

Is that what you call those nasty things?

Yes. Her voice sounded stressed and the rhythm of her flight slowed as he watched.

You can't go on.

I must. You cannot help me. The steady pace of her wings faltered.

Allow me.

To do what?

In answer, he swooped below her and matched her pace. Timing the strokes of his wings to hers, he slowly rose beneath her. *Put your weight on me, and I'll do the work.* He felt rather than heard her sigh of relief as her weight bore down on him.

Where are we going?

An image of a clearing in the forest came to him, with the landmark on the cliffs where he should turn inland.

Once her wings folded out of the way, he began to work in earnest. He'd thought flying to be carefree but with her added weight, even his great strength neared its limits.

Without warning, the load on his back lightened. Before he could ease up, the downstroke of his wings sent them soaring. Slender arms closed around his neck.

She had shifted back to her human form and now lay on his back, straddling him just in front of his wings. Damn, the problem of mass conversion bothered him. There was no way she could compress her dragon bulk inside her human form. If she'd done that, she wouldn't be any lighter now, and she was a lot lighter.

The laws of physics are constant throughout the universe, so this had to be a dream. That also explained why he wasn't experiencing any symptoms of shock, which he would expect after surviving a crash. No shivers, no sweats, no shortness of breath, no dizziness.

No other possibility. Shit, that meant he was severely injured after all. His mind shied away from the implications of that conclusion. Until the docs eased up on his meds and he woke up, he'd just go with the dream.

He tried to remember if he wore clothing after he changed form in his dreams. He didn't think so.

Which meant she was lying against him, stark naked. Damn, his scales weren't sensitive enough for him to tell if her pubic hair pressed against the ridge of his spine.

The mental image of her cunt spread open on him gave him a raging hard-on. Well, it did if dragons could get raging hard-ons. Whatever they did get when turned on, he sure had it.

How could he be thinking about sex when she was hurt? He mentally shook his head in disgust. *Asshole.*

Wait, he wasn't an asshole. He'd just decided the laws of physics dictated that this had to be a dream. Ergo, she wasn't real. Ergo, she wasn't hurt.

Whether she was real or not, whether she was hurt or not, he couldn't erase the mental image of her slicking his scales with her juices every time she shifted her weight.

She was shifting her weight too often. In spite of his conviction that she wasn't real, he found himself asking, *Are you uncomfortable?*

Yes. Your back is bony and ridged. That is why we do not often carry others in such a manner, but now there is no danger of exhausting you.

The landmark outcropping of rock appeared ahead and he turned inland in a long sweeping curve. In a moment, the trees parted to reveal the clearing she'd shown him.

Let me down before you change, please.

Christ, his dreams always picked up right after that part. He didn't know how to change.

How *did* he change?

Coming straight down, more like a chopper than a jet, he landed neatly in the center of the clearing. Damn, this dragon gig was versatile—and still way fucking cool.

He bent his legs on one side and felt her slide down.

"Change, and come with me."

Yeah, right. He was too embarrassed to tell her he didn't know how to shift back to being human. Working to catch his breath after the strenuous flight, he watched her sashay to the edge of the clearing.

Clothing didn't make it through the change, or at least hers hadn't. Her long silver-white hair fell in a sheaf, almost to her narrow waist. The sway of her wide, naked hips and the soft jiggle of her ass mesmerized him. Damn. He could feel the tight wet heat of her cunt welcoming his cock in his memory. Without thinking, he took a step after her.

A shimmer in his vision interrupted his train of thought.

What had she told him to do?

Oh, yeah, change and follow.

When he stepped forward, it was with a human foot and not a dragon's claw. His snort of surprise was just that, a nasal exhalation with no accompanying smoke or fire.

How could he have expected to get stuck as a dragon? It was his dream, after all. That meant he was in charge.

He hurried to catch up with her, his hard-on bobbing in front of him. He probably looked like an idiot. Good thing there was no one around to see him.

Chapter Four

Harna walked past the fire pit and ducked under the low overhang in front of the shelter. Despite her exhaustion, her step was light and her heart raced with excitement. Her Chosen was here!

Pulling aside the cloth that covered the opening, she stepped inside. In the warmth and darkness, she sensed the presence of her two companions. Yiman was as close to her as only a brother can be. Ajan had long been a dear friend of their family.

Had she known she would meet her dreamwarrior on this passage, she would have insisted two of the doubters come with her. The sooner her Chosen asserted his leadership, the better it would be for the enclave.

"You were not long, sister."

"No, Yiman, I was not."

Her eyes adjusted to the dim interior. Her brother lay at ease propped against the bench in the back of the space. Ajan had her usual spot, curled up against her pack near the door.

"We have trouble." Harna crossed to her pack and opened it. With an effort she kept her voice level and her hands steady. Strangely, she found it difficult to speak of him, even to her brother and her close friend. "I was attacked by a swarm of harriers. They have spread far faster than the bards told us to expect."

"Dear gods, Harna!" Ajan's voice rang with horror. Both she and Yiman jumped to their feet. "But you changed and walked in on your own. How did you survive? Were there only four or five harriers?"

"There were more than enough, perhaps a score." She failed to keep the smugness from her voice. "My warrior has arrived. He saved me."

Ajan squealed and leapt to her feet. "He is here? Oh, and I am without my torque and my hair is a mess!"

"Relax, Ajan, he is not expecting a ceremonial welcome." Harna rummaged through her pack for a robe. She felt an elusive touch of silk slip away and dug after it, catching it before it disappeared again under the wool and linen. She wanted to look her best when she greeted her Chosen for the first time.

"Hello?"

Ajan sucked in a breath. "Is that your Chosen?"

"Aye." Harna pulled the silk gown over her head and hastened to smooth the folds down so the hem hung below her knees. "Come and meet him."

Ajan and Yiman rose to follow her.

Outside, her Chosen stood tall and straight, highlighted by the full sun overhead.

She had forgotten he was naked.

She hadn't known he was aroused.

Sweet weres and wings, was he ever! Her pulse kicked up a notch. His cock thrust out from his belly like a lance. He stood looking into the woods, presenting his profile.

Blocking the doorway with her body and shoving Yiman back into the shelter, she ignored his grunt of surprise. She turned her head to murmur over her shoulder. "Brother, bring one of your garments."

She remained where she was until he returned and thrust a linen shirt into her hand.

"Wait a moment, both of you. Do not come out right away."

Ajan made a small noise of protest but didn't appear. Harna just knew her young friend was ogling the warrior from the shadows.

Approaching her Chosen, she had to smile at the way he stood straight and tall, hands at his sides, bold in his nakedness. "Here, you will be more comfortable once you've garbed yourself."

At the sound of her voice, he came to face her. The dappled shade painted him in splotches of light and dark. Never had she seen such sculpted muscles, such strength and power in a man's body.

He moved closer, one large hand extended, and her breath hitched in her chest. What had she done to deserve such perfection?

As he took the shirt, she said, "I am called Harna."

"My name's Doug." His voice was a little rougher than she remembered from her dreams, but the timbre was the same.

So was the effect it had on her. Her knees weakened and her belly trembled. Reality struck her hard. He was finally here!

All would be well. He would defeat the harriers. Her people would survive and her future was secure. No longer need she fear a return to her lesser status. She could stop fretting about that and concentrate on becoming a leader.

She waited while he pulled the shirt down, trying to think of what to say first. There was so much to speak of, so much she had to tell him, so much she had to learn.

When his face reappeared, he solved her dilemma by speaking first. "What were those harrier things that attacked you, Harna? And why aren't you injured? I saw wounds all over you but now they're gone."

"Harriers are a vicious sort of flying lizard. And I am fine because the change heals us." How did he not know this? He had changed upon landing. That meant he was of her people. Didn't it? Concern rippled through her. What exactly was he? In her dreams, she had gotten the impression he hadn't really known what it meant to be her Chosen. He had claimed his world was different. Exactly where had he come from?

Behind her, Yiman cleared his throat and Ajan giggled. Harna tore her eyes from Doug and remembered the courtesies she had to perform.

"Warrior Doug, this is my brother Yiman and our friend Ajan." Harna approved of the way her Chosen promptly extended his pale hand, although he looked a little surprised when Yiman laid his dark forearm along Doug's and clasped his elbow, in the formal greeting of their people. Doug recovered quickly, gripping Yiman's elbow firmly in return.

Now that Yiman was full-grown, he was among the tallest of the enclave's men, yet Doug had to bend his head slightly to look him in the eye. Harna sighed in relief. Her Chosen was expected to be a strong warrior, and he would have no problem asserting his authority in a physical manner.

"We are honored that you have come to us in our time of need." Yiman released Doug's arm and they both stepped back. "You cannot know how much we would suffer without you."

"If those, ah, harriers I saw attack Harna are an indication of the problems you've got, I can understand. They're nasty. How many are there?"

"We can only tell you a portion of it. Harriers hunting dragons is something we've never heard of, or it was until recently." Yiman looked at Harna and jerked his head toward the structure behind them. "Shall we make ourselves comfortable?"

"Indeed. Come, let us do just that. We have food and drink to share." Harna indicated a low plank table surrounded by stools. Nearby, wood arranged in a low stone hearth lay ready for lighting. "Take a seat while I start the fire. Ajan, please prepare refreshments for our guest."

Ajan grumbled and balked until Harna pinned her with a glare. She lifted the curtain over the doorway and disappeared inside. Harna followed her, retrieving a chunk of pitch from the secure cabinet where a large supply of it was stored. When she rejoined Doug, he had selected a stump and sat watching her.

At his questioning look, she explained, "We use a pitch-based mixture to start our fires. Every camp like this, which is set up to host traveling parties, has a sizable supply. All of the things we might need are safely shut in stout cupboards. They must be, or the harriers will destroy them."

Ajan returned with a tray heavily laden with food and began to set out cups for drink. Yiman took the pitch and stuffed it among the logs. Harna handed him a flint kit and a few deft flicks of his wrist sent sparks flying among the wood. One went into the center of the pile and the pitch flared up.

Harna set an unlit torch beside each of them before she chose a seat. "We will be safe here, even if the harriers followed us. We know they fear fire, as do most creatures."

"Smart of them." Doug edged back a little as the flames roared up, engulfing the stacked wood.

She turned to face him. "Harriers have long been scavengers, clearing the remains of dead animals from forest and field. In the past, they presented a nuisance more than a threat. Occasionally one would invade our pastures to attack a young or ailing beast. We recently received word that a mage taught harriers to hunt together. But he has lost control of them and the behavior is spreading. Until today, they have not been seen doing so this far from their original territory. At least this is the first time I know of." She shuddered at the memory of those sharp teeth tearing into her tail and wings. "We believe a number of our settlements have been lost, destroyed by them. Your arrival is our salvation."

Yiman broke in. "They are now a threat unlike any other. Not only to us in flight, but as we are now, we are close to helpless against them. As are our livestock. We have begun traveling in groups to avoid attack, but when we are not in flight…"

She shared a look of understanding with Yiman. There was no need to dwell on what would happen should a harrier swarm come upon a group of them in their two-legged form.

Doug cleared his throat. "Are they carnivores?"

Yiman nodded. "They eat anything and everything."

"Then you gotta go after them. Find them where they nest or whatever it is they do when they hang out. They've gotta live somewhere. You carry an unbeatable weapon with you, always ready to use. Flame 'em."

Something within Harna sprang to life at his words. This was the solution they needed! None of her enclave would ever have suggested this, but once it had been voiced, she knew hunting the harriers, taking the fight to them instead of waiting for their attack, was undeniably the correct course of action.

A chill followed the recognition of truth. The assembly would be loath to accept it. By tradition, her people butchered animals for food. Harriers, ⁻being both scavengers and uncomfortably close to dragons in appearance, were not food.

She hoped she could help him convince the enclave of the necessity to kill, by stressing it was only the harriers and only until they were no longer a threat. Years of tradition and custom would have to be overcome. If they fought alongside both fisherfolk and magefolk, surely the gods would not make them pay the steep price they had once before, at the end of the Great War.

"Please, be welcome in our shelter and accept our hospitality." Ajan handed a cup to Doug and placed a plate of grain cakes, dried meat and peeled roots before him. He nodded as he took the cup, sniffed it once and sipped. A smile spread across his face and he drank deeply.

"The water of our homeland is the best in the world, or so we believe." Harna took the heaping plate Ajan offered her and attacked the food. Changing may have healed her wounds but she needed to eat and drink heartily and rest during the next few days to restore her body completely so she could accomplish the next change unharmed.

When they all had plates and drinks, Yiman raised his brows. "You ask us to *chase* the harriers? We would count ourselves fortunate to escape them!"

"There's no other way to get rid of them. Hunt 'em down and kill 'em!"

"They are too much like us." Yiman's tone was flat and adamant. "Our people do not kill what we cannot eat."

Doug didn't react with anger at being contradicted, as Harna expected. He made no attempt to argue. He simply responded, "Then it's time you did."

Yiman sat back on his heels, astonishment clearly written on his features.

Harna knew just how he felt. She had not expected her Chosen to be, well, so blunt. Her surprise faded as she thought about it. Did they not need a strong leader? Was he not a warrior?

"This is a kill-or-be-killed situation, pal, so you'd better get with the program if you're going to come out on top." Doug pursed his lips for a moment. "What are their weaknesses?"

Yiman's jaw worked soundlessly. Fearing he was speechless with shock, Harna answered. "They have none!"

"Bullshit. Everything has limitations. They've got to have an Achilles' heel."

She caught Yiman's frown, returned it and shrugged. Her Chosen spoke with strange words but also with confidence and wisdom. Since the dreams told her that he had come to save them, she would put her faith in him. And in the First One who sent him.

Convincing the assembly would be another matter. They had not shared her dreams of him. Thank the gods. At the thought of her enclave elders knowing the erotic nature of her dreams, her skin heated with more than the memory of Doug's hands and mouth on her.

Doug set his plate aside and leaned forward. "Every enemy has a weakness. The trick is to find it. Let's see. Do they hate sea water? Do they have limitations on flight speed or range?"

Yiman roused himself and spoke. "We do not know." His voice rose in a nervous squeak.

Harna suppressed a smile. At times he was clearly a man, and then something like his voice cracking would make her aware of just how young he still was.

"The only time we are safe from them is at night." Yiman spread his hands and shrugged. "They appear suddenly, from who knows where, and no one has ever tried to follow them. That would be unwise. They fly a little faster than we do."

"I know a pissed-off dragon can burn them to a crisp. Can they be poisoned?"

"Until today, they have never attacked us. We know them as solitary creatures, and as such they have never been a threat. As Harna just said, occasionally one will appear to eat a dead herd beast in the field. That we can tolerate, for we would not eat what we have not butchered." Yiman exchanged a glance with Harna. "No one has ever tried to kill them."

"Then it's past time to start. You're going to have to develop some new tricks." Doug looked at Harna. "Where's your base?"

"Base?" She grew tired of repeating what he said and appearing foolish, but she had not heard these words before. What might an Achilles' heel be? Where did her Chosen come from that they spoke so strangely?

"Your home. I saw a city far away from the coast. What looks like white towers and walls. Is that where you live?"

"No, that is the City of Light, the easternmost dwelling of the mages."

His eyes lit up. "Mages? Cool."

"It is no warmer or cooler than here." Harna watched him closely. In her peripheral vision, she saw Ajan tilt her head and frown.

Was his strangeness a good thing or not? She couldn't decide. Would his odd manners help his ability to convince the assembly his way was their salvation? She would have to wait and see how he dealt with the enclave's leaders. Surely the Mother of All would not send her a Chosen lacking the skills to help them.

"No, I meant that's good. I like it. I want to go there, but not until we get this harrier thing taken care of."

Harna glanced at Yiman. His face reflected her unease. Her Chosen spoke with strange words and now he expressed a desire to visit the mages' city. By the First One's wings, her Chosen in the flesh was not what she expected.

She knew his kiss but not his character. She knew his touch but not his intentions. Perhaps the dreams were to be feared because they focused on mating and not on learning what was necessary.

Doug leaned back once more. "Now, where do you live?"

"Near the foot of the mountains, to the north. We come to the coast to trade with the fisherfolk."

"Are there more harriers here than where you live?"

"These are the first we have seen on this passage, and before they began to swarm, we did not trouble to notice one or two." Yiman shrugged again. Harna bit her lip. Her Chosen was asking so many questions they could not answer. "As I said, they left us alone. Until today."

"You weren't surprised to see me, Harna. Why not?"

"I have seen you before, and I knew you would come to us soon. Surely you dreamt of me?"

His eyes widened. "You had the dreams, too?"

"It is an old prophecy, that the warrior dreams begin when the warrior is due, and they come only to his Chosen. The more intense the dreams, the closer his arrival." Harna had an awful thought. "You did not know this?"

He shook his head. "You used that term in the dreams. What does it mean to be your Chosen?"

Harna's cheeks heated. This was not a conversation she wished to have in front of her brother or Ajan. How could she phrase it, to conceal the sexual aspects of their dreams? "That we are fated to lead my people, side by side, together in all ways." She met his eyes and gave a small jerk of her head toward the others.

"Oh. We don't have that myth in my world."

"Then why did you come?"

His smile was grim. "Let's just say it wasn't my choice."

"But now that you are here, you will defeat the harriers, will you not?" Yiman's voice was a bit panicked.

"You people have a problem and I'm here, so I guess I will. What have I done all that training for, if not to fight? This may be the only real combat I ever see." He grinned again, a full predator's grin, his teeth shining very white in the dimness of the shelter. Harna shivered at the sight, very glad she was not a harrier. "You don't know your enemy's capabilities. The first thing I need to do is learn more about the harriers. We'll start in the morning."

* * * * *

Harna set about sorting out the bedding, taking a bit from each of them to provide for Doug. While she smoothed a blanket out for him, he leaned close and took her hand. "Can't we be alone?" Tracing the outline of her palm with his tongue, he lapped up to her wrist and nipped the tender skin.

Her belly clenched. Sweet gods, she was growing wet from just his touch on her hand. He eyed her taut nipples, pressed against the silk of her gown, and grinned again. There were traces of a predator in that expression, as though he might eat her whole. Harna shivered again, this time from desire. Dear gods, she wanted to be in his arms, to feel his cock fill her in reality and not in a dream, but there was no other shelter than this.

"Later. Not tonight."

"I can think of any number of ways for you to thank me for saving you. Why not tonight?" He pulled her close enough for her to feel how much he wanted her. She pulled away. The outline of his erection showed clearly beneath his borrowed shirt.

She reached down and gave his cock a gentle squeeze. "There will be other nights." She made it a promise. "I wish it were otherwise."

"But it's my dream, and I can do what I want."

She blurted out, "What?"

"You heard me. This is my dream and I should get what I want. What I want is to fuck my brains out. Tonight. No, make that right now."

"Are you insane? What makes you think this is a dream?"

"Everything! No one can really turn into a dragon. Other ridiculous factors aside, the mass differential is impossible." He held up his hand and ticked the points off on his fingers. With each one, he grew more agitated. "There are no little flying sharks that look like lizards. Instead of wasting time farting around here, I ought to be recovering from the crash. In fact, I should be dead. I deserve to be dead but I know I'm not, 'cause this sure as hell isn't heaven—not if I can't get laid when I want to!"

He jerked his thumb toward the door, where Yiman and Ajan spoke quietly by the fire outside. "Get rid of your brother and what's-her-name so we can get down and dirty, fuck like bunnies. No, I'll do it." He leaned out the door and said, "Why don't you two take a walk for a while? We've got Chosen business to discuss in private."

Yiman and Ajan glanced at each other but got up and did as he bade them.

Doug let the curtain fall, shrouding them in gloom. "Come here."

Chapter Five

ɛᴏ

"Don't do this. I don't want to."

"Oh, give me a break, you're always hot for me. Three minutes ago, you were longing for me to fuck you senseless, like in every other dream I've had of you. I'll bet your cunt is dripping with cream right now, begging for my cock."

"I don't want this," she repeated. "Not while you're angry."

"Then make me feel better." He grabbed her shoulders and massaged her with his thumbs. "Maybe your head says no but I'll bet your body says yes. You can't deny it, can you?"

He was right. Even through her anger, her disgust at his attitude, she did want to feel him buried inside her. He was her Chosen, her destined mate. The key to a bright future for her, away from weeding and plowing and baking in the sun.

Could she deny him? Should she?

"Come here." His voice was flat and emotionless. When he held out a hand to her, she took it, cursing her body's weakness and the legend that decreed they were fated to be together.

He claimed her mouth with his, thrusting his tongue between her lips. His kiss was rough and invasive, his embrace tight enough to rob her of breath. His breath came harsh and fast.

Where was the tender lover she'd met in her dreams?

Determined to find that man again, she met him halfway. Stroking his tongue with hers, she sought to soften the edges of his anger, an anger she didn't understand.

Her hands crept up to his hair and stroked the contours of his head and down his neck. It occurred to her that this was much like calming a field beast. She'd never thought that her Chosen would need to be treated thusly.

His rough breathing eased. He moaned into her mouth, running his hands up and down her back in a caress. She responded with growing desire. She reached down and gently squeezed the firm length of his cock, to show him she was pleased. His hips rocked against hers and she spread her legs to bring him closer.

Her anger faded as desire grew. She tried to hold onto it and failed. She didn't want to want him, not after what he'd said, but her body had other thoughts.

Oh, gods, this was what she wanted. The welcome touch of her Chosen, the man she'd gladly share her life with.

She helped him draw her gown off over her head, leaving her naked. He reared back and examined her. His eyes darkened with desire and she felt his gaze move over her skin like a heated touch. She shivered. *Perfect.*

He spoke in her mind! Her people could only do that in their dragon forms. This must be part of the sharing between a woman and her Chosen.

I am pleased you think so. She pulled him down for another kiss. He pressed closer, grinding his hips against her. The thin linen of her brother's shirt let her feel the heat of his thick shaft.

Suddenly it no longer mattered that Yiman and Ajan could return at any moment. The open doorway would permit them to be both heard and seen. She breathed in the scent of him, male and strange yet very familiar. After all, he was her Chosen. They were meant to be together.

But why wouldn't you be perfect for me? I made you up. He moved away long enough to raise the hem of his shirt. With one swift thrust, he slid his cock deep inside her.

She was more than ready for him. Sweet gods, having him in reality was so much better than the dreams. He stretched and filled her completely. She trembled as the head of his cock probed the entrance to her womb. Satisfaction filled her, along with a sense of rightness. He was right where he belonged, buried deep inside her. He began to move, driving in and out without pause, demanding wordlessly that she rise to meet him.

When he cupped her breast, it was with a force that made her gasp. She broke their kiss and locked her mouth shut, knowing her brother and Ajan were not far away. The cloth curtain over the doorway made a flimsy barrier.

His grip eased. She drew in a shaky breath, only to expel it forcefully as he found her nipple with his thumb and rubbed the tip firmly. Sensation shot straight to her womb, a streak of fire that left hunger in its wake. He rasped across the sensitive nub again and wrung a moan from her. She tightened around him and he answered her with a low growl.

She'd waited so long for him to arrive. How could she not make him welcome? That he was rude didn't change fate. Nor did it change how much her enclave, and she, needed him. She brushed aside her disappointment at his attitude and redoubled her efforts to seduce him into gentler touches.

He responded by quickening his pace. The glide of his cock stoked the fire of need within her and she rose to meet each thrust. He rode her hard, releasing her lips to lean forward and suck her neglected nipple into his mouth. She stifled a gasp when he scraped his teeth across the sensitive tip. Sweet wings and weres, she felt that all the way down to her toes. As he plunged deep, his balls slapped against her. Knowing that her brother and Ajan would hear increased the heat building within her.

She sensed the coming eruption, both in herself and her Chosen. His urgency fed hers. Tickles of delight spread across her skin in waves. He thrust ever harder, until he bit her nipple, bringing a spark of pain that flooded through her as pleasure. She clenched around him, rising on a tide of pleasure as he jerked and roared his release.

Before she reached her climax, he pulled out and left her.

Anger surged within her, so strong she couldn't speak for a time. She lay on the bedding, staring up at him as he calmly used her gown to clean himself.

She finally found her voice. "By the First One's wings, you are not the man I thought you were!"

He pulled the shirt over his head and stared back at her. "No, I guess I'm not. What's the difference?"

Harna rose to face him. She didn't care that she was nude, only that she was furious. "What do you mean, what's the difference? You are my Chosen, my destined mate and the only hope my people have of surviving."

He shrugged. "Big deal. It's not like they matter. None of you do, since you don't really exist."

"I don't exist?" She hissed, trying to keep her voice down, hoping he would do the same so that Yiman and Ajan didn't hear the insanity he was spouting.

"No, you don't, except here in my dreams." He threw his hands in the air, a wild gesture that made her take a step backwards. "I'm beginning to think this is a nightmare." With that, he stormed out the door and across the clearing. His hands were clenched in fists. If she hadn't known better, she might have believed he was about to have a temper tantrum.

She stared after him. What had happened to the strong warrior of her dreams? She'd been wrong about his arrival securing her future. He was more likely to ensure her doom. Why had the First One sent a raving lunatic to be her Chosen?

They were all doomed.

Harna picked up the silk gown he'd ruined. She looked at the stain and cast it aside. Huffing her anger, she found another garment in her pack and yanked it over her head. The First One had sent a bull-headed, arrogant man as her Chosen. Could she live with that? She wasn't fool enough to think she could change him.

Ajan slipped into the shelter, casting a glance over her shoulder at Doug. He'd stopped at the edge of the woods and just stood there, tension screaming in the rigid lines of his body.

Even as angry as Harna was, she longed to comfort him, to smooth out the frown she was sure he still wore. She tamped down the part of her that ached for him and focused on deciding what to do now. If he did not change his attitude on his own, she would have to make him want to stay and become a warrior once more. No matter what he said or thought, he was too important to let go. For all of them.

"What happened?"

Harna blinked back tears and tried to decide how much to reveal. She loved Ajan, but her young friend loved to talk. She had to safeguard her status. Letting everyone know her Chosen was not committed to helping them would not be prudent. To put it mildly.

"I'm not sure. His world is very different. He might be having trouble adjusting."

"He said that he did not choose to come here," Ajan pointed out. "I would think that moving between worlds by itself would be confusing, without finding you'd dropped into a boiling crisis. He asked intelligent questions earlier. I think he needs time to figure out what's going on and what he's supposed to do about it."

Harna stared at her. Ajan was young but now she showed a wisdom found in older and more experienced weres. Had Harna closed her eyes, she would have thought an elder spoke those words.

What was going on with those around her? Doug had turned out not the caring lover she'd met in her dreams and Ajan was showing an unexpected depth of character. Her world was spinning out of its normal orbit, into unknown territory.

"Time is one thing we may not have." The words came out more tartly than she'd planned. She slanted a look at Ajan who merely shrugged and began helping her spread out the bedding.

The sun was setting by the time they finished preparing the evening meal. Here among the trees, night fell earlier than across the fields at home. Harna helped Yiman bank the fire for the night and when she looked up, Ajan had cajoled Doug into returning to eat. The two came across the dusky clearing arm in arm. She tried not to be jealous when he walked past her without even a nod.

* * * * *

In the morning, even before they had broken their fast, Doug took a stick and began drawing in the dirt beside the fire pit. Harna watched, still angry and hurt but pleased he had chosen to make good on his intention to learn more about the harriers. At least he acknowledged her.

"You've followed a policy of leaving them alone as long as they left you alone. The problem is that you don't know enough about the harriers to hunt them effectively. I need to figure out a few things if I'm going to help you." He drew a series of lines, one under the other. "First, we find their weaknesses. Second, we find where they live. Third, we exploit those weaknesses.

"If we discover they die in water, we can provoke an attack and dive. From what I observed yesterday, they fly fast and close as they attack. That means they probably can't avoid a dunking. If that doesn't work, they can be toasted, which we know."

He looked around and met each of their eyes with a steady gaze. "I cannot impress upon you how important this is. We must understand the enemy. Your lives and those of your family and friends, the very existence of your people, are at stake. If we do not succeed in finding out how to destroy these creatures, soon there will be no more dragonfolk. There will be no more fisherfolk. There may still be mages, but I doubt they'll survive without the support system you provide."

"What does that mean?" Ajan asked.

Harna shot a questioning look at Doug and waited for his slight nod before she answered. "It means there will be no one to trade with, and the unchanging do most of their work. The mages won't be able to sustain a spell to protect everyone—mages and retainers—from the harriers for long."

"Our mission today is to gather information. We want to see how they act. And react. Maybe stir them up a bit."

"How do we do that?" Yiman spoke with his mouth full of fruit.

"Good question. First we have to find them. Then we put them through an obstacle course and see what happens. We need to know just how much faster than us they can fly. How far they can fly before they tire. How high they can go. Height is *always* a tactical advantage. At least one of us needs to be above them at all times, just in case they get out of control." He paused and looked at each of them in turn. "The four of us should be enough to try a few things, to test their limits and gather some data."

"Three of you." Harna talked around a mouthful of toasted grain cake. "I cannot change yet."

Doug frowned. "Why not?"

"I have not regained my strength. I would still be injured in my dragon form."

"Hmm...I need to figure out what limitations you have as well as understanding the harriers, but that can wait. For now, you're out of commission." He looked around, from Yiman to Ajan. "So it's the three of us. Are you game?"

The two exchanged looks. Yiman chewed a large mouthful. Ajan spoke. "I do not understand."

"Are you up for it? Are you in? Do you want to see what we can find out on our own?"

"Ah." Yiman's eyes lit up. He gulped water before he elaborated. "Yes. You are the warrior. We must follow you."

"No, you don't have to follow anyone. There's no draft here, no forced military service. If you're not willing, you don't go."

"But we are! You are our leader." Concern crept into Yiman's face. "We have always avoided harriers, and now you ask us to seek them out. Ah, you have hunted something like this before, have you not?"

Doug's grin was wolfish. Harna could think of no other description. "Yes, I have. Many times, in the air, and I would call it fighting more than hunting. Prey runs from the hunter. I expect a harrier, like what I have hunted, will fight back if it can. We must be ready."

"I will learn." Yiman's tone left no doubt.

He was willing and Harna loved him more for it. Although Doug had said they were gathering information, he also made it clear that they might have to kill the harriers they tested. Killing was what the unchanging did, not her people. It took a great deal of faith to agree to kill for the first time, and under the guidance of a stranger. It took even more to agree to hunt harriers as their first prey.

"I am willing." Harna echoed her brother. "I will accompany you next time."

They all turned to look at Ajan.

She stared back for a moment in silence, fidgeting with a fig. "Oh, I don't like it, and I'm still worried about what might happen later, with the Sea Hag and all, but if everyone else does, I will, too."

Harna frowned. "Ajan, that's rude. You should not risk offending the Ocean Mother."

"Sorry." Ajan didn't sound at all apologetic. "You just have to tell me what to do exactly, so I don't get hurt."

"As long as you are still able to change, it matters not how badly you are injured," Yiman assured her. "We will be alongside you."

"I carried Harna last evening when she could barely fly," Doug said. "You'll be fine." He looked at Harna for a long moment. "Leaving you here alone is a problem, though. You need a way to protect yourself if the harriers show up while we're gone. Got any weapons in those cupboards?"

"There must be a bow and a sling."

He shook his head. "Not good enough. Both are too slow. You'll need something you can use continuously, like a sword. You don't have one of those, do you?"

"No. Only a few knives that might be suitable for butchering or skinning."

"Since you don't eat harriers, I'm guessing you won't need those."

Yiman chuckled and Harna breathed a sigh of relief. Doug appeared to have recovered his good humor. Maybe a good night's sleep was what he'd needed, after all.

Doug got to his feet and turned around once, looking intently at the trees. After one revolution, he clapped his hands together. "Okay, here we go. Build up the fire, Yiman, and Harna, find those knives. We're going to make you a couple of spears. It won't take long."

* * * * *

Harna watched the dragons take flight. Her Chosen's stately form led the way. His matte black scales absorbed the light, drawing her eye away from the gleaming shapes of her brother and their friend.

Never had she seen such a dark dragon.

Never had she been so torn.

Killing was done by barbarians, by the people they had fought to leave in their past. Not by the people they were now. His ideas felt right where it counted, deep within her, but she knew the assembly would need to be convinced that the enclave must hunt harriers.

Doug had not expressed a wish to kill every harrier he saw, but she knew that, should the opportunity present itself this morning, he would be unable to resist.

What else could she expect? He was a warrior, after all.

Harna longed to be flying with her Chosen and her family. Instead, she sighed and set about straightening up the camp. Packing away the remaining food was important. Although she felt more confident of her ability to fight off a harrier attack on her own now that she had the spears, attracting them was something she didn't want to do. Not for the first time, she cursed the evil luck that had led the harriers to her the day before.

Had she not been injured, she would be accompanying this "recon party" on its flight.

Had she not been injured, she might have a chance to circumvent any killing today.

But had she not been injured, might her Chosen have passed her by? The thought that she might have missed meeting him was unbearable. He was her people's salvation and her hope for a better life.

Was this all part of the First One's plan?

Sometimes being a living legend wasn't what she'd expected.

Chapter Six

ಐ

"Higher!" Doug commanded. The two dragons followed his lead, spiraling into the sky.

He had a squadron again, or the beginnings of one. If this dream lasted long enough, he might just wind up ruling the were-dragons. The thought of him as a ruler sent a shot of smoke streaming from his snout in a chuckle.

When he figured they were high enough, he leveled off to cruise. Yiman, who proved to be a muscular gold and tan dragon, pulled out to flank him on the right. Ajan, slender and the pale blue of the morning sky, mirrored the move to his left. The next recruit he gained would take up the rear. For some reason, he kept picturing Harna there, her dark scales glistening in the sun as she watched his back. For now, he'd have to remember to keep an eye out behind them. The harrier things might be smart enough to plan an ambush.

From this height, he could see from the City of Light in the east clear beyond the fields to where the forest took over in the west. The tide had come in again. Below, the sea crashed against the base of the cliffs.

No sign of any harriers.

Well, he'd always wanted a chance to be a hero in a real fight. He wasn't sure this qualified as heroic since he was just roasting a bunch of small pointy-toothed birds, but it was as close as he was likely to get.

When planning this expedition, he hadn't told Harna the truth, but what the hell. Since she didn't exist, it wasn't like that counted as a lie. He planned on killing as many harriers as he could find, as fast as he could. He was still pissed off about the crash and the deaths of his squad. It made no sense that he should be the chance survivor.

He should have followed them in, the way he was trained.

He should have died with them.

Once this mission was over, he'd have tonight with Harna. He wanted another real fuck, with deep penetration and sweat and screaming and a mind-blowing orgasm. Maybe two. What surprised him was his body's insistence that it be Harna. Ajan was cute but definitely not who he wanted.

Getting his rocks off the day before hadn't helped. He'd thought it would release his frustration but it only added to his guilt. Harna had let him fuck her like it was a chore she had to do. She deserved better than being used like that. He wanted her to respond with enthusiasm.

Like she had in his other dreams. He'd bet plunging into her willing participation in reality would be better than any dream.

Whoa! When had he started thinking of this as reality? No, this was just a drug-induced dream. Just because it was a dream didn't mean he had to act like a jerk. He'd work out his grief and his anger here, and after a while, he'd wake up to agony and the welcome faces of Wingnut and Jet Wake.

I see something, down there, at the edge of the field.

Doug searched the field until Yiman sent him a clear picture of what he'd seen and where he'd seen it. *Stay here. I'm going down to investigate.* Dropping swiftly, keeping his eyes on the moving speck, he flew until he could identify it.

Harriers!

Not just one, as he'd thought. A small flock streaked up to meet him. A sense of excitement filled him, intensifying as they approached. They flew faster than he expected. Excitement turned to bloodlust, a need to bite and tear, to taste blood in his mouth.

What the hell?

Before he could rise again, they were on him in a chittering mass. Tiny stinging bites covered his tail, back and wings.

We're coming to save you! A chorus of the two dragons' voices filled his head.

No! Wait! He labored to rise, each powerful pump of his wings dislodging a few of the nasty critters and pushing him higher. As fast as he flung them off, others took their places. A protest sounded from above and he repeated his order. Striving to ignore the pain, he concentrated on gaining altitude.

With one more push, he was clear of the harriers. He looked down, soaring a little higher just to be sure. Below them, the harriers milled and chattered but rose no further.

Jesus, Mary and Joseph, but those bites hurt.

He didn't have nearly as many as Harna had gotten from those little bastards. Son of a bitch, he could barely control himself and keep flying. How had she remained so calm? He struggled to speak without screaming with pain and frustration.

Do you feel the pressure at this altitude? Will you know it again?

Yes, Doug! Their joint response made him smile. A squad during inspection couldn't have been more prompt. Now that they were obeying him, could he convince them to kill the beasts, get them both blooded on this mission?

A sense of elation filled him, an eager anticipation of the coming war against the enemy. He looked down to see what the harriers were doing and his smile fled.

The swarm was arrowing away, back the way the dragons had come.

He cursed and lowered his head, pulling his wings in tight against his body to reduce wind resistance. As air rushed over him in an ever-faster flow, gravity speeding his descent, he called out to the others. *They're headed for the camp!*

Toward Harna.

With cries of dismay, Yiman and Ajan followed.

Harna contemplated the materials spread in front of her. Her Chosen had yet to make the decision she needed him to make. That he was developing plans to learn more of the harriers was a good sign, but she did not yet trust him to become the committed warrior they needed. Nor the mate she desired. His behavior the day before proved the dreams had lied.

If they were to lead as equals, she must do her part in the coming struggle. Darya and her father had always led from the front, doing no less than they asked of others. Harna knew she had to set a good example, both to preserve her status and to save her people should Doug fail her.

Her enclave would be proud of her work this morning, she was certain. Not even her Chosen had thought of using any of the other supplies they had against the harriers. She discovered that, with some imagination, common household objects could become lethal weapons.

"A pissed-off dragon can burn them to a crisp," Doug had said of the harriers. She may be unable to change and breathe fire at them, but she'd found other means of toasting them should they get too close.

She stepped back and surveyed the things she'd pulled from the various cupboards and the surrounding woods.

The four spears they'd made lay by the hearth. Around her, large balls of pitch sat atop dry logs in a large circle. The hank of heavy string she held would soon connect them. If she had no warning, the cord would carry the flames from one to the next and complete the ring of fire while she fought off the attackers. True, the heat might grow to be uncomfortable, but what was that in the face of dying? Once the whole thing was alight, even a child in this form should be able to hold off a swarm of harriers.

She hoped she wouldn't have to burn up so much of the supplies at this camp, but if she needed it, she had it almost ready. Should she not need it, they could dismantle it quickly and return the various items to the cupboards.

The cord was the only thing left to arrange. She picked up the first ball of pitch and began working it between her hands, softening it enough to shape it around the string.

Something prickled at her, making her uncomfortable. Her unease grew. Shielding her eyes with her hand, she saw what looked like a flock of small birds approaching.

No, they were not birds. And they were coming too fast. She grabbed a burning stick from the hearth and lighted the nearest chunk of pitch. As the flame caught, she moved to the next. A high-pitched chattering urged her to greater speed

There was only time to light a half-circle of fire. She grabbed a spear and dropped back into the protected area behind the hearth. That left only two ways for the harriers to reach her. She snatched up another spear and kept one in each hand, poised on either side of the hearth.

The harriers milled about above her, shifting and shoving each other. A wild hunger rose within her, a desire to rip and tear them wing from wing. The feeling increased when the swarm grew larger. Another swarm was joining them!

Where was her Chosen?

She'd forgotten about the small area above her, where they could dodge the flames. The first harrier swooped low behind her, biting her leg. She kicked it away. The second landed on her shoulder, gripping her dress with its sharp talons and tearing a gash in her ear. She dropped one spear and fought with it. Pain lanced through her. Dear gods, in this form she lacked any defenses at all. Another attacker dropped onto her back. Her world contracted to pinpoints of agony and a growing lethargy.

Flame the bastards!

Her Chosen's cry penetrated the fog that surrounded her. Yiman and Ajan were there, too, calling out assurances and begging her to hold on.

Hurry, she managed to whisper into the mist settling over her. She could no longer feel her fingers where she clutched a harrier's leg, or the sting of the repeated bites.

Doug spewed flame into the crowd of harriers seething above the camp, sweeping his fiery breath across the mob. Harna had fallen silent after that single, pain-filled word. Desperation filled him. Damn it, he was not going to lose her, too!

This swarm was larger than the one that had been chasing him. Those must have somehow joined up with another group that found Harna. He cursed his quest for intelligence, which had kept the enemy alive. He should have killed them all as soon as they reached the height limit, while he had the advantage.

This was all his fault.

Redoubling his efforts, he hosed the creatures with his fiery breath. Ajan and Yiman followed his lead. Yiman clearly wanted to save his sister, toasting the harriers like a madman, while Ajan acted more in self-defense than on the offensive.

A few survivors turned tail and fled. He let them go, focusing on Harna. She lay still, surrounded by dead harriers and dying fires.

He and Yiman changed as they landed, reaching her at the same time. She was smeared with blood from head to toe. Doug dropped to his knees at her side. Nasty gashes showed in her shoulder and left leg. None of her injuries were pumping blood, so at least he wouldn't have to deal with a nicked artery. Still, the way she lay without moving made him worry. No, it was more than that. The way she lay so still made him crazy with worry. He shoved his emotions aside and dredged up everything he'd ever learned about first aid.

"She's lost a lot of blood." Doug looked around for something to start cleaning her up with. He needed to assess the extent of the damage. "Get me a cloth or a bandage."

"Yes, Doug." Yiman ducked into the shelter, returning with a pile of what looked and felt like linen strips and pads. He held them out and squatted on the ground beside Harna.

Doug began applying pressure to her shoulder, which was bleeding more than the wound on her leg. It took both his hands to cover the large area the harrier had savaged. "Clean water?"

"I'll get it." Ajan ran off.

"Press a pad against her leg," Doug ordered. Maintaining constant pressure on her shoulder, he watched Yiman's steady hands as he did as he was told. The kid was okay in a crisis.

But damn, she wasn't stirring and she'd gotten awfully pale. Only her rapid, shallow breathing indicated she was still alive. On the other hand, it might be a blessing. She wouldn't feel them clean the bites.

Water slopped over the rim of the bowl as Ajan set it down.

"Any sign of the harriers coming back?" That was all they needed. A sneak attack while they were like this would be deadly for them all.

Ajan shook her head.

Doug indicated the cloths Yiman still held. "Start washing off what you can. We need to see what's what."

She dabbed at the crusted blood and dirt on Harna's face. "We should have a healing salve that will help prevent festering."

Yiman said, "I saw it when I was searching for the knives. The whole healer's pack is intact. There should be stitching supplies as well."

"Get it."

"We usually don't have much need for medical stuff since the change heals us, but the camps are always stocked for emergencies."

"It's a good thing. Will she have enough energy to change?"

Yiman shook his head. "No. Her injuries from the first attack were too extensive. Although we heal quickly, not enough time has passed for her to recover. It is easier to bandage her in this form."

"You know a lot for someone so young."

Yiman's teeth flashed in a quick grin. "I am not so young. Harna has only two years on me."

Doug had to admit, the kid was quick. He'd already picked up a bunch of slang expressions from Doug. He'd make a good leader someday.

Ajan returned with several small crocks. After removing the corks, she smeared goo from each of them across the clean scratches and cuts on Harna's face.

"Jesus, those already look awful." One of her eyes was almost swollen shut. Reddened lacerations criss-crossed her cheek and ran down her neck. He could see worse ones under the edge of the pressure dressing he held.

"Harriers are not the cleanest creatures. They eat dead things, some long dead," Yiman reminded him.

As if he needed that mental image. "I hope that goo is good enough to battle the infection."

"It has healed worse. Dragonfolk heal more quickly than mages or the fisherfolk," Ajan assured him.

Doug attempted to turn his mind away from speculation about what types of bacteria and viruses lived in scavengers' mouths, but it was like trying not to think of pink elephants. He couldn't focus on anything else.

This whole thing was his fault. If he hadn't wasted time showing off and teaching the young dragons, if he'd waited until after the harriers were dead, Harna might not have been attacked.

Bullshit, another part of him argued. If he'd waited, the first group of harriers would have reached her while he was lecturing, and there would have been nothing to warn him that she was in danger. She would have faced them completely alone.

But he and Harna could communicate mentally, even in human form. Why hadn't she called him?

Because he'd been a real asshole. She was pissed at him.

It was all his fault.

Harna stirred and groaned. "By all the gods, I hurt," she whispered. Her eyelids flickered several times before staying open.

"We got here in time," Doug told her, leaning close to be sure her pupils were normal. They were.

She reached out a hand. Her gaze slid past him. "Yiman?"

Christ, her dismissal of him cut like a knife. How could it hurt that bad?

Doug backed off and let Yiman take his place, gripping her hand as Ajan smoothed more ointment over her swollen skin.

It was all his fault. He valued her more than he'd thought. How could it be a dream, if he hurt this much? It wasn't physical hurt, like he'd expect after the crash. No, this was an emotional agony that went deeper than any wound. His whole chest actually hurt, and not with symptoms of a heart attack. Was that the pain of his heart breaking?

No, that wasn't possible. Not when he'd just gotten here, not when he'd only begun to get to know Harna. Yet he tried to dismiss the pain and couldn't.

Did it matter if this was a dream or not? It felt all too real, as impossible as that seemed. Maybe it was like the chaplain said, if you turned your back on faith and were wrong, you were really screwed. It didn't take much to live your life as a good man.

Maybe he needed to act like this was real, just in case it was. What would it cost him? If he acted like an asshole and it was real, it could cost him a lot. Starting with Harna.

If being an asshole hadn't cost him Harna already.

"Doug," Ajan called. "There is a pack with the healing supplies on the bench inside. I need the bundle of dried roots, the longest ones."

His feet didn't want to obey him. He stumbled into the shelter, found the pack and fumbled through the contents. There were four bundles of what he guessed were roots. The longest smelled like licorice.

He went back to where Yiman murmured encouragement to Harna and handed the roots to Ajan. She bit off a piece and put it in Harna's mouth. She chewed it until she lost the glaze of pain in her eyes.

Would chewing on that root help him stop feeling the agony of Harna's rejection? He doubted it. That blow had struck deep in his spirit rather than his flesh. The analgesic or narcotic qualities of whatever was in the root would suspend physical pain. Even if it could work on his emotional state, he wouldn't expect much from it. Some wounds were too great.

Numb with worry and in pain himself, he watched Ajan work. The young woman proved to be competent with the needle, suturing the deep gashes neatly and efficiently.

When he realized Harna never looked at him, he walked off, aimlessly poking around the clearing. Now that the adrenaline rush was fading, it hit him how weak he was. Once Harna was stitched up, they'd all need food and rest. He plopped onto a stool and rested his arms on the table.

The extent of the fire Harna had started intrigued him, breaking through the haze of pain and weakness, making him thing about something outside himself. The hearth lay at the center, but around that was a lot more than the remains of their morning cooking fire.

What had Harna done?

There was a ring of ashes and hot coals a few feet outside the hearth. Harna lay inside its limits. He walked around it on the outside, examining it as he went.

"She sleeps. That root is powerful." Yiman came to walk with him. "Did you feel anything different when the harriers spotted us?"

Doug thought about it. "Yes. I felt their excitement."

"So did I. I think they send out emotions, sort of like the way we talk to each other in our heads when we're in our dragon form."

"Yeah. Initially I felt both hunger and excitement. Once the first one bit me, the excitement turned into a frenzy. It's some kind of empathic broadcast."

"Whatever you call it, I think it's a way to find them."

"Or if not to find them, then a way to tell when they've found us. Everyone needs to stay alert while flying. If you feel even a hint of that excitement, fly high. Remember, if you go far enough above them, they can't follow you."

"I'll remember that. And tell anyone and everyone I can. We're all going to need to know that." Yiman went back to examining the camp.

"Look at what she did here." Doug gestured at the circle, both the burned and burning parts.

"Interesting. I would not have thought of using the pitch." Yiman stopped moving. "My sister is better at this than I expected. You are fortunate to have her as a mate. She is a worthy leader for our enclave."

Doug barked a cynical laugh. "She just asked for you, not me. Is that a woman who considers me her mate?"

Yiman regarded him for a long moment in silence. Doug could tell he was weighing his words, deciding how much to say.

"You have disappointed each other, I think, despite the dreams that bind you together."

"I didn't just disappoint your sister, I failed her. If I hadn't spent so much time thinking of how to get you two to go ahead and kill the harriers we flushed out, even though you didn't really want to, I would have gotten here sooner. If I'd toasted those bastards right away, she wouldn't be lying there now, maybe dying." Yiman would have interrupted but Doug kept going. "Dreams and legends can't make two people love each other," Doug said.

He spoke the words with a shudder. Just when had love entered the picture? He didn't know how or when it happened—he just knew he loved Harna.

Shit. And she thought he was an asshole. With good reason.

Yiman placed his hand on Doug's shoulder. "She will recover. And you will make amends. Our people need both of you."

Yiman stood in front of the shelter, facing Doug who sat next to Harna inside. "We know the harriers do not fly at night." He squinted at the darkening sky. "We are three hours' flight from home. Ajan and I will leave now. We plan to return with more supplies in a day or so." His tone brooked no argument. Doug could make no valid objection anyway.

"I think a day or two will be just fine." Doug looked at Harna. Now dressed in a short gown, she'd fallen back asleep on the pile of bedding. Good. She needed all the rest she could get. Already, in less than three hours, the swelling had subsided and the scratches were not as red. Ajan had not lied. Dragonfolk did heal quickly.

"My sister needs to regain her strength, and you two have a few things to resolve between you." He exchanged glances with Ajan, an expression Doug couldn't interpret. "You're vulnerable here by yourselves, without the ability to change. It is best we shut you inside the shelter."

Yeah, right. There was just the curtain, no door. "Shut us in here? How?"

Yiman's eyes held a sparkle that Doug did not trust, not at all. "There's a panel that fits over the opening. Did you think we leave the camps open when we aren't using them? It can only be secured from outside. That's how we can tell from a distance if a camp is occupied. On arrival, travelers remove the panel and when they leave, they replace it."

Doug racked his brain, reviewing the contents of the camp. He recalled nothing resembling a door. "But I haven't seen anything like that."

"We ate our meals sitting around it." Yiman grinned as he picked up the plank that had served as a table and fitted it against the opening. He yelled over Doug's sputtering protest, "I lit the lantern for you and checked all of the supplies. You'll be fine for at least three days."

"Why didn't you lock Harna in today while we were gone?" Shit, she wouldn't have been attacked if she'd been safe inside.

"She would never have let me. She's just as hard-headed as you are. Talk to her. You'll see."

Doug jumped to his feet and rapped a fist on the door. "You can't do this! You can't just go off and leave us in here!" The snick of bolts being driven home was the only response. He thought quickly. "What if the harriers kill everyone who could come free us?"

"In three days you will both be healed. If we have not returned, change and burn a hole in the wall!"

Ajan called out, "Don't forget to give Harna the broth every time she wakes up. And be nice to each other!"

"Hey! Come back here!" He beat his fists against the inside of the door. Through the walls he heard the amused trumpet of a male dragon, joined by a higher, female note.

"Son of a bitch! I can't believe they actually did that."

He sat beside Harna's sleeping form and thought. They were vulnerable. And there was no other way to leave them. Realizing Yiman was right did nothing to improve his mood.

They'd left him stuck here, with a woman he wasn't sure how to care for. A woman who by all rights needed hospitalization.

A woman who hated him.

He was afraid he was in for a long two days.

Chapter Seven

❧

He managed to keep the lantern going and find the food he needed. For what he figured was the whole first day and night, he did nothing but eat and sleep. Every time he woke up, he shook Harna until she surfaced enough to swallow the broth Ajan left.

Harna woke him the next time. While he slept, she'd peeled some roots and gathered together two plates of food. When she turned up the lantern, her skin fairly glowed, clear and unblemished.

"Eat."

He took the plate she offered. As he bit into a grain cake, he eyed her cautiously. "Your brother locked us in here."

"I knew he would."

An uneasy silence fell between them.

Once he'd finished eating, he set the plate aside. "Listen, I'm sorry."

She just looked at him. Christ, this was harder than facing his commanding officer after a bad drill.

"Um, I'm sorry for everything." He shifted position and tried to find the words he wanted to say. Now he remembered why he hadn't dated in a long while. Women always wanted the open-your-heart-and-talk shit. He'd rather open his veins. It hurt just as much. Since it was Harna, he'd keep trying. "I treated you like a jerk. It's my fault you almost died."

"You did treat me badly, but how could you have prevented the harrier attack?"

"It's my fault they attacked you. I meant to get Yiman and Ajan to kill them, and I wasted too much time trying to figure out how to push them into it. I should have roasted the bastards right away."

Her features softened a little. "There were two separate swarms, Doug. You could not have stopped them both."

"I should have. I'm your Chosen, after all."

"Are you really?" She searched his face. "I thought I was just your dream-fuck."

He winced. "Ouch. Did I really say that?" She nodded. "No wonder you hate me. I don't expect this to change your mind, but I am sorry for using you the way I did. I can be such an asshole."

He dropped his head between his knees. "Now I really wish I was dead."

She put her hand on his shoulder. "No, you don't."

"Yes, I do. I've lost everybody I love. Buffalo and Wingnut and Renegade, those guys all died." The moments before the crash replayed in his mind. An awful realization spread through him, making his eyes burn. He pounded his fist on the floor.

"Dammit, I know what that sound was—Buffalo sneezed. They all died because of a fucking sneeze! Jet Wake and Wingnut were clear, but they need me and I'm not there." Tears trickled down his face. Oh, Christ, he'd lost it completely. "And I treated you like shit and now you hate me. I've failed everybody."

Her hand slid across his back and she drew him down into the bedding, where she curled around him. He went into her arms, not caring that she'd reject him, knowing only that he needed her.

"I can't take your grief away. It took me months to recover after my husband died." She rubbed his back. God, no one had done that since his mother died. It felt good. He felt, well, cared for. Like he belonged.

"You were married?"

"For two years. He was as kind to me as he knew how to be, but he was a hard man. That was another selfish reason I had for wishing you would come soon. You are a much more considerate lover."

"Until I treated you like shit."

"I didn't understand why you were angry. Even when I was angry with you, I wanted to make you feel better. I knew what you were like from the dreams. I don't hate you."

"You don't?"

"No, I don't. I am not sure I could, although you did make me, what do you say, pissed off."

"The proper way to say that is that I pissed you off."

"Yes. You pissed me off. You really pissed me off." He could tell she was playing with the way the words felt in her mouth.

"I piss you off, you piss me off, he pisses me off."

She laughed. "How did you know that's what I was doing?"

"I could hear it in your voice. That's how we learn our language, too, by practicing the different forms of the verb."

"You know me so well."

"You're perfect. And not just because I made you up. I don't think I did anymore."

"While we're doing as Yiman wants, getting to know more about each other, I have to confess that I'm not perfect, not by anyone's measure. Before we heard about the harriers and I knew why the First One had given me a Chosen, I wanted you here soon because I was selfish. I was tired of working in the fields. Being a leader meant I would have an easier life."

He stared at her in disbelief. "This is an easier life? Getting savaged by harriers? Jesus, what do you farm, rattlesnakes and killer bees?"

"No, we raise grain, fruit and vegetables. Field hands have long days and heavy work, at least from spring until harvest. Then we move to the weaving sheds or gather firewood."

"Heavy physical labor." He rubbed his thumb over the calluses on her fingertips. "I can tell you work hard."

"Do you think less of me, knowing that I am selfish and lazy?"

"Honey, I'm not fond of weeding gardens, and the work you've done is worse than that. I'll bet you worked just as hard as anybody else. Besides, I've been pretty selfish myself. How can I criticize you?" Running one hand down her thigh, he squeezed the lean muscle he found there. "And since all that hard work gave you such a great figure and such good muscle tone, why aren't you on top more often?"

She relaxed against him and sighed. "I don't deserve you."

"Seems the First One would disagree, since I'm your Chosen and not somebody else's." He drew her close, wrapping his arms around her.

"And I'm glad you are mine. The dreams were nothing beside the reality of having you here." Pulling his head down, she kissed him.

He rapidly concluded that this was better than his dreams. Ergo, it had to be real. Come to think of it, he could smell stuff he never had in the dreams. This time, he'd felt hunger. He'd felt pain. He'd felt...oh, shit, he felt *her* like he never had.

She'd never kissed him like this while he lay asleep in the barracks. Her hot, sweet tongue invaded his mouth to duel with his. She kissed like she wanted to swallow him whole.

Jesus, Mary and Joseph. This was beyond mind-blowing. He turned down the lantern. Closing his eyes, he waited for his vision to adjust to the gloom. When he opened them, he discovered he could see better in the dark than he had before.

Harna had shed her short dress. In one swift motion, he yanked his borrowed shirt off and tossed it aside. Hardly seemed worth putting it on. The three weres he'd met so far were pretty casual about their naked bodies, not often bothering with clothing. He hoped the rest of them were. He could get accustomed to this nudity thing.

When he reached for her she arched into his hands, rising to meet his touch. The soft globes of her breasts invited him to knead and explore. Her hips moved against him, sending shocks of sensation through him, straight to his hard cock.

She traced the line of his jaw and ran her hand down across his chest. Her fingers feathered across his nipples. He hadn't known he could be so hard and not explode.

Her breath came faster, in time with his. He rolled atop her. Bringing his knee between hers, he parted her thighs. He explored with his hands, found wetness and heat. He suckled at her breasts, moving back and forth between them while his fingers teased her, tracing the folds of her cunt and entering her to stretch her just a bit, until she pounded on his shoulders and cried out.

She grasped his head in a fierce grip. "Now! Please," she pleaded.

He obliged her, sliding into her slick heat in one thrust.

Her tight sheath undid him. He managed one more thrust then another before he exploded inside her. His release struck him with the force of a lightning bolt.

To his wonder and delight, she joined him, that fast, clenching around his spurting cock, squeezing him like a tight fist.

Their labored breathing gradually slowed.

Shit. He'd come so damned fast, like it was his first time.

"I'm sorry. That was too quick."

"Hmmm." She smiled up at him, a lazy smile that made something inside him turn flip-flops. "Sometimes that happens. But we can do it again, can't we?" She moved something inside her that increased the pressure and his cock began to harden.

"Oh, honey, we can do it as often as you want."

"Is that a promise, Warrior Doug? I want to watch your magnificent cock slide in and out of me. I want to sit on you in the hot mountain spring and feel you fill me. I want to live the dreams we shared."

"It's a promise." He lowered his head to take her dark nipple in his mouth. He'd not thought about the contrast between their skin colors, but now he watched his pale fingers move across her dark skin and found it made the blood rush to his cock. He promised himself he'd pay closer attention to the shades of skin she had.

He reared up and pulled out of her, looking down. His glistening shaft pulled her pussy lips outward into a pout, as if she didn't want to let him go. She was even darker there, the color of garnets, where she gripped his ruddy cock. He slowly thrust back into her, watching as the silver hair curled around him, wondering what this would look like from a different angle.

Did they have mirrors here? If not, did he know enough to make one?

Maybe he *had* somehow come to a place where he could use his skills for something more meaningful than entertaining a crowd. Maybe he *had* found the woman of his dreams.

Maybe he really *was* a fire-breathing stealth dragon.

How fucking cool was that?

* * * * *

Harna replaced the top to the cook pot and rose. Since Yiman and Ajan had locked them in the shelter, they'd not bothered with clothes.

Doug drank in the sight of her, full breasts, full ass, nipped-in waist. She looked like a magazine centerfold, only better, because she was his. He knew the taste of her, the texture of every bit of her skin, how she felt beneath him and on top of him. Hmmm…they hadn't tried doggy-style yet. He'd like to see her on her knees in front of him while he held onto those generous love handles and pounded into her. He shifted on the mound of furs to accommodate his growing cock.

She came to sit opposite him, folding herself gracefully to the furs cross-legged. Her position revealed all of her best features, from her large breasts to her dark pussy half-hidden by her silver hair.

"If I'd known what this was like, I'd have come sooner." He reached out to trace the folds of her cunt through the soft curls. He was rewarded by a flood of moisture that he gathered on his fingertips. "You are the best thing that's ever happened to me, honey."

She clasped his hand in hers, raising his fingers to her mouth. Her eyes met his and she gave him a satisfied little cat-smile. The slant of her eyes emphasized the resemblance. He shuddered as her tongue swept across his fingertips.

"Do you like the way you taste?"

"I'm savoring the taste of us both. I love the way *we* taste." She sat up straight.

His eyes were drawn to the enticing jiggle of her breasts. He'd never thought stick-thin women were attractive, but Harna had driven home to him the appeal of a full figure.

No one, even from afar, would ever mistake her for a boy. She definitely was soft, very soft, in all the right places, even though she was clearly used to hard work. When he stroked her, he felt the muscle beneath. He could hear Renegade's voice, "The bigger the cushion, the better the pushin'."

God, he missed the guys. A pang of sorrow ran through him, grief for their senseless deaths. It was a sneeze during a training exercise, for Chrissake, not even a fighting maneuver. Death was just as unfair as life.

"You are thinking of them, aren't you?" He nodded. "I can see the sadness in your eyes. There is no greater honor than living on in a friend's memories."

"Harna, you're way too good for me." He gathered her close, breathing in the now-familiar scent of her.

She stuck her tongue out and tickled his ear. "It's much more fun to be bad. Teach me some more of those words that are not polite. You can show me what each means. If you do, I'll teach you some of ours."

"Oh, so it's you-show-me-yours-and-I'll-show-you-mine, is it?"

"Yes. I always drive a hard bargain."

"Let me show you what hard is."

The sound of bolts being released awakened them. Doug looked up from the pile of bedding. A flood of sunlight poured into the shelter as the door panel fell away. He spread a blanket across Harna's bare back.

"Hello!" Yiman shaded his eyes and peered in. "Woo-hoo! I see you've worked out your differences. That's great!"

Doug lay staring at the people moving things around outside. "I don't think the harriers got them."

"No." Harna sat up and pulled on her gown. "I was hoping we might have a little more time."

"Me, too." He reached for her but she twisted out of his grasp. He sighed and looked for his shirt. His time alone with Harna had been all too short.

Yiman's face popped back into view. "You'd better get up, Doug, it's time to work."

When he stumbled out of the shelter, it was to find the door once more serving as a table. Piles of food covered it. His stomach rumbled as he sat down. When had they last eaten? In the gloom of the shelter, there had been no way to tell the passage of time. And they'd had more fun things to do.

Yiman introduced him to Keena, Orda and Young Nodda who had accompanied him from the enclave.

Doug evaluated them from the perspective of having to train them and was pleased. The weres were young and physically fit. Yiman and even Ajan had done well in their first hunting flight, and he expected no less from these three.

Before Harna could make further introductions, the men accosted Doug with exclamations and questions.

"Can we really fly higher than they can?"

"What is it like when they broadcast their emotions?"

"Can we hunt them tomorrow?"

"Wait!" Harna's raised voice cut through their babble. After they all subsided and gave her their undivided attention, she continued, "We cannot fly safely until dusk, even with so many of us. There is plenty of time for everything today. Once we have eaten, we will discuss the harriers. Until then, you should get to know each other."

She motioned Doug toward her. He stepped up beside her, filled with pride at the way she commanded a group of grown men. "This is Doug, my Chosen." She pointed at each were in turn.

"Orda is Ajan's brother." Orda nodded. He shared Ajan's fair skin, medium hair and brilliant blue eyes.

"Young Nodda is a member of the assembly and has been blessed with nine children."

"So far," Nodda added. His hangdog face lit with a boyish grin.

"You've got your own baseball team!" At their questioning looks, Doug added, "It's a game in my world. I'll explain later."

Harna threw her arms around the last man, a hulking giant with skin darker than hers and black hair. "And this is Keena, my eldest brother."

Keena gathered her against him. "I'm sorry I wasn't here to protect you from the harriers, little one," he said into her hair. Turning to Doug, he offered his hand. "I thank you for your timely arrival. My only sister is our family treasure."

"Now you embarrass me, old man." She softened her words with a smile. "I'm starving. What did you bring for us to eat?"

"More than you will need, little one. We knew you would need to eat, both of you, so we brought all that we could carry."

Over a meal of fresh fruit, dried meat and the water Doug found so delicious, he and Harna told the story of the harriers' first attack, his rescue of her and the exploratory foray he had made with Yiman and Ajan, ending with the second attack and Harna's recovery.

It didn't take long to discover that Yiman and Ajan had been persuasive in their recruitment of volunteers to join him and Harna in the camp. Hearing their story so soon after the bards' warnings, the three were convinced of the need to kill the harriers, and enthusiastic and impatient to start their first hunt.

Doug needed to talk them out of their impatience. "We need a plan, and to only hunt harriers that have adopted this behavior. Scavengers like the harriers fill an important role in your world. We can't go off flaming harrier colonies willy-nilly, at least not until we confirm that they are all hunting dragons."

Keena let out a hearty laugh. "Yiman warned us that you use strange words. I don't know what this willy-nilly is, but you speak sense." A speculative gleam came into his eyes. "What can you teach us that we will need to know when we do attack harriers? I suspect a flock of them will put up more of a fight than the deer I have hunted."

These men might not be used to waging war, but damn they were intelligent. Doug had expected to have to convince them they didn't know it all already.

"I have a few ideas, but first, I want Harna to tell us about what she cobbled together to protect herself. I'll take notes." Doug swept the ground in front of him clear and began to draw in the dirt.

Chapter Eight

ฌ

Oh, no! Harna's distressed thoughts reached Doug clearly, along with the smell of smoke rising in the darkness.

Below them lay a village. Lights shone in windows and streamed from doorways. Figures raced around the remains of several structures, lit by glowing embers and an array of what he took to be lanterns.

Yiman trumpeted and everyone on the ground looked up. They began yelling and waving their arms long before the six dragons touched down and changed.

My house! Harna started running as soon as her feet hit the ground. Doug took off after her, catching up with her easily. *My house burned!* She turned into his embrace and sobbed. *I told you I was selfish.*

Ajan ran up to them. "A huge swarm of harriers attacked us this afternoon. In the fight, a few of the houses caught fire. Yours was the worst, Harna, and the guest house. Misma's shop was crushed."

Harna straightened and pulled away from him, eyes wide and worried. "By what?" Her tone had become brisk, without a trace of concern remaining for her own loss.

"One of the elders collapsed in flight. I think his heart gave out. He fell through the roof like a boulder."

"Who?"

Ajan's eyes shifted away before she answered. "Darya's father."

"I thought he'd live forever. Anyone else?"

"Just a few bites here and there. Nothing the change couldn't heal. But we can't find Asok."

"Who?" Doug asked.

"Darya's younger son."

The guest house would require repairs but wouldn't have to be replaced completely. Harna's house, where she lived with Yiman, was a total loss. Doug shied away from the memories that the charred timbers evoked. Nothing remained of their furnishings or possessions beyond a few pieces of ironwork. Despite her protest that she was selfish, she turned her back on the wreckage and set about the task of getting the wounded patched up and everyone else accounted for.

When she got it all sorted out, Asok was the only one missing and Darya's father the only death. If you didn't count harriers, Doug thought as he stepped around another carcass lying in the street.

Doug stood in the street and stared at the assembly hall for a moment before he walked up and pushed open the door. Inside, he continued to gawk. He had no choice. The stone chamber was impressive as hell.

So were the occupants. The entire enclave gathered here. They ranged from small children to wizened old men and women—at least he thought both genders were represented in the elders. Amidst all the wrinkles it was hard to tell what they were, and the layers of shapeless garments they all wore were no help.

What really got him was that every one of these, every man and woman, old and young, could become a dragon. Just like he could.

Doug sat in the front row until Harna introduced him. She sat down and he took the floor. Shunning the dais, he strode back and forth while he spoke.

"We have no time to waste in formal greetings and all that folderol, so please pretend that I've said all the right things. As you have experienced for yourselves, there is a crisis at hand. It seems I've been sent by the First One to help Harna lead you out of this mess." Around the room, heads began bobbing up and down.

Encouraged, he continued. "There are a few things we've learned about the enemy we face. The harriers warn us of their approach by broadcasting their emotions. Before they attack, we will all feel their excitement, their hunger and bloodlust. If any of you, at any time, feel an urge to just get up and do something or tear something apart, let everyone know and find shelter or change immediately. As dragons, we have a better chance at surviving than we do now."

He made eye contact with as many of his audience as he could. He guessed the red-eyed woman in the front row was Darya, and the child she clutched was her remaining son.

"While we were at the camp, Harna came up with a few interesting tricks that just might let us defeat the harriers." He outlined her plan to build a ring of fire around herself, using the pitch and string.

"Now, what I'm thinking about is trapping the harriers inside a structure or a cave, somewhere that we can kill them all at once, in a big fire. Using the pitch, we can start it quickly. I figure as dragons we can herd the nasty critters without getting too close. There should be enough of us to do it."

A man in the middle of the hall waved his hand. When Doug nodded, he asked, "But that only kills the ones that fly. We don't know where their colonies are. What about the eggs that hatch later?"

"Good question. If none of them swarmed until Perdin taught his harriers and they taught others, then it's a learned behavior and not instinct. If the abandoned young manage to survive on their own, they won't swarm unless someone teaches them to. I don't think we need to worry about the eggs."

A muttering ran through the chamber. He hoped it meant they were with him. They'd need every available dragon to herd a swarm the size of the one that had attacked the enclave.

Orda raised his hand and Doug nodded. "What about that old shed out in the east field? No one's used it in a couple of seasons. Couldn't we burn that down with 'em in it?"

The muttering grew into sounds of agreement.

"Fine. We'll do it. When?" Orda asked.

"We need to set it up tonight."

That sparked a protest from the back of the room. "Tonight? We just got the enclave cleaned up."

Harna came to stand beside him. "The harriers will be back. We must be ready for them."

No one had an adequate answer for that. For the next few hours, people ran around gathering pitch and wood. Some worked the pitch until it was soft enough to press into the bark of the wood. Others carried the prepared wood out to the shed.

Doug inspected it and deemed it large enough for their purposes. A set of double doors opened one whole side, and a smaller door was almost opposite it. He couldn't have asked for a better layout.

They lined the interior with the pitch-packed wood, all the way up to the ceiling. He had them line the rafters as well. None of the harriers could be permitted to escape, even though he planned to have hovering guards ready to flame any that did.

Four weres volunteered various field beasts to leave tethered in the shed as a final lure. Harna asked the assembly to decide. They chose the oldest one, a bull well past his prime.

Finally, all was ready. Doug told everybody to go home and snatch several hours of rest before the show started at dawn. He and Harna found space with her brother Keena's family.

Harna fell onto the pallet in Keena's main room, exhausted by the long flight, the meeting and preparing for the destruction of the harriers. Doug lay beside her, close enough to touch. Yiman and Keena's youngest son lay between her and the door.

The sounds of breathing slowed, until she knew Yiman slept. Beside her, Doug's breathing remained fast and heavy. Much like her own.

After the breathing of the others softened into sleep, he reached for her. She went to him gladly, shifting her bedding closer to him. Only so far, though, for Yiman had stirred until he trapped the edge of her blanket. Should she move farther, he would awaken.

The sensation of Doug's hands playing across her bare skin was better than in her dreams. The need to remain silent increased her excitement.

She wasn't surprised when the touch of a calloused fingertip, feather-light, caressed her thigh.

She turned to face him in the darkness, reaching out. Her hand encountered his cheek. He turned and kissed her palm. His lips parted and he lightly nipped the fleshy base of her thumb.

A shiver ran through her. Her brother and her nephew slept close by. What was he thinking of doing?

She found out soon enough. His hands reached under the blankets, seeking her shoulders, stroking down to find the sensitive skin above her breasts. He paused there, gently rubbing his thumbs in circles.

An ache sprang into being beneath his touch, where her nipples tightened in anticipation of his next move. Heat and dampness grew between her legs. He pulled away for a moment, holding the covers up and allowing cool air to wash over her skin. Her nipples puckered into tighter points and she had to remind herself to breathe.

A tiny gasp caught in her throat when he unerringly touched the tip of her left breast. His finger moved around the areola, barely touching her while slowly drawing ever-tighter circles. Her breasts grew heavy and her nipples puckered into tighter peaks as she anticipated the moment when the spiral he drew would reach the sensitive nub. Tension hitched her breath.

Sweet wings and weres, she had never thought to feel so much from so light a touch.

The covers drifted down as he raised his other hand and pressed his finger against her lips. The reminder that they were not alone forestalled the whimper in her throat. How had he known she was about to make a sound?

She swallowed that question along with her whimper. He was her Chosen and he knew things she did not. That was why they were destined to lead the enclave together, to complement one another and become more together than they were individually.

Doug ran his hand down her arm, took her hand and guided it to his erect cock. She clasped her fingers around his girth and marveled at the smooth texture. With him here in reality, everything became so much more vibrant. She felt his touch more keenly. His scent provoked an intense response deep within her.

Under the blanket, his hips moved slowly into her hand, encouraging her to stroke his cock. He was hotter than she remembered from their dreams, firmer beneath her hand. Tonight they were restricted to touching, but tomorrow, tomorrow they would manage to be alone. Tomorrow, she would make him scream, she promised herself.

His finger resumed circling her areola, reaching her nipple. With a flick, he lightly scraped the edge of one fingernail across the sensitive tip, and she stifled another sound. The effort of keeping quiet made her shudder. Her fist tightened on his shaft and he jerked beneath her hand.

A sensation of rightness flooded through her, along with a liquid warmth between her legs. This was so right. She belonged with him.

For a moment, time hung suspended between them. She couldn't have moved had her life depended on it. Despite her stillness, sensation rioted through her, trailing fire from her breasts to her womb and back again.

Doug broke her trance by pinching her nipple, little more than a quick sensation of sharp pressure before he engulfed her entire breast in his warm hand. She almost arched her back, seeking to press herself against him, and remembered Yiman's weight on her covers just in time. She slid from beneath the sheet that trapped her and into the night air. The tantalizing touches Doug was torturing her with were not enough. She wanted more. She wanted skin on skin. She wanted, no, she *needed* to taste him.

As if he read her mind, once more he acted on her thoughts. He leaned forward, pushing his head beneath the blanket and drawing her nipple in his mouth. She felt as though he drew her soul into him. Her dreams had never been like this!

With one final suck, he released her nipple. Cool air made the sensitive tissue pucker tighter — until his breath engulfed the taut peak and it bloomed in the heat. He left her breast and kissed his way up to nuzzle her neck.

He nudged her hand where she held his cock, and she remembered to breathe as she stroked him. When she ran her thumb over the swollen tip, a drop of moisture greeted her touch and she spread it over him.

He hissed between his teeth and they both stilled, waiting to see if the others awakened. The hair on the back of her neck rose. Should Ajan awaken, she might as well resign her position before the assembly removed her. Ajan was one of the biggest gossips in the enclave.

They waited long enough for her to count ten even breaths. When no one stirred, she murmured encouragement and squeezed her fist up and down his shaft. Was it her imagination, or had he grown thicker since she first touched him?

With a firm hand, she took her time exploring his contours. He was here in reality and as long as they did not disturb the others, they had all night. He tried to push her hand away, but she shook her head. She longed to taste him, to take him fully into her mouth, but that could wait until they were alone. She would at least welcome him to their enclave by giving him what pleasure she could.

He jerked in her grasp and she responded by smoothing her hand up and down once more. She increased her tempo to match the motion of his hips. Once she had to lick her hand to increase the wetness, and relished the lingering taste of his pre-cum.

Doug trailed his hand over her ribs and down toward where the strongest ache lay, between her legs. She shifted as much as she dared, trying to keep breathing and massaging his cock while lightning sparked under his touch. He paused and gently caressed the swell of her belly.

In their dream encounters, they came together in urgency and haste. Never had the lust between them been a thing of softness. The tenderness of his touch reached inside her and wrapped around her heart. The physical craving of the dreams was no longer all she felt. Affection tempered her desire. Was this part of her bonding with her Chosen?

His hand dipped lower, one finger tracing a path into the curls between her thighs. No, not just one, but two. When he spread them, cool air flowed across her heated, damp flesh and she shivered. She shivered again when he touched her swollen clit. Just a light contact before he spread her labia and thrust one finger into her. Her hips bucked, trying to take in more of him. His thumb began circling her clit, tracing a path that denied her the stimulation she craved. She bit back a moan as he pulled away.

In the dim light of the shelter, his eyes held hers as he lifted his hand to his mouth and suckled her juices from his finger. A wave of heat flooded through her and she flexed her legs together. Gods, how she wanted him to fill her with his hard cock!

Doug licked his finger one last time. Still holding her gaze, he unerringly found her cunt and this time, he thrust two fingers inside her. She met him with an eager jerk of her hips.

He didn't pull away again. His thumb circled her clit while he kept up a steady rhythm with his fingers, alternately reaching deep or spreading her open and stroking the inside walls.

She gave up trying to maintain any kind of control over her massage of his cock and held him in a tight fist as sparkling sensations poured through her. Tension winched tighter and tighter within her, finally reaching a point where a flash of light filled her vision and her cunt spasmed around him. Fire spread through her, racing up her spine and down to her toes. Her head jerked back and Doug covered her mouth with his, swallowing her cries of ecstasy as her world contracted to the penetration of his fingers and the stimulation of his thumb. He drank in her moans as she climaxed.

After the shudders and sparkling joy subsided, Harna slumped against him, her hand still gripping his cock. She whispered, "Wow."

He lifted his head and smiled. "You think that was good? Wait until we have our own home, with a big bed and privacy."

Yiman's chuckle was soft in the darkness. "Speaking of privacy, how soon can you find me someplace to live?"

Chapter Nine

∽

Doug hung above the shed, slow beats of his great wings holding him steady. In the distance, near the village, he could see the large dragons flying back and forth and frequent blasts of flame as they learned to herd harriers.

It is beginning to work well. Harna flew high above them all, keeping him updated. *They have mastered the technique.*

Good. When they reach the halfway mark, let me know. I will begin to stir up the bull. A few bellows should encourage them to come this way.

Just make sure you leave enough time for your escape.

Not a problem. No way would he linger any longer than necessary in a building that was about to blow up.

The plan was for him to poke the bull into loud activity and, once the harriers began to stream into the wide opening, run out the back and when Harna gave the all-in signal, pull the ropes that would shut the doors. He'd change and, once in dragon form, flame the primer cord before he took off.

He'd timed it at the camp three times, and he'd have enough time to clear the blast. He suppressed a shudder. He hoped. The variable was whether the shed would burn or explode. If it blew apart, he had no clue how big the explosion would be. He'd had no way to practice that.

For the next time they'd know, but for now they were guessing. He didn't even know enough to risk a SWAG. He made a mental note to tell Harna about making a Scientific Wild-Ass Guess. Gee, it had been days since he'd last heard an acronym of any kind. Had he explained to Harna about TLAs? He couldn't remember.

They're almost there! Harna's call pulled him back to the task at hand. *Get ready, get set, GO!*

The approaching harriers' panic tickled at him as he ran into the shed and stopped up short. The bull had fallen asleep. Or it was dead. He started toward it when movement outside caught his attention. Christ, were the harriers here that fast?

No, it was a boy, running across the field toward him.

He stepped outside and waved his arms. "No! Go back! Hide!" The child kept coming.

That's Asok! Harna called. *You have to move. Now!*

He looked up and found the harriers, getting closer by the second. He could almost pick out individuals in the swarm. Their flight became purposeful instead of random. It was clear they'd spotted him. *No! There's no time.*

There was no time for any of them. He grabbed Asok and ran into the shed. "Shit."

"Is that a bad word?"

"Yes. Now, don't move, no matter what happens." He changed and draped his big dragon body over Asok.

I'm coming.

*No! Harna, listen to me. There's no time for you to get clear. Stay there. T*he first harriers streamed through the doorway and fell upon his back. *Don't let them send you back to the field*s.

When he could no longer stand the pain of his ripped flesh, he braced himself and breathed a gout of flame onto the nearest wall. *I love you.*

Doug! No! Wings tucked tight against her sides, body and head aligned to increase her speed, Harna was halfway to the shed when it exploded. A rising cloud of flame and dead harriers buffeted her. Heated air laden with smoke caught in her throat. She spread her wings to stop her descent. Splinters and shards of wood peppered her, gouging holes in her hide and tattering her wings.

Out of the way, sister! Yiman screamed past her to dart a fiery breath at a flapping harrier.

She jerked to one side only to bump into Misma.

Whoo-ha! It worked! That Chosen of yours is one hell of a planner! We've got to send word of this to the other enclaves. He rushed off to spear flame at another harrier.

The air filled with more dragons, calling congratulations. Their words barely registered. All she could think was that Doug could not possibly have made it out of the shed. Nor could Asok have survived.

How much of the debris around them that she'd thought were harrier parts were actually Doug parts? Her stomach clenched and she gagged a spurt of flame.

Settling to the ground with the last of the wreckage, she changed. Falling to her knees, she sobbed, "Doug, why?" She knew the answer as clearly as if he had voiced it himself. Her people had become as important to him as they were to her, important enough to die for.

Ajan appeared and gathered her close.

"He died to save us all." Harna wept into Ajan's shoulder. "Why couldn't he have lived for me?"

No wonder the First One didn't deem her worthy of her Chosen. She was so fucking selfish, she'd pissed off the gods.

"What's wrong?" Yiman pushed his way through the crowd of weres. "It worked just as we planned." He looked at the sober faces surrounding Harna. "Didn't it?"

"Doug, oh gods, Doug was in the shed," Harna managed to get out. "With Asok."

Darya collapsed with a wail.

"Ah, shit." Yiman turned and stamped away. He picked up a charred log and threw it as hard as he could into the remains of the shed. "Shit!"

"That's a bad word," came a muffled voice.

Darya's head jerked up. "What?"

"And you shouldn't throw things." The voice was stronger. Harna recognized Asok's timbre.

If Asok lived, Doug might as well.

She tore herself from Ajan's embrace and ran barefoot into the ankle-deep embers. "Doug!" Ripping at the heaped rubble with her hands, she barely noticed when Darya joined her, others right behind her.

"Here!" Orda shouted. "I've found a wingtip!"

Something stirred beneath her feet.

"Here, too!" she yelled. "Back up!"

Everyone stepped away to clear the area. A mass of debris shifted and raised up. Asok crawled out of the revealed cavity, into his mother's arms. They watched as the rubble shifted again before falling in on itself. When everything stopped moving, there was a deep hole in the center where Asok had been.

Harna walked forward. It couldn't be. She'd pissed off the gods.

It was. Doug lay in the bottom of the depression, looking up at her. Somehow he'd managed to change. And heal.

I love you.

And I you. While the rest of the enclave gaped, she fell and landed in his arms. She grinned up at him like an idiot. *But how did you survive?*

How did the First One bring me here? It's her will. After all, I am your Chosen.

* * * * *

Doug ran his hand over Harna's naked back. The morning light filtering through the shutters played up the difference in the shades of their skin. In the weeks since they defeated the harriers, the sun had darkened him to a golden tan, but he was still pale next to Harna's gorgeous mahogany.

She shifted in his arms. "Good morning, Dugga my love."

He smiled down into her sleepy eyes. "Every morning is a good morning."

"Mmmmm." She hummed her agreement and nestled closer. Her hip pressed against his cock and desire stirred within him. God, could he ever get enough of her?

He loved the feel of her skin sliding against his. He loved their snug new house and he loved waking up next to Harna every morning. "You look like you belong here."

"Mmmmm, yes. My place is with my Chosen." She breathed a sleepy sigh and buried her face in his chest. "As your place is with your Chosen." It came out in a whisper that tickled his skin.

"That would be you." He caressed the soft globe of her ass. Flight drills and an experiment with balls of burning pitch awaited him, but he was not ready to leave his warm bed — or his hot mate.

"Mmmmm. We are a team." She wriggled against him.

Good. She was waking up. He wouldn't disturb her if she really needed to sleep. "You and I are nowhere near a baseball team. We need at least nine players for that."

"Mmmmm. Baseball. We play the Hedge Hoppers tomorrow?" She stretched and treated him to the sight of her full curves. He could swear her breasts kept getting bigger.

"Yup. And the Pasture Piglets two days after that."

"How many teams are there now?"

"Seven that I know of." He watched her rub her eyes and chuckled at the way the weres had taken to baseball like ducks to water. Four of the neighboring enclaves and two fishing villages now had teams, and he had hopes of forming a Coastal League by the end of the summer. By his best calculation, the planetary tilt here was less than that of Earth, so summers were long and winters mild. That meant a longer baseball season, which was fine with him.

She reached up and kissed him, a quick press of her lips that did nothing to tamp down his desire. He pulled her back and devoured her with a long, intense mating of their mouths. Her lips opened and her tongue met his eagerly, twining and delving deep. When he released her, they were both breathing heavily.

"I'm so glad the enclaves have adopted your baseball. Everyone needs a hobby."

"Forget baseball. Playing with you is my favorite hobby."

"I can't forget baseball. You talk about it in your sleep!"

"I do not talk in my sleep!" She teased him often with this nonsense.

She tapped his chin with her finger. "You do indeed, and I know what your fondest wish is."

He waited for her to drop the other shoe. Last time she'd said this, she'd unveiled uniforms the women had made for his team. Screaming Dragon jerseys, or as close as he'd get to them in this world.

"We *will* field our own team one day, to play the Nodda Nine." She placed his hand over her belly. "By next summer, we will have doubled the size of our family."

He stared into her eyes. Through her skin, he could actually *feel* life. Two lives. Twins. Their sons. Dear God, he was going to be a father.

A wave of protectiveness washed over him. His head spun. He clutched her shoulders to keep from passing out. He'd barely gotten the hang of this mate thing and wasn't anywhere near getting a handle on the leadership stuff. How was he supposed to deal with being a father?

"Don't fret. You'll do fine."

He gaped at her. "How did you know what I was thinking?"

Harna laughed. "All men go through the same doubts and worries when they hear they are going to be a father for the first time. Don't you think we women ever discuss our mates?"

He covered his ears. "I do not want to hear any more. Save me from women's mysteries."

She pulled his hands down and placed them on her breasts. "I can't tell you any more. You haven't been initiated. And you don't want to know what that involves!"

Her eyes sparkled at his groan. She had kept her hands over his and began a gentle massage. Her nipples tightened under his palms and he forgot about baseball, babies and gossip as his cock surged to attention. "Can we? It won't hurt the babies?"

"Oh, yes we can, as much as we want, until much later." She wrapped her hand around his cock and gave him a sly smile. "I've heard women claim being loved while filled with a child is the most intense pleasure they've ever felt."

"Do not tell me any more!" He captured her laughter with a kiss.

She met every light pinch he gave her taut nipples with a whimper of pleasure. He was right—her breasts were massive, overflowing his hands with a bounty of softness. He moved to the gentle swell of her belly, marveling that new life lay so close, just beneath his hand. Not just any new life, but a blending of his and hers.

Harna trailed one hand down his chest, circling his nipples before she reached lower. Mimicking her, Doug trailed his hand lower. He tangled his fingers in her pubic hair as she palmed his balls. Parting her cunt lips with one finger, he discovered she was slick and very ready for him.

The scent of her arousal filled his head. "God, you smell good enough to eat. And I haven't had breakfast."

Her laughter rang out as she pushed him away and scooted up the mattress. "You'll get no complaints from me." She caressed his cheek. "You're very good at this. I hear that other men—"

"I don't want to know any of this!" He plunged his face down, pulling her thighs close to cover his ears. He could still hear her laughing, so he busied himself teasing her clit. Christ, even that was bigger than he remembered! Softer and larger than her nipples, it stood up and just begged to be suckled. He complied, sealing his mouth to her flesh and sucking while he played with his tongue, drawing patterns around her erect clit.

Her juices flooded his chin. He lapped up a succulent swallow. She even tasted different. Richer. Fuller, if that made sense.

He reared back and sat on his heels. God, he'd never tire of looking at her. Using both hands, he spread her legs wide. Dark skin gave way to silver curls that framed her garnet-red, pouting inner lips. Her cunt bubbled with her juices, ready and waiting for his cock.

His cock was more than ready for her. Leaning forward, he spread out over her.

Harna shuddered and clutched the sheets with both fists. She loved the way Doug liked to look at her body. She loved his sweet torture. He nuzzled her breasts, taking one nipple in his mouth and tugging as he moved between her thighs. Lightning arced from his mouth to her womb. Sweet wings and weres, would he always make her feel like this? She sincerely hoped so. She made a small sound in the back of her throat and arched into him. She wriggled in a silent plea until he jerked his hips and drove deep.

He filled her with his length, stretching her almost to the point of pain. As his balls slapped against her ass, his hair ground against her clit and she soared on a tide of intense pleasure. By the First One's wings, if she was this sensitive now, what would she be like as her pregnancy progressed? Those other women might well be right.

The tendons stood out on his neck like cords as he fought to pull out. She fought too, against the muscles that gripped him like they would never let him go. Holy Mother of All, she was going to climax right away. Doug always made sure she was satisfied, but she had never been this responsive. She worked to contain her pleasure. She wanted this to be special.

He thrust back into her slowly, taking his time. She wrapped her arms around him, whispering, "Fuck me, Doug."

She loved to use words and phrases he'd taught her, especially the ones he told her weren't very polite. She'd learned just how to get him revved up. He plunged back into the tight heat of her, pulling out just as she said, "I want your hot cock buried deep in my juicy cunt. Fuck me hard, Doug. I want it all."

He gave it to her, filling her, sheathing his cock to the hilt before withdrawing to pump into her again. All she could do was hang on for the ride of her life.

She managed to hold on to her sanity by a thread, putting off her climax until he lowered his head and pulled her nipple into his mouth. Pleasure poured through her, streaking from her nipple and her clit throughout her body. He took her nipple firmly in his teeth and fire flared up her spine, burning through her flesh to sizzle across her skin.

He kept the pressure on, not letting go. Sensation mounted and became sweet torture, wave after wave of ecstasy that carried her aloft. Higher and higher they flew, until the ever-faster climaxes became one, an unending blaze that consumed her. She threw back her head and screamed.

Doug freed her nipple and thrust one last time. He roared his release, jetting spurt after spurt of his cum as his body went rigid, buried to the hilt inside her.

He collapsed on the bed next to her. "Jesus, Mary and Joseph. I don't think I'll ever walk again."

"Mmmmm." She snuggled up to his side. He lifted an arm and pulled her close. "I think we need thicker walls. The women will be full of questions."

"Tell them to mind their own business."

"I like to brag about you. What is wrong with that? Let them be jealous."

"Maybe I can live with that. I just can't live without you."

"Mmmmm." She knew she couldn't live without him, either. And they not only needed thicker walls, they would soon need a much larger house, with more space around it. The Flying Phoenixes would need lots of room for batting practice.

Taking Shape

By Tielle St. Clare

ဢ

Also by Tielle St. Clare

About the Author

Tielle (pronounced "teal") St. Clare has had life-long love of romance novels. She began reading romances in the 7th grade when she discovered Victoria Holt novels and began writing romances at the age of 16 (during Trigonometry, if the truth be told). During her senior year in high school, the class dressed up as what they would be in twenty years—Tielle dressed as a romance writer. When not writing romances, Tielle has worked in public relations and video production for the past 20 years. She moved to Alaska when she was seven years old in 1972 when her father was transferred with the military. Tielle believes romances should be hot and sexy with a great story and fun characters.

Tielle welcomes comments from readers. You can find her website and email address on her author bio page at www.ellorascave.com.

Prologue

ഇ

Edward Branch takes pompous to a whole new level, Nicholas Conner thought, watching his latest client simultaneously raise his chin and look down his nose as he stared at Nick across his ornate, well-polished desk. The smooth surface practically begged to be marred by fingerprints...or maybe it was the owner—a little too slick and smooth—who inspired that response.

"Now, Mister Conner, your reputation gives me some assurance that you will be able to resolve this issue but I must demand complete discretion and secrecy. Ms. Hayward can know nothing about this investigation."

Nick allowed none of his irritation to show on his face. If the man knew anything about the reputation of Conner Investigations, he knew that discretion was their agency's second most prized skill.

Get in, blend in and get out without being noticed.

His family's peculiar gifts made that part of their investigations routine.

"Don't worry. She won't even know I'm there." He flipped through the file. It didn't hold nearly enough information about the target. It had her work history, her address and the reasons AirPress Incorporated thought she was embezzling but none of the stuff he would need—who she dated, what were her habits, what did the inside of her house look like? Nick made a mental list. His brothers and sister were working their own cases but it shouldn't be difficult to learn what he needed to know.

"Why not just fire her?" he asked, nailing Branch, AirPress's president and CEO, with his stare, practically daring him to explain the real reason CI was being hired.

"A segment of the company is being sold," Martin Jessup, AirPress's chief financial officer answered, drawing Nick's attention to him. That seemed to be the pattern. Branch gave orders but any questions were immediately answered by Jessup. The CFO was used to shielding his boss. The uptight accountant offered a weak smile. "We don't want any questions about our reputation. Embezzlement is an embarrassment under the best circumstances."

"And you know women like this…" Branch interjected. "They sue over any little thing. We have to have evidence — collected by a third party — so she doesn't have grounds to take us to court."

The condescending sneer made Nick's knuckles ache. His mother or sister would have been over the desk with their fingers wrapped around his chauvinistic throat. Nick settled for placing his boot against the front of Branch's desk, leaving a visible footprint. It was petty, he knew, but his sister would be proud.

"We need to move quickly on this," Branch said. "The sale will be finalized in the next quarter. I don't want anything hanging over our heads."

"We'll need a few weeks to gather some background information."

"That's fine. Keep Jessup in the loop. I want to keep this perfectly legal so when you want to search her computer here, give Jessup a day's warning and he'll arrange it." Branch rose from his chair and waved to the door, indicating he was done with Nick.

Nick was slow to come to his feet. He'd never been one to take orders well. Nick made a mental notation to have Jameson check out AirPress and its CEO. Something didn't quite feel right with this job. His internal sensors were all on full alert. He considered just walking away — they didn't need the work — but Branch offered access to a whole different clientele.

Don't judge the client.

He heard the mental advice and easily recognized the voice. It was his. He'd repeated as much to his brothers and sister on numerous occasions. Their job was private investigations. Not righting wrongs or criticizing the people who hired them — most of whom were sleazier than their targets.

Nick said his goodbyes and exited the building. He didn't go far. It was almost lunchtime and it was a beautiful spring day. Surely Ms. Hayward would take her lunch outside. He waited. Finally, about two-thirty she appeared, walking two blocks to a coffee shop. Nick followed at a distance. She didn't speak with anyone except the counter staff then took her paper cup and sat by the window. She stared blankly at the world. After twenty minutes, she sighed, stood and went back to her office.

She walked past him, never seeing him. Her long-legged stride spoke of a woman with energy and determination. He followed her back to the door, trying not to notice the swing of her cute little ass beneath the slim skirt she wore. It wasn't until she'd disappeared into the building that Nick realized he had spent the last half of her walk wondering how her ass would feel in his hands as he fucked her. He took a slow breath and willed away the beginnings of an erection he didn't need right now. Just as it wasn't wise to judge the client, it was truly stupid to lust after a target.

Though it wasn't strictly necessary, Nick hung around outside the building, staying out of sight. The building cleared out about six with a few stragglers coming out at six-thirty. No sign of his target. At seven-thirty he finally saw her leave, her briefcase clutched firmly in her hand and her brow furrowed in concentration. From the distance he couldn't see the color of her eyes but he didn't doubt they were steady and strong. He smiled at his own musings. He was supposed to be observing her, not cataloguing her. Her long brown hair hung down to the middle of her back, the strands messy and tangled as if she'd run her fingers through the length too many times during the day.

She opened her back seat and tossed her briefcase in. Her chin tilted up and her head dropped back as if she was pulling the tension from inside her body. Nick shifted in his hiding place, watching the lithe form arch and stretch, like invisible fingers were working her spine. Her breasts pressed against her blouse, creating a well-defined line—round and full. She rolled her head to the side and Nick could see the stress slipping from her body. His fingers twitched. It was too easy to imagine him, straddling her back, her tight ass beneath him as he worked the tension from her muscles.

His cock twitched, liking the idea.

She's a target, his overdeveloped conscience chimed in. He clung to that thought as she got into her car. He made a note of the license plate and let her drive away. There was no need to follow her. He could get what he needed off the computer. It was time to learn more about the thieving Ms. Tally Hayward.

Chapter One

ഔ

Tally Hayward rolled her shoulders back, trying to ease the strain in her muscles. Please God, would this week never end? At least it was Friday and she had the weekend to look forward to. She glared silently at the glass walls of her favorite coffee shop. Sometimes she hated work. She loved her job but lately…the pain at the back of her neck shot down her spine. She took a deep breath and forced the muscles to release. The tension eased enough that she could move without wincing. Damn, she needed to relax, in bed, flat on her back. The image made her smile. *Preferably with a studly man above me*, she thought. Or behind. The spread of her lips widened into a full-fledged grin.

Her phone chimed once — alerting her to a message. She sighed. Had to be Richard. He did this when he didn't want to talk to her — to make a clean getaway. He didn't actually call, he just left messages. She flipped the phone open and dialed her voice mail, listening as her boyfriend's voice slid through the line.

"Hi, baby doll." He used that low sensual tone that Tally called his "don't you think I'm sexy" voice. It did nothing for her. It reminded her of a bad porn actor. "I just wanted to say I'm off to Chicago. Back in a few days. See ya!"

A little of the stress in her neck eased. Well, that was one thing she didn't have to deal with for a few more days — breaking up with Richard. It had been weighing on her mind for the past week. Not that it was a surprise. She'd known for weeks it wasn't going to work out but she'd stuck it out. She hadn't wanted to bail on a potential relationship too early. After all, Richard looked good on paper — great job, nice car, friends with all the right people—and he looked good in person. If ever there was a human model for the Ken doll it was him.

Complete with being anatomically incorrect.

Tally covered her mouth to hide her smile and stop the full-blown laughter. That was rotten of her. It wasn't that Richard was physically inadequate. He had all the requisite parts in reasonably good proportions. It was a rhythm thing. He had none. Or at least none that matched Tally's. She sighed as she snapped the phone shut. She'd never been bored in bed—until Richard. And he didn't take suggestions well. Once she'd suggested maybe he go down on her. He'd shook his head sadly and explained that women today were responsible for their own orgasms and surely she didn't need "tricks" to make her come. Tally rolled her eyes at the memory. She wouldn't have minded a few tricks. Richard had one trick—fuck, roll over and play dead before slinking away in the early morning hours. Not that she necessarily wanted him to stick around for a second try but still, it would be nice to have her lover smile at her in the morning.

No, it was definitely time to let him go. Move on. Find someone new. Someone who actually seemed to enjoy having sex with her. He didn't have to be perfect…just trainable.

Gorgeous didn't hurt, with a tight ass and long strong legs. Broad shoulders, large hands. Oh yeah. Mystic blue eyes and black silver-tinted hair. She moaned softly and the sound made her realize she was no longer fantasizing about Mister Perfect—she was staring at him. Her dream man stood in front of her ordering a latte. Again.

He glanced across the curved counter, his eyes catching hers. His smile filled his face, creating delightful crinkles around the edges of his eyes. Smile lines eased the harsh lines of his cheekbones.

He accepted his paper cup and wandered around the corner of the bar to where she stood. Slowly she dropped her phone to the counter.

"Good afternoon."

A warm shiver curled down her spine as he spoke. It was like vocal sex. Since the first time they'd spoken, she'd become fascinated by the power of his voice. She was pretty sure she could come just from listening to him speak. *I wonder if he's silent in bed — or if he likes to talk, whisper all sorts of wicked things.* Not that she would ever find out. They were friends and brand-new friends at that. Casual meetings at a coffee shop did not a relationship make, even if he had started starring in her late night dreams.

"Uh, hi," she remembered to answer after a long time.

"It's good to see you again."

She smiled. He always sounded so sincere when he said that — as if seeing her had made his day better. It certainly improved the hell out of hers.

"You too." They wandered over to "their" table. The coffee shop wasn't crowded. It rarely was at this time of day. They probably wouldn't have even spoken if the little café hadn't been unusually busy one day last week. Every table had been full and Nick had asked to join Tally at hers. They'd talked and Tally had been late getting back to work. The next day about the same time, she'd returned to the coffee shop and he'd been there. He'd invited her to share his table even though there were plenty to choose from. Since then, they'd met almost every day and Tally had the sneaking suspicion that he was timing his visits to coincide with hers. If he'd been the least bit creepy or aggressive, it would have bothered her.

"Are you all right? You've got this worried look on your face."

She shook her head. "It's nothing. Stress at work. Stress in the personal life."

"Yes, you'd mentioned you were working on a big project. How's that going?"

"Fine. I guess. I'm having some trouble with it. Don't really know who to go to." She didn't want to say any more than that. It wouldn't be appropriate to draw him in. He was a stranger after all. And she wasn't sure how to explain it. The numbers weren't adding up.

She waved her hand to indicate she wanted to change the subject. "I went to that bookstore you recommended," she said.

The edge of his mouth bent upward. It was the only sign he'd heard her but she could tell he was pleased. "And did you enjoy it?"

"Fascinating." She launched into a discussion of the books she'd bought and the temptations she'd resisted. An hour later, she glanced at her watch. "Eeek, I've got to get back to work."

Nick stood when she did. He cleared their table and met her at the door.

She grabbed her purse, digging in the side pouch. "Drat."

"What's wrong?"

"Oh, I can't find my access badge. I hope I left it in the office. The guards know me. They'll let me sign in today but I need it to get into the building over the weekend."

"You work too much from what I see."

"I have to get this project done."

He looked like he had more to say on the subject but kept his mouth shut. Instead, he tipped his head toward the coffee shop. "Want to get together tomorrow? Here, a little before noon."

Tally's heart leapt into her throat. It was the closest Nick had come to asking her out. She couldn't actually go on a date with him of course. Not until she'd officially broken it off with Richard. That would be just plain tacky. But coffee wasn't really a date.

"That's sounds great. I'll see you then."

He nodded then turned and walked away. Tally couldn't resist watching him. Pure masculine beauty. She stared until he was out of sight then whimpered. She had to get back to work. Damn.

Nick walked away, fighting the urge to turn around and see if she was watching him. He kept moving, formulating the plan. They'd make their move this weekend. He'd get Tally out of her office and keep her busy for a few hours tonight while his brother Devon checked her office computer.

She would have to be a pretty stupid embezzler to keep documents on the company computer but they had to check. Tally was many things but she wasn't stupid.

It had been relatively simple to gather information about her. Her address, friends, family, lovers, even her favorite kind of pizza. Between the Internet, observation and a few well-placed questions, Nick had found out all he'd needed to know to move forward. When nothing had seemed out of the ordinary, he'd approached her in the coffee shop last week. He'd filled the other tables with his employees and then introduced himself. Since then, he'd tried to steer the conversation toward her work but she always closed down when he did. Something was bothering her about work, something she didn't want to talk about.

Arriving home, Nick flipped through the information he had on her boyfriend. If all went as planned, Richard would be on a plane in about thirty minutes. All Nick had to do was take his place.

Nick shook his head. Unfortunately, too many of his thoughts lately had been about him taking Richard's place. In Tally's bed, in her body. His cock hardened. It was easy to imagine her naked, stretched out on his bed, his cock pumping hard between her sleek thighs. He gripped the edge of the dresser and tried to fight off the image.

"She's a target. Don't forget that. Get in, blend in and get out without being noticed." He'd said the same thing to his brothers and sister dozens of times.

He glanced at the clock and decided it was time. He stripped off his clothes and stood in front of the mirror. He rolled his neck to the side, pushed his shoulders back and stared at himself. His naked body looked golden in the dying evening light.

Everyone in the family had their own little ceremonies to ease the change. Nick liked to see himself — to remind himself who he was, what he was. It was something he needed to remember.

He took a deep breath and called up the image, the fundamental energy that made up Tally's boyfriend, Richard. He waited until the picture was clear in his mind and then poured himself into the image.

Nick gritted his teeth as the change began. He hated this. Animals — fine. Even inanimate objects. But turning into another person was dangerous — both physically and psychically.

To turn into another form, Nick first had to touch the thing. Through that contact he absorbed the object's basic energy, the fundamental essence of the person. When turning into another human, some of the psychic baggage came along with it. That little bit would become part of Nick. If a shifter touched a truly evil soul, it could be deadly.

Richard wasn't evil — just dull. Nick left a pleading note with the universe that none of Richard's blandness remained in him when the transition was complete and then concentrated on the change.

Muscles and bones stretched and cracked. His face lengthened — his chin drawing back, his ears sliding down. Of all the sensations, Nick hated that the most — the loss of his face.

He waited until the change was complete and the form firmly locked in his mind before he opened his eyes and stared at this new face.

He leaned closer, seeking himself in the eyes. That was the only part of him that didn't change. No matter what form he took, the color of his eyes remained the same.

He turned away and pulled on the clothes he hoped would fit. He'd ordered them from the upscale store Richard patronized so he knew they matched the image. Once he was dressed, Nick picked up his phone and dialed his brother.

"It's me."

There was a moment's hesitation and Nick knew Devon was adjusting to the foreign voice coming from Nick's phone.

"Are you ready?"

"As I'll ever be. I'll get her about six. After you see me leave, get in and get out."

"Want me to sign in as you?" Devon asked. "You said they gave you permission to search."

Nick thought about it for a moment. Nothing had changed since the first meeting. He didn't quite trust his client and wasn't sure he wanted Branch or Jessup to know he'd searched Tally's office. "No. Shift into someone leaving the building. I don't want them knowing I've been inside."

"It's your gig. Call me when you're done."

Nick nodded, getting used to the way Richard's muscles moved. "I'll talk to you later." Nick clicked off his phone and stared at the mirror. He took a deep breath. It was time to be someone else.

* * * * *

Tally chewed on the edge of her thumbnail, gnawing at that short nail before ripping her hand away from her mouth. No, she'd spent three months breaking this habit, she wouldn't let one little stress at work make her start again.

Okay, so it was a big stress.

Something was wrong with these numbers. She'd been through them twice and there was something wrong. Seriously wrong.

She glanced at the clock. Six o'clock. It was Friday and she had no plans. She could work a few more hours before heading home.

The audit of the Georgia plant had originally been assigned to her but then a month ago, she'd gotten a promotion and Martin had suggested she wouldn't have time to complete it. She hated leaving a project half-done so she'd told him she'd do both jobs until the audit was complete—even it if meant working lots of overtime.

But now, something wasn't right. She tapped her fingernail on the keyboard. The Georgia plant was reporting far higher profits than what she was seeing. Maybe her expenses were off. She clicked on the file—

"Hey, baby doll."

Her head snapped up at the sound of Richard's voice. *What the hell is he doing here?* She spun around and faced the door. He leaned against the doorframe looking gorgeous and debonair. Elegant. She watched him for a moment and felt a slow flutter deep inside her body. There was something different about him. A new energy that seemed to fill the room.

"Richard?" The name fell from her mouth as a question and then she felt silly. Of course it was Richard, unless he had a twin. "Uh, what are you doing here? I thought you were in Chicago."

"Change of plans. I don't leave until tomorrow. I thought I'd stop and take my best girl to dinner."

She cringed at the almost paternal way he talked about her.

"Well, I was planning to work for another few hours." Richard always understood that work came before everything.

Except tonight he tilted his head toward the door. "Come on, baby doll. Let's go get something to eat." He winked. "You have to eat, right?"

She tensed at the teasing sound of his voice. He might make subtly sarcastic comments about her plebian tastes but never did he tease her.

"Come on," he said. "I'll take you out for pizza."

She stared at him for a moment as she waited for her mind to process his offer. "Pizza? *You* want to get pizza?"

He shrugged but the movement didn't seem as casual as she thought he'd intended.

"Sure, why not?"

"You hate pizza."

"I'm turning over a new leaf." He sounded exasperated. "Now, can we go?"

Shocked into submission, Tally closed down her computer and slipped the disk back into her briefcase. She never went anywhere without that disk. After discovering that someone had been snooping through her computer three weeks ago, she'd started carrying everything on disk.

Suddenly unsure of herself, she closed her briefcase and stood up. Richard smiled and held out his hand, offering to carry her bag. She hesitated for a moment then handed it over. Richard had particular tastes in leather gear. Briefcases had to be made by a certain company from a certain cow. She waited for a moment, expecting a disparaging remark. When none came, she looked up. Richard watched her, eyes glittering with heat and hunger as if he wanted to bend her over the desk and fuck her. Hard. The image filled her head making it almost impossible to think. It didn't take long for the fantasy to change. It wasn't Richard doing her on the desk, it was Nick—with that wickedly sexy voice and deep blue eyes. Like Richard's.

She shook her head. That wasn't right. Richard had brown eyes.

"Colored contacts?" she blurted out.

He nodded. "What do you think?"

Strange, pretentious, vain.

"Uh, unusual color."

He laughed softly. "I thought they made me look sexy. What do you think?" He lifted his chin as if posing for a sculptor.

She stared at him for a long time before answering. He did look sexy tonight. No, not sexy. Sexual. But she didn't think it was the eyes. Something deep inside her was responding to him as it hadn't before.

"They look great," she said, because they did. The color was almost a teal. The new shade seemed to give his eyes hidden depths. The edge of his mouth kicked up and Tally felt a warm shiver in her pussy. His smile widened like he sensed her body's reaction—and he approved.

He led her down the hall, politely stepping to the side to let her enter the elevator first. She hesitated. Something didn't feel right. Richard was always polite but tonight it seemed more innate—as if he did these things to ease her, not because someone was watching.

"How's work?" she asked as the doors closed.

He shrugged. "The same."

"Okay, what's up?" she demanded folding her arms across her chest. Richard always wanted to talk about his work. His eyes widened, making him look a little too innocent.

"What do you mean?"

"You're acting…weird."

"I'm in a weird mood." He leaned down and put his mouth next to her ear. "It must be the contacts. I feel like a whole new man tonight."

The words, his voice, circled through her head and made a beeline for her sex. She put her fingertips against the elevator wall to steady her weakening knees. Where had this "new" Richard come from?

She still didn't have an answer when she led the way into her house three hours later. She only hoped he'd stick around. The evening had flown by and she'd enjoyed herself more than any other date with Richard. He stepped inside and glanced around the living room. Papers were scattered across the dining table and she tensed, waiting for Richard's usual admonishment about keeping her house tidy. He said nothing.

Just another first. Whatever alien had snatched Richard's soul away…

The rest of the thought drifted away as he turned his focus from the room to her. Richard's teasing touches and subtle innuendos all night had kept her body humming and tight—and now she wanted the rest.

She smiled as he walked to her—anticipating his suddenly sexy voice to whisper that they should go upstairs.

"I'd better get home," he said. Counter to his words, his voice rumbled low and hungry. He didn't want to leave. He looked at her for a long time, the regret visible in his eyes. He leaned down and pressed his lips against hers. It was a good night kiss. Sweet and pleasant. Not passionate or overwhelming. At least that's the way it started. Then he moved his mouth against hers, opening his lips just enough that she could taste the sweet wine from dinner. He flicked his tongue across the peak of her upper lip. She groaned and leaned in, opening herself to his silent request. He started slow, not controlling or demanding but searching—as if this was their first kiss and he wanted to learn her. In fact the whole night had seemed brand new. Like a first date.

Her ability to focus on anything except Richard was lost as he eased his tongue into her mouth. Her body reacted instinctively—bowing to the command of his and taking her own pleasure, curling her tongue around his, sucking lightly, holding him deep inside her. His hand fell to her backside and pulled her forward, pressing his cock against the V of her thighs. Their bodies fit together well and a wicked little shimmer fluttered through her sex.

Tally lifted her mouth away, drawing in much needed air. His lips moved along her jaw, leaving a trail of heated kisses until he reached that secret space beneath her ear. He'd never been able to find it before but now it was perfect. He kissed, licked and raked his teeth across her skin.

Her head tilted to the side, giving him more access but instead he pulled away.

No! The very essence of her rebelled at the thought of losing the sweet pressure of his mouth. She wrapped her arms around his neck, holding him close. The heat in his eyes gave her confidence. She pressed forward and kissed his neck, mirroring the kisses he gave her.

"You could stay," she said, her words breathless against his throat.

"I really shouldn't. Early flight in the morning."

She opened her mouth against his neck, scraping her teeth along the tight straining muscle. He groaned and she licked the same place. She felt wicked and sexy. Seductive. Strange, she'd never felt seductive before with Richard. As if she was luring him away from his responsibilities, tempting him. And tonight, that's exactly what she wanted to do. Her body hummed with his delicious kisses and she wanted more.

"Stay," she whispered against his mouth.

Chapter Two

ଥ

"Stay," she said again with more force. She watched his blue eyes darken and knew she had him.

"Maybe for a while."

Tally stepped back but didn't go far. The seductive power of a woman in need flowed through her veins.

"Come with me." The husky words echoed through the living room but she felt no embarrassment. The heat in his stare was more than enough to tell her he wanted this as well.

She led him up the stairs to her bedroom. The room was her private retreat designed in a rampant mixture of the colors she loved. Richard rarely came over. He was more comfortable at his place. A faint twinge of irritation flickered through her as she saw that the bed wasn't made. She hadn't expected to bring anyone home when she'd crawled out of bed this morning. Richard was sure to comment and she didn't want anything breaking the sensual mood.

She stood in the doorway, blocking the entrance with her body. Maybe she could tidy the bed before he noticed.

His arm wrapped around her waist as she hesitated— pulling her back against him, his cock pressing against her ass. The world around them stood still. He rubbed against her as if seeking entrance, promising what she'd only imagined in dark dreams. Need pulsated through her pussy and she pushed back, letting him rock into the split between her ass cheeks.

"Watching this sweet ass move up the stairs has made me very ready to fuck."

The words slid from his lips into her ear, seducing her with wicked intentions. The comment was accompanied by a hard roll of his hips as if he warned how deeply he would enter her.

"Just let me fix the bed," she said breathlessly.

He lifted his head. "What's wrong with it?" he asked, the confusion in his voice making her smile.

"It's unmade. It'll just take me a moment." She moved out of his grip but he stopped her, yanking her back into his embrace.

"We're just going to tear it up again," he growled against her ear.

Tally squeezed her lips together to stop a whimper. It was just like her fantasies. Richard had miraculously turned into her dream lover.

It felt like their first time together — that excitement and fear of what it would be like to take him into her body. Excited and a little bit frightened by what might happen if she took this next step, she walked slowly into the room. Richard stayed at the door, his arms crossed over his chest, his shoulder propped against the doorframe and his eyes on her.

She raised her eyebrows in silent question, unsure what this "Richard" had in mind.

"Take off your clothes," he ordered. The brusque command made her knees tremble. She stared at him for a long moment to see if he was joking or teasing but the power she'd sensed all night seemed to have bubbled to the surface. He was a man in control.

It was definitely the eyes. They were a pirate's eyes — a tough, harsh captain about to ravage his willing captive. And he was waiting for her to follow his instruction.

Blushing furiously, she fumbled with the buttons on her blouse, not sure where to look. Her fingers trembled and her pussy wept, flowing hot and hungry. Anticipation surged through her in steady waves. She needed to be fucked. God, she hoped Richard was up for a hard ride — for a change. She jerked off her blouse and went to work on her dress pants. As they slid to the ground, she stepped clear, leaving her dressed in her bra and panties. They matched. That was good. Richard liked that.

She brushed the lower edge of her hair forward. He followed the movement as the ends curled around her breasts. The heat burning from deep in his eyes strained her nipples, drawing them forward, pressing against the lace of her bra. Her arms twitched in an unconscious urge to cover herself from his gaze.

"Don't hide yourself." His voice was different tonight as well. Stronger and more powerful. "Take off the bra. I want to see those beautiful tits," he commanded.

Nick cursed himself as he watched the light flare in her eyes. Damn it, he'd forgotten for a moment that he was "Richard". Somehow Nick couldn't see the stuffy financial planner calling them "tits". He probably called them bosoms, if he mentioned them at all. But these were breasts, delicious full breasts with tight hard nipples. Nick felt his cock stretch, pulsing inside the expensive suit.

What the hell was he thinking? This was one of the fundamental family rules and he was about to break it. Even knowing that, he couldn't tear himself away. Not when sweet Tally was easing her bra forward, lowering it to the floor. She looked up at him—her eyes a contradiction of passion and hesitation, as if she didn't know what his reaction would be.

Nick swore silently. What kind of shit was her boyfriend? She shouldn't be feeling anything but desire, hunger. Maybe a little power. She was in control. It was her body that he was desperate for. Didn't she realize that?

His irritation evaporated as she straightened, shyly presenting her breasts to him. Tight pink nipples just like he'd imagined tipped the full mounds. He could easily picture holding them in his hands—pinching her nipples while he fucked her from behind. Again, her arms fluttered at her sides like she wanted to cover herself. The animal that perpetually lived inside him snarled its disapproval.

"The panties," he ordered. The words came from deep inside him — the part of him that demanded he fuck this woman as he desired — hard and long. Deep and fast. A slightly more civilized voice tried to insert itself but Nick ignored it. Tally wanted this. Something in the way she moved, the luscious scent that filled the air as she inched the scrap of material down her legs, told him she was as hungry for this fuck as he was. She wanted a guy who would be just a little wild, a little untamed.

"Get on the bed." The light in her eyes flickered again and he knew that her "lover" never treated her like this. Logic told Nick he had to leave. Now. Or at the worst, give her a fast, emotionless fuck. Something that would send her to sleep — with boredom no doubt — so he could get the hell away.

But her hunger reached for him and Nick knew he couldn't leave her like this. *Can't leave yourself like this,* that irritating voice inside his head mocked. And it was true. He'd been nursing a hard-on for almost a week now. He needed relief and he needed it inside her. She sank back onto the mattress. Her legs fell open, revealing the succulent pussy he'd been dreaming about for days. He took a quick look up to her eyes. Fear and insecurity were blended with the eager fire of lust.

"Beautiful," he said as he entered the room. "Delicious." She shuddered beneath his words and he knew then she loved the sounds as well as the touch of fucking. The insecurity faded from her eyes as he spoke. "I've dreamed about seeing you like this, spread open before me." Seductive shivers raced through her body. Her legs moved restlessly across the sheets as if she was aching between those sleek thighs.

The sweet, almost shy woman from the coffee shop was disappearing before his eyes.

Unable to resist touching her in some way, he eased his hand up her thigh, pressing against the wet V of her sex. She gasped as she pumped her hips upward, pushing herself against his hand.

"Please, Richard. Touch me."

The sound of the other man's name on her lips drew him back. The voice of his conscience finally broke through, screaming its objections. He couldn't make love to her. There were too many potential complications. But he also couldn't leave her like this—her beautiful body spread before him, hungry and aroused. He couldn't leave her without some satisfaction. It would make her more suspicious if he suddenly left.

Mocking his own silent justification, he crawled over her, stretching out beside her, still fully dressed and hating the feel of the silk shirt against him when it should be her skin.

He wouldn't fuck her, he silently vowed. He would just tease her a bit, give her a little pleasure then he'd notice the time and remind her that he had an early flight. Richard seemed like that kind of guy.

She reached for him but Nick leaned just out of reach and shook his head. She seemed to hear the silent command and lowered her hands to the mattress. Nick groaned at the subtly submissive position. Damn, he wanted her hands on him but knew he wouldn't be able to resist if she touched him. That's what had happened downstairs. A few kisses and he was leading with his dick.

He propped himself up on his elbow and looked at her— memorizing the curves and lines of her body. He would never have another chance to lie beside her like this, see her and touch her freely. Tomorrow he would report to his client and then he'd disappear from her life. As he watched, she blushed, the pale pink adding a delicious shine to her breasts.

"You're incredible." The temptation of her skin was too much to resist any longer and he smoothed his hand across her stomach, absorbing the satin surface and welcoming the heat into his body. He trailed his fingers in random patterns circling closer to her breasts. The tight peaks rose and fell with each shallow breath, tempting him like berries to a wild animal.

"Delicious," he whispered.

Another of those wicked shivers scurried down her spine and Tally didn't know how she could bear it.

She clawed her fingernails across the sheet, desperate for something to cling to, something besides Richard. She held herself still as he slipped his fingers across her stomach and up the slope of her breast. The cool, light caress left a trail of heat that spiraled into her pussy. She felt like a canvas as he painted his touch across her skin, every stroke leaving her alive and vibrant. Warmth pooled in her sex and the urge to move was strong. He teased her, moving close to her nipple but never quite touching it.

Bracing herself to endure the delicate caresses, she forced her breath to remain slow. None of this made sense. Richard never lingered. He squeezed, fondled and then climbed on board. But tonight he'd transformed into a slow, exotic lover. The stuff of dreams. Her eyes drooped shut and the shape of her dream lover changed. Richard's hair grew darker, longer and those wicked blue eyes were real. Nick. Damn. Even now he was invading her world.

"So beautiful," he whispered, the words sliding across her skin. Heat enveloped her breast as he exhaled across the peak. The light flicker of his tongue across her nipple sent a jolt straight into her pussy. "So delicious."

Hot, open mouth kisses, wicked laps of his tongue, moved from one breast to the other as if he was exploring, sampling her. He sucked her nipple into his mouth and Tally couldn't contain her groan. He lifted his head, watching for a moment, then repeated the caress. It was like he was learning her responses for the first time.

She slid her hand up his shoulder, holding him in place. His expensive silk shirt was a lovely caress against her palm but she wanted more, wanted to feel his skin beneath her fingers. She reached between them, slipping the top buttons free. He leaned back and, for a moment, she thought he was going to leave. Instead, he reached over his shoulder and yanked the shirt over his head, tossing it on the floor like it was twenty-dollar cotton flannel.

The shirt was quickly forgotten as he pulled her to him, her breasts meeting his chest, the tight nipples rubbing against him. One large hand closed over her ass and pressed her close to him, reminding her that he was hard. Her mind swirled with the possibilities. His mouth covered hers, blocking out all thought. This was no seeking, gentle kiss. He conquered her mouth, driving his tongue deep and binding her to him with his hunger even as he pulled her thigh up, opening her pussy and sliding his knee between her legs. The slow, wicked friction ran across her clit. Delicious little shocks moved through her pussy and she squirmed trying to create more. He clamped his hand on her hip and held her in place. The violence of her need wouldn't let her remain passive. She pulled her mouth away, grabbed in a breath and then leaned down to scrape her teeth against his neck. Richard was usually worried about marks on his skin but tonight she didn't care. She needed to claim him as hers.

She nipped him again with her teeth and began to inch down, peppering kisses across his chest, laving her tongue across his nipples. Hunger surged inside her. She wanted to taste him. All of him. Run her fingers and lips over his body and make him twist in desire. She slipped one hand down, sliding it between his legs. The hard line of his cock pressed back as she massaged him through his trousers.

"Damn," he sighed as he grabbed her hand and pulled her away.

"What's wrong?" She leaned forward and gave him another gentle bite on his collarbone. It was like she wanted to eat him alive…and, fuck, he couldn't get that picture out his head. He took a deep breath, trying to send cooling, softening thoughts to his cock. Her hand slipped from his and she zeroed in on his groin, tripping her fingers lightly over him. He had to do something before he let her open his pants. If that happened, he would be lost. He would be on top of her, inside her.

Even as he mentally commanded himself to move away, his hips pumped up, rubbing his cock against her hand.

A wicked, feminine smile formed on her lips. She knew just how she was tormenting him.

Her. You're supposed to make her *come and then run.* He heard the voice in his head and nodded. He grabbed her hands and pulled them up, moving on top of her as he trapped her wrists against the mattress, her body below his.

"Yes," she sighed, arching against him, her pussy massaging his cock, heating it and promising warmth and pleasure. His teeth snapped together to keep the moan inside.

"Let me," he said, leaning down and placing breathless, reverent kisses on her breasts, her nipples, vowing one day to come back and learn her every curve, sample these treats with his own senses. He kissed his way down, losing himself in the flavor of her skin and the soft flutter beneath his lips as he drew closer to her sex. The sweet scent of her arousal muffled the logical voice in his head. The heady scent washed over him as he sank his fingers into her pussy. Damn, he needed to taste her. He inched down—the deep pink flesh before him, ready, open and hungry. He bent forward, focusing on the target in front of him.

Her legs snapped shut and she curled them upward. Nick looked up, surprised at the sudden change in her body. She'd been pure liquid passion up until this point. "What are you doing?" she demanded.

"I would have thought that was obvious." Even as he said the words he realized he'd made a critical error. This was one of many reasons why it was unwise to take another human's form. There was no way to know all the nuances of a relationship. Maybe she hated oral sex. Damn, he hoped she didn't hate it. He had a fondness for the activity.

"But you don't do that."

"What? Go down on you?" She nodded. The tiny lines around her eyes deepened. Suspicion and confusion flickered through her gaze, along with a flash of interest. "Well, I think it's time I tried it...again." He let his desire rumble through his words. "Let me taste your pretty cunt."

Her eyes widened, hunger returning to their green depths. He waited—patient and prepared to withdraw. When she didn't move, he curled his hand over her knee, pulling her leg down. She relaxed, moving with him until she was once again open to him.

"May I taste you?" he asked, placing a kiss on the inside of her thigh. She nodded, slowly and cautiously. A gentleman probably would pull away but he couldn't—not when she was staring at him with those wide, increasingly hungry eyes. He trailed his tongue across her skin, drawing closer to her pussy. Forcing himself to go slowly, he was rewarded when moments later, the tension eased from her muscles and her thighs opened wider. He leaned forward, cautiously licking the peak of her mound.

He looked up and hesitant pleasure stared back at him—as if she was afraid to enjoy it. He silently cursed her boyfriend. *Bastard.*

He continued the slow teasing strokes, monitoring her reactions. He trailed his tongue up the inside folds of her pussy, lapping at her wet flesh. Delicate strokes until she moved against him. The subtle rocking of her hips made his cock twitch. She would be so hot when he fucked her. He moaned against her clit, imagining the tight grip of her cunt as he slid into her. The reasons for not having her were fading fast from his mind and the voice of his conscience became a whisper. He wanted her. Needed to have her, fill her.

He slipped two fingers into her pussy—testing her first then thrusting hard inside her. She cried out. The shocked sound quickly changed into a groan. Yeah, she liked it. He lapped at her clit, rubbing his tongue across her in time to the deep penetration of his fingers. The slow movements of her hips picked up as she pumped against him, fucking herself onto his hand. Her delicious moan reached deep inside him—driving him on.

He opened his lips over her clit and sucked lightly, countering the motion with another hard thrust inside her. The shocked cry told him he'd found the right spot. He scraped his fingers softly across the inside of her sex, rubbing the delicate flesh. Her body tensed beneath him. He repeated the motion, building the tension until he felt it in his own body.

Desperate hunger—the need to feel her come—drew him on. He licked and sucked, stroking her inside, massaging that spot that made her groan, working her hard until her body shuddered with release and her wild cry filled the room.

Tally bolted upright, her body jerked forward by the orgasm that swirled through her body. She stared down at the man lying between her legs, his mouth still teasing her clit, his fingers moving inside her. As she watched him he raised his head. There were no words to speak—nothing to say. She needed him.

They came together—both reaching for the other. She grabbed his shoulders and pulled him over her. The orgasm that had ripped through her core seconds ago was gone and all that was left was the desire for more. More of him. She worked at his pants, fumbling with the zipper, loving the way he tensed with each brush of her fingers along his erection. Laughing softly, she undid his fly and pushed the pants and briefs down. Richard took over, sliding them the rest of the way off. With the same casual disregard he'd shown for his shirt, he threw his pants over the side of the bed like they offended him.

He stared at her and Tally felt it all the way through her body. The blue of his eyes glittered bright and hungry. He wanted her, was desperate to have her. Always before she'd felt that Richard had sex with her because it was expected—that's what couples did after a date. This Richard *wanted* her. His body was taut and tight, as if he was fighting the urge to overwhelm her. Her pussy vibrated with delicious tension.

"Please," she whispered, pulling him close. She ran her hands across his chest and shoulders. She'd seen him, touched him, dozens of times but tonight he was a different man, like there was something wild and hungry inside him.

He moved with her, taking her mouth with his. The warm musky flavor of her own sex melted on her tongue. She curled her leg around his back. Pulling him close, she lost herself in his kiss. It was pure hunger. She closed her eyes and savored the power of his lips and tongue, the hot pressure of his hands sampling her body.

The first intrusion of his cock snapped her back to reality.

"Wait!" She pressed her hand onto his shoulder, holding him two painful inches away. "Condom." She kissed him again, not moving far. She reached behind her and grabbed a condom that she kept in the bedside drawer. She was on the Pill but for some reason had never told Richard he didn't need to wear a condom. Not that she didn't trust him. Or maybe she didn't. Either way, they still used them. He drew back, kneeling between her legs and putting too much space between them — as if he had to pull away or risk fucking her without protection.

He made no move to take the condom from her. His cock stood hard and thick between their bodies as his hands curled into fists at his sides. Heat, hunger and a shot of male arrogance flashed at her though his eyes. Sexual power spun through her core and she met his gaze with an arrogance of her own. Knowing he watched, she placed the latex on the tip of his penis and slowly rolled it up the shaft, stroking him, squeezing him as she sheathed him. It wasn't merely a practical act — it was a caress.

His forearms clenched as if he fought the urge to reach for her. He was at the edge of his control. Tally wrapped her hands around his cock, letting her fingers pet him as she drew back, luring him forward.

"Damn," he whispered as he followed, guiding her back until she was supine and he lay between her spread thighs.

She held her breath, waiting and waiting. Finally she looked up. He was looking at her as if he'd never seen her before. As if she was a fascinating new treasure before him—a treasure he wanted but couldn't touch.

"Richard?" she asked, concern squeezing through the lust pumping through her veins.

He said something softly under his breath, so soft she couldn't hear, but she could feel him pulling away. *No!* Her body screamed its silent protest.

He lifted his head and stared down at her. The torment in his eyes was balanced by a vivid hunger that couldn't be denied. They didn't speak. He reached between their bodies and placed his cock to her entrance. Heat flooded her pussy as the very tip slipped inside. *So good.* Her hips rolled in unconscious response, trying to draw him into her, but he shook his head.

He held her hips and slowly pushed into her. Tally grabbed at his rib cage, holding on as he penetrated. Slow and deep until he was seated fully inside her. She gasped in her breath. It had never felt this good before. Richard was big enough but he usually fucked her in a rush. Tonight, it was like he didn't want to hurry, didn't want to miss any sensation. He pushed deeper as if to assure himself he was as far as he could go, then drew back. It was the same long lovely slide.

"You feel so good," he murmured as he filled her again. She could only groan her agreement. "I'm not sure how long I can last, baby," he warned.

Tally smiled. "Don't worry. Just fuck me." She never dared command Richard like that but tonight it felt right. And it was an honest answer. She'd come once—gloriously—now she wanted to feel him, wanted him moving inside her.

"As you wish." He placed a seductive kiss on her lips and began to move, riding her slowly. Tally sighed as he entered her again and again, heavy, sensual thrusts. Despite his comment that he wouldn't last long, he seemed in no hurry. Even when he seemed to be fighting himself, he moved slowly, finding the way she liked to be fucked. She didn't know how long he moved inside her, only that each stroke was a streak of pleasure. Coils of heat built inside her, drawing every part of her body into her core. With each penetration and retreat he bound her tighter until her physical world was concentrated between her thighs — and she needed more.

She wrapped her legs around his back and dug her heels into his ass. "Harder," she said, her voice muffled by his neck. Her body was riding a thin ledge and all she needed was a little push to send her over. "Please." The desperate pleading to her voice didn't bother her a bit. She was lost in the world of Richard. Needing him.

As if that was the signal he'd been waiting for, he thrust in hard. Tally cried out. *Yes, that was it.* She rocked against him, using all her strength to counter his penetration, wanting him deeper, harder. He seemed to want the same thing, filling her over and over again until she could only take what he gave her, her body overloaded and all she could do was accept him.

His breath was harsh as he surged into her. It was sweaty and messy and she loved every minute of it. He wanted her. This was no casual-just-because-he-paid-for-dinner fuck. He wanted her.

Tally felt her fingernails bite into his skin but couldn't release her grip. Every muscle in her body was locked in anticipation. *Oh my God, it's happening again. He's doing it again.* His finger rubbed the side of her clit and Tally screamed. She couldn't stop the sound. Didn't want to. She wanted the world to hear. She let her whole body explode into the orgasm that flowed from her pussy then felt another jolt of pleasure as Richard pumped into her again. A harsh masculine cry rumbled through his chest as he arched his back and drove into her one final time. He held himself above her for one breath before sinking down. She wrapped her arms around him, accepting his weight, loving the feel of his softening cock inside her.

Yes, *this* was what she wanted.

Chapter Three

∞

Nick killed the light in the bathroom and stood in the doorway, staring at the woman asleep on the bed. A thin sheet covered her breasts and shoulders but her pussy and her legs were bare and still slightly spread as if she anticipated his return. Her sleeping form was a wicked contradiction—sexual satiation and defiant hunger. His cock grew again. Her legs were open. It would be so easy to slip between them, drive himself back into her. Fill her.

He growled at the thought that he'd used a condom. That his seed hadn't filled her, hadn't found a home inside her body.

He shook his head, trying to blank the image of her delicious body rounded with his child. Damn. His father had warned him this might happen some day. The urge, the primitive desire to fuck and procreate would drive him. It was part of their nature.

Nick backed away. She was much too tempting for his peace of mind. He'd already gone too far over the line...and unfortunately he wanted to return.

He glanced at the clock and silently swore. Devon would have expected him to call three hours ago.

As Nick walked down the stairs, he released his hold on Richard's form and allowed his natural shape to return. Tension bound his shoulders, just one of the hazards of holding another form for so long. Standing on the bottom step, he looked around. First order of business—he needed to check in and his cell phone was in the pocket of "Richard's" pants upstairs. He glanced around the living room, taking in an impression of the woman who lived here as he looked for a phone. The room was homey and well used. Not too tidy. Nick appreciated cleanliness as much as the next person but it was unnatural to never have anything out of place. From observing her for the past three weeks, he'd seen the rigid control she kept on the work areas of her life. It was comforting to see she relaxed those standards a bit at home. He couldn't live in a place where he couldn't make a mess.

The fact that he was looking at her house as somewhere he could "live" made him intensify his search. He had to get out of here—away from Tally's influence—before he starting planning where he'd put his couch. He finally found the phone crammed between two sofa cushions. Nick laughed softly as he grabbed the handset and dialed.

"Hello?" There was no sleep in Devon's voice so Nick knew his brother had been awake, waiting for his call.

"It's me," Nick said.

"Where the hell have you been?"

"I got…caught up."

"You got caught?"

"No, I got caught up with Tally."

There was silence on the end of the phone. "Tell me you're not calling from a target's house at two in the morning." The reprimand and warning in Devon's voice prodded Nick's conscience.

"Can we deal with that later? What did you find in her office?"

Devon paused for a minute and Nick knew his brother was deciding whether to let it go or not. "Nothing. Work files, general stuff. There was actually little there. I went through her desk and computer. Nothing seemed out of the ordinary. I was out by about eight." He paused. "Just waiting for your call."

"Yeah, I know. Well, she's asleep. Let me check around here, see what I can find. I'll talk to you tomorrow."

Nick hung up before Devon could make another comment about the situation. He didn't delude himself and assume Devon was done with the discussion. Nick had broken the first rule of shifting and he was going to hear about it.

Moving quickly, he searched the downstairs, finding her home office just off the living room. A small space with a desk, computer and file cabinet. The information was probably on her computer but if she was smart she'd long since removed it and placed it in paper files—something easily destroyed. He quickly flipped through the pages, finding nothing of interest. Most of it was personal business.

He turned on the computer and went through her electronic files. There were a few financial statements that he didn't understand. That might be what they were looking for. If she was stealing money, she had to put it somewhere. He flipped open her email and logged on. The high whine of the computer as it dialed her phone line made Nick wince and move to the door, listening for Tally. He waited until the computer was connected then sat down and emailed Jameson the questionable documents. He quickly deleted the note from her sent file and shut everything down.

He'd look at the information tomorrow. For now, he had to go back upstairs, get his clothes and slip away. He closed his eyes and let his body reshape itself, once again taking on Richard's form.

* * * * *

Tally rolled over and rubbed her hand across the empty sheet. He was gone. Damn. A thread of disappointment swirled around her heart. Richard usually left after sex or gently kicked her out of his apartment but she'd hoped, thought, that after tonight's experience he might stay. Cool air tripped over her skin and Tally pulled a blanket over her, trying to make up for the warmth she'd lost when Richard had left. She draped one arm over her eyes, letting her mind wander through the night. There had been something definitely different about him.

He'd been exciting, commanding. Sexual. She tipped her head back, remembering the sweet pressure of his mouth on her sex. For a man who claimed to not like oral sex, he seemed to know his way around a pussy. Her sex began to tingle. Damn, why tonight of all nights, when he'd miraculously turned into the lover she'd always craved, did he have to disappear?

It was late, or early actually, but she wasn't sure she could fall asleep. She could always get up and work. She had a briefcase full of stuff that could be done. The thought sounded wholly unappealing. What she wanted to do was Richard.

A footstep on her top stair gave her a jolt. She sat up, clutching the blanket around her. He stepped into the room. The light of surprise in his eyes matched hers.

"You're still here." The breathless pleasure of her voice curled through his insides like streaks of fire. His cock rose, stretching to reach her. Even as he told himself this was a bad idea, he placed one knee on the mattress and crawled onto the bed, unable to resist the chance to have her one more time. One last time.

One hand immediately went to her thigh, slipping up under the soft material of the blankets. "I thought you'd left," she whispered.

"How could I leave you without one more taste?" He pushed the material up and out of his way, baring her pussy. "Spread your legs for me, baby. Let me see you."

A shiver zipped through her body and flowed into his like an electrical current. The intensity of the sensation penetrated the back of his mind—the center of his shifting power. The image of Richard wavered in his brain. Nick clamped down on the picture, locking it into place.

Tally pushed her legs apart and the intriguing scent of her arousal again commanded his senses. He bent over and placed a light kiss on the very top of her sex, teasing her clit with his tongue. Her body tightened, tensing with the delicate stroke. More liquid flowed down her pussy and Nick couldn't resist. He placed the flat of his tongue at her opening and licked long and up, gathering her taste. The picture in his brain shimmered. His form—his *natural* form was fighting to come through. His jaw tightened as he struggled to control the shape.

He jerked back, knowing the abruptness startled her.

"Wha—?"

"Don't worry, I'm not leaving you, baby." He pushed his finger into her pussy, filling the place where his tongue longed to touch. He should leave—this was dangerous—but there was no way he could deny his body this pleasure. He had to have her. One last time. "Roll over."

The heat in her eyes flashed for a moment and he wondered again if he'd made a mistake, if this was one of the ways that Richard didn't like to fuck. *Damn, is the man just stupid? He has a sexual, sensual creature like this to take to bed and he doesn't take advantage of it.*

"What's wrong?" he asked when she didn't move. He'd moved into another tricky area. Maybe *she* didn't like it from behind. Tension clamped down his shoulders as he waited for her answer.

"You've just never wanted to do it like this before." The blush on her cheeks made him harder.

"That was before I saw your ass in those silk pants you wore tonight." He pumped his finger into her again and felt her grip him. "I've been thinking about it all night." It was the truth, as far as it went. In reality, he'd been thinking about it since he'd first seen her wearing a skirt. He rubbed his hand across her stomach. "Imagining how it will feel to fuck you hard and deep. Have you push back against me." His words sent the images into his brain, weakening the control he had on his form. "Roll over," he urged. She groaned and twisted as if the combined prompting of his hands and his words were too much. "That's it, baby."

She turned, easing onto her stomach, her tight rounded ass presented to him. Nick smoothed his hand over her skin, conforming his palm to her curves, loving the satin of her skin. The shy but excited look she flashed over her shoulder heightened the need in his cock. He gripped her hips, pulling them high and easing his cock between her spread thighs.

"Have you ever taken a man like this, baby?"

Tally responded to the low sensual question. She shook her head. She'd been intrigued by the idea but had never found the courage to ask any of her lovers — until Richard, and he hadn't sounded interested so she'd dropped it.

"I'll feel even bigger inside you." He pumped his cock against her pussy lips, gentle pulses that promised more. Tally gripped her pillow and smashed it to her face. She couldn't believe this was happening. Energy spun through her body, pooling in her pussy. She'd never felt so alive — so wickedly sensual that every touch, every brush of his fingers was like a mini-orgasm. "You'll be sore," he promised. "Because I'm going to fuck you. Hard. Is that what you want?"

"Yes." The answer came out soft and breathless.

"I didn't hear you, baby. If you don't answer me, I'm going to think you don't want this. You wouldn't want me to leave, would you?" He punctuated his question by grinding his hips against her ass. The rough hair around his cock was like hundreds of little fingers stroking her.

"No."

"So tell me," he commanded. "Do you want me to fuck you hard?"

"Yes!"

"That's it, my sweet Tally. Let me hear how much you want me to fuck you."

"Yes, please fuck me." She pumped back against him, feeling sexy and wild as she offered her pussy to him.

He placed the tip of his cock against her opening and began to push in. Just as he'd promised, he felt thicker and larger. She groaned, loving the almost painful sensation of being stretched.

"Tally, you are so wet. You'll take me, won't you, baby?" She nodded her head and rolled her hips, encouraging him deeper. He slid into her—countering his slow, steady penetration with shallow delicious pulses that left her hungry for more.

"Please."

Her plea was so quiet he barely heard her but the wiggle of her hips told him all he needed to know.

Nick pushed a little more into her and had to grit his teeth to keep from shouting. It was perfect. Like coming home. She accepted him and held him, pulling him deeper. He growled as he gripped her hips and punched forward, driving the last two inches deep into her pussy.

"Richard!" she cried, her face buried in the blankets.

The sound of another man's name on her lips while *he* was buried inside her made his blood burn. It should be *his* name that she cried. *His* cock buried in her tight cunt.

Even as he thought the words he felt his body shift, flowing into his natural form. He clutched at Richard's image, the illusion he'd created, trying to stop the transition—but as he did, Tally surged back, fucking herself on his shaft. The wet heat of her pussy was too much for his overloaded mind. All his focus contracted to his cock.

Distraction was deadly. He knew it but he couldn't fight it. His body swelled, stretching and filling out to his natural form.

"Oh my God." Tally's fingers dug into the pillow. She groaned. "What did you just do? It feels like you grew two inches inside me."

The grip of her sex tightened around his cock. He opened his mouth, preparing the sensual command to relax and enjoy but realized he couldn't speak. When he'd slipped out of his borrowed form, his voice had returned to normal. He no longer spoke with Richard's smooth, slick tones.

"Let me have you," he urged, deliberately keeping his voice soft and low. "Just like this, let me have this sweet little cunt." He accented his words with a long slow retreat and a heavy penetration. He wished the lights were on so he could see the delicate flush of her skin because he knew she was blushing. "It's mine. Let me have it."

She nodded and hid her face between her hands. Words wanted to burst from his throat — how sexy she was and how much he loved fucking her — but he couldn't say them. He squeezed his lips together and let his body move, a small part of him secretly hoping she recognized the difference in her lovers.

He held her hips and pulled her back as he thrust forward. The long slick slide of his cock into her cunt was a sensual journey. He held himself inside her for a moment, savoring the tight grip, but he couldn't fight the need for long. The need to move and take her, consume her senses. He drew back and began to fuck her. Hard, just as he promised her.

Tally buried her face in the pillow as he pounded into her. Her body was screaming with exhaustion and future soreness but she didn't want him to stop. He felt so good inside her. Richard had never filled her this way before. He'd never fucked her this way before. Not just the position but with such intensity. It was as if he couldn't tolerate being away from her. That each time he withdrew he had to be back inside her.

And he felt huge inside her. She knew this position made a man feel bigger but he seemed to touch every inch of her pussy. He was silent with none of the sexy words he'd used the first time they'd made love tonight. She found herself missing the guttural utterances, wanting to hear as well as feel his desire.

Without his voice, her mind took control, picturing him as he fucked her. The hard deep thrusts continued to power into her pussy but it wasn't Richard who moved within her. It was Nick. Riding her, loving her. Nick with his mysterious blue eyes and seductive power.

She groaned and shoved the pillow into her mouth, fighting the urge to scream his name. A twinge of guilt drifted through her but the worry faded as he slid his finger between her folds and began to rub. The tiny pulses along her clit perfectly matched the heavy thrusts of his cock inside. Lights began to twinkle behind her eyelids. She crammed the pillow against her mouth to hide her screams, not wanting it to end but she was so close. Each time he slid into her he reached that one spot that made her eyes water.

"Come for me, my sweet lover. Come for me." He punctuated the command with a deep thrust and Tally gasped. Molten waves radiated from her sex, melting her body from the inside. "Yes, that's it." As he thrust into her she had the vague awareness that it wasn't Richard's voice but then he burst inside her, filling her with his cum. Heat and shock drove the concern from her mind. Her body, relaxed from her climax, struggled to hold her up but she collapsed face down on the bed. Richard quickly followed, rolling behind her and pulling her back against his chest. Even here, after his cock had slipped from her body, he felt different. Larger. A different man entirely.

She mentally mocked the idea but the memory of his shout kept bringing it back. She knew that voice. She'd heard it before.

From Nick.

This was bad. Her fantasies of Nick were becoming too real.

Taking a deep breath, she rolled over, ready to face Richard. He lay beside her, his eyes shut, his jaw tense.

"What's wrong?" She waited, silently praying she hadn't called out Nick's name.

His eyes snapped open. The false blue depths looked stormy and dangerous. "Uh, nothing." The dismissive way he shook his head told her she hadn't cried out Nick's name but Richard was clenching his teeth for a reason. The warm, liquid satisfaction of her orgasm quickly faded.

"You didn't like it?" she asked, latching onto the only possibility. He'd seemed to enjoy it. Drat, there went her chance of having him that way again.

"What do you mean, didn't like it?" He pushed himself to sitting, staring down at her with an intensity that brought a blush to her cheeks. "Didn't like what?"

She shrugged and looked away. "The position. I mean it's okay if you didn't, it's just that sometimes—"

His hand curled around her shoulder, turning her around to face him.

"Baby, I loved fucking you that way. Feeling that tight little ass pressed against me." He released her arm only to slide his hand between her legs. The warmth of his skin flowed through her aching pussy. "I could barely get it in you before I wanted to come." He pushed one finger inside, timing the gentle pulses with his words. "But you felt so good, so tight I couldn't stop. I had to have more of you." He rubbed his fingertip along the inside of her pussy. She inhaled sharply and arched up. "You like that, don't you? You like knowing how addicted I am to this sweet cunt."

She sagged back onto the bed. Nick moved over her but didn't try to penetrate her. He couldn't. His control over this form was tenuous. She was so fucking sexy and her asshole lover didn't seem to know it. He slipped a second finger into her, determined to give her one more climax before he disappeared from her life.

Her pussy tightened around him and his cock lengthened, responding to the delicate grip. He shoved his arousal away and concentrated on her, on making her come. It didn't take long— her body was primed and slick. He countered the firm thrusts of his fingers with a light massage of her clit—all while he stared at her, watching the passion illuminate her face.

"That's it, baby. I love watching you come. Let me feel it again. Let me hear you." His words encouraged her along. She moved against his hands, her fists pulling him to her. Her thighs slid open and he knew she would accept him if he wanted to fuck her. He shook his head, gently rejecting her silent offer but he would make sure she didn't go without. He increased his pace, fucking his fingers into her. The soft cries flowing from her mouth were too much for him. He leaned down and captured her lips. Her tongue whipped around his, drawing him in, binding him to her.

He accepted her scream as she came and felt the soft flutters of her cunt along his fingers. He didn't stop moving. Kept pumping into her, slower, drawing out each bit of pleasure.

When she finally seemed done, he lifted his head. Her eyes were wide and glassy and a delicate blush had bloomed across her cheeks and breasts. She looked sated and sexual. His cock stretched. Damn, he wanted her again. Him, not this made-up version of a body he was inhabiting. He wanted to fuck her, ride her until she screamed his name.

"Sleep, baby," he whispered. Silently, she curled into him, her legs entwining with his. He ground his teeth together as her smooth skin slid over his, hoping she settled soon. He had to get out of there. Before she woke up and looked at him with those warm green eyes and he said to hell with the case.

Chapter Four

🔊

Nick walked into the office at nine, grateful to be back in his own body and his own clothes. Without greeting his brothers or sister, he went into his office and shut the door. He wasn't in the mood to talk to anyone. His mind was still trying to come to terms with last night.

He dropped into his chair and stared up at the ceiling. He'd managed to successfully avoid thinking about it all morning—focusing on escaping from Tally's house and getting to the office. But now there was no escaping it. His conscience was screaming and it asked the same question repeatedly. What the fuck had he done? He'd had sex with a target. That alone wasn't that big of deal. Sometimes that was the best way to get close to a mark—but doing it in her boyfriend's form... It was just wrong. Unethical. And quite possibly the most erotic experience of his life.

He couldn't even blame it on anything—except lust. He'd known what he was doing. He hadn't run when he'd had the chance.

She had no idea who she'd been in bed with last night—who'd come inside her body. His stomach did a slow, sickening roll.

A light tap on the door was the only warning he had before his door opened and Devon walked in. He shut the door behind him. The grim look on his face warned Nick that his brother was going to ask the same question he'd been asking himself.

"Tell me what you found," Nick said, hoping to forestall Devon's inquisition. He needed to get this case moving, get Tally off his target list and what? Into jail? Into bed?

Devon didn't take offense at Nick's brusque question. "Like I said last night, nothing unusual. Work-related stuff. I couldn't find anything proprietary. She spends her time dealing with the financials. Seems to be interested in this plant in Georgia they're selling but again, that didn't seem to be classified information." Devon dropped into a chair. "Maybe they're looking at the wrong person."

Nick didn't like the way his stomach clenched at the idea. He was supposed to be proving her guilt, not searching for the reasons she might be innocent.

"Or she might keep the information with her," he said. "She carries a briefcase. It's either with her or it's locked somewhere safe. I'm guessing she'll have any important information there."

Devon shrugged. "Your call but from what you've said and what I saw on her computer, I think we're heading the wrong direction."

Nick stared at his brother. He trusted Devon's instincts. "While I keep working on her, let's try to find out as much as we can about the guys who've hired us."

"Sure."

Devon nodded but didn't move.

"What?" Nick finally demanded.

"Want to explain what you were doing in a target's house at two a.m. when you left with her eight hours earlier in *her boyfriend's* form?"

Nick knew there was no way he was getting out of this discussion. Devon would keep pushing.

"I slept with her."

Devon waited but Nick wasn't going to fill in the silence. "As…" Devon finally prompted. He knew the answer but wasn't going to give up until Nick admitted to it.

"As her boyfriend."

"Damn it, Nick, are you crazy?!" Devon's shout shattered against the window. He slapped his open palm onto the desk.

"The first rule of shifting is no intimate contact with a target while in another person's form. You know that."

"Of course I know that."

The door swung open. "What's all the commotion?"

Nick glared at Devon, warning him not to say anything to their sister and brother who stepped curiously into his office. It only took him a moment to realize they'd been waiting outside for a chance to burst in. They'd obviously known something was up. There were no secrets in this family.

"Nick slept with a target while he was in her boyfriend's form," Devon announced.

"What?" Caitlin laughed. Her wide eyes locked on Nick. "But the first rule is no—"

"I know the blasted rules. I wrote them and yes, I know it was wrong."

"Then why did you do it?" The logical question came from Jameson, the youngest in their family.

Nick faced the wide-eyed stares of his brothers and sister and wasn't sure he could explain. Hell, he *couldn't* explain but maybe he could come up with a plausible excuse. "I hadn't planned on it but there she was and she was so sexy and her boyfriend's such an asshole. He's fucking his secretary and Tally doesn't even know it. And from her reactions, he's lousy in bed and—"

"And you thought you'd show her what she was missing?" Caitlin asked. The smirk on her face inspired Nick to glare right back.

"I think it was better than what she's been getting."

"Did you manage to hold your form?" Devon asked. Nick didn't respond for a moment. He wanted to tell them it was none of their business but it was. If he screwed up, they could all be exposed. Finally, Nick shook his head. "Damn it," Devon threw himself out of the chair. "And now we have to—"

"Wait. I don't understand." Jameson had only recently begun shifting and didn't grasp all the nuances or hazards.

Devon sent another disapproving glare to Nick before turning back to Jameson. "The problem with having sex with someone while you're in another form, besides the tacky moral complications—" Another glare at Nick. "—is it's difficult to maintain the form you've chosen. All those endorphins running through your body make it difficult to hold a complex shape. Especially another human."

Jameson looked confused but nodded. "But if you lost your form, what did the lady say?"

"She didn't notice."

Caitlin coughed as if his answer choked her. "How could she not notice something like that?"

Nick felt his cheeks heat up and waited, hoping that someone would change the subject. Or that aliens would land on the roof and distract his family. Nope. Nothing.

All three siblings stared at him, eagerly awaiting his answer. Finally he sighed.

"I was behind her at the time."

Caitlin held up her hand. "More information than I needed to know."

"And more than I wanted to share but you were so damn curious." He waved his hand, indicating he was done with this conversation. "Let's forget it happened and move on. Devon checked out her office computer last night and found nothing. I searched her home office and there was nothing. I sent Jameson some information last night from her home computer." Nick looked up and raised his eyebrows.

"Still working on it. Nothing looks out of the ordinary."

"Keep on it. She carries a briefcase. I need to see the inside of it. Might have what we're looking for."

"What are you going to do?"

"Go back into her house."

"How?" Caitlin rested her hip against the desk and smiled innocently. "The boyfriend?"

"No. He's out of town," Nick answered, ignoring her attitude. "I could fudge it for one day but I can't risk it another. I thought I'd have her 'boyfriend' send her a present while he was gone. A little something to remember him by. It will get me inside and then I'll be able to search as she's sleeping."

He looked at his family. They nodded and shrugged in agreement but he could see a mixture of concern—and in the case of his sister, amusement—at his situation.

"What are you going in as? Flowers?" Devon said with enough mockery to show he didn't approve of Nick's plan.

Nick shook his head. "Too complicated. Too many separate pieces."

"A box of candy?" Jameson offered.

"She might eat me—don't say it," he said to Caitlin, knowing the words were on her lips.

Caitlin snapped her fingers. "I've got it. A vibrator."

All three men stared at her and Nick knew his brothers had the same stunned look on their faces.

"What?" he asked.

"A vibrator. It's all one piece. She's going to take it out of the package because no woman—particularly not after a night of really wild sex, which I'm assuming is what you had but I really don't want any more details—is going to be able to resist. Even if she doesn't use it, she'll open it up." She fluttered her eyelashes. "It's a sexy gift from her guy when he's out of town."

Nick tapped his fingers against the desktop and considered the idea. The objections rose fast and furious in his head. One, he hated the thought of "Richard" sending Tally anything remotely sexual. He didn't want to end up making Tally like the guy even more. Plus, inanimate object shifts muffled the senses and bound the shifter into the form. Nick wouldn't be able to bring himself out of the shape. He would have to wait until the form released him. Something that small would probably be about four hours.

Physically, he could do it. It had been years since he'd attempted anything this complicated. Images of Tally, stretched out on her bed, rubbing a vibrator up the insides of her thighs, slipping it into her pussy filled his head. He could almost feel the heat enveloping his body. He knew just how hot and wet her pussy could be.

"What if she doesn't open the box?" Jameson asked, interrupting Nick's fantasy. "Some women aren't into sex toys or might feel shy about using it. What if he comes out of the form, she hasn't opened it—he bursts out of the box and scares the shit out of her?"

Caitlin swallowed and Nick could swear she was trying to hold back her laughter. "Trust me. She'll open it. If she's not into sex toys, she'll leave it downstairs and you'll have free rein of the house."

"I'm going to pop out of the form about four hours after I'm put into it." Larger shapes didn't blind the senses quite as much, making them a little easier to control.

"We'll deliver it at bedtime."

"What about in the morning? How am I going to get out of her house? I'll be naked and she might—"

"You're just stalling because you don't think women should play with sex toys," Caitlin huffed dramatically.

"I don't believe that. Hell, I love to watch—" Caitlin held up her hand. "Why am I suddenly discussing my sex preferences with my sister?"

"I don't know but it's creeping me out. I've given you a viable option. You're the only one in the family who could possibly do this."

Nick nodded. It was true. He had an affinity for shapes— any shape, any size. None of his siblings could shrink their bodies into tiny forms. They were stuck with almost equal-sized objects and even then, Jameson hadn't mastered being inanimate.

But turning into a vibrator? It seemed a little tawdry, he thought righteously, but no other option came to mind and that image of Tally sliding a thick cock into her pussy dug itself into his mind and wouldn't let go.

"I guess—"

"Great," Caitlin interrupted before he could finish his thought. "Now, you just have to go buy one."

"What?"

"Well, you've got to have something to sample, unless you've turned into a vibrator at some point in your life, which I'm assuming not. And you need something to leave behind when you disappear tomorrow morning."

Damn, she was right. To turn into an object, he needed to touch it, copy its shape and energy into his body.

"So you go pick it out."

Caitlin's lips squished together as she considered her brother. "Okay."

Trepidation filled Nick's chest as she walked away. That had been way too easy.

The concern was still weighing on his mind when he walked into the coffee shop thirty minutes later. Being a Saturday morning, it was crowded with the weekend late breakfast crowd but he immediately found Tally sitting in the corner. She stared out the window. He watched for a moment, trying to gauge her mood. The relaxed, sexually satisfied woman he'd left a few hours ago had disappeared. This one had a deep thought crinkle building in her forehead.

As if she sensed his stare, she turned and looked toward him. The grim set of her mouth disappeared and she smiled, though some hesitancy lingered in her eyes. He worked his way through the tables and sat down across from her.

"Good morning."

"Morning," he replied.

The low sexy greeting sank into her core and a warm shiver slid down Tally's spine. It would be so easy to imagine him rolling over in bed, greeting her in that bedroom voice and then making slow lazy love on a Saturday morning.

"Hellooo, Tally." She snapped to attention and smiled at Nick. "I lost you there for a moment."

"Oh, sorry. I have a lot running around my head this morning." She pushed the second paper cup toward him. "I got you a coffee. The line was getting long."

He smiled his thanks. "Great." She watched his lips as he carried the cup to his mouth and took a sip. Her pussy fluttered with a strange combination of memory and anticipation. Trying to ease the ache, she rocked forward in her chair. The subtle motion only made it worse. *Damn, you would think I'd be immune after last night but it seems great sex makes me crave more.*

Richard. Remember Richard. It was sex with Richard that made you feel this way. She looked at Nick, trying to remember what Richard looked like. The memories from the night before washed over her but instead of Richard's body, Richard's voice, it was Nick. Over her, inside her, *his* mouth tasting her pussy. The hungry growl as he pumped inside her.

"Tally? Are you okay?"

She flinched and felt her cheeks burn. "Sorry."

"You keep wandering off. Something you want to talk about?"

"Yes. No. I don't know."

Nick leaned back in his chair. "Come on. You can tell me anything." There was no smile in his eyes. Something seemed to be weighing on his mind. Maybe her minor problems—having great sex shouldn't be a problem, right?—would take his mind off whatever was bothering him.

And it would help to have a second opinion. "Okay, so I had a date with…" *My boyfriend?* No. That didn't sound right. She wasn't planning to continue the relationship, was she? One night of hot sex couldn't make up for the months boredom. Or maybe it could. "With Richard—this guy I've been seeing." Nick's lips tightened at the corners and she almost stopped but she needed to talk to someone. "And well, it was great. We had a wonderful time. Or I did. I'm assuming he did."

"He did," Nick said, moving forward and propping his elbows on the table.

"How do you know?"

He licked his lips like he was thinking through his answer. "Because you exude positive energy and if you're happy, it's hard for the people around you not to feel the same way."

Unexpected tears pricked her eyes. It was so sweet. He knew the right thing to say.

"Thank you."

Nick nodded. "So you had a good time, what's the problem?"

"It wasn't right. This wasn't Richard. I kept expecting a snobby comment about the pizza place or my house but it never came." She sank down, feeling her body collapse onto itself. "And the sex." She remembered who she was talking to and straightened. "Sorry. Shouldn't have said that."

He tensed but shook his head. The words sounded a little forced when he said, "No, it's fine. Think of me as one of your girlfriends. What about the sex?"

Tally laughed. She could barely imagine him as one of her male friends let alone a girlfriend. But he'd asked and he was here.

"It was great. Amazing."

"And it's not usually like that?"

"God, no." She slapped her palm across her mouth, stopping the flood of words. "Sorry, I shouldn't have said it quite like that."

Nick's eyes twinkled but it didn't look like he was laughing at her. More that he was pleased with her outburst.

"It's just, Richard's always been very, traditional, I guess is the best way to say it."

"And last night he wasn't?"

"Not at all. It was like he was a different man. All night. Not just the sex." She fiddled with her empty coffee cup. "Now I don't know what to do. I mean, I was all set to break up with him…"

"Yes."

"…but now? I don't know. Last night he was the man I'd always dreamed about and I don't want to miss the chance with him. And why am I telling you this?" She rubbed her hand across her eyes. "I'm sorry. It's rude, isn't it, for me to be talking to you about another guy."

"I wouldn't be sitting here if I wasn't willing to listen."

"I'm done with my wishy-washy stuff." She looked around the coffee shop, anxious to find a new topic of conversation. "I've never seen it so busy here. I'm usually only downtown during the week."

"Going into your office this afternoon?"

"I was but it's too nice. Plus, I didn't ever find my access badge, so I'd have to sign in and it's not worth it. I keep all my files on a disk so I can work anywhere."

"You work too much," he said, reminding her of their conversation yesterday. "You need to have fun once in a while."

She laughed. Last night had been fun. Lots of fun. She could do with that kind of fun but she wasn't going to say that to Nick. He'd heard enough of her issues this morning.

Determined to keep her thoughts away from her night with Richard, she asked about Nick's plans for the weekend and listened as he talked about his house. The sound of his voice was almost hypnotic, holding her attention until she finally jerked back and looked at her watch. It was almost two.

"Eek. I have errands to run," she said, smiling.

"I should go as well." They cleared their table and walked to the door. "I doubt I'll see you tomorrow but Monday? About two?" She quickly agreed but recognized the disappointment in her chest that she wouldn't see him tomorrow. It had only been a week but she'd become used to seeing him every day. No, it wasn't right. She had to break up with Richard. Even after last night, she didn't think she wanted to keep seeing him. The disappointments of the past three months couldn't be wiped out by one night.

"See you Monday."

Nick started to turn away and stopped. "Tally, you know, if you ever need anything or you're in any kind of trouble, you can call me." He handed her his business card.

She took it, more confused by the verbal message than the card. He sounded like he expected her to be in trouble. "Thanks."

She tucked the card into her pocket and looked at him. It just seemed natural to lean forward and brush her lips against his cheek. His hands lightly touched her waist, holding her near for a just a moment before releasing her. "See you Monday."

* * * * *

Nick stormed into the office at five. Guilt continued to circulate through his body but frustration was starting to bubble to the surface. He'd followed Tally as she'd run errands and visited her sister. And every time she climbed into her car, her jeans stretched across her ass and Nick thought he would come in his pants. His only consolation was that never once did she head toward her office. Whatever she was doing, it was being done either during business hours or on that disk in her briefcase. Jameson had picked up her trail a few minutes ago. He'd stay on her for the rest of the night.

Nick walked to his desk and stared at the box sitting on top.

"What the hell is this?"

"Caitlin left that," Devon said, having appeared from his office again. "That's your form for the night."

Nick picked up the box. "It's a rubber ducky."

"It's a vibrator shaped like a rubber ducky," Devon clarified, amusement dripping from his voice.

"This is what Caitlin picked? She expects me to turn into a rubber ducky vibrator? She couldn't have picked something a little more…" He scrounged for the word. "I don't know, penis-like? Macho?"

"Look at it this way," Devon said, obviously enjoying himself. "Do you really want your girlfriend more impressed by her sex toys than you?"

Nick looked at the smiling duck and shrugged. "You have a point."

"If she stays true to form, your girl will go for a walk about nine. I'll place you on the front step so you'll be there when she gets back. That makes you coming out of form at about one."

Nick nodded absently, his mind still on the fact that he was going to turn into a vibrating rubber duck.

Chapter Five

&

Tally walked up to her door and saw the package lying on the steps. Strange. She'd gone out for her nightly walk and didn't remember seeing it before she left. She picked up the box and went inside. It didn't have a mail stamp but there were official markings on it, like a delivery service had brought it by. She glanced at the clock and saw it was almost ten. Must be an after-hours delivery.

Curious, she set down her water bottle and carefully opened the package. The box inside had a familiar logo. It took her a moment to recognize it. There was a store on Fifth with that logo—a sex toy store. Tally had never been inside, preferring to do her sex toy shopping online.

Who would be sending her something from that store? Richard? Not likely.

She flipped the box open.

For a woman who needs to have fun.

Nick

Her breath exited her lungs in a rush. Nick had bought her a vibrator? She snagged her lower lip between her teeth and lifted the duck out of the box. He'd sent her a sex toy. A fun sex toy. She laughed. It was the kind of thing one of her girlfriends would send her—except Nick had sent it. Nick, the man who had starred in her most lurid fantasies.

She turned the duck around in her hands. It was warm to the touch as if it was alive. She glanced at the clock. It was late enough and it had been awhile since she'd pulled out her vibrator. Her pussy tingled with anticipation. Strange how the lack of good sex made her not want sex at all—but one night of really good fucking and it was all she could think of.

Tally walked upstairs and tossed the ducky on the bed. The box said it was waterproof but she couldn't bring herself to carry it into the shower with her. Weird pictures of her being electrocuted in the bathtub by her rubber ducky vibrator made her wince. She would never be able to explain that to her parents.

She rushed through her shower, feeling the urge to get back to her ducky. She laughed as she rinsed the conditioner out of her hair. She hadn't been this excited to go to bed since...well, since last night with Richard. *Maybe I'm just suddenly sex crazed.* She considered the idea as she dried off. It actually comforted her. That could explain why Richard seemed so phenomenal last night when every other night he'd been mediocre.

She grabbed a cotton nightgown from her dresser, resisting the urge to wear one of the lace negligees that lay at the bottom of her drawer. She was *not* dressing up for her vibrator.

She crawled into bed and picked up the rubber ducky. Its bright blue eyes stared at her. Its dopey smile made her grin in response. It was like the little beast was as eager as she was. She quickly read through the instructions and precautions. It explained how to use its beak and tail as stimulators. Tally tossed the paper on the floor. She could figure it out for herself.

Knowing her body, she needed a kick before she turned on the vibrating ducky. She flipped the light off and lay on her back, forcing her thoughts to Richard—him moving over her, thrusting inside her. The memories from last night came sharp and clear but were soon crowded out by nights of blandness. She opened her eyes and took a deep breath. She would try a different fantasy. One that she knew would inspire her response.

Nick's voice filled her head—hot and hungry. Begging to fuck her.

Let me have you. Let me inside this sweet cunt.

They were the words Richard had whispered last night but it was Nick speaking now. She arched her neck, feeling his mouth against her skin, sensing his presence. Her pussy wept in silent appreciation as she rolled the fantasy through her head.

Taking a deep breath, she flipped the switch to turn on the vibrating duck. The little body began to shake, rocking her hand. She skimmed the beak across the inside of her thighs, long teasing patterns, drawing closer to her sex. She tickled her clit and pulled away, flicking the toy along her lower lips.

Let me have you. So delicious.

Her body reacted to the wicked words that echoed through her mind. The ducky's beak grew slippery as she slid it around her sex. She closed her eyes and imagined it was Nick using it with her. Gliding it over her pussy. She rubbed it around her clit, pulsing it against the edge, feeling the delicious build.

That's it. God, you're beautiful. Come for me. Come on.

The voice commanded her response and she pressed the ducky low into her opening. The sharp vibration sent a smooth jolt into her system, triggering the clear, quick orgasm. Tally opened her eyes and stared up at the ceiling, giggling as she rolled over, her body eased, her mind relaxed. She heard the soft thump of the ducky hitting the floor as she drifted off to sleep.

Nick felt his body explode, shedding the illusion of the little rubber toy. It was quick and slightly painful as he stretched and expanded. His mind slowly caught up with the transition, shaking off the film that covered it. He froze, crouched on the floor beside the bed, listening for screams or any sign that he'd been caught. The only sound was the slow, breathy sighs of Tally. Shaking off the disorientation of having his senses muffled for so long, he slowly stood and stared down at her sleeping form.

Long, sleek legs stretched out from beneath a rather plain white nightshirt. He took a deep breath. The scent of her cunt filled his head and he realized it was all over him, lingering remnants as the rubber duck. His cock hardened at the sight and smell of her. She'd used the toy—rubbed it across her pussy.

Lust locked him in place, holding him there when he knew he should be leaving. As if she sensed his presence, Tally's eyes flickered and opened. She looked up at him and her lips curled into a sleepy smile. The instinct to escape ran through his body but he didn't move. His gaze wandered down her body landing on the hidden V of her thighs, hoping for a glimpse of the secrets beneath the white cotton gown.

"You're back." Her dreamy voice sent a shockwave through Nick's system. He nodded slowly, not wanting to startle her, wondering why she wasn't screaming. The haze of sleep lingered in her eyes. She was partially asleep, probably thought she was dreaming. He just had to ease her back into the full sleep state then he could slip away and find the disk.

"I couldn't stay away," he said, accepting the truth in his words, deliberately keeping his voice low and soothing. *Tell her to go back to sleep. Tell her to close her eyes.* He opened his mouth to speak but she moved, rolling over and reaching out. Her fingertip connected with his thigh, inches away from his erection. So close. He held himself still, unsure of what she was planning and damn, if he didn't want to find out.

She stroked her hand up, along his hip, across his stomach. He felt himself moving closer, allowing her full access. She didn't touch his cock but she came close.

Sleep. Get her back to sleep.

"Uh, maybe you should close your eyes and rest for a bit," he offered, realizing how lame the words sounded even as he said them. Damn, this woman affected more than his cock. She drove his brain to insipidness.

She laughed softly. "I'm already sleeping. Why would I want to close my eyes?" She pushed up onto her elbow and spread her fingers across his stomach muscles. "Yum. This is the best dream I've had in a while." She slid her hand down, curling her fingers around his cock. "Okay, this is the best dream I've had ever. You're so big and hard. Just like I imagined."

Nick clenched his teeth together and inhaled sharply as she stroked him. He needed to pull back—and he would, in just a minute.

It's just a dream. She thinks it's a dream.

At least this time she doesn't think she's fucking her boyfriend.

Was this any better? She thought he was part of some wet dream, a fantasy. Funny, she hadn't been surprised that it was Nick standing by her bedside—not Richard. This would be his chance to hear his name on her lips.

"Lift your nightgown for me, baby. Let me see you."

Her eyes glowed in the pale light as she rested back and pulled the nightgown up, lifting her hips to free it from below her backside. Nick grabbed the lower edge and helped her, pulling it over her head and tossing it over his shoulder.

"So beautiful." He kept his voice soft, hoping to maintain the dream-like atmosphere for just a little longer. Just long enough that he could touch her again. "Have you dreamed about me?" She nodded. "Often?"

"Every night."

Her sighed confession made his cock infinitely harder. Damn, he wanted to fuck her. Instead, he slid his hand between her legs and groaned when he encountered her moisture.

Tally pumped her hips up, unconsciously guiding the tip of his finger into her cunt. Nick couldn't resist going just a little deeper. The warm, wet pussy clung to him, almost dragging him inside.

"Oh yes," she groaned.

Oh, no, Nick thought. He had to get out of here before he did something really stupid.

"More," she sighed. She reached between her legs and grabbed his wrist, holding him in place as she moved against him. His cock rose, eager to take the place of his finger sliding in and out of her. "Please, Nick, fuck me."

Her words were like a hook dragging him forward. Even as his mind screamed that he was going to screw up the whole job—hell, his life—he couldn't stop himself, climbing onto the bed, moving between her legs. She spread her thighs eagerly as he moved over her.

"Oh, God, yes."

The warm scent of her arousal filled his head, making him dizzy with the need to taste her. He licked his lips, trying to capture her flavor from the air. He'd tasted her last night but it had been through the senses of another man. Nick wanted her for himself, wanted her flavor to linger on his tongue, in his memory. He crouched down, until his mouth hovered over her sex. With a quick flutter of his tongue, he teased her clit. His memories from last night told him where to stroke, how much pressure to apply. He circled the tight point, massaging the side until she cried out. His name. It was *his* name that was on her lips.

All logic, all sensibility told him to back off and disappear but the desire to hear her begging him, calling for him to come inside her was too much for him to control. He drew a long stroke up the length of her slit, teasing her flesh before returning and tasting, sucking on her sex lips, slipping the tip of his tongue into her opening. The now familiar sound of her gasp told him she liked the sensation. He applied pressure to the top of her entrance, rubbing the sensitive spot.

"Oh, wow, that's nice."

Very nice, he silently agreed. He reached between them and pushed two fingers into her pussy, stroking the inside as his mouth worked her clit. Licking and sucking, light strokes to carry her higher. The slow roll of her hips became sharp, erratic thrusts, as she sought the climax he held just out of her reach. The desire to feel her come pressed him on. He sucked her clit between his lips, strong and steady.

"Yes, oh, yes, that's it, Nick. Right there." Her body tightened—her knees closed around his head and her fingernails bit into his shoulder as she came.

He kept on her, easing her through another wave of orgasm. Her soft cries dragged him up—his body instinctually responding to their combined hunger. The need to have her controlled him.

Oh my God, this is the most incredible dream, Tally thought. Nothing had ever felt this good. He moved over her, holding his body above hers. She smiled up at him and stroked her finger along his cheek. "I didn't know my fantasies were that good," she giggled.

He turned his head and kissed her palm "My pleasure."

"It was *my* pleasure but I'm glad you enjoyed it." She smoothed her hand down his chest. It was just as she'd imagined—hard and strong, a faint trace of dark hair that clung to her fingers as she stroked him. "Will you come inside me? I've thought about it for days." She trailed down his breastbone to the faint ripple of stomach muscles. "What it would feel like to have you inside me. Hard and deep."

"Do you like to be fucked hard?" His voice was raspy and harsh and Tally smiled. She loved the fact that she could tempt him, make him hungry for her. Even if it was just a dream, she loved it.

"Sometimes." She curled her hand around his cock and caressed his length. "I want to be taken and fucked, loved like you're desperate to have me."

"I am," he groaned.

"Do you want to fuck me? Slide this huge cock into my pussy?" The words that fell from her mouth were more suited to a romance novel than real life but she didn't care. She liked the way they sounded. Liked the way his eyes glowed when she said them. She pumped her hand up and down his erection. His jaw tightened and his chest rose and fell in fast, harsh breaths. He wanted her. "Please, Nick," she begged, doing her best porn star imitation. "Come inside me."

He groaned and the resistance seemed to flow out of him. He drew out of her grasp but didn't move far. She tensed as he placed the thick head of his cock to her opening.

"Do you want this?" he demanded, teasing her with the first inch.

"Yes. Nick, I want you." He hesitated then drove in, filling her in one hard thrust. Tally pressed up on her shoulders her body shuddering at the sharp invasion. There was a bright sparkle of pain but it was quickly overcome by the pure pleasure of having him inside her. *This* was what she wanted—what she dreamed of every night. He hesitated for a moment and Tally waited, fearing the dream was over. That she would be left hungry and aroused as she came awake.

He took a long breath and slowly pulled back, almost leaving her. The delicious pleasure was too much for her to lose. "No, please," she begged, clutching at him.

"Oh, baby, I can't leave you. Not now."

Comforted by his assurance, she released her tight grip and rested back on the bed. "That's it," he whispered. "Let me move in you."

His words drifted over her and she rolled her hips, widening her thighs. He seemed pleased with her actions and pulled her hips up, placing her backside high on his thighs, settling his cock even deeper.

"Oh, yes, baby. God, you feel so good."

She chuckled softly. "You too."

He smiled and she felt a zing inside her chest. It was the patented Nick smile—sexy and alluring. And wicked. There was something decidedly dangerous about him. As she watched him, heat built between them. He didn't thrust, just held himself deep inside her, filling her, drawing her into him. She didn't know how long they stayed—locked together—when he began to move. Slowly pulling out before driving in deep. She cried out and held on.

She moved her hips in subtle pulses, matching his heavier thrusts. He stroked her deep—finding that place that enticed the climax from inside her pussy. She gasped as the waves broke through, holding onto him, clinging as her world spun out of control.

Nick clenched his jaw and fought the urge to come. He wasn't wearing a condom, hadn't even thought about it. Hadn't thought about anything but fucking her the way she wanted to be fucked. Hard and deep. Now that he was inside her and the sweet grip of her cunt held him, he realized he couldn't come. He might, just might, be able to convince her this was a dream— but not if she woke up the next morning sticky with his cum.

The pleasure of being inside her, of hearing his name on her lips and feeling her pussy shimmer to climax was almost enough. Almost. No, it would have to be enough. Even though he couldn't come, he couldn't pull out of her just yet. He slowed his thrusts, needing more control.

"No, hard, you promised me hard."

He laughed softly and leaned over, kissing her, nipping at her lower lip in sensual thanks for her demand. "And I've given you hard. You've come twice." He slowly drew back, crushing his own groan.

"I want more." She wrapped her legs around his back. "It's my dream, I can have more." She pumped herself against him, fucking him inside her in short, powerful thrusts. This time Nick couldn't stop the moan. She was so sensual—so lost in her own pleasure.

"One more. Let me have one more," she begged.

One more, he vowed as he pulled back and began to move hard inside her. He kept his thrusts short and deep, rubbing her pussy far inside as he stroked her clit with his finger. Her eyes widened as the double caresses built within her body. She was open and exposed. There was no effort to hide her reactions. It was as if he could see inside her mind. He pulsed within, watching her eyes widen as the pressure grew in her cunt.

"That's it, baby, come for me. Let me feel you come on my cock."

Tally pumped against him, her body caught in the pull of the pleasure. Never before had she experienced anything like this. *It's a dream, it's a dream.* It didn't matter. Need surged through her body and she moved with him, rocking her hips in sharp, fast strokes. Deep inside her—like someone had tickled her—the pressure released, fast and hard through her body. She grabbed his shoulders and pulled him down, clutching him as her body floated in the stratosphere.

He pulled his still hard cock from between her legs.

"You didn't come," she said, her words were blurred by the sensual exhaustion that dragged at her. She placed her hand against him. He was wet from being inside her, and slippery. She rubbed her hand along his shaft. Nick tensed as if her touch was painful but he didn't move away. He moved forward, urging his cock into her palm. The tiredness seemed to fade from her body as she rolled to her side. She wanted to taste him. Bending over, she flicked the tip of her tongue across the thick head. The musky flavor of her own sex floated across her tongue. She wanted more—wanted to taste him. She opened her mouth—but he jerked back.

Disappointment and embarrassment battled for control in her brain as she looked up at him. He didn't want her mouth on him?

"I'm sorry, baby, but tonight's just for you," he said. He leaned down and covered her mouth with his, pushing her back until she was flat on the bed and he was once again over her. "One day, I'm going to fuck that beautiful mouth." He licked the corner of her lips. "But now I have to go." He backed away. "Now close your eyes and sleep again. I'll be back. Soon."

He moved into the shadows, watching her as she followed him with her eyes. Finally, she sighed and closed her eyes. He waited, afraid to move, afraid to startle her.

Her breathing evened out but he knew she wasn't deeply asleep. He glanced behind him, considering the option of slipping downstairs and searching for the disk. He took a step back and her alarm screamed through the room.

Nick stared at the clock. Who set their alarm for five o'clock on a Sunday? Frozen for a moment, he saw Tally snap awake. She rolled over, moving away from him to the other side of the bed where the clock sat blinking and buzzing. Seeing no other choice, Nick gathered his form around him, pictured the rubber ducky and poured himself into the image. His body collapsed and he lost his senses.

Tally groaned as she rolled toward her bedside clock. Damn, she'd set it last night out of habit, forgetting today was Sunday. Her heart pounded in her ears and threatened to vibrate out of her chest as she collapsed back onto the bed.

Wow, what a night. She dragged her arm up and over her eyes waiting for her heart to slow. The subtle movement shifted the sheet across her skin. Her bare skin. Tally looked down. She was naked? When had that happened? She'd been wearing a nightgown when she'd gone to bed.

She pushed up onto her elbows and looked over the bedside. Her nightgown lay in a puddle on the floor. The dream came crashing back. Nick, stripping off her nightgown, throwing it down as he knelt between her legs, licking her, fucking her. It had been so clear, so real. She rolled over and the muscles inside her thighs twinged. She cupped her hand to her sex, surprised at the sudden ache between her legs. Like she really had been fucked hard last night.

"That was some wild dream," she said aloud, sitting up. She fluffed her hair back away from her face, trying to get the images out of her head. She rolled her head to the side, working out the kinks, and saw the rubber ducky lying on her floor in her doorway. "How did you get over there?" She climbed off the bed and picked up the toy. Looking back at the bed, she laughed softly. The sheets were crumpled and wrinkled as if she *had* spent the night in wild sex. She'd obviously been so caught in the dream she'd removed her nightgown and somehow flung the rubber ducky toward the door. She carried the toy into the bathroom and set it on the counter. She looked in the mirror.

Her eyes were bright and tired but there was an energy flowing through her body. The glow that surrounded her seemed real and sexual.

"Hmm. It's a bad sign when my dreams are more exciting than real life." She gripped her toothbrush and saw the rubber ducky staring at her in the mirror. The ducky's smug smile made her blush. "Great. I'm embarrassed by my own sex toy."

Chapter Six

ঙ

Nick strode into the office and stopped. Caitlin and Devon leaned against the receptionist's desk. Damn, he thought, he didn't need this. Not this morning. His mind had been circling through explanations since he'd come out of the duck's form on Tally's bathroom counter. It was by the sheer grace of God that Tally hadn't been standing beside him when the change had occurred. Thankfully, Caitlin had planned ahead and checked Tally's usual Sunday schedule. She met her friends for breakfast early Sunday morning. When Nick came out of the form, he'd called Jameson who had appeared with clothes and dropped Nick back at his place. Now, Jameson was tracking Tally. Keeping her in sight. With the exception of a few hours yesterday morning, someone in their family had been watching her all weekend. It usually came to this at some point in every investigation. Thankfully with their family's particular skills, very few people ever figured out they were being tailed.

Nick started to walk by his brother and sister, hoping to ignore them, but their smiles stopped him.

"What?" he demanded.

"How was life as a sex toy?" Caitlin asked, letting go of the laughter she'd been holding back since yesterday.

"Sometimes I hate you." He moved past them into his office and dropped his coat onto the chair. Devon and Caitlin followed, naturally. He glared at his sister. "It was your stupid idea in the first place."

"I was joking."

"What?!"

She laughed again and he could see the tears welling up in her eyes. "I was kidding. I thought you'd laugh and reject the idea but poof—you actually considered it."

"So you just had to egg me on."

"What else could I do? It was my sisterly duty to see if you'd actually go through with it. How was it?"

Nick just glared at her in response.

"Did you get the disk?" Devon asked, dragging them back to their purpose.

"No."

"What happened? Surely you didn't stay in that form all night."

Nick could hear the panic in Devon's voice. That was a shifter's greatest fear—trapped forever in a form from which he couldn't free himself.

"No, I came out of it."

"And you decided not to search…"

Caitlin chuckled. "I think big brother got distracted by a certain accountant."

"Again?" Devon asked.

"Yes," Nick admitted. "And she took that damn briefcase with her when she left."

"So you have to go back in," Caitlin pointed out. The twinkle in her eye made Nick snarl.

"I'm not going back as an inanimate. I need something that I can control." Unlike my libido, he thought, keeping the snide comment to himself. He looked at his brother and saw the same silent response.

"I'll handle it," Caitlin announced. Nick started to protest but she shook her head. "Don't worry. I'll really do it this time."

Nick stared at her for a long moment but didn't see any mockery in her eyes. She was serious this time. "Fine." As they left, he saw the message light on his phone glowing. He dialed in and waited impatiently as the smooth voice of the voice mail greeter went through her spiel. Finally, he hit "0" and heard the message.

"Mr. Conner? Martin Jessup. We've decided we won't be needing your services any longer. It appears that Ms. Hayward is not a problem after all. Thanks for all you've done. If you'll send me a final bill, I'll get a check cut."

Nick tapped his pen on the desk. That was odd. Nick had left a message on Branch's phone on Friday saying they were moving ahead. Why pull him off now? And strange that Jessup hadn't said they'd decided Tally was innocent or they'd made a mistake, just that she wasn't a problem.

He heard Caitlin moving around her office. This case was officially closed and they all had plenty of work for other clients. Nick could send Caitlin and Devon home, call off Jameson. They could all have the day off. It was Sunday after all.

But something didn't sit right.

Nick let his pen drop to the desktop. He would give it one more day. One more try to see what she kept on that disk she protected so well, then he'd back off. Jameson had reviewed the information Nick had sent him and found nothing unusual. Nick opened his computer and pulled up Tally's file—everything they knew about her. She wasn't stealing from AirPress. Nick would bet his reputation on it but she was hiding something and maybe that something was why he was hired in the first place.

*   *   *   *   *

"What's this?" Nick stared at the puppy squirming in Caitlin's hands. After a day spent plowing through computer files, he wasn't in the mood for any more of her jokes.

"Your way in."

He raised his eyebrows waiting for her to explain.

"Same concept as the vibrator but you'll be able to move around. Change into the puppy, I'll deliver you. You'll have free rein of the house."

He stared at the dog, currently licking his sister's fingers, his little tail wagging with perky ecstasy. "I hate turning into little animals. Too yappy. It's hard to keep control of their minds." Everything had its own energy—even that stupid vibrator—but when dealing with a living creature, there was the added complication of psychic energy. In an animal, this energy revealed itself as instinct. If he took on the puppy's form, he would actually become a puppy with a human mind inside it. The human had to control the animal, fighting the natural instincts and innate responses. Some animals were easier than others. Baby animals tended to have very short attention spans.

"You'd rather turn into an inanimate object?"

No, but at least I had a chance of getting near Tally's pussy. And that had worked so well.

"Fine." He took the dog from his sister and concentrated, absorbing the animal's essence. It slipped into his system like a streak of electricity. The puppy stretched up and licked him across the chin. Nick smiled, no more able to resist the adorable puppy than hopefully Tally would be. He could easily imagine Tally on the ground, rolling around with the puppy—her eyes alight with laughter. The picture made his chest ache.

Steeling his spine, he pushed the dog back in to Caitlin's hands.

"We'll do it tonight. Late. So she doesn't have a chance to get rid of the dog before bed."

Tally stared at the papers spread out across her kitchen table. No matter how she looked at the numbers on the Georgia plant, they didn't add up. Profits were being tallied but she couldn't find the source. She'd checked and rechecked the math but still it looked like money was appearing out of nowhere. She grabbed the expense lists for the factory. Maybe there was some savings realized that she hadn't—

The doorbell broke her chain of thoughts. She peered up at the clock. Nine forty-five? Who would be coming by at this hour? Richard? A warm shiver skipped down her spine at the thought. A repeat of the other night might have been part of her unconscious fantasies throughout the day. But as quickly as the thought came to her, it died. Richard had called and said he was safely in Chicago. He'd even called her "baby doll". Ugh. She much preferred the hungry, growling "baby" when he was buried deep inside her.

She dropped her pencil on the table and went to the door, smoothing her clothes. The bell rang again. She peeked out the window. A woman in a crisp blue suit waited. Her lips were moving as if she was talking to someone.

Still cautious, Tally opened the front door, keeping one foot behind it to block it from opening further.

"Yes?"

"Tally Hayward?"

"Yes."

"I have a delivery for you." She stretched her arms forward, pushing a brown bundle through the small opening of the door. Tally had little choice but to accept it. The door swung wide but that was no longer her biggest concern. It was the puppy twitching in her hands. The fluffy mound of fur was squirming and wiggling, as if trying to get closer to her. She pulled it against her chest and he began to lick her neck, up to her earlobe.

"He likes you. Imagine that?"

The puppy turned his head and released a little growl. The sound was low but hardly dangerous. The other woman chuckled and looked as if she was holding back a full belly laugh.

She set a bag at Tally's feet. "Here's everything he needs for the next few days and a list of instructions on puppy care." She started to turn away.

"No, wait. What is this? You can't leave him here. I didn't order a puppy."

"He's a gift." She looked at a slip of paper. "From Nick Conner."

"Nick sent me a puppy? But I can't keep a puppy." She pushed out her hands, holding the dog away. He started to cry as soon as their bodies separated—the mournful, heart-wrenching cries of a puppy. The sound was so pitiful, Tally cuddled him back against her chest. He settled down and his little tail flipped back and forth in joy.

"He doesn't seem to want to leave you." Again the woman looked on the verge of laughter. "But don't worry. He's housetrained." She reached out and petted his head. "The best in his class at puppy school." Another growl in her direction.

"But why would Nick send me a dog? Can you keep him until I figure this out?" It was a sweet gift but she'd didn't have pets. With the hours she worked, it didn't make sense. Pets took time and energy. The puppy licked her chin. And love. She looked down into his deep blue eyes. They seemed to be pleading her with her...*keep me, keep me*. "He's adorable—" Just like the man who sent him. "But..." She pled silently with the woman.

"I'm sorry. It's against policy. Once an animal has been delivered, it's your responsibility." She smiled and tilted her head. It was a friendly welcoming smile that seemed out of place with the casual relationship of a delivery person and her client. "It was nice to meet you, Tally." She tapped the puppy on the head. "Be good." There was a stern warning in her voice that the dog ignored. He rested his head against Tally's chest and closed his eyes. "You're going to have a time with that one. Good night."

The woman walked away. Tally could have sworn she heard her laughing as she went down the porch and back to her truck.

Tally stood for a moment, thinking it had to be a joke. Nick couldn't have sent her a dog. Why? Did he think she was in need of companionship? If so, he should have come himself.

With a sigh, she stared down at the puppy, now sleeping contentedly in her arms, his chin resting on her breast. He looked happy and pleased with himself. Almost as if his little mouth was smiling.

There was nothing she could do tonight. She'd have to keep him tonight and return him to Nick tomorrow. She grabbed the bag of supplies and dragged it into her living room. Carrying the puppy carefully, she set him on the couch. She was two steps away when the cries started. He'd woken up and was standing at the edge of the cushions—alternately looking at her and the ground so far away.

"You want to come with me? Okay, but no tinkling in my house, okay?" She doubted the puppy actually agreed but she picked him up and put him on the floor. With those sweet little puppy eyes staring at her, there was little chance she was going to get any more work done. It was time to admit defeat. The numbers were wrong and that meant someone was stealing. She'd have to talk to Edward Branch or Martin Jessup in the morning and tell them what she'd found. She gathered up her papers and tossed them into her briefcase. The puppy whimpered at her feet.

"Are you hungry?" She looked through the bag that had come with him and pulled out a water bowl and puppy food. The dog sniffed the food and growled. "No good, huh?" She stood and stared at the cute little guy. He sat on the ground looking up at her with quiet adulation, melting any resistance she had to him. "Well, I'm ready for bed. How about you?" The puppy's tail wagged furiously until she thought it would knock his little body over. "Need to go outside first?" She let him out into her backyard to do his business. He ran behind the one tree in her yard like he was shy then returned moments later looking as cute and adorable as ever. He ran back to her side and wagged his tail as if thrilled to see her again. Oh, he would be hard to give back. She crouched down and collected him in her arms, carrying him upstairs with her.

"You really are too cute but I don't think I can keep you." The puppy whimpered as if he understood her. "Well, we'll see."

The light immediately returned to the dog's eyes. He sighed and snuggled against her, resting his head contentedly on her chest.

* * * * *

Nick stared at the closed bathroom door and wondered if it was safe to risk changing into his human form. This puppy mind was driving him nuts. The puppy had no control over his reactions. Every emotion Nick felt the dog immediately amplified and showed. He briefly wondered if Tally thought it strange that the dog was reacting to her words.

The thought passed quickly. Nothing stayed long in this puppy's mind.

The indignity of it all. First he'd had to pee in her backyard. Nick had been able to control the puppy enough to run behind a tree. Not that he was overly shy in his human form but he didn't want Tally's memories of him to be him lifting his leg.

And then she'd locked him in the bathroom for the night.

He heard a rustle of skin on sheets. *Damn, I want to be with her.* The puppy mind immediately reacted and the dog released a pitiful cry. And kept crying.

"Oh, puppy, please be quiet," Tally called from the other side of the door. But he could hear the guilt in her voice. He was getting to her. He kept crying and added a little scratching to the bottom of the door. She was silent for what seemed like a long time—though it was difficult to track the passage of time with the puppy's short attention span. Finally he heard her move. Seconds later the door popped open and he skidded back.

She was huge to him in this body but still adorable. Her scent was especially tempting. The puppy instincts took control and Nick felt his body twitch and shake with joy.

"Okay, sweetie, you can come sleep with me."

Oh yeah. The tail whipped up into a frenzy.

She held him against her chest all the way back to the bed. She lay down and placed him beside her. He crawled over her, cuddling between her breasts as she lay on her side. The warmth and her spicy scent enveloped him. The puppy's mind responded to Nick's pleasure at being beside her and instantly relaxed. Everyone had gotten what they wanted. Nick felt his eyes shutting and couldn't keep them open. The puppy was exhausted and content. There was no way he could fight sleep.

"You really are just way too cute," Tally whispered. It was the last thing he heard before his mind faded to black.

He woke with a start—the frantic puppy dream still racing through his head. He'd been bounding through a field of tall grass chasing butterflies.

Nick recaptured the zipping little mind and lifted his head. He was snuggled up against Tally, practically sleeping between her breasts.

The dog mind tugged at his attention but Nick managed to keep control. He had to get moving. Regretting the loss of her warmth, he slipped out of Tally's embrace and padded to the edge of the bed. He peeked over the side. It was a long way down. He braced himself and jumped. The dog's instincts took over and he landed gently on all four feet.

Crouched on the ground, he willed his human form to return. The slow stretching of his muscles was a silent, painful process. The thin layer of baby fur faded from his skin and his human hair returned. It didn't take long to make the switch but it took a moment for him to recover.

He lifted his head and looked across the mattress. Tally was deep in sleep, her mouth slightly open, almost begging for his kiss. Her leg was curled up to the side and Nick knew if he lifted the bottom of her nightgown he'd see the deep pink of her cunt. Damn, he'd become obsessed with her pussy in the past three days.

With a sigh, he stepped away from the bed. He wasn't here to make love to her. Again. He hurried downstairs and found Tally's open briefcase on the kitchen table. Papers were casually stacked inside. He glanced through the financial reports she seemed to be reviewing.

He kept part of his mind focused on noises from upstairs and with the rest he reviewed the pages and the calculations. She didn't seem to be hiding information—she seemed to be searching for it. The disk lay in the bottom of her briefcase.

He grabbed the disk and went to her office. It took only a few minutes to bring up her computer. A quick scan of the disk's files revealed that this was her high priority disk. It appeared that anything of importance was on this disk. There were lists of subordinates' salaries and employee reviews. She was smart and protective.

He looked through the files and there was nothing to indicate that she'd been stealing. More notes about the Georgia plant sale. He dialed into the network and sent some of the files to Jameson for review.

Nick glanced at the clock. It was getting late and he needed to get back into puppy form. He meticulously returned everything to its place and went upstairs. He listened at the door for the slow steady pace of Tally's breathing.

Instead there was a soft gasp. Nick recognized the sound. She'd made it the night before when he'd licked her clit. He pushed open the door, inching it wider so he could see her on the bed. The cool moonlight that drifted through the window was enough to illuminate her pale body. Her nightgown was raised, baring her sleek legs and that hot pussy. He licked his lips at the memory, hoping to find some remaining trace of her flavor. He took a step back and leaned against the wall as the memory of her sighs and groans flowed into this crotch and hardened his cock.

Another breathy sigh from Tally didn't help the affliction. Unable to resist, he looked back through the opening. Her hand lay between her legs, pumping and pushing. Her knees pulled back as she thrust her fingers into her cunt. His hand pushed the door open even as his mind — the distant portion of his brain that was functioning — commanded that he draw back.

But the exotic vision of Tally spread before him, her own fingers plunging into her pussy, was too much for his desperate body to resist. He stepped to the side of the bed and stared down. Her eyes were shut, her lips open as she gasped for air.

Get out, change, move. Do something. He knew he had to follow the strident commands of his mind but there was something so compelling about the slow pump of her hand between her thighs and scent that arose from her sex.

Her eyes fluttered open. Nick tensed. The haze of sleep was gone from her gaze and he could see the fear building in her body. He had to do something.

"It's just a dream," he whispered.

As his words drifted into the air, he began to change. His body shrunk and...turned furry. Tally blinked and sat up, staring at the puppy wagging his tail. She'd been so sure she was awake — on the verge of coming — and when she'd opened her eyes Nick had been standing in her bedroom. It had seemed too real.

Right up to the point where he turned into a dog.

The puppy yipped. Tally jumped, the sound giving an extra jolt to her heart. She was awake now. With the tilt of his puppy head, he bounced on his hind legs, trying to get to her. After a moment, she reached over the side and picked him up. He jumped over her leg and crawled up until he was again nestled against her chest. One quick sigh later, he closed his eyes and collapsed into sleep. Tally watched for a moment then shook her head. It had all seemed so real.

She rubbed the puppy's head and stared into the darkness. The dream lingered, keeping her awake until the sun rose. Finally, she dragged herself out of bed and got ready for work. Before she left the house, she let the puppy out, fed him — which he again refused to eat — locked him in the laundry room and ran from the house before she had to endure any of his mournful cries. The guilt at leaving him alone all day was bad enough.

Still trying to shake off the affects of the dream, she arrived at work in a daze.

Tally stepped off the elevator and was immediately hit with the wave of concern and fear that permeated her office. She looked at the receptionist, hoping to get a sense of what was happening. Bethy's eyes grew wide and filled with tears.

"Bethy, what's wrong?"

"Doug, the security guard?" Tally nodded. She knew him. Saw him most nights when he made his rounds and she was working late. "He's dead."

"What happened?"

"I don't know but the police are here." Bethy took a deep breath. "They found him in your office."

"What?"

"Tally?"

She whipped around at Edward's low, serious call. Martin hovered in the background as Martin tended to do.

"Edward, I just heard. What happened?"

"I really can't say much. The police would like to talk to you." He nodded to two men standing beside him.

"Of course."

One of the men stepped forward. "We'd like to talk to you at the station if that's all right, Ms. Hayward."

Tally felt her heart skip a beat. Oh, she'd seen enough TV shows to know that was never a good thing.

Nick stared at the numbers on his phone. This couldn't be good. He flipped the phone open. "What's up?" he asked Jameson.

"We've got major problems." Energy raced down Nick's spine and he was immediately on his feet and moving to the door.

"What's happened?"

"The police just took Tally in."

Was this why Branch hadn't needed Nick's service? He'd decided to have Tally arrested. It didn't make any sense. Devon, Caitlin and Nick had gone over everything they knew about Tally and all agreed there was nothing to indicate she was stealing.

"What's the charge?"

"It's not official yet, but they think she murdered someone."

Chapter Seven

ᔇᔿ

Tally stared at the gunmetal gray walls, trying to get her mind around the fact that they thought she'd killed Doug. Oh, they hadn't arrested her. The police just wanted to "talk" but it amounted to the same thing. They thought she'd killed someone. Her initial panic was eased slightly when she learned that Doug was probably killed on Friday night. She was safe. She had an alibi. Richard. He'd been with her all night. Well, he'd disappeared for a little bit but he'd been naked at the time. Somehow she doubted he'd gone far.

She tapped her fingers on the tabletop and waited. She hadn't asked for a lawyer—not yet anyway—because she was innocent. All they had to do was make a phone call to Richard and he would confirm that she was home all night. With him. In bed. There was no way he could forget that night, she thought with a smile. It was indelibly burned into her memory.

The door opened and she slowly stood, expecting Detective One—she'd long since forgotten their names—to tell her she was free to go.

"Did you talk to Richard?"

"Yes, ma'am," the detective answered, stepping into the room and closing the door. "And he says he was in Chicago on Friday night."

"But he didn't go to Chicago until Saturday."

"No, ma'am, we checked the airlines and Richard Chalmers was on the plane Friday afternoon so he couldn't have been with you." He nodded to the chair, indicating she should sit back down. "Now, is there anything you'd like to tell me about that night? Maybe it was an accident. You were startled, thought the guard was a burglar and you hit him before you realized who he was."

"I didn't hit him. I wasn't there. I was at home, with Richard." Why would Richard say he hadn't been there? It didn't make sense.

"Your boyfriend says different. Are you sure you want to stick to that story?" the detective asked softly.

"It isn't a story. It's the truth. Let me talk—" Her plea to talk to Richard was interrupted by a knock and the door swinging open. Nick, looking strong and comforting, entered without acknowledging the detective's presence. Two other men walked in behind him. One was the other detective. The other was a man she didn't recognize but he had the aura of "lawyer" about him. Nick immediately came to her and pulled her into his arms. The warmth of his body melted the strength she'd been fighting so hard to maintain. Tears welled up and crept over her eyelids. She wrapped her arms around his neck and began to cry.

"Shh, shh. It's okay, baby. I've got you. Don't worry. Everything's going to be all right." She knew the others were there but she didn't care. All that mattered was Nick had come for her. She didn't know how or why but he was here. He continued to whisper to her, soothing nonsense that somehow reassured her. A long time later, when her tears were cried out, she lifted her head and looked into his blue eyes. "Okay now?"

She nodded, the strength she'd been faking no longer an act.

"What's going on?" Detective One said.

"This is her legal team," Detective Two announced from the doorway.

Tally blinked away the last tear and took a good look at the well-dressed man.

"Tally, this is my brother Devon. He's going to act as your lawyer." Nick settled her against his side. "But I think we can clear this up right now."

Devon stepped forward. "I'm hoping to forestall any more inclination in my client's direction with regards to this murder. She couldn't have killed that security guard. She was in her house all night."

Somehow she felt comforted when the lawyer said it with such official tones. She knew it was true but it sounded better coming out of his mouth.

"So she says," Detective One said. She felt the hairs on the back of her neck stand up. "But her building access badge says different. Shows her entering at twelve-thirty Saturday morning."

"I lost my badge on Friday," she protested. Devon nodded. At least *he* believed her.

"Tally couldn't have been downtown at twelve-thirty on Friday night," Nick said. "She was in bed." He paused and she could see him bracing himself. "With me." Heat spun through her chest and stomach. He was lying for her? Why?

The two detectives smirked at each other and then turned to her. "That's interesting, because she told us she was with another man all night."

"She's confused."

Tally's overwhelmed brain snapped back into clarity. "What?!" She stared at Nick but he kept his attention on the detectives. He looked so confident — but he was lying. She'd been with Richard.

"Friday night, I picked her up at her office, we took her car to dinner and then went back to her place. All night." The wicked glint in his eyes revealed clearly what they'd been doing *all night*. But that had been Richard. Hadn't it?

The sexy words, the exciting lovemaking. So not like Richard. No — she stalled her wayward thoughts — it had been Richard. She'd seen him. Confusion and fear that she was losing her sanity pounded at her already stressed temples.

"Then why would she say it was someone else?"

Nick had the grace to look sheepish. "I'm pretty good at disguising myself. I dressed up like her boyfriend, clothes, wig, makeup, and stayed in low light. It wasn't that hard to fool her." He looked at her and she could see the apology in his eyes. She turned away. Why was he lying? She'd seen him in full light — in her office and at her house. There was no way that was Nick.

"Check her phone records," he said. "I made a call about two in the morning and I dialed in to the Internet and sent an email. I was there." He sounded so definite, Tally was starting to believe him.

Either she was crazy or stupid. She moved forward so she could look directly into Nick's face. Into his eyes. His *blue* eyes. The same color that Richard's had been on Friday night.

"Oh my God." She didn't know how it was possible but somehow it had been Nick, not Richard, in bed with her that night. The air that had seemed in such short supply suddenly flooded her lungs. She gulped in a deep breath. Her hand snapped out and came into sharp contact with Nick's cheek. His head rocked to the side. He paused then nodded.

"I guess I deserved that."

The other men backed away, as if they knew the true power of an infuriated woman. He'd made love to her — fucked her. She felt her stomach roll over and she thought she might throw up. A warm hand on her back counteracted the sick feeling. Damn it, even when she was furious with him, his touch seemed to comfort her.

Devon snapped his briefcase shut. The definitive click seemed to declare the conversation complete. "Check her phone records, detectives, and confirm the time of death of your victim. I can assure you, it would be physically impossible for Ms. Hayward to be your killer. And if you want to talk to her again, you can call my office." Devon handed him a card. "We'll be going now."

Her mind reeling, Tally followed the command in Devon's voice along with everyone else in the room. Devon led her out of the station house and to a silver sedan. Nick opened the passenger door and helped her inside. Exhaustion from the tension that had bound her body for the past three hours tore at her strength and Tally collapsed into the seat.

"Get busy on finding out what more the cops know," Nick commanded his brother. "And find out where Branch and Jessup were on Friday night. Get Jameson working—"

"I got it, Nick. We've done this before. We'll have all the information we need in a few hours."

The words entered Tally's head but she wasn't sure she was processing the information fully.

"You'd better take care of her."

She looked up and saw Nick nod—the grim face of a man who didn't want to confess his sins.

Nick climbed into the car and started it, pulling out into traffic without speaking.

"How—?" she started to ask. Nick shook his head.

"I'll explain it all when we get to your place."

She was vaguely aware of Nick driving through town, stopping at her house and getting out of the car. He'd obviously been here before because he didn't ask for directions. He followed her up the front walk, waiting patiently as she opened the door and went inside.

She looked at him, remembering the first time she'd seen him—in the coffee shop. A casual meeting—an accident. Or maybe it wasn't.

Tally walked into the living room and spun around to face him. She was done waiting for answers.

"Who are you? And how—" She jabbed her finger into his chest. "How did you do it?"

He winced. "If you'll give me a chance, I might be able to explain some of this."

"I don't know how you're going to explain how you disguised yourself as my boyfriend, fucked me and then provided me with an alibi for a murder I didn't commit. It's not possible. I saw Richard that night. Not you. Explain that."

"I'm a shape shifter."

A cough came out of her throat—a mixture of laughter and choking. "What the—" A yip from the laundry room grabbed her attention. The puppy.

"Go get the dog and I'll explain."

She laughed this time. "You'll explain." Somehow Nick's answer eased some of her anger. He was crazy. That was something she could understand since she was feeling a little insane herself. She walked to the room off the kitchen and opened the door. The brown little puppy crouched on the floor. Once again its tail was flapping back and forth. "Hi, sweetie." She picked him up. He licked her face and then scrambled his legs like he wanted to get down. Strange, last night he'd wanted her to carry him around.

She brought him back to the living room and placed him on the carpet. The puppy immediately ran to Nick's side. Nick knelt down and scratched the dog's ears.

"Hey, little guy. Remember me?" The puppy wagged and bounced, the excitement obviously too much for his little body to contain.

Fighting to regain some of her anger, Tally dragged her attention away from the puppy and back to Nick. "Well?" she demanded.

He stood up and faced her. "I'm a shape shifter," he said again.

"You know how crazy that sounds right?"

"Yeah but it's the truth." He sat down on the arm of the couch. "My whole family can do it. It started back in the mid-1600s and it's just passed to every generation."

"A whole family of shape shifters," she said, not even trying to keep the disbelief out of her voice.

"Exactly. So on Friday night I turned into Richard—or at least made myself look like him—and took you out to dinner, brought you here and made love to you." He stood up and walked toward her. Even though he was patently insane, she didn't feel the urge to back away. "You admitted it yourself— that he hadn't acted like himself that night."

"It's not possible."

"Anything's possible."

He took a deep breath and his body changed. It shrunk and grew furry. Tally's throat closed up as she watched him. His clothes fell into a pile as the form beneath it collapsed. One moment he was standing in front of her. The next—he was a puppy. She shook her head, trying to erase the picture in front of her. It wasn't possible. It wasn't. But there it was. She pinched herself to make sure she wasn't dreaming. The dream. She'd seen this in her dream, the one that had felt like reality.

Nick sat on his haunches and looked up at her. His tail fluttered with little doggie excitement.

Oh my God. He's a shape shifter.

The other puppy bounded around the end of her couch and pounced on the dog in front of her as if thrilled to find a friend his size. The two puppies rolled around together until Tally couldn't tell which was which. They were exact copies of each other. Moving in slow motion, she sank down until she sat on the floor and reached toward the dogs. One of the puppies detached itself from the other and ran to her, immediately licking her hand and trying to crawl onto her.

Oh yeah, this one was Nick. She picked him up and inspected him, holding him close. Deep blue eyes stared back at her. His pink tongue flicked out and lapped her nose.

"Stop that." He did it again. She laughed. "You are going to be a handful."

As she spoke the dog began to wriggle like he wanted down. She put him on the ground and he began to change, rising and growing until a very naked Nick crouched before her. He lifted his head and smiled arrogantly at her.

"Somewhat more than a handful, I think," he said.

She started to respond—to ask how it was done—but he was there, his mouth on hers, his lips moving against hers as if he was hungry for her taste. Despite the amazing revelation she'd just witnessed, he was still Nick, the man who occupied her dreams. The man who'd made love to her three nights ago.

Her confusion at how Richard could have become her dream lover disappeared as she tasted Nick. This was right. She wrapped her arms around his neck and pulled him closer, opening her mouth beneath his. His tongue took immediate advantage, sliding gently between her lips. The warm masculine flavor combined with a touch of coffee made her sigh and draw closer.

Heat rose from his body as he curled his arms around her, pulling her closer even as he guided them both to the floor. His hands were slow, almost hesitant, as if he was giving her space to pull away. One concern niggled the edge of her consciousness. Nick had known where she lived—he'd known about Richard, he'd known enough to turn into Richard.

Tally sat up, forcing inches between their bodies.

"Why?"

"What?"

"Why did you turn into Richard in the first place?"

He sat up as well, resting his wrists on his bent knees. He looked at her for a long time before he nodded. "My two brothers, my sister and I run a private investigations firm— Conner Investigations. Edward Branch hired us to find evidence that you were embezzling."

"What!?"

"He hired me about three weeks ago to prove you were embezzling."

Energy zapped her body, re-igniting the anger from before. She rolled over and got to her feet, walking away, needing to expend some of the violence surging through her body. Edward thought she was stealing? He'd hired Nick to prove it. And that's why Nick had slept with her.

"You bastard."

He didn't deny the title.

"Did you turn into Richard hoping to search my house? Wait. You did search my house. That's what the phone call was. That's why you dialed into the Internet."

"I was searching for proof."

A stab of pure betrayal pierced her heart and forced tears into her eyes. "Did you have to fuck me? You couldn't have found some other way?" She wrapped her arms around her waist, feeling vulnerable. He'd been her dream lover and she'd been part of his job. She gulped down air trying to keep the tears in control.

"I didn't mean for that to happen."

She flipped her hair out of the way and glared at him. He'd gotten to his feet and stood within punching distance. "Then why did it?"

He hesitated but there was something in his eyes that told her he wasn't pausing to come up with a good lie. He looked at her with that turbulent blue gaze. "I was just supposed to keep you busy so Devon could search your office but then I kissed you and…" He shook his head. "I couldn't help myself," he confessed. "I knew it was wrong but you were there and you so sexy and sexual and all I could think is—'I might never have another chance to have her.'" He pressed his lips together. "I am sorry. I've never done anything like that before—making love to a woman in another's form. Devon's been kicking my ass about it for the past two days."

Nick probably didn't realize the way his honest regret eased her soul.

"Then I kept thinking about what an asshole Richard is and I guess I wanted to show you that you could have better."

"And that would be you?" she asked, unable to keep her smile in check.

A weaker man would have blushed but Nick just shrugged — and his eyes flashed at her with lust and confidence.

"You did say that night was — what was the word you used? Oh, yes, amazing."

She shook her head. "I'm not sure that kind of arrogance is going to get you back in my bed," she warned but even she could hear the laughter in her voice. He raised his eyebrows and Tally felt her stomach sink. He might not want back in her bed. Innate insecurity bubbled to the surface. Tally opened her mouth to explain, draw back the offer, change the subject, anything.

Nick held out his hand open palm. "Meeting you started out as a job but from the beginning I looked at you as more than a target. You fascinated me by the way you walked and talked. And nothing I've learned since has changed that first impression. I'm more intrigued than ever. I want to know you and I want you to know me."

Tally had to fight not to melt into a warm puddle of feminine goo. Once again he'd said the right thing. She looked into his eyes. The liquid depths were stormy and a hint of his own insecurity flashed at her through the warm blue haze. His pupils were mere pinpricks and the tops of his cheeks were painted with the merest shade of red. These weren't reactions he could control.

She looked away, needing to retreat from the power of his stare. She was confused and hurt. She wanted him, liked him, was probably halfway to being in love with him, but still — she glanced down. His cock was thick and hard. Another reaction he couldn't seem to control. Her pussy warmed in reflected response.

Chapter Eight

ဢ

The need to forget, to be taken away from everything that had happened and been revealed in the last few hours, overwhelmed her. She moved toward him, craving that moment away from reality.

"Nick—"

He was there, strong and solid, knowing what she needed. Their lips met—and bells rang. Tally jerked back, staring at him for a moment before her mind connected the sound with her doorbell.

"Expecting visitors?" he asked.

"No."

"I'll get it." He moved toward the door. Tally grabbed his arm.

"You're naked. I'll get it."

She passed him, hearing the muffled masculine protests as he dragged on his clothes. She peeked out the front window and saw Devon.

"It's your brother."

Nick arrived shirtless and adjusting the top of his pants as she opened the door and let Devon in. Another younger man and a woman who looked vaguely familiar followed him. Tally stepped back to let them in.

"You're the delivery lady," she accused.

"Hi, I'm Caitlin, Nick's sister. And this is Jameson our younger brother." Caitlin looked at Nick and widened her eyes. "Oooh, did we interrupt something?"

"Yes," Nick answered.

Caitlin laughed. "Good."

Nick ignored her. "Why are you here?" he asked, stepping close to Tally, silently announcing his claim to the other males in the room. He knew it was a primitive reaction but didn't care. He wanted his brothers to know that Tally belonged to him. At least he thought she did. Or she eventually would. She'd handled everything that had been thrown at her today — even seemed willing to forgive him — so he had to believe there was hope.

"I think we need to move on this today," Devon said. Devon had good instincts.

Nick led them all into the living room, sat down on the couch and pulled Tally down beside him. The puppy bounded around the corner and ran to the nearest human, sniffing and inspecting each one in turn until Jameson finally picked him up and held him on his lap.

"What did you find?" Nick asked.

"According to the police, the guard was killed about one a.m. Saturday," Devon said. "He checked in at twelve-twelve and said he was starting his rounds through Tally's building. Starts at the top and works his way down. He didn't check out when he was done. Not unusual. A lot of the guards forget to sign out. The body was in her office on the floor."

Nick saw Tally's cheeks turn white and he squeezed her fingers. She flashed him a weak smile but stayed firm.

"The weekend guards just walk the halls occasionally so they didn't see the body until the cleaning crew came in at midnight last night."

"While Devon was talking to the police, I went to Tally's building and had a look at her computer," Caitlin said.

Tally sat forward. "But — how — they just let you look at my computer?"

Caitlin smiled. "They didn't know it was me looking. Anyway, it seems that on Friday night-Saturday morning, someone loaded some interesting documents on Tally's computer. I'd say someone was trying to set her up for embezzling."

"That's why they wanted to know when I was going to check out her computer," Nick said.

"I don't understand."

"When Branch hired me, he wanted to know when I was going to look at your work computer. He said it was to allow me access to the building but it was really so he could put the incriminating information on your computer." It all made sense in a stupid-criminal sort of way. "If he'd put it on weeks ago, you might have noticed."

"Obviously, whoever did it doesn't know that a computer tracks when a document is created," Caitlin added.

"I'm sure they didn't care," Nick said, thinking back to his meeting with Branch and Jessup. He'd known something was hinky but hadn't listened to his instincts. "They probably just wanted to leave a big enough trail to get rid of her. Enough to threaten her with so she'd quit."

Tally spun on her seat to face him. "Why would they want to get rid of me?" She squinted her eyes and he watched that fascinating mind process the information. "The Georgia plant. I knew something was wrong. They're inflating profits to make the selling price higher."

"That would do it," Nick agreed.

"Martin tried to take me off the audit team shortly after we started it. He gave me a promotion and then said I'd be too busy. I hate leaving in the middle of a project, so I told him I'd make the time."

"When they couldn't get rid of you that way, they must have decided to get you fired or make you quit." Nick scanned the faces of his brothers and sister. They were all ready to go. "Devon's right. We should probably move on this before Branch and Jessup know Tally's been cleared."

Tally's shoulders slumped a bit.

"What's wrong?"

"Do you really think they are after me?" She looked up him with liquid eyes. It was just another blow in an already overwhelming day.

"I think they are trying to protect themselves and you're in their way." The plan he'd been formulating in his mind changed as he saw the hurt and fury battle for control of her body. She needed to be a part of it. He took her hand and squeezed her fingers in a gentle show of support. "Don't worry. You and I are going to take them down."

"What have you got in mind?" Devon asked.

"Jessup is the weaker of the two, right?"

Tally nodded. "He does whatever Edward tells him to, but I can't believe he'd kill someone if that's what you're thinking. Or that Edward would order it."

"Well, let's find out what he would do."

"How?"

Nick smiled, finally able to offer her something that might fix the situation.

"Did you acquire Branch?" Devon asked before Nick could respond.

"Naturally. I think it might be an appropriate time for the police to question Branch. Devon, you'll handle that?" Devon nodded. He stood and Nick followed suit. "Caitlin, we'll need a wire."

"It's in the car."

"I just need some clothes and—"

"Everyone stop," Tally commanded, standing and holding up her hands. She turned until she faced Nick head on. He had to work to hide his smile. She was tired and confused and probably more than a little frightened but she wasn't backing down. He liked that kind of strength in a woman. "What is 'acquiring' and how can Devon make the police do anything?" Tally said.

Devon started toward the door. "While you explain it all to her, we'll get moving and meet you outside the building in thirty minutes. I'll have clothes."

Nick waited until the front door shut behind his siblings and then explained.

"Acquiring is when I collect the shape of a thing or person. I have to touch something to turn into it."

"So when you met Edward, you 'acquired' him?"

"I thought it might come in handy and it has." He grabbed his shirt and pulled it on, pleased to see a flash of regret on Tally's face when he closed it. Good. Since he truly enjoyed her body, he hoped she felt the same way about his. "Let's get going and I'll explain what I have in mind."

* * * * *

Tally paced in front of Edward's desk. Her heart pounded so loud she wouldn't be surprised if it was picked up on the microphone she wore beneath her shirt.

"Relax," Nick said, though it came out of Edward's mouth. Tally looked at the distinguished gentleman behind the desk and had to readjust her mind again to remember that was Nick—just in Edward's body.

Devon had arrived five minutes ago, looking disturbingly like Detective Two, and had asked Edward to go with him to Tally's office. Once they'd left, Nick and Tally had slipped into Edward's office and summoned Martin.

"Is this going to work?"

"Yes. Don't worry. We're good at this." Nick leaned forward, his blue eyes glittering back at her. They seemed to be the only thing that didn't change on him and gave her some comfort that the "real" Nick was somewhere inside. He winked. "How about giving us a little kiss? For luck."

"Eww. Not in that body."

Nick laughed. "When we go home though, baby, I'm going to—"

"Your sister's listening," she warned.

She saw a flicker of fear in his eyes and almost laughed. The sound was cut short by the door opening and Martin Jessup walking in. He jolted when he saw Tally standing close to Edward's desk but after a moment his face cleared and he looked like the passive, wimpy accountant she'd always seen before.

"You wanted to see me, Edward." He didn't walk all the way in, hovering at the doorway.

"Yes, get in here and shut the door," Nick commanded and dang if he didn't sound just like Edward. Not just in voice but in tone and attitude. "We've got a problem."

Tally knew it was time for her act. She crossed her arms and placed her hip on the edge of the desk, doing her best to look pissed and cocky at the same time.

Nick lifted his chin toward Tally. "She knows."

Martin swallowed but didn't flinch. "Knows what?"

Nick looked at Tally and she knew it was her turn to take over. Nick's voice couldn't be on this part of the tape.

"Everything," she answered. "I was willing to overlook that you two were inflating the profits for the Georgia plant. I figured I'd get my cut later, but I'm not willing to take the rap for murder." She realized she sounded like a bad-action movie but figured Martin was so panicked he wouldn't notice.

"Murder?"

"You murdered that security guard and then you sent the police to me." Nick and Caitlin had told her to use the word "murder" often. Martin wasn't a hardened criminal and a reminder of what he'd done might trigger the guilt and confession. "I'm not taking the blame for a murder."

"It wasn't murder." Martin looked at Nick, looking for guidance. Nick did an excellent job of looking disgusted and a little afraid at the same time. He waved his hand toward Tally as if indicating Martin should explain. Martin gulped again. "It was an accident. I didn't want him to see me so I covered my head and ran for the door and I ran into him. He fell against the wall and cracked his head."

The tears in Martin's eyes comforted Tally. It hadn't been intentional and he obviously felt horrible about it.

"Then why send the police my way?"

"We didn't really—" he started to protest.

"We?" she demanded, needing a name. Needing Edward's name.

"Edward," Martin said, nodding toward the man behind the desk. "I called him after it happened." He glanced toward Nick but he remained silent. "It was just to get you out of the way. I wouldn't have let you go to jail. I wouldn't."

Tally let silence fill the air. They had enough. If not to give to the police, at least to threaten Martin and Edward into talking to the cops.

"You've said enough," Nick said, standing up. He definitely had Edward's commanding tone down. "Go back to your office. I'll deal with her."

Martin hesitated then his shoulders drooped forward and he turned to go, his head down, the energy seemingly sucked from his body.

Tally felt sorry for him—she was still going to turn him in to the police but she felt sorry for him.

"We've got to go," Nick said, taking Tally's hand and pulling her to the door. "I don't know how long Devon can keep Branch busy." Nick stopped beside the door, bent his neck to the side and slowly began to change. His face shrunk back, the lines of his cheekbones once again had definition. His chest expanded, threatening the seams of the suit he wore. She shivered as she watched her lover re-appear. It was almost less disconcerting to see him change into the puppy.

When he'd finished changing, he hiked up the now too-big trousers and opened the door. They stepped into the hallway, pulled the door shut behind them and had taken two steps when Devon—still in the detective's form—came around the corner walking with Edward.

"I couldn't have believed it of her myself but she's obviously not the angel we all believe—" Edward pulled up short. "Ms. Hayward."

Strange, she'd been "Tally" since day one—now suddenly she was "Ms. Hayward".

"Edward," she replied.

"Uh, I thought you were—" He looked at Devon. "I was under the impression that she was under arrest."

"Oh, did I say that? No, she's actually cleared. She was with Mr. Conner all night."

Edward's eyes widened but that was the only visible response to the announcement. "Conner? You were working for me."

"Precisely. I was 'investigating her' that night." Nick knew a threatening smile would be perfect right now, but he was afraid that if he moved it would be to punch Branch in the face. He nudged Tally forward. "Let's go, honey." He leaned down as they walked by Branch. "And you fucked with the wrong man's woman."

"I'll be going as well," Devon announced and turned around, walking away with Tally and Nick. They entered the elevator and faced Branch as the door closed. Tally leaned into Nick, keeping her chin lifted as she stared down her soon-to-be-former boss.

Now, Nick smiled.

Nick followed Tally into her house and greeted the puppy. The little dog ran around the room in a frenzy of not knowing what to explore first before collapsing beside the couch and promptly falling asleep. Tally tossed her purse on the table and sighed, dropping her head back as if the weight was too much. She'd stood like this the first day he'd seen her, and even then he'd wanted to ease her tension, soothe her, have her.

He walked up behind her. She straightened but didn't move away. Anticipation hung between them. Moving slowly, not wanting to rush her but needing to touch, feel her body, he placed his hands on her waist and leaned his head forward, brushing a light kiss on her throat. She tipped her head to the side, giving him the access and permission he sought. The warmth of her body called his. He inched forward until her back was pressed to his front, the hard line of his erection pushing against her ass. It reminded him of the first night, when he'd been inside her, fucking her from behind. When it had been *his* cock and *her* pussy, nothing between them.

As he nibbled at her neck, feeling her relax into him, he smoothed his hands up her sides, close but not quite touching her breasts, remembering how sensitive her nipples were, teasing her, drawing her out. She rolled her hips back, rubbing against his cock.

He gently bit her earlobe, rewarding and reprimanding her in one gentle bite. She groaned—and then reluctantly spun out of his arms, stepping away.

"I can't."

Nick snapped his teeth together to hold back the growl that wanted to be freed. He could understand her reluctance. He *would* understand. She'd had a lot of shocks today. And she wasn't completely in the clear yet.

They'd left the recording with Caitlin and Devon who would contact a few friends in the police department and get them looking at Branch and Jessup. Normally Nick would have stayed to follow through but he'd wanted to get Tally away from it all—and alone.

Walking out of her office, his mind had been focused on claiming her—and having her accept him, but he was obviously moving too fast for her. He would be a gentleman and wouldn't push. He'd take it slow, he'd ask her to coffee and dinner and a movie and all that shit but he wasn't letting her go.

"Okay, I guess—"

"I need to talk to Richard." It was all Nick could do not to snarl at the mention of the other man's name. "I really should, you know, break up with him before we do anything. Else."

That was her concern? Breaking up with her boyfriend? Nick grabbed his cell phone off his belt, flipped it open and handed it to her. "Call him."

She dialed the number but Nick could see her weakening. She bit her lip and looked at him.

"I hate to do this on the phone."

"He's fucking his secretary."

"What!?"

"Richard. He's having an affair with the chirpy little blonde that works in his office."

"How do you know?"

"I had to check him out. I took on his form and went into his office one night. She seems quite fond of sex on his desk."

Tally's eyes tightened and pure emotion flowed through them. "Did you...?"

"No." He answered as fast as humanly possible.

Her anger turned to disgust and irritation. "He had sex with her on his desk? In his office? I couldn't even get him to do it in the living room." She lowered the phone and the energy seemed to drain from her body. "Maybe it's me. Maybe I don't inspire that kind of lust." She seemed to be speaking to herself, almost forgetting that he was there.

Nick grabbed her hand, raised the phone, hit send and pushed it toward her ear. "He's an idiot and, from what I can tell, a lousy fuck. You inspire all kinds of lust and if you'll just tell him to take a flying fuck, I'll have you right now. And then later on the kitchen table."

Her eyes widened and she seemed to unconsciously move closer.

The tinny sound of the voice on the other end of the phone line made her flinch.

"Oh, Richard, it's me, uhm, Tally." She spun around, turning her back to Nick but he wouldn't be ignored. Not now.

"Over the end of the bed," he whispered in her other ear. "I'll take you from behind. I know how much you like a hard fuck." He nipped her neck. "Remember how big I felt inside you? I'll ride you until you scream my name."

She whimpered. "Uh, what? Oh, it was a misunderstanding. The police thought I'd killed someone."

He could feel her tensing as she focused on the conversation and not on him.

"Finish it. Let me have you." He cuddled up against her back, running his hands down her side, skimming the edges of her breasts. She leaned back. Nick spread his thighs and pulled her into him. "Hard and deep, all night." He slipped his hand down her waist and pushed his palm between her legs.

"Richard, I think we should stop seeing each other."

He fluttered his fingers against her pussy in reward and heard her gentle gasp as he pressed the heel of his hand over her mound.

"No, it's just...oh damn."

"Finish it," Nick whispered again. "I need to fuck you."

"It's over, Richard," she said firmly. She opened her mouth like she was going to continue speaking. Nick pulled the phone from her fingers and hit the disconnect button.

"He doesn't need an explanation. He lost you. It's his own fault." He tossed the phone onto the couch and spun her around so she faced him, almost fearing the look in her eyes. Had he pushed too hard? Taken too much for granted? She smiled as she looked up at him.

"You like being in control, don't you?"

"Yes," he said, baldly acknowledging that weakness in his character. "But ask my brothers and sisters—I can back down and, baby, if you ever want to command me in the bedroom, you just say the word and I'm there for you."

She nodded and waited. Nick didn't move. Knowing his tendency to bulldoze his way through things, he didn't want to overwhelm her. The thought that she might regret what they were about to do would haunt him for the rest of his life.

Finally she opened her hands. "So were you just kidding when I was on the phone? Or did you really mean it about, you know, the living room and the kitchen?"

The edge of his mouth pulled up into smile. In trying not to push, he'd made the lady impatient. "And the end of the bed. I definitely meant it."

"Now?"

"Oh yes." He whirled her around and eased her down onto the couch as he reached for the buttons of her blouse. They would get more creative later, but for now, he just needed to be inside her. Needed to be a part of her. He opened the zipper of her trousers and pulled them down, tossing them and her panties to the side.

He slipped his fingers between her legs, testing her, needing to know she was ready for him. Her moisture and heat almost undid him. He couldn't stop himself. He placed his cock at her entrance and pushed in, one long hard stroke.

"Nick!" Her excited cry filled the room and blocked all sound from his mind. It was perfect.

She was calling *his* name.

"Say it again."

She looked directly into his eyes and he felt it down to his toes.

"Nick," she whispered.

"Always."

Why an electronic book?

We live in the Information Age—an exciting time in the history of human civilization, in which technology rules supreme and continues to progress in leaps and bounds every minute of every day. For a multitude of reasons, more and more avid literary fans are opting to purchase e-books instead of paper books. The question from those not yet initiated into the world of electronic reading is simply: *Why?*

1. *Price.* An electronic title at Ellora's Cave Publishing and Cerridwen Press runs anywhere from 40% to 75% less than the cover price of the exact same title in paperback format. Why? Basic mathematics and cost. It is less expensive to publish an e-book (no paper and printing, no warehousing and shipping) than it is to publish a paperback, so the savings are passed along to the consumer.

2. *Space.* Running out of room in your house for your books? That is one worry you will never have with electronic books. For a low one-time cost, you can purchase a handheld device specifically designed for e-reading. Many e-readers have large, convenient screens for viewing. Better yet, hundreds of titles can be stored within your new library—on a single microchip. There are a variety of e-readers from different manufacturers. You can also read e-books on your PC or laptop computer. (Please note that Ellora's

Cave does not endorse any specific brands. You can check our websites at www.ellorascave.com or www.cerridwenpress.com for information we make available to new consumers.)

3. *Mobility.* Because your new e-library consists of only a microchip within a small, easily transportable e-reader, your entire cache of books can be taken with you wherever you go.

4. ***Personal Viewing Preferences.*** Are the words you are currently reading too small? Too large? Too... ANNOYING? Paperback books cannot be modified according to personal preferences, but e-books can.

5. ***Instant Gratification.*** Is it the middle of the night and all the bookstores near you are closed? Are you tired of waiting days, sometimes weeks, for bookstores to ship the novels you bought? Ellora's Cave Publishing sells instantaneous downloads twenty-four hours a day, seven days a week, every day of the year. Our webstore is never closed. Our e-book delivery system is 100% automated, meaning your order is filled as soon as you pay for it.

Those are a few of the top reasons why electronic books are replacing paperbacks for many avid readers.

As always, Ellora's Cave and Cerridwen Press welcome your questions and comments. We invite you to email us at Comments@ellorascave.com or write to us directly at Ellora's Cave Publishing Inc., 1056 Home Avenue, Akron, OH 44310-3502.

THE
☥ ELLORA'S CAVE ☥
LIBRARY

Stay up to date with Ellora's Cave Titles in
Print with our Quarterly Catalog.

TO RECIEVE A CATALOG,
SEND AN EMAIL WITH YOUR NAME
AND MAILING ADDRESS TO:

CATALOG@ELLORASCAVE.COM

OR SEND A LETTER OR POSTCARD
WITH YOUR MAILING ADDRESS TO:

CATALOG REQUEST
C/O ELLORA'S CAVE PUBLISHING, INC.
1056 HOME AVENUE
AKRON, OHIO 44310-3502

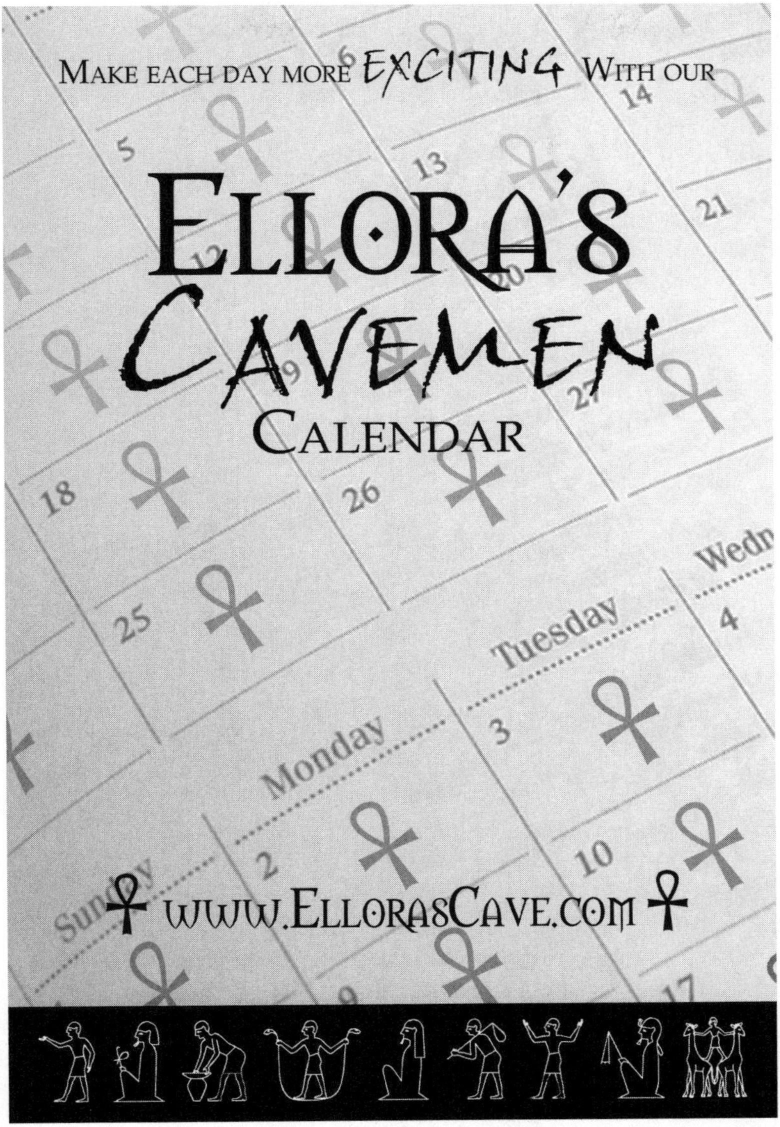

Make each day more *EXCITING* With our

Ellora's
Cavemen
Calendar

14

5

13

21

20

27

18

26

25

Wedn

Tuesday

4

Monday

3

Sunday

2

10

www.EllorasCave.com

17

Now Available!

Ellora's Cavemen

Dreams of the Oasis I

A special edition anthology of six
sizzling stories from Ellora's Cave's
Mistresses of Romantica.

Edited by Raelene Gorlinsky

Featuring:

Myla Jackson, Liddy Midnight, Nicole Austin,
Allyson James, Paige Cuccaro, Jory Strong

erridwen, the Celtic Goddess of wisdom, was the muse who brought inspiration to storytellers and those in the creative arts. Cerridwen Press encompasses the best and most innovative stories in all genres of today's fiction. Visit our site and discover the newest titles by talented authors who still get inspired - much like the ancient storytellers did, once upon a time.

Cerridwen Press

www.cerridwenpress.com

Discover for yourself why readers can't get enough of the multiple award-winning publisher

Ellora's Cave.

Whether you prefer e-books or paperbacks,

be sure to visit EC on the web at
www.ellorascave.com

for an erotic reading experience that will leave you breathless.